SLEEPING BEAR

EMILY
BESTLER
BOOKS

ATRIA

An Imprint of Simon & Schuster, Inc.
1230 Avenue of the Americas
New York, NY 10020

First Emily Bestler Books/Atria Books hardcover edition July 2021

EMILY BESTLER BOOKS / ATRIA BOOKS and colophon are trademarks of Simon & Schuster, Inc.

For information about special discounts for bulk purchases, please contact Simon & Schuster Special Sales at 1-866-506-1949 or business@simonandschuster.com.

The Simon & Schuster Speakers Bureau can bring authors to your live event. For more information or to book an event, contact the Simon & Schuster Speakers Bureau at 1-866-248-3049 or visit our website at www.simonspeakers.com.

Interior design by Erika R. Genova

Manufactured in the United States of America

1   3   5   7   9   10   8   6   4   2

Library of Congress Cataloging-in-Publication Data

Names: Sullivan, Connor, author.
Title: Sleeping bear : a thriller / Connor Sullivan.
Description: First Emily Bestler Books/Atria Books hardcover edition. | New York: Emily Bestler Books/Atria, 2021.
Identifiers: LCCN 2021008720 (print) | LCCN 2021008721 (ebook) | ISBN 9781982166397 (hardcover) | ISBN 9781982166410 (ebook)
Subjects: LCSH: Women veterans—Fiction. | Missing persons—Fiction. | Fathers and daughters—Fiction. | Political fiction. | GSAFD: Spy stories.
Classification: LCC PS3619.U4145 S58 2021 (print) | LCC PS3619.U4145 (ebook) | DDC 813/.6—dc23
LC record available at https://lccn.loc.gov/2021008720
LC ebook record available at https://lccn.loc.gov/2021008721

ISBN 978-1-9821-6639-7
ISBN 978-1-9821-6641-0 (ebook)

SLEEPING BEAR

A THRILLER

CONNOR SULLIVAN

EMILY BESTLER BOOKS
—
ATRIA
New York   London   Toronto   Sydney   New Delhi

For Alan

Since 1988 more than seventy thousand missing person reports have been filed by the Alaska State Troopers. Many of the missing were last seen in and around a gigantic, triangular-shaped wilderness above the 60° North Parallel latitudinal line that forms the raw, unforgiving heart of the most remote state in America.

Prologue

PAUL BRADY WOKE up with a start and went for his rifle. Sweat poured down his face, his cotton T-shirt sticking to his sleeping bag. For nearly a minute, he sat up breathing deeply, trying to figure out where he was.

He wasn't in Ramadi.

That was nearly fourteen years ago.

He wasn't in the Korengal.

That was twelve years ago.

Heart pounding, he fumbled with the switch on his head lamp and turned it on, illuminating the small one-person tent.

Rushing water, the rustle of leaves, and creaking trees sounded outside.

Then he remembered.

It was 2019. He was in Alaska, six miles south of the town of Chicken, camping on the bank of the Fortymile River.

He had thought coming up to Alaska would clear his mind. That the fresh air and seclusion would mitigate the stress and anxiety that had plagued him for the last four years.

Over two years ago, Paul Brady had been diagnosed at the San Diego VA with PTSD.

It explained all the nightmares. The short temper and the jumpiness. It explained the depression, anxiety, and the manic episodes.

As a former chief petty officer in SEAL Team Two, Paul Brady never thought he'd have to deal with the effects of the trauma he'd experienced in his nearly seventeen years in the Teams. He'd always thought SEALs were impervious to such symptoms. It was true that he'd seen terrible things on his deployments. War was hell, no doubt, but he'd thrived in those environments. It wasn't until he'd left the navy and moved from Virginia to San Diego with his family that his life started to spiral out of control.

It started with the night terrors and then escalated to a point where he couldn't hold down a job.

The VA-sponsored psychotherapy didn't work.

Neither did the medications. He pushed everyone away, including his wife and two boys, who, after nearly two years of trying to help, finally packed up and left.

He'd lost nearly everything in the divorce: his job, the house, the kids, and most of his money.

After the divorce was settled, the former SEAL found himself left only with his Ford truck and the meager amount of money in his savings account, which was spent quickly on Bud Light and whiskey.

For three months he lived like a bum out of his truck near Mission Beach, close to Coronado where he had gone through BUD/S training, until one day he was struck with an idea.

What if I can just get away from it all?

What if I can go to some far corner of the world and just live?

It took him three days to sober up, and another five to drive to Canada's Yukon territory, where he stayed at a quaint hotel near the Alaskan border.

The owners had been welcoming and, when hearing his plan to camp in Alaska for the summer, had given him a list of their favorite spots.

That's how he'd found this little plot of paradise on the river.

Brady kicked out of his sleeping bag and unzipped the door to his tent. Grabbing his bear rifle, he stepped out into the cool night and stood on the sandy shore.

Small wisps of smoke rose from the dying embers of his fire pit and caught wind, blowing out over the river. It was that time of night in the great north where you could see the stars and the Milky Way, that three hours of darkness where the forest finally took a break and went to sleep.

Brady paced in circles around the camp, trying to get his mind under control. He found that the pacing helped rein in his thoughts. He'd been sober nearly eleven days—the longest he'd gone in years—but, damn, could he use a beer right about now.

Directing the beam of his head lamp over to the group of trees twenty yards behind his tent, he gazed up at his food box hanging by a rope from a tall branch and considered what was inside.

He'd bought the pint of Jack Daniels as a test for himself as he left Southern California.

A test in self-control.

For too long, he'd been self-medicating with alcohol.

And look where it got me.

I can't go back to that.

Brady turned his head away from the swaying food box, stopped his pacing, and closed his eyes.

You've come here to start again. You've come here to recover.

It was a mantra he'd repeated to himself during his long drive north, a quasi affirmation to keep him on the straight and narrow.

For nearly ten minutes, the former SEAL stood in this meditative state and had finally started to relax, when a sharp sound snapped him out of his trance.

Instantly, the hair on the back of his neck stood on end, his senses elevating. He spun to look at the dark forest behind him.

His food box continued to swing in the wind, and he primed his eyes for any sight of a potential threat.

The sharp snap had sounded like a heavy stick being broken under a great weight.

The dark shadows of the forest continued to dance in front of him and suddenly he got the eerie sensation that he was being watched. He'd had that feeling many times before, the calm before an ambush.

Brady clicked the safety off his rifle and brought the stock of the weapon into his shoulder, his eyes still scanning for any movement. His mind scoured through the list of potential predators in the Alaskan wilderness—wolves, mountain lions, and inland grizzlies.

Snap!

Brady whipped the barrel of his rifle to the left in the direction of the new sound.

Snap!

Another stick broke to his right. Brady started backpedaling sideways toward the river, cutting off the angle to potential threats when a large, hulking figure stepped out of the forest.

The figure looked like no animal he'd ever seen, it looked—

"Hey!" Brady shouted. "What the hell are you doing?"

Aiming the rifle directly at the figure, he started to apply pressure to the trigger. He was just about to shout again when a loud sound—*pop!*—cut through the midnight air and something thudded to a stop in the sand at his feet.

Brady squinted down at the mysterious object. In the starlight, it looked like some sort of thermos. Then, suddenly, a loud explosion rocked Brady off his feet. The brilliant flash of orange and red blinded him as he was thrown onto the sand.

Something hissed loudly. He clawed at the sand, desperately searching for his rifle. Ears ringing, he finally grasped the wooden stock of his weapon.

His world suddenly began to swim. Vibrant colors kaleidoscoped all around him.

Then Brady gasped deeply and felt a sharp burning sensation.

His body locked up and he pitched backward, darkness engulfing him.

Chapter 1

THIRTY-TWO HOURS BEFORE Cassie Gale went missing, she was driving her green Toyota Tundra west on Yukon Route 2 through dense forests of spruce and aspen. Though it was late June, the air was cool, and in the light rain that fell from dull gray clouds, it almost smelled like fall.

Every so often there were breaks in the trees that flanked the highway, and Cassie caught glimpses of pristine valleys and faraway peaks, and slowly grew calmer, at ease, not at all the troubled woman who'd left Montana three days before.

But just as quickly, the vista was swallowed by thick, gloomy claustrophobic woods that seemed to gnaw at her mood. On impulse Cassie reached for the center console. When she did, the regal, male German shepherd in the passenger's seat cocked his head, and his eyes narrowed.

Cassie stopped her hand short of the console and willed it back to the wheel.

"Sorry, Maverick," she said, reaching over and scratching the dog's head. "I promised I wouldn't go there today, didn't I?"

Maverick nuzzled Cassie's arm as she drove past a sign that read: Dawson City, Yukon 50 kilometers.

Thank God, Cassie thought, fighting a yawn. *Just thirty miles.*

It was past seven in the evening by then and she'd been driving nearly twelve hours. She had come all the way from Watson Lake in the southeastern corner of the territory and had sat through dozens of summer highway work delays on the route. She looked forward to a shower, food, a cold beer or two, and a clean bed in Dawson. She desperately wanted one more good night's sleep before she pushed on into the great unknown.

That thought made her feel better. The great unknown. Adventure. Wild places. A break from the hustle and bustle of the modern world and the pain she was leaving behind. The thought made her smile and take an appraising glance at herself in the rearview mirror.

Cassie was in her early thirties, five foot five, and very fit, with short ash-blond hair, and dark sapphire eyes. She wore little makeup, and her skin was deeply tanned and sun spotted due to many years out in the extreme elements. As a result, she was more handsome than beautiful, and at this stage in her life that suited her just fine.

And so did traveling alone with Maverick. Cassie believed she and the shepherd were more than capable of handling themselves in any situation. She was just trying to enjoy the sheer newness of every turn in the road ahead.

But then, in the deep recesses of her mind, a little pang of familiar misery ran through her. She reached for the center console again, only to stop.

Returning her hand to the wheel, she rolled her shoulders back, and lifted her chin up high. It was something her dad had taught her as a young girl when she was feeling down.

Act like you are queen of the world, Cassie, stand like you're queen of the damn world, and everything else will fade away, he used to tell her when she was young and moping about some minor tragedy.

Crossing a bridge, she glanced down to the creek below, swollen, silted, and rushing with runoff from the snowfields high above.

The frothing water triggered another memory, a bad one, and before she could stop herself—raw, stinking emotion as swollen and roiling as the creek below filled her chest and throat. Tears blurred her eyesight until she had to pull over beyond the bridge.

Throwing the truck in park, she rested her forehead on the steering wheel and sobbed. Maverick began to whine and snuffle at her cheek and ear.

"I know," Cassie said, wiping her eyes, then hugging the dog. "I love you, too, big guy."

Maverick's tail wagged as he licked the tears off her face. Ordinarily, that would have been enough. Cassie would have bathed in her dog's unconditional love and driven on. Instead, she lifted the center console lid and got out her Globalstar GPS satellite phone.

"I know you don't like it, but I have to," Cassie said, turning the phone on.

Against a voice in her head commanding her to stop, she dialed the moment she had a solid connection. At the other end of the line, a phone rang four times before going to a voice mail.

"This is Derrick," the voice said. "You know what to do. In the meantime, remember, only dead fish swim with the current."

The current, Cassie thought before the beep.

She wiped at her eyes and spoke into the phone, "Hi, I know I promised I wouldn't call. But I was missing you, and . . . I'm going to Alaska, just like we said we always would. I'll probably be there tomorrow, and I . . . I'm doing well, for the most part. Taking it minute by minute." She paused, "Derrick, I need to tell you a secret. I need to say that—"

The phone chirped—she'd lost the satellite connection.

Cassie cursed and put the phone back in the center console before putting the Tundra back in drive.

Rolling west again, she turned on the radio and got the weather report on an AM station out of Haines Junction, which called for localized showers before clearing up with warmer weather for the next few days.

That's good. It could easily have been pouring buckets.

She'd no sooner had that thought when the iron gray skies opened and lashed the highway with sheets of water so thick it forced her to slow to a crawl.

As the water pounded on the windshield, Cassie's memories leaped back years. She saw herself at fourteen, crouched under an overhung cliff, watching a spectacular summer storm roll up an alpine wilderness valley where granite crags soared like cathedrals on all sides. A fire burned beneath the overhang, the smell of coffee wafted, and she remembered feeling safer and surer of herself than ever before.

How old was I that day? Fourteen?

Fourteen, and I already knew.

He was the one.

Chapter 2

AS QUICKLY AS it came, the squall passed, and the sun broke through the clouds. Just before eight p.m., she pulled into Dawson City. It was nestled comfortably on a narrow shelf at the confluence of the Yukon and Klondike Rivers and took Cassie by surprise.

She expected a desolate, abandoned nineteenth-century mining town. Instead, Dawson hummed with activity. Tourists milled up and down the main streets, snapping pictures of the flowing Yukon and the various historical sites.

The roads were dirt, and most buildings sported freshly painted frontier-style facades—a former ghost town now revamped and reconstructed for summers filled with tourism.

Cassie went from hotel to motel and found them booked straight till the end of the month. A friendly clerk at the last hotel took pity on her and suggested she try the Northern Breeze Lodge & Smoke House Bar just an hour west of town on Route 9.

"Last bit of civilization until you hit Alaska. It ain't the Ritz, but the food is decent and the owners are nice," the clerk said. "Beats sleeping in your truck."

Cassie thanked the clerk and drove out of Dawson and waited on the ferry that took them across the Yukon River. She paid the toll and drove her truck onto the barge. When they got to the other side, she jumped on Route 9 and headed west for another thirty-seven miles, sighing with relief when she saw the lodge's flashing green Vacancy sign. The Northern Breeze Lodge & Smoke House Bar was a two-story log cabin building with a rough-looking bar connected to its side. A dirt road flared off Route 9 and headed north behind the building.

Cassie grabbed her yellow rain jacket, opened the door, and climbed out. She tugged the jacket on, aware of Maverick watching her. Cassie whistled, and the dog bounded out of the truck and sat at her feet.

"Go pee pee, Mav."

Maverick trotted across the parking lot to some bushes, sniffed about, did his business, and came back to Cassie's side.

"Good boy," Cassie said. "On me, now. Best behavior."

The dog fell in beside her as they entered the lodge, a peeled and varnished log affair with a vaulted lobby and wings that flared out to either side. A beautiful elk antler chandelier hung over a sitting area next to the stone fireplace. A massive bull moose with paddles that jutted out five feet wide sat mounted above the hearth. The moose was so impressive that Cassie stopped for a moment to admire it.

"Big, isn't he?"

Cassie turned away from the moose to find a plump woman with silver hair pulled up in a tight bun, smiling at her from behind a wooden counter.

"He looks prehistoric; is he local?" Cassie asked.

"Who, Boris? No, he's not from around here," the woman said pleasantly. The badge pinned to her front lapel read, "Darlene."

"Boris?" Cassie said, reaching the counter.

"Boris Badinov. My husband, Ned, insists on calling him that. Shot him on the Kamchatka Peninsula, oh, must be eleven years ago. Are you looking for a room, dear?"

"Yes, ma'am."

"Well, would you look at this big handsome fella," Darlene said, leaning over the counter. "And so well behaved. Will he be staying with us?"

"As long as dogs are welcome."

"He's more than welcome, just need to put down a deposit and keep him on a leash. Insurance thing."

Cassie handed Darlene her credit card and dug out her passport.

"You two traveling alone?" Darlene asked, opening the passport.

"Just me and Maverick."

Darlene smiled again at the dog. "Hi, Maverick."

The dog's hind end wiggled, which caused Darlene to titter; she looked down at the passport. "Cassandra Ann Gale. From Lincoln, Montana. You're a long way from home, dear."

"We're pushing on to Alaska in the morning."

"Pushing on to Alaska. We get a lot of that, as you can imagine."

Darlene put Cassie's credit card on file and then held out a room key. "Two-oh-one, overlooking the creek. Best view in the whole lodge."

"Is the kitchen in the bar still open?"

"Open till midnight. Food's nothing fancy, but it's tasty and reasonably priced."

Cassie thanked the woman.

"My pleasure. Enjoy your stay. Oh, and breakfast's included, eh? Starts at six, ends at nine."

Outside, the sun was still high above the horizon when she retrieved her overnight bag, a small daypack, and Maverick's bowls and food. She thought about unlocking the pickup's cap to get out the steel-sided case that was buried under several duffels in the truck bed, but decided against it. Canada had certain laws that she didn't particularly agree with, but she wasn't going to flaunt her defiance of them and get thrown in jail out of principle. Instead, she took Maverick to room 201.

The room was bright, airy, and adorned with rustic furniture. Cassie dropped her bags on the bed, then opened the double-glass doors to the little deck and looked down at the creek riffling below her. She stood there for a minute, admiring the creek before her thoughts seized on the image of a fourteen-year-old boy wading out into a river carrying a fly rod. Mayflies were swirling in a coppery light as the boy cast his line next to a whirling rapid.

Maverick whined, tearing Cassie from that warm yet heartbreaking memory. She put kibble into one bowl and filled the other with water. Drool fell from the shepherd's mouth, but he sat obediently in front of the bowl waiting for his mom's instructions.

"Eat up, boy," Cassie said. The dog dug into his food and then lapped up the water in his bowl while Cassie took a shower.

Refreshed, she put on fresh jeans, boots, and a light sweater before scratching Maverick behind the ears. He made a nest for himself on the foot of the bed and settled into a postmeal nap. Cassie turned on the TV for the dog, something she always did, and went to the door.

"Mommy's going to get some dinner, I'll be back in a bit," she said, and left.

Chapter 3

OLD-FASHIONED GAS LAMPS lit the bar, casting a warm glow on the oiled log walls, the rough-hewn plank floor, and the booths and chairs whose red-cracked upholstered leather sagged under drinking customers.

Business was brisk, the place jam-packed with rough-looking patrons drinking beer after a hard day's work. One rowdy group shot pool by the jukebox.

Cassie could feel the attention on her as she crossed the room and took the only empty stool at the bar between a scraggly young man scrolling on his iPhone and two older women who were having a hell of a time over a bottle of Black Velvet whiskey. The two women broke into laughter as Cassie sat next to them, their long black braids swishing over denim vests. Their hazelnut-colored skin would have looked like fine Italian leather had it not been for decades of drink and cigarette abuse.

The bartender leaned against the bar top and stared at the TV above him, focused on an episode of *Shark Tank*.

Cassie glanced over at the game of pool and was met with a half-dozen curious faces gazing back at her. A tall man in a bright red flannel shirt, sporting a five o'clock shadow, raised his beer and blew her a kiss. One of his buddies nudged him and the group laughed.

"Wouldn't encourage them if I were you."

Cassie's gaze went to the scraggly kid to her left, his eyes never leaving Instagram on his phone. She asked, "Encourage who?"

"Everyone in this damn place."

"You get Wi-Fi in here?" Cassie asked.

"Barely."

Cassie reached into her pocket and took out her own iPhone, placing it on the bar top. The bartender peeled his attention away from *Shark Tank* as an order rang up from the kitchen. He grabbed the plate and placed a heavenly smelling pork chop in front of the kid.

"Password is 'Northern,' uppercase N," the bartender said.

The kid put his phone down and sniffed at his dish. He looked at Cassie for the first time and grinned. His Oakley shades sat on the bill of a dark green Sitka ball cap, hiding a swath of tangled blond hair. He looked like he hadn't seen a razor in months. To Cassie, he fit the mold of the stereotypical environmental science major—an outdoor enthusiast on a four-year track, but procrastinating through seven. He seemed nice enough, so Cassie returned the smile.

The kid jabbed the chop with his fork. "There is a great force for good in the universe. It's being proven to me all over again."

The women to Cassie's right snorted into their drinks. The bartender cleaned a glass with a hand towel. "I swear, kid. That wilderness messed you up something good."

The kid's mouth was too full to answer.

The bartender rested a hand on the bar in front of Cassie. "What will it be, young lady, dinner or just drinks?"

"I'll have one of those pork chops," she said, studying the bartender.

Silver haired, blue eyed, and clean-shaven, his face said early sixties, but his build said fifteen years younger. He was wiry and strong—the flexing muscles on his exposed forearms looked like taut telephone cables—the kind of guy Cassie's father would call "all sinew and rope." He wore jeans, a denim shirt, and an apron that was monogrammed across the breast with the words: NED. MY PLACE. MY RULES.

"You got it."

"You're Darlene's Ned?" Cassie asked.

"Thirty-two years this September," Ned replied, and adjusted the sleeve on his shirt, exposing a faded anchor-shaped tattoo. "Anything to drink?"

Cassie scrutinized the familiar-looking tattoo, then ordered a local ale.

"You got a name?" the kid asked.

"Cassie."

"Billy." He held out a hand.

She took it. "You just come out of the bush, Billy?"

"Eighty days solo free trekking."

"Is that like a walkabout?" Cassie asked.

One of the women to Cassie's right said, "It's what these new age hippie white kids do to find themselves."

"Trespassin' on our ancestors' land what it is," the other added.

Billy put his fork down. "I told you, all the land I enter is public." He looked to Cassie and said, "And yeah, it's kinda like a walkabout, more of a vision quest. You find the biggest, wildest terrain, and just dive in with no connection to the outside. Without any of this."

He picked up his iPhone. "Whole world is addicted to this device. I was unplugged for almost three months; first thing I do when I come back to civilization is turn it on and start scrolling away. Next thing I know, three hours have gone by, and for what? That's why I decided I'm going back in tomorrow. I need to continue the cleanse."

Billy explained that he grew up in Oregon, got a degree in philosophy from Reed College in Portland, then committed himself to go full Christopher McCandless for the next couple years. "*Into the Wild* changed my life, man. But I'm not an idiot like that kid. I grew up in the woods. I'm prepared for it."

Ned returned and plopped Cassie's meal in front of her.

Billy continued, "You ever get a chance to spend some time alone in pure, unadulterated wilderness, you gotta do it."

Cassie cut into her chop. "My family runs an outfitter and dude ranch in the Bob Marshall Wilderness in Montana. Spent my whole childhood there."

Billy whistled his approval. "I went into the Bob last summer from the Rocky Mountain front. Country's beautiful, too many people though. You want to go into deep wilderness alone, you come to Alaska or the Yukon, makes Montana look like Disneyland."

Cassie was too hungry to disagree with the kid. She'd had enough friends from Alaska over the years and knew it was frivolous to argue whose state was more "wild" or "dangerous." Montana could be a rough place no doubt, but Alaska and the Yukon were different beasts.

She took her first bite of the chop and voiced her approval. Ned gave her a thumbs-up.

Behind her, there were snickers from the group at the pool table. Cassie glanced in the mirror behind the bar, seeing the reflection of the tall, bullish man in the red flannel approaching her.

The woman to Cassie's right saw him, too. "Like a wolf on an elk carcass."

The man came to the bar. He was tall, cowboy strong. He held a beer in his hand and leaned between Cassie and Billy. He looked down at Cassie's chest unapologetically.

"Is there a problem?" Cassie asked.

"Quite the opposite," the guy said.

More laughs from the pool table. Cassie glanced over at them. A squat man with red hair filmed the interaction with his phone.

The tall guy flicked his head to the pool table. "Name's Jake. Wanna join us for a game?"

"I'm good here, thanks."

"No need to be rude; c'mon, I'll buy you a round, what are you having?"

"Already got myself a round," Cassie said, "and not being rude, just hungry."

Jake's lips tightened. "Around here, someone offers you a beer and to shoot some pool, the polite thing to do is say yes."

"And I politely decline."

The snickers at the pool table quieted.

Jake leaned in, his breath smelling like ale. "Then why don't you finish your drink and we can go somewhere else—"

"Hey, man," Billy said, tapping Jake on the shoulder, "she said she's not interested."

Jake glanced to where Billy's finger touched his holy Canadian flannel.

Cassie moved her plate away and shifted her weight on her stool so her right elbow had more leverage on the bar.

"I'm sorry," Jake said, "I didn't ask a little hippie shit for his opinion."

The redhead moved in for a closer angle with the phone.

Billy looked like he instantly regretted opening his mouth. The fork in his left hand shook. "She . . . she's not interested."

Jake said, "Who do you think she's interested in, you?"

Billy's furtive eyes jumped to Cassie's calm face, then back to Jake's. He seemed to wrestle with his next line and settled with putting his fork on his plate and standing to face the man.

Jake had a foot in height and an easy seventy pounds on the kid. Billy stared at his brutish physique.

"I didn't say she was interested in me . . . she's just not interested in you."

"Looks like Cheech and Chong here left his bong at home and found his balls." Jake laughed and took a confident sip of his beer. Then he looked at the bottle and swished it in a circular motion. "You know kid, you look like you need a shower." He raised the bottle and emptied the frothy suds on Billy's head.

Billy closed his eyes and let the beer fall down his face. He reached up and took off his hat and wiped at his eyes.

The redhead extended his arm even further.

Cassie stood. "You know what I can never get over?"

Jake turned.

Cassie continued: "Canadians always have the reputation for being polite. It's all 'sorry 'bout that, sorry about this—yes ma'am, no sir—you all right there, bud?' But as soon as one of you gets liquored up, you're no different than any other dip-spitting, hockey-loving, flannel-wearing asshole in cowboy boots."

She put her face right up to Jake's. "So why don't you and your jailhouse friends let us eat in peace?"

Jake burst into laughter, then addressed the bar, "She's got quite the way with words."

"Just get outta here, man," Billy said.

Jake pivoted, unleashing his right fist into Billy's left eye. The crack of cartilage on bone sounded like a deer rifle going off. Billy staggered backward, falling over his stool. Jake cocked his elbow for another blow.

Cassie grabbed the man's balled-up fist, found his pinkie finger, and yanked. Jake screamed.

Cassie held firm and wrenched the finger even farther out of place, using it as leverage to force Jake's head and torso onto the bar top.

"Lemme go, bitch!"

Ned exploded out of the kitchen. "What in Christ's name—!" His face contorted in rage. He came around the bar and grabbed Jake by his collar. Cassie released the finger and Ned dragged Jake over against the wall.

Ned said, "You ever start shit again in my bar, Jake, you're out, you hear me? For good!"

"Cool down, Ned, he was just messing," the redhead said, lowering his phone.

Ned turned. "Curtis, you shouldn't be egging this on. Hotheadedness has got no place here or in the field, you hear?" He turned back to Jake, slammed him against the wall again. "Understand, son!"

Jake didn't like it, but he nodded, and Ned released him. Jake massaged his throat. Ned motioned to the group of men. "Up to Clinton Creek, all of you. Triple shifts until I say otherwise."

The group dropped their pool sticks and reluctantly collected their things. Jake muttered under his breath, held his injured finger, and threw Cassie a bitter look as he passed.

Ned offered Billy a hand, righted his stool, and guided him back on the seat. "Let me get you something for that." He went behind the bar, scooped ice out of the cooler, and placed it in a Ziploc before handing it to Billy, who placed it over his eye.

Ned mopped up the spilt beer on the bar top and said as he looked at Cassie, "Those boys are hard workers, but that doesn't mean they ain't stupid sometimes. Food's comp'd for the rest of your stay."

"That's nice of you."

"Least I can do."

Cassie sat back down. "Those guys work for you?"

"I run a small logging outfit on the side up north in Clinton Creek near the river. Helps pay the bills. Where'd you learn that finger trick? I've never seen that one."

"Picked it up in the military."

"US military? Which branch?" Ned asked.

"Army," Cassie replied.

"What'd you do in the army?" Billy asked, wincing as he lowered the ice.

"This and that," Cassie said.

"I was in the military myself," Ned said. "Canadian Armed Forces."

Cassie pointed to the anchor tattoo on Ned's forearm that read: *Parati Vero Parati*. "You were Royal Canadian Navy?"

Ned laughed. "Back in the old days it was known as the Maritime Command. Spent most of my career on a Halifax-class frigate out of Esquimalt doing sweeps in the Bering Sea. Froze my ass off for the better part of my life patrolling for Soviets. Swore once I was done I'd never subject myself to that kind of cold again."

Cassie laughed as she said, "Yet you live in Dawson?"

"I like to call it between Dawson and the middle of nowhere, but I enjoy the summers here. In winter everything is shut down so Darlene and I vacation somewhere warm. My goal is to retire on a boat in the Caribbean. Maybe St. Thomas . . ." He pointed to their empty beer glasses. "Another round?"

Chapter 4

THE NEXT MORNING Cassie leaned against the front counter and looked down at the large map of Alaska between her and Ned.

"I just need a place to camp for a day or two," she said. "Detune a bit, maybe do some fishing. I don't have to be in Fairbanks for work until Monday morning."

Maverick nudged Cassie's leg with his nose. Cassie stroked the top of his head. "I'll get you breakfast in a second, bud."

Ned roved his finger over the map. "If you're heading into Alaska, I usually send people here"—he put his finger on a tributary jutting off the Yukon River—"just north of Eagle. One of our favorite spots."

He showed her the direct route to Eagle, where the Taylor Highway ended and the Yukon River ran into the vast Alaskan wilderness. He marked a dirt road that traveled north and showed her a place to camp and fish off the beaten path.

Maverick whined when Darlene came into the room with a steaming cup of coffee.

"I want to apologize again for last night," she said. "I'm sick to my stomach just thinking about it. We want to comp your stay."

"That's not necessary," Cassie said. "Ned's already paid for my dinner, but I'd like to pay for the room, please."

Darlene reluctantly agreed and stood next to her husband.

Cassie turned back to the map. "What's the bear situation up there?"

"Helps if you think they're around, so you get no surprises," Ned said. "I'd carry spray, or a gun if you've got it. But it's been years since I've seen grizzlies where I'm sending you."

After giving Cassie more details, they shook hands, and Cassie thanked them for the hospitality. Darlene apologized again for the bar scene.

Ned said, "Speak of the devil."

Billy entered the lobby, a stuffed backpack slung over one shoulder. His left eye was a mosaic of blues and reds, but he smiled when he saw them.

"Where you off to now?" Darlene said.

"Gonna hitchhike back to the US border and figure it out from there. Probably head back into the Alaskan wilderness," he said, then looked down and saw Maverick. "Oh, hey, look at you!"

He went to put a hand on Maverick's head and the dog growled.

"Easy, Mav, he's a friend," Cassie said. "Sorry, he can be extremely protective."

"Damn, he looks like he could be a police dog or something."

"Ex-marine, actually."

"You were a dog handler in the military?" Billy asked.

"No, Mav's just family," Cassie said, scratching the shepherd behind the ears.

Billy looked confused but decided to not push the subject. He said his good-byes to the group and went for the door. Cassie watched the kid go.

"You take a shower this morning, Billy?" Cassie asked.

"Yeah, why?"

"I can give you a lift across the border, take you as far as . . ." She looked to Ned.

"Jack Wade's where you take the Taylor Highway north," Ned said.

"Jack Wade, unless you want to head to Eagle," Cassie said.

Billy considered her proposition. "I'll take you up on that."

In the parking lot, Cassie had Billy stow his stuff in the back of the already crowded pickup bed.

"That a raft all rolled up in there?" Billy asked.

Cassie put food into Maverick's bowl and the dog attacked the kibble.

"It is," Cassie said. "Oars are up top."

"Going rafting?"

"Next week," she said, locking the cap and taking Maverick's now empty bowl from him. The dog sat outside the passenger's-seat door and whined.

"No, Mav, you're in the back seat. Humans up front."

The dog did not look happy and Cassie had to pick him up and place him in the back seat.

"Big guy's stubborn," Billy said.

"He can be a bit ornery."

They watched Maverick make a spot for himself in the back seat among the pile of duffels.

Billy climbed in shotgun and Cassie started the truck, pulled out onto Yukon Route 9, and headed toward the US border crossing at Little Gold.

"Where you going rafting?" Billy asked.

"Arctic National Wildlife Refuge."

"No kidding. You flying in?"

"I'll fly from Fairbanks and land on one of the gravel bars."

"Guide waiting?"

"I am the guide," Cassie said. "One of two on the trip, anyway."

"So you do know your way around the wilderness."

"I'm competent."

"Who are you guiding?"

"A group of ecotourists from Japan."

"You married?"

The question caught Cassie off guard, she glanced over at him; he pointed to the white, untanned ring of skin on her ring finger.

Billy put up his hands. "Sorry, none of my business."

"It's complicated."

"Fair enough."

While they drove, Cassie learned that Billy had loved backpacking and nature from an early age. He told her he had enough money saved up to fund several more long backpacking trips into the wilderness. It wasn't until they reached the border crossing at Little Gold that she found out his last name was French.

A bored-faced US Border Patrol agent barely glanced at their passports and cleared them through immigration and into Alaska with a wave of her hand. Five miles down the road, Billy said, "Do me a favor. Up here, pull over for a sec?"

He pointed out three towering spruce trees in a cluster ahead, and Cassie pulled over on the shoulder and put on her hazards.

"Be right back," he said, jumping out of the truck and dashing down the embankment into thigh-deep grass.

Cassie reached back and petted Maverick, figuring Billy had just gone to relieve himself, but he came back quickly, carrying a small waterproof daypack and a steel rifle case. He leaned through the open passenger-side window and asked, "Can you unlock the back for me?"

Cassie did. "That yours?"

"Of course," he said, sliding the rifle case and pack below Maverick. "You think I'd go into the Alaskan wilderness without a gun?" He slid back into the passenger seat. "I hope you have one?"

"I've got two," she said.

"You registered them for Canadian transit?"

She arched an eyebrow. "No," she confessed with a smile, pulling back on the highway. "Just keep them well hidden."

When they reached the abandoned mining community of Jack Wade an hour later, Cassie let Maverick out of the truck to go pee and run around in the small creek next to the remnants of an old perpetual motion gold dredge.

Billy soaked his feet in the creek and threw sticks for the dog and looked at the dredge. "Crazy how this stuff is still standing."

Cassie stared at the rusty machine. "Back in the nineteen hundreds they used to pull a couple hundred thousand bucks' worth of gold out of these streams with this kind of equipment."

Billy let out a low whistle and pointed to the run-down living quarters, the corroded tin siding stained orange and brown. Flanking the living quarters was a large garage, with a security shutter rolled down over the old wooden doors. Over the shutter, heavy steel throw bars locked into the building's wall.

"Don't know why they keep this place locked up like Fort Knox, looks like it's going to fall down any minute," Billy said.

Cassie looked at the beer bottles scattered around the creek bed and replied, "Keeping the drunk kids out I suspect."

Behind them, they could hear Maverick sniffing through the heavy grass.

"Someone caught a scent," Billy said.

As he said it, a grouse flushed and Maverick bolted after it. Cassie called to the dog, but he was already off and running.

"Shit, I gotta go get him," Cassie said. "Mind following me in there?"

The forest was thick with conifers and willows. Cassie trudged through the woods and called for the dog. She could hear his excited panting ahead and the sounds of small branches breaking. She quickened her pace until she hit a large clear-cut.

Timbered ridges surrounded the cut, and long green grass moved in a lazy wind. Cassie could see Maverick's tail bobbing through the grass.

Billy came huffing up behind her. "What's this place?"

"Logging cut from the looks of it." Cassie moved through the high grass, calling for Maverick.

When they got to the middle of the field, they stopped. Two long, parallel strips of grass were matted down and ran the length of the field.

"This looks like a landing strip," Billy said. "What the hell is a landing strip doing out here?"

Cassie knelt down to examine the pressed grass when Maverick came running over with a dead squirrel in his mouth.

"Maverick, drop it!"

The dog dropped the squirrel at her feet and wagged his tail proudly.

"Great," Cassie said, securing him to his lead and walking toward the woods. Billy lingered for a moment longer, staring at the landing strip, then followed.

Back at the truck, Cassie wiped Maverick's paws and put him in the back seat again.

Billy leaned against the hood. "Where are you heading exactly?"

Cassie shut the door. "Past Eagle. Ned showed me a place to camp along one of the Yukon's tributaries."

"Yeah, I'm thinking of doing the same thing."

Cassie looked at him suspiciously. "I planned on camping alone. I need some time to clear my head."

"Oh, no, of course. I wasn't saying we camp together. If you're able to drop me at the preserve north of Eagle, I'll just walk the river bottom and find a place to pitch my tent. I can throw you some gas money if you want."

"Don't worry about it, it's on the way for me," Cassie said, opening her door and climbing in. "Come on, I'd like to get up there before noon."

Chapter 5

THEY MADE IT to Eagle just shy of noon and Cassie parked the truck in the parking lot of the Eagle Trading Company, the only grocery store in town, and got out.

"Lunch?"

"Sure," Billy said, pulling out his wallet.

Cassie waved it away. "I'll buy if you take Maverick down by the river, let him run around a bit."

Billy didn't argue and Cassie headed inside and grabbed two premade sandwiches at the deli. She paid with her credit card and headed outside and walked to the shoreline where Billy threw sticks in the river for Maverick to fetch. Cassie sat down at a picnic table on the gravelly shore and looked from Billy and Maverick over at Eagle. The place reminded her of the countless small towns she'd passed through growing up in Montana—western settlements frozen in time, their purpose for survival chewed up and spit out by the turn of the twenty-first century. But considering the harsh Alaskan environment, Eagle still had its charm and the residents had an easiness about them—like the worries of the modern world were irrelevant—which Cassie thought was probably true.

"They have an airport here, you know," Billy said, coming over and sitting down. "About a quarter mile east of the village where all the natives live." Their drive to Eagle consisted of Billy rattling off conspiracy theories about the landing strip they had seen in the clear-cut. "Could be used for the wild animal trade."

"What?"

"That landing field, what if they're using it to ship bears and exotic animals? I read an article that they are worth a fortune on the black market."

"It's most likely for fire crews or getting supplies in for local authorities. I think all that time alone in the wilderness has made you a bit paranoid."

Billy laughed and took a bite of his sandwich. "Yeah, Ned was probably right. I'll tell you, though, around day fifty in the bush, I started seeing shit."

"Seeing shit?"

"Hallucinating."

"What kind of things did you see?"

"My dead mother for starters. She's been dead for fifteen years, but there she was, clear as day."

Cassie looked skeptical.

"Okay, let me explain better." Billy set his sandwich on the table. "Day fifty, I'm camping on the side of this small river, thirty miles from any sort of civilization and I just felt something. It was like a warm breeze on the skin; then I just look up, and there she was. Standing in the middle of the stream, smiling at me." He smacked his hands together. "Then boom! Every good feeling I've ever had about her came rushing at me all at once and she was gone. From that moment on, it's felt like her death isn't so finite."

Billy rested his chin on his knuckles and he watched the water drift lazily by. "But on the flip side, I also ran into dark patches, felt like a bad acid trip—bad spirits maybe. The natives up here call them *Kigatilik*."

Cassie lifted an eyebrow.

"I know, I know. I sound crazy," he said. "But you ever come to a place by yourself that raises the hair on the back of your neck? Like your body recognizes a threat that your brain can't comprehend?"

"Sure."

"Means dark spirits live there. At least the native shamans say so," Billy said. "I took an anthropology class at Reed that focused on the northern Native Americans. Part of the reason I came up here. I'm pretty sure the natives in this area are descendants of the Hän people, means people of the river. One of the first tribes up here to have made contact with the Europeans."

Maverick came running over, soaked from the water. He shook and drenched the pair, panting and smiling. Cassie leaned forward and kissed the dog on the head. "Well, as long as I have Mav with me, I think I'll be safe from dark spirits."

Billy gave her a wide grin. "No doubt about that."

Ten minutes later they were back in the truck and heading down Front Street going north. The dirt road flanking the Yukon River was treacherous and twice Billy had to get out and guide Cassie over the deep ruts and crevices.

After a little over four miles, Billy had Cassie drop him off in a heavily wooded area. He grabbed all his belongings and leaned through the open passenger-side window and said his good-byes.

Cassie wished him luck. "Stay away from those evil spirits."

"I'll be okay. Thanks for the lift, Cassie."

"Any time, Billy."

Picking up the rest of his stuff, he turned toward the river. She waited until he disappeared before driving on.

Cassie kept going north for another three miles, until, a half hour after dropping off Billy, she finally came to a flat section with an opening in the trees well off the side of the road. A fire pit sat in the middle of a small campsite.

She put the car in park and consulted her map where Ned had marked the spot and announced to Maverick that they'd arrived.

Cassie stepped outside, let the dog out of the truck, and looked over the campsite. It was surrounded on three sides by low-hanging willows, ferns, and small spruce trees. A large poplar dominated the northern edge of the site and looked like the perfect place for her to hang her antibear food container. The sound of rushing water could be heard from the east and Cassie found a small opening in the vegetation that was most likely a trail that led to the river.

Ned wasn't lying when he said it was the perfect place to camp.

Cassie rummaged in the back of her pickup and took out a pistol case she had hidden below the seat. She opened the case and took out a Colt Python .357 with a bone-white hilt. Engraved in the bone was the etching of a bucking horse and the name *Cassandra*.

Cassie opened the cylinder, loaded six bullets, and slapped it shut. Next she grabbed a leather holster from under the seat and cinched it around her belt and put the .357 in its place.

Camp was set within an hour. She dragged a dead log from the woods and set it next to the fire pit so she would have a place to sit. She decided that she would sleep in the back of the truck with Maverick, not wanting to trust the bear situation. But she pitched her red Cabela's tent nevertheless and used it to store her clothing and supplies.

With everything done, she got out the satphone, locked her food box in the truck, and started putting together her fly rod. She collected Maverick and together they used the game trail that headed east to the river.

The summer season had turned Alaska into a tapestry of green and faraway blues and made the mountains that jutted above the Yukon seem more painted than real.

As Maverick basked in the sun, Cassie fished on the fringe of a small eddy next to a large, flat-topped boulder. Two hours and a sizable trout later, she took out her satellite phone, and climbed up on the boulder.

She lay down, resting the phone on her stomach, closed her eyes, and felt the sun beat down on her face. Despite the heat, she remembered snow falling over mountains. She saw the silhouette of her father trudging away through knee-deep powder, and the voice of Emily, her older sister.

He blames himself, Cassie. You can't do the same.

Cassie recalled how pale Emily's face had been that day, how she held a steaming bowl of chicken noodle soup, how it trembled in her hands as she placed it on the table next to Cassie's bed.

Cassie's eyes jolted open.

To the west, a dark nimbus cloud lingered on the horizon. The scent of rain hit her nostrils. Cassie contemplated the satellite phone, then sat up and dialed. The call cut straight to the familiar voice mail: *Hey, this is Derrick—*

The recording ended and the answering machine beeped. Cassie kneaded the bridge of her nose, and tears welled in her eyes. She needed to let it out. All the pent-up emotion and anguish that had been building for months. Everything she'd masked in front of her family, friends, and doctors had to be let go.

Cassie finally choked out, "Derrick, my secret is . . ."

She paused and looked down at the glinting sun on the swirling water, felt her throat constrict, and said, "Deep down I know it was my fault. I ignored the signs. I . . . the truth is, I'm not doing better. It's all a sham, I'm not doing better at—"

The phone beeped and an animatronic voice told her the voice-mail box was now full. She hung up and placed it by her side. It had been over six months since that fateful morning, and in that time, she'd refused to cancel Derrick's phone service. Against everyone's advice, she'd needed to keep hearing his voice.

Cassie remembered waking early that winter morning to the slap of barn doors in the howling, snowy wind. She remembered going outside to shut them, then collapsing into the snow at the sight within the barn. Her screams had been so animal she hadn't recognized them as her own. Then the strong hands of her father holding her upright. She recalled how sore her throat had been in the days that passed.

As she sat on the boulder looking out at the Alaskan wilderness, Cassie put a hand to her flat stomach. She questioned her place in the world, if the impulsiveness of her trip was yet another way to escape the harsh realities of the past year, or if it was the exact kind of therapy she needed.

Whether it was muscle memory or not, Cassie took out the worn photograph from her wallet and unfolded it, gazing at her favorite picture of her family. Derrick, Emily, Trask, her father, Maverick—and herself, three years prior, all smiles in the sweltering Fort Benning heat. It was one of the happiest days of her life. She remembered how proud everyone was of her.

How proud Derrick had been.

Cassie's eyes welled and spilled tears as the wind picked up. She rocked back on the boulder and looked at the impossible blue sky and then at the billowing dark clouds moving in.

She thought of Derrick and the life they might have had together.

She wondered if her own life was worth living without him.

Chapter 6

SHORTLY AFTER MIDNIGHT, Maverick lay curled up like a donut against his mom's purple sleeping bag in the back of the truck.

A summer rainstorm had passed through quickly, and Cassie had spent most of the evening by the fire trying to read a paperback, but her thoughts kept drifting to Derrick. Around ten she gave up and cleaned up camp, storing her food in the food box and hanging it from a high branch in the poplar tree.

As she slid into her sleeping bag, she secured her .375 H&H Magnum rifle by her side and pinned the Colt Python in its holster between her air mattress and the wheel well. She then shut the truck cap's back window and latched it before checking to make sure the side windows were locked. She wasn't going to make any mistakes when it came to the dangers that crept around in the Alaskan wilderness.

Not tonight.

Not ever.

‖‖

Hours later, Cassie woke to Maverick's growling.

The shepherd was standing, his ears trained. Cassie knew every nuance of the dog's personality and understood how quickly Maverick could switch from a loving family member to a consummate professional—*to a marine.*

"Maverick, down."

Instantly, the dog dropped on his haunches, but his head remained high, and his ears planted still. Cassie opened the side window of the truck cap.

It was well past midnight and the forest was cast not in darkness, but in deep blue shadows. Other than the low murmurs of the river and the chirping of crickets, the camp sat in near silence. A light wind blew from the west, causing faint smoke trails to rise from the dying fire.

She put a hand on Maverick's back. The hair along his spine was stiff, standing on end. That low growl rumbled from his throat once more. His nose was tracking—his pointed ears searching.

Crack! Crash!

The sounds came from toward the river where she could not see—a large branch breaking under tremendous weight, and what, something falling?

Maverick found his feet again. Cassie snatched up the .375, turned on her head lamp, and aimed the beam in the direction of the noises. She stared at the large poplar on the northern edge of her campsite where she had stashed her food.

"Shit," she said, her mind flashing on the image of a bear meandering into camp.

Maverick's nostrils flared.

Cassie shouldered the rifle, rested it out the window, and then turned the light back on the poplar where her food hung. Nothing broke the dense cover toward the river. Nothing stirred.

After five minutes, Cassie shut the cap's window, turned off her head lamp, and went back to sleep. Probably just a moose.

||||||||||||||||||||||||||||||||||||||||||||||||||||||||||||||||||||||||||||||||

She woke an hour later to the dull drumming of a faraway motor and sat up. Maverick had returned to the same position, his eyes fixed out the back window. The motor wasn't coming from the direction of the road; it was coming from the river.

Cassie checked her watch: 3:05 a.m.

Who would be out on the river this time of night?

The drone of the motor grew louder. It was approaching from the southeast.

The motor slowed and crept closer. Cassie could hear it idling for a few moments before it sputtered and threatened to stall. But then the engine roared, and it passed her camp and soon faded away. She rested a hand on the dog.

"Go to bed, Mav—"

CRASH!

Maverick sprung to his feet. Cassie fumbled for the rifle again before pushing up the cap window.

A small light blinked in the direction of the river.

She thought she heard muffled voices.

Her mind raced. Was someone in trouble? Was it just a couple of drunks out for a midnight cruise? Why did they stop in front of her campsite?

Cassie cinched the head lamp over her head and turned it on to find the pistol and holster. She threaded the holster through her belt and unlocked the rear window before climbing out of the pickup bed.

"Maverick, heel."

The shepherd leaped out and buttonhooked to her side. With the holster snap undone, and the pistol within easy reach, she gripped the rifle at port arms. She pointed the head lamp toward the river, the beam scanning the willow thicket and the game trail. She walked past the fire pit and stepped over the log, pausing next to her tent.

The forest went eerily quiet. The hair on the back of Cassie's neck started to rise and she had the uncanny sensation she was being watched.

"Anyone there?"

There was no reply. Maverick started to growl.

She waited for what seemed like an eternity, before hearing the crunch of dried dirt to her left, beyond the poplar tree.

Maverick reacted first and pivoted. Cassie whirled around. Her head lamp beam found the tree and then a figure standing at the base.

The explosion came from behind her in a flash of orange and reds, the concussive force knocking her over.

Cassie's face smashed into dirt. Stunned by the blow, her ears rang, and she felt dizzy and realized her head lamp was gone.

Her mind went to her rifle. She groped the ground for the gun, seeing Maverick stagger up a few feet away. He barked, though she could barely hear him over the ringing. Then the dog went into full attack mode, reared, and tore off into the woods.

"Maverick!"

But he was gone.

She forced herself up onto her knees, and her right hand instinctively drew the Colt Python.

There was a loud *thwack*—like two heavy bodies colliding off in the forest. Then, Maverick's howls of pain pierced the air.

Cassie got up fast, thumbing back the hammer on the pistol.

"MAVERICK!"

Something metallic clicked twenty yards to her right—Cassie tracked the sound and fired a shot. The pistol barked. The muzzle flash lit up the campsite. Something dark and hulking moved in the shadows. She fired again, blinking hard. Gun still up, she tried to determine if she hit her target.

A faint sound—*pop*. Something seemed to hit the dirt by her feet with a dull thud.

A hissing noise engulfed the campsite. A wet mist drifted across her face and clawed at her eyes. Cassie gasped. A sharp chemical odor seared her lungs.

She sputtered and choked. Her mind swam. Her limbs felt disjointed and her body began to spasm. She toppled to the ground.

Maverick's wailing echoed in the distance as Cassie clawed at the dirt, wanting to stop the tremors that dominated her, desperate to fight the darkness she felt coming.

But the seizure only got worse before she felt herself falling away.

Chapter 7

JIM GALE TOOK his attention off the reddish cloud billowing on the western horizon, and the bits of gray ash falling from the sky, to gaze at the young, extremely rank mule thundering around his feed corral as if looking to murder someone.

Gale spit tobacco. "Alvin, I'd rather break ten pissed-off mares than another damn mule."

Gale was in his midsixties, and though extremely fit, his body ached from sitting and his mind felt edgeless, the usual sensation one gets after driving six-odd hours straight. Plus, his damn allergies were kicking into overdrive with all the wildfires and smoke.

The record heat that gripped Big Sky country only made it worse and gave Gale the sensation of being in a constant dry sauna.

Alvin Petit, Gale's senior ranch hand, hoisted a leather saddlebag over his shoulder and tipped his sun-bleached cowboy hat over his eyes. He leaned against the corral's rusted metal gate and gazed at the angry mule still pounding around the corral in circles.

Petit said, "They make damn good pack animals once they're broken in."

"We don't need another mule. I don't want another mule."

Petit smiled. "How about your new son-in-law breaks him for you?"

Gale looked beyond the other side of the corral fence to the three ranch hands loading saddlebags and leather panniers onto a train of horses in front of the lodge. The largest of the three men, Gale's new son-in-law, Peter Trask, dropped one of the big panniers, and the other two ranch hands shook their heads and laughed.

"He'll get the hang of it," Gale said to Petit.

As a matter of fact, Gale was warming to his new son-in-law. While Trask's outward appearance teetered on domineering, Gale knew he was a good kid at heart, a gentle giant who treated his eldest daughter like a queen. So Gale was trying to make Trask's transition to ranch life as smooth as possible. Something Petit was reluctant to agree with.

"You can't be too easy on him or he'll never learn a thing," Petit said, "and it pisses off the others seeing him get a free pass."

"He's not getting a free pass, Alvin. It's just new to him."

"I'm just saying, the Davis brothers have been working here for two years, and they feel like they've been treated a bit unfairly."

"Unfairly?"

"It's time to cut them some slack, Jim."

"Not a chance," Gale said. "They start bar fights in town, they've got to live with the consequences. It affects my reputation."

"It's been two months, Jim, and they've been itchin' to get off the ranch."

"Like I told them, they're on my shit list till hunting season starts. They're lucky I didn't fire them in the first place. The amount of strings I had to pull with the sheriff." Gale shook his head.

Petit looked to Gale's truck pulled next to the corral—it was still running—and eyed Gale curiously. "How'd the trip go?"

"Politicians want what's best for their pockets; ranchers can't compete with the incoming developers. Same shit, different day."

"What did the ranchers from Bozeman have to say?"

"What ranchers from Bozeman? Whole Gallatin Valley looks like a miniature Portland. High-end suburbs in every direction, next thing you know there'll be a Whole Foods. Montana's changing, Alvin." Gale looked out over the golden rolling foothills of his ranch. "Only a matter of time until the rest of the world reaches us in our little plot of paradise."

Petit sighed. "I know I sound like a broken record, but it's time you ran for office. Get Bill Cronin at the Rocking R Ranch to back you. Cronin throws a long net, not just in the county, but all over the state. If you ran, Jim, you'd win."

"You know I could never be in the public eye, Alvin. Not with my history. Plus I couldn't put my family back in the spotlight," Gale said, looking over to the barn, and recalling the horrible memory. "Not since Derrick—"

Gale's voice cut and he couldn't finish the sentence.

"You'd get the veteran vote, too; half of Lewis and Clark County has served," Petit said, in a soft voice.

"They'd just think I was politicizing a tragedy."

"No, they—"

Gale held up his hand. "I stopped over at Tuck Cemetery on my way back. You picked a beautiful place, Alvin."

"I didn't pick anything," Petit said. "The boys in his platoon did. Good bunch of kids. You would have liked them."

Gale lowered his head, studied his dirty cowboy boots, and shifted his weight and grimaced.

"How's the hip?"

"Doesn't like long car rides," Gale said, stretching his hamstring, as he looked at the mule. "We still set for a three o'clock walk?"

Petit looked toward the pack train. "Emily needs another half hour getting everything of hers ready to load. Two of the clients have food sensitivities."

Loud laughter reverberated over to them.

Gale turned and looked at his place, the Whitehorse Ranch Lodge. The sprawling log cabin featured a wraparound front deck and wide, floor-to-ceiling windows that offered a tremendous view of the peaks of the Bob Marshall Wilderness to the north. Gale and the ranch hands had built much of the lodge themselves almost thirty years before: four bunk rooms in the lodge's western wing, an industrial-size kitchen, living room, and dining room in the center, and his private residence in the east wing.

A dozen men came out of the front door and stood on the deck, overlooking the pack train, getting ready for their trip in the mountains. The men sipped from beer bottles. They all wore matching bone-white cowboy hats, new Levi's, and matching blue flannel shirts.

Petit grumbled, "Never thought we'd be hauling dudes."

"Like I said, Montana's changing," Gale said, eyeing the men. "What the hell's with the getups? They look like a Chippendale act."

Petit laughed. "Corporate retreat, app developers out of Silicon Valley, guess they wanted matching outfits to develop brotherhood or some nonsense. They brought enough gluten-free beer to drown a herd of steers."

"Maybe we should send them to Bozeman," Gale said. "They'll fit right—"

A loud yell erupted from the horse train.

Trask stumbled backward into the lead horse. The horse whinnied in fright and kicked its hind legs. The big man took a hit and tumbled to the ground.

Sensing the lead horse's alarm, the dozen other horses reared in panic, tearing at their lead ropes.

"Oh for Christ's sake!" Petit roared.

Gale didn't hear him; he was already over the corral's feed gate and blowing by the mule. He jumped the second gate and sprinted to his son-in-law, grabbed him by the armpits, and dragged him away from the flying hooves. Petit came up behind them.

Trask pointed to a heap of saddle blankets on the dirt next to the lead horse and shouted, "Big snake! Big snake!"

Gale heard the rattling before he saw the diamondback. It was coiled in a defensive posture three feet from the horse's front legs. The frantic horse rose and came down hard. The diamondback retracted its head, then struck, venom-soaked fangs missing by inches.

The horses in the middle of the train slammed into the hitching post and thrashed at their ropes.

"Untie them and get them into the corral!" Gale shouted, lifting his son-in-law to his feet. "Trask, get the gate open!"

Petit and the Davis brothers fought to untie the bucking horses.

Gale snuck up behind the snake, which coiled for another strike. Gale shouted to his ranch hands, "Where's the snake stick?!"

Trask swung the horse corral gate open and yelled, "I don't know!"

Gale knew he had to do something fast. He came up behind the snake and grabbed it by the shaking rattle. In one fluid motion, he pivoted and slammed the rattler on the ground.

It was still moving.

Gale's hand flew to his belt and he drew his Colt Anaconda .44 Magnum from its holster.

BOOM!

The diamondback's body jolted, then ceased moving.

Gale holstered his weapon. Trask and Petit came up behind him.

Picking up the snake, Gale handed it to his son-in-law.

"We kill something around here, we eat it. That's the rule. And from now on, keep that snake stick with you when you're working with my horses, you hear?"

"Yes, Jim," Trask said.

Gale gazed over his son-in-law's shoulder. The lead horse continued to whinny in agitation as the Davis brothers tried to calm him down.

Gale called the brothers off and approached the horse.

"Easy boy, easy now," he said, his voice soothing.

The horse calmed down slightly, his eyes glued to Gale.

The clients on the deck watched in stunned silence.

Gale got under the lead rope, the horse snorted and pawed at the dirt. Gale put a delicate hand in front of its nose. Hot steam blasted his knuckles.

"You're fine old boy, easy does it," Gale said, as he unfastened the lead rope with his other hand. "C'mon, let's go for a walk."

Gale led the horse onto the driveway cul-de-sac and walked him in slow circles.

One of the dudes on the deck clapped his hands together and said loudly, "Talk about being in man-freaking-tana!"

Gale walked the horse back to the hitching post, and a shrill voice sounded over the commotion.

"What is going on out here!"

A small, pretty young woman with short, jet-black hair and piercing green eyes stood in front of the lodge's entrance.

Petit wiped his hands on his Wranglers and walked away from the dudes, pointing over his shoulder.

"That damn husband of yours nearly let a diamondback make mincemeat of our horses!"

Trask dropped the snake and hurried toward his wife, holding his right arm.

Gale's eldest daughter hopped down the stairs and went to her husband. Gale walked over and had Trask roll up his sleeve.

A welt the size of a baseball was swelling below the elbow where the horse's hoof had clipped him.

"I'll be fine," Trask grumbled.

Gale said, "Get some ice on it before we head out."

"And for the love of God, don't be leaving saddle blankets out overnight for rattlers to be crawling in them, this ain't the damn city!" Petit said, storming off into the lodge.

"That old bastard needs to cool it," Emily muttered. "Pete's still learning."

"Alvin's of a different generation, give him time," Gale said, watching the old cowboy disappear inside.

"When did you get back from Helena?" Emily asked her father.

"About ten minutes ago." He flicked his head to the large cloud on the eastern horizon. "That fire in Wolf Creek jumped the highway, had to turn back and take the Helmville route."

"How'd everything go?"

"I'll tell you about it later. All the meals packed?"

"Breakfast and lunch for five days. Petit said he's got venison and that elk backstrap in the freezer he's going to bring up for dinners," Emily replied.

"Good, let's get that diamondback skinned and into one of the coolers. I'm sure these California boys are itching to try it," Gale said with a sly smile, then walked toward the lodge.

Emily called after him, "Oh, Dad. Someone's been calling the office line all morning. I told him you were out of town and had your cell off. His number's on your desk."

"All right," Gale said, his mind elsewhere. "Trask, pull my truck in the garage, keys are in the ignition. And let's not serve the clients any more beer. I don't want them drunk on my horses."

Gale took his cowboy hat off and entered the lodge's main room. It was a spacious living area containing a set of full grain leather couches, a flat-screen television, and a billiards table. European mounts of monstrous bull elk and mule deer bucks adorned the walls. He walked through the room to the stairway and could hear Petit cursing in the kitchen.

Gale climbed the stairs to the second floor and into his cluttered office. A blue sticky note sat on his keyboard. He went to the window, cranked the air conditioner, and loosened his collar.

Sinking into his desk chair, Gale grabbed the sticky note. The area code on the handwritten scrawl read: 907. *That's an Alaska number.*

The name written above the number read: Dennis Price.

"Shit."

He picked up the receiver on his office phone and dialed. A gruff man's voice sounded on the other line, "High Water Rafting Expeditions. This is Dennis Price."

Gale introduced himself, leaned over his desk, and grabbed a small snow globe with a miniature version of the Eiffel Tower in it. He shook the globe and watched the shards of white plastic create a faux blizzard in his hand.

Price cleared his throat. "I have you listed as an emergency contact for one of my new guides, Cassandra Gale; she's your daughter?"

Gale stopped shaking the snow globe. "She is."

"Well, Cassandra never showed up on Monday and she's not answering either number I have listed for her."

"Never showed up?"

"Her group left for the Arctic refuge yesterday, I was wondering if you've heard from her?"

Gale felt the muscles in his shoulders tense. He put the snow globe down on the oak desk. The afternoon light cut above the air conditioner and flooded across the rug-covered floor. He told Price that Cassie had left eight days before and he hadn't heard from her since.

"She's put me in a helluva bind," Price said. "I had to scramble to find another guide last minute. You get ahold of her, tell her I'll give her until tomorrow to get here before we'll have to move along and find someone else."

Gale thanked the man and promised he'd get back in touch. He hung up the phone and stared at his reflection on the computer screen. The lamp on the table next to him was on, and the plasma screen on the far wall displayed muted images of the fires in Wolf Creek. Petit must have been using his office while he was gone, Gale thought, before his gaze settled on the black-and-white framed photograph of a woman on his desk. He stared at the photograph and frowned, his attention flitting to the far wall.

He stood and walked to the wall, his gaze settling on another picture, framed amid the others—the picture that brought him the happiest of memories and consequently the saddest—a young man, his arm hung around his youngest daughter. Her posture relaxed, her green cammies taut around a small but muscular frame. Her head was tilted back, her brilliant white teeth flashing a million-dollar smile. *She was so happy,* Gale thought, his eyes going to his own figure next to them, holding the large German shepherd by the leash, his other arm draped around Emily who leaned into Trask. It was one of the happiest moments of his life. One of his favorite photographs—one of Cassie's favorite photographs. He knew she kept a wallet-size version of the photo with her at all times.

She was so happy. We were all so happy.

He touched the picture with a dirty thumb as he said softly, "What have you done now, Cassie Gale?"

Chapter 8

GALE TRIED CASSIE'S cell phone first. It went straight to voice mail. He rummaged in his desk drawer and found the number listed for the satellite phone he bought her and like the cell, it was turned off. Then he fired up his computer and got the number for the Alaskan State Troopers out of Fairbanks.

A bored man's voice answered and identified himself as a desk sergeant.

Gale introduced himself and asked if there had been any car crashes or anyone showing up in their system with the name of Cassandra Ann Gale. He gave the trooper the make and model of Cassie's truck and license plate number. The man put him on hold, then came back on the line. There had been two auto accidents in southeast Alaska the week before. None involved a green Toyota Tundra. And none of the victims were identified as his daughter.

His next call was to the Canadian Mounted Police in the Yukon territory.

The Mounties ran Cassie's information through their database and came up with nothing.

He then tried the border crossing at Sweetgrass in northern Montana and the border crossing into Alaska at Little Gold, via the Yukon territory. The station at Little Gold didn't answer, and an agent in Sweetgrass said his supervisor would get back to him.

Gale hung up and stood over his desk.

Excited laughter echoed up from his Silicon Valley clients outside. He crossed the room and shut his office door. When he sat down, he stared out the window and up at the Bob Marshall Wilderness.

Cassie could very well just be running late to Fairbanks. Her phones could be off and she could have just gotten stuck in summer work delays.

Or, Gale speculated, maybe she just decided to spend an extra day or two camping. But why hadn't she contacted anyone about her new plans? That wasn't like his youngest daughter. The fact that she hadn't shown up to her first day of work, let alone notified someone of her absence, didn't sit right. Something was off.

He had a puckering thought—the same dark thought that had pestered him almost every day for the last six months. But he wouldn't allow himself to go there, not now. Gale took that dark thought and put it in a box along with all the other boxes he had stashed away in the deep recesses of his mind. He picked up the snow globe again and stared at his reflection.

Compartmentalize, he thought. *Look at this objectively, keep the emotion out.*

He opened the door to his office and called down for Petit to come up.

The old cowboy leaned against the doorframe and pulled a tin of Copenhagen Long Cut out of his pocket, proffering it to Gale. When Gale shook his head, Petit shrugged and opened the tin, popping the chewing tobacco into his mouth and maneuvering it to his bottom lip.

"If this is about yellin' at Pete, the only way that boy is gonna learn is if someone gets tough on him."

"It's not about Trask." Gale told Petit about the call with Dennis Price. When Gale finished, the old cowboy sat down on the couch opposite Gale's desk and remained silent for about thirty seconds, then said, "Nothing from the authorities?"

"Nothing," Gale replied. "US Border Patrol said they'd give me a call back."

Petit scrutinized the patterns in the rug. "Well, if you want to stay here until you get things sorted out, I can take this crew up to base camp tonight. Trask and Emily should be more than enough help for the week."

"No, Emily can help me track her. Trask, too, they're both good with that stuff. I'll take the Davis brothers off my shit list for the week. But they're not allowed to touch any beer. I don't care if it's gluten free, or not."

"They can do that."

"If we're not at base camp by morning, head to the lake on schedule. Second we hear from Cassie, I'll call you and we'll meet up there."

When Petit got up to leave, Gale asked him to send up Emily and Trask.

When they walked in, Trask held an ice pack over his injured forearm and Emily looked irritated. "If Petit is still bitching about the snake, let me remind you—"

Something about her father's face made her stop short, and she eyed him, alarmed.

"What happened?"

Gale leaned against his desk and explained the situation.

When he finished, he said, "I'm going to need you to help me access her satellite phone's data, it should give us a position from where she last made a call."

Emily's face dropped. She planted herself on the couch and shook her head in disbelief. "You don't think she—"

"No," Gale said, sternly. "We can't be thinking like that. Just get me that satphone information."

They both said they would and left the room to go downstairs to use the house computer.

Gale's phone rang.

It was the Immigration and Naturalization Services supervisor at the Sweetgrass crossing. He told Gale he couldn't release any information on Cassie's passing without a state or federal warrant. He told Gale his best option would be to contact the Alaska State Police or the Canadian Mounted Police and get a missing person report filed and a petition to INS for a release of records.

Emily poked her head through the doorway. "Pete got access to Cassie's call log."

Gale thanked the supervisor, hung up, and followed his daughter downstairs. Out of the front windows, he could see Petit leading the pack train of dudes toward the Bob Marshall Wilderness.

His son-in-law's large frame was huddled over the computer in the living room.

"Globalstar account was listed in your name, Jim. I've got her time logs."

"Show me."

Trask pulled up the page. "She made twelve calls from the time she left here on the eighteenth, looks like nine went through, three didn't. She called the same number."

"That's Derrick's number, Dad," Emily said. "She never canceled his phone service."

"Last call was four days ago, twenty-second of June, out of Alaska at 6:32 p.m.," Trask said.

"Does the company log the GPS coordinates from where the calls were made?" Gale asked.

"They should."

"Then find out exactly where it was made."

Trask noted the coordinates from the latest call entry and copied and pasted them into Google Earth. The screen zeroed in on a tributary of the Yukon River some eight miles northwest of Eagle, Alaska.

The area was an ocean of mismatched hues: jagged mountains and green valleys, with the Yukon River slithering through the satellite image like a brown snake. Trask zoomed in as far as he could. The coordinates pinpointed Cassie's last call from the remote bank on a narrow tributary of the Yukon. An old dirt road ran parallel to the river coming up from Eagle and ended abruptly a mile to the northwest of where she made the call.

"Hell of a place to camp," Trask said.

"She was looking for desolate. You're positive that was the last call she made?" Gale asked.

"Last one that's recorded."

"We can work with this. I'm going to call the troopers again, see if we can get anyone up there to check on her." Gale ran up the stairs and redialed the Alaska State Trooper office in Fairbanks.

The same desk sergeant answered the phone and Gale got him up to speed with the situation. The sergeant was quiet on the line for a moment then told Gale he would transfer him to the Alaska Bureau of Investigation.

"I'll patch you through to the sergeant that runs point on that region," the man said.

The phone rang again and was picked up abruptly; a sharp woman's voice answered, identifying herself as Sergeant Meredith Plant with the ABI.

Gale gave the blow by blow as fast as he could, asking once again if he could get a trooper up to the tributary to check on Cassie.

"Give me a minute," Plant said. She came back on the line five minutes later. "The only trooper I've got in the area is stationed in the town of Tok, some four hundred miles from Eagle. He's on assignment for the next couple days in Delta Junction. Let me see if I can get in contact with the village public safety officer in Eagle."

Plant's voice returned a couple minutes later.

"The village public safety officer isn't answering his phone. You'll want to deal with him on this. I left him a message to get back to me—"

"What's his number?" Gale grabbed a pen and paper. The sergeant read it off for him. Then Gale asked, "And if he's unreachable, could someone be flown over from Fairbanks?"

Sergeant Plant gave a sigh of resignation. "My detachment covers two thousand, three hundred square miles, and I've only got ten troopers on the job, and they're overworked as it is. I can't just tell my guys to drop everything and travel that distance because your daughter is a couple days late for work. Unless there are any circumstances that would lead you to believe she's in danger, either to herself, or at the hands of someone else, I can't really be of much help other than to say, contact the village public safety officer."

Gale eyed the picture on the wall.

"Mr. Gale?"

"My daughter," he tried to say as controlled as possible, "has been going through a rough time lately."

He gave the sergeant a brief overview of what had happened to his daughter in the last six months. When he finished, Plant remained silent on the other line.

"I'm really sorry to hear that, Mr. Gale," she said, finally. "I'm . . . truly sorry for her."

Gale swallowed hard.

Plant continued, "Given the circumstances, I can expedite a missing person report into our clearinghouse."

Gale spent the next fifteen minutes giving Sergeant Plant all the information he had on his daughter as well as faxing over a picture of her. Trask and Emily came into the office and stood with their backs against the wall.

When Gale hung up, Emily asked, "Someone's checking on her?"

"Hold on," Gale said, dialing the phone number to the VPSO office in Eagle. It went to voice mail. Gale left a detailed message and asked the officer to get back to him ASAP. When he hung up, he looked at Emily.

"I filed a missing person report. The troopers can now request information from the INS, but it'll still be two days before a trooper can get up there, and the village public safety officer in Eagle isn't answering."

"Then we do it," Emily said.

"How long is the drive to Eagle?" Gale asked.

"Google Maps said forty-one hours, more to get to the tributary," Trask said.

"I'll check flights, see if I can get into Fairbanks tonight."

"We're coming with you," Emily said.

Gale wiggled the mouse on his computer. "You can't, I need you here."

"Call Bill Cronin, he can cover for us, they owe us a ton of favors."

"Em—" Gale said, shaking his head, his attention glued to the computer screen.

"If you seriously think I'm just going to sit here while my little sister might be in danger, you're out of your mind. What if she's hurt? Are you going to single-handedly pull her out of that wilderness with that bum hip of yours?"

"My hip is fine and the troopers will be able to help me—"

"They won't be up there for another two days!"

Gale remained silent, pondered what his daughter said, then shook his head.

"What if she broke her back, what if she's sick—you would need our help!" Emily yelled.

Emily could handle herself in most situations but Gale wasn't so sure of her abilities in the wilderness. As a young girl, she had shied away from hunting trips into the mountains and the second she turned eighteen, she had moved to Salt Lake in search of a life in the city.

Compared to Cassie, she was also more emotional. He worried how his eldest daughter might act if they got up there and the situation was more dire than they had anticipated. What if Cassie had planned all along to use the trip as cover to get away from therapy—to get away from everything forever?

Gale considered that idea. One dark box in his mind started to crack open. He felt the terror of the memories in that box spill out like acid. It made his ears ring. The ringing got louder, the box opened wider.

"Dad, answer me!"

"What if it's worse!" Gale said, his voice harsher than intended. "Your sister has obviously been lying to us all, and lying to her therapists. She's been calling Derrick's phone nonstop from the moment she left here." He pointed at Emily. "Are you prepared to find your little sister hanging from some goddamn tree?!"

Emily's face looked like Gale just slapped her.

Gale kneaded his brow and walked to the window, the open box in his consciousness unleashing a tidal wave of fear. His hands shook. He rested them on the air conditioner and looked down again at the rank mule in the feed corral.

"How dare you," Emily said coldly. "I've put everything on hold for this family, my education, my career—everything! I was the one sitting by Cassie's bed all January. I was the one feeding her, making sure she wouldn't harm herself. And where were you, huh?"

Emily took a predatory step closer. "Taking those walks by yourself in the mountains, crawling into that shell of yours. You couldn't even show up for the funeral!"

"Em," Trask said, reaching for his wife.

"No!" Emily slapped her husband's hand away and glared at her father. "I might not be as physically tough as you and Cassie, I get that. But I'm the only one capable of holding this family together when shit hits the fan. I basically raised my sister until she was ten. I watched over her while you mourned for Mom for the better part of a decade. All the drinking—those solo trips in the mountains. What kind of mature adult would force that on his kids?"

"Stop!" Gale snapped.

"Stop what? Talking about Mom?" Emily pointed to the black-and-white picture on the desk. "You keep it there like some sort of shrine, but God forbid we speak about her!"

"You don't know what you are talking about."

"That's right," Emily shot back. "I don't know, because you never talk about any of it. Your time in the service, the embassy work in Moscow, Paris—Mom's car accident, and now Derrick."

She let Derrick's name linger in the air like a dark cloud. When she spoke again, her voice was serrated. "If my little sister is in trouble, or God forbid she is dead and hanging from a tree—I will *not* let you jump back into that shell of yours. I will not let you block out the rest of us. I'm going with you and that's that."

"*We* are going with you," Trask said.

Gale clenched his jaw so hard he thought his teeth might splinter. He stood staring at his eldest daughter and her husband. "Fine," he finally said. "Get the rifles out of the safe and into locked, hard-side cases. We're going to Alaska. Tonight."

He waited until they left the room and shut and locked the door to his office. Emily's words still rattled in his ears. He felt his heart rate spike. Felt the boxes overflow in his chest—those dark thoughts boiling up, and his worst fear—the fear of losing his daughters.

He almost lost them once, all those years ago. He'd been a different person then.

Gale trembled as the memories of his past life washed over him. The dark cobblestone Moscow streets, the Paris high-rise—

His attention dropped to the carpet he stood on, his mind's eye visualizing what lay hidden beneath the floorboards. After a long moment, Gale yanked the carpet from the floor, wedged his fingers between the semiloose board and lifted, exposing a pitch-black space below.

More memories flooded through him.

The gray concrete edifices swarming the Kremlin. The biting wind and deep snow-drifts of the Khimki Forest.

Gale reached down into the space and pulled up a green metal box.

Inside was a reminder of his past—

A promise he'd made himself.

He'd almost lost his little girls once.

That would never happen again. They would outlive him, raise families, have children, grandchildren.

Gale opened the box and snatched and pocketed the envelope within. He carried the envelope with him for nearly ten years after his wife died, after they'd been relocated to Montana. He carried it with him in January after—

But he'd never opened it. Not in over thirty years.

The thought of having the envelope on his person anchored him.

Made him never forget who he once was.

What he once did.

Cassie would be safe.

Gale would make sure of that.

Chapter 9

THE CESSNA 172 Skyhawk shuddered and lurched from side to side before dropping seventy feet through thick cloud cover.

Gale cinched his seat belt tighter around his waist then gripped the seat rest. Two decades before, he had gotten his private pilot's license to scout for elk in the off-season around the ranch. But he quickly realized that he didn't have an affinity for flying, plus the fuel it required was too expensive. He hadn't flown a plane in nearly eighteen years and much preferred to either keep his feet on solid ground or let a professional do the flying.

Over his headset, the pilot yelled: "Hold on!"

As the plane rolled left then fell, the vibration in the small cabin made Gale feel like he was a conduit in an electric current. Trask and Emily groaned behind him. Raindrops ran off the plane's windows, and a clap of thunder sent a violent tremor through the cockpit.

Gale sat next to the pilot, who backed off the throttle. The plane dipped and bounced, but the pilot held firm and just when Gale thought he couldn't take it anymore, they finally descended into clear air.

Gale could hear the pilot's sigh of relief through the headset speakers, then he pointed.

"That'll be Eagle over there."

Gale looked out the Cessna's windshield at the cappuccino-colored water of the Yukon River stretched out beneath them. Countless tributaries jutted off from the main channel, and Gale could see the colored specks of houses in the distance on the far southern shoreline.

After the heated exchange in his office the day before, Emily and Trask had packed in a hurry while Gale made the necessary arrangements to get them all to Alaska as fast as possible. He'd alerted Sergeant Plant of their intentions to head north and she confirmed that Cassie's missing person report had been entered into the state's clearinghouse. Their request of a release of records at the US Border Patrol station could now be issued.

The flight out of Helena to Seattle had gone off without a hitch. So had the red-eye from Seattle to Fairbanks. They landed at six that morning, and Gale chartered the small, four-seat, single-engine Cessna from a sight-seeing operation to get them to Eagle.

While they loaded their rifle cases and daypacks onto the Cessna, Gale had taken the opportunity to dial and redial the Village Public Safety Officer Support Office in Eagle.

His calls went unanswered.

This communication problem bothered him. He had found out through Sergeant Plant that the VPSO in the area was named Max Tobeluk, a six-year veteran of the Alaskan volunteer service and that Plant, too, had been trying to get ahold of him to no avail.

The Cessna sailed smoothly over the vast expanse of wilderness and banked above the small town before it straightened out in front of the muddy runway and touched down. The pilot hit the brakes and taxied to a small, two-plane hangar. An orange wind sock flapped against its lashes next to a sign outside the small building that read: WELCOME TO EAGLE AIRPORT.

The pilot helped them unload their equipment, then shook Gale's hand. "You need a ride out of here, give me a call."

Gale thanked the man and watched as the plane taxied down the runway and took off again.

It was nine a.m., and the tiny airstrip sat deserted.

"Map said it's a half mile to town, guess we're walking."

Gale took the hard-plastic case of his Colt Anaconda out of his luggage and unlocked the clasp. He cracked the cylinder and loaded the pistol, put on his holster, and cinched the weapon in place.

Emily did the same with her weapon. Trask carried most of the supplies.

Eagle seemed asleep when they arrived, but the VPSO's office on Front Street was easy to find. It was an elevated, brown shanty that stood on six feet of cement cinder blocks a mere fifty yards from the Yukon's shoreline. Gale climbed the front steps and hammered on the door. He waited several moments, then peered through the window, trying without luck to catch a glimpse between the shades and the sill.

"Em, does your phone have reception?"

"Half a signal."

"Call that VPSO's number for me."

Gale pressed his ear to the door as Emily called; he heard a faint ringing from inside then heard it go to voice mail.

"Should we ask someone where this guy is?" Trask said.

Gale told them to stay put and he circled the building and found a white Ford Expedition with the VPSO logo painted on its side sitting next to a garage. He was about to go back to the front of the building when he heard something across the street.

A man with the body composition of a pear dragged a two-wheel dolly to a stack of crates that lined the side of a storefront.

Gale hurried over to him.

"We don't open till ten today," the man said, without looking up. "Cisco truck didn't show up until late last night and I'm the only one on shift."

"I'm trying to find the public safety officer, you know where he is?"

The man turned his chubby face to Gale. "Who, Tobeluk?"

"Max Tobeluk. He's not in his office and he's not answering my calls."

"Yeah, he wouldn't be."

"Why's that?"

"'Cause he's probably piss drunk somewhere." The guy squinted at Gale, his eyes going from his cowboy hat to the pistol on his hip. "What're you, some sort of cop?"

"Not a cop, just need the public safety officer."

The guy looked at Gale for a long beat. "Villagers won't talk to him anymore. He's staying in town now. If he's here, check the lime-green piece of shit on Chamberlain and Fourth. There's a busted-up truck in the front lawn."

Gale started back to the office to grab Trask and Emily.

"Oh," the guy called after him. "Make yourself known before you start banging on his door. That drunk bastard's trigger-happy when he's surprised."

Gale thanked the man and collected Trask and Emily and led them up Chamberlain and stopped at Fourth. A lime-green, dilapidated shack sat against the forest. A 1970s Bronco sat in the front yard; tall saw grass grew out of the empty chassis.

Gale approached the shack's warped door and knocked, calling out, "Max Tobeluk!"

There was a loud crash and the sound of glass bottles breaking. Someone cursed from inside.

Gale hammered on the door again.

A dead bolt was thrown and the door creaked open exposing a shirtless man with high, sunken cheekbones. The man leaned a supporting elbow against the doorframe and squinted through bloodshot eyes.

Gale almost recoiled from the stench of booze.

"What do you want, man?"

"You're Max Tobeluk, the public safety officer?"

"Sorry, off duty."

Tobeluk made to shut the door; Gale slid his boot between the door and the doorjamb.

"I've been trying to get ahold of you since yesterday."

Tobeluk blinked.

"Sergeant Plant has been trying to get ahold of you, too."

This seemed to awaken the man and he looked at Gale as if seeing him for the first time. Like the fat guy down the street, Tobeluk stared at Gale's cowboy hat before his gaze settled on the revolver at his hip.

"I'm sorry, who are you?"

"Jim Gale. I need you to take me downriver so I can find my daughter." He gave Tobeluk a brief explanation of Cassie's last known location via the satphone, how she didn't show up to work three days before. "I need an authority on scene just in case the troopers need to be called in."

Tobeluk shook his head. "You need an MPR filed—"

"A missing person report was filed last night. Sergeant Plant faxed it to your office."

Tobeluk swayed, then saw Trask and Emily waiting on Chamberlain Street, their luggage at their feet.

"You brought friends."

"Get dressed and meet us at your office before I call your sergeant and tell her you've been partying on the clock."

||||||||||||||||||||||||||||||||||||||||||||||||||||||||||||||||||||||||||||||||||||

Tobeluk eyed Emily as he fumbled with his keys and climbed the front steps to the VPSO building. His brown uniform looked like it hadn't seen an iron in months, and his belt was cinched two notches too loose, causing his Taser to rest halfway down his upper leg. He noted the pistol in Emily's holster and smiled smugly.

"Everyone in the family own a Colt pistol with a cattle bone grip?"

"Every public safety officer armed with a Taser?" Emily retorted.

Tobeluk's smirk fell, and he opened the door.

The office was small and consisted of a cluttered desk with a blinking fax machine and a phone. Papers spilled out of the fax machine tray and onto the floor. A massive topographic map of the region hung on the wall. Tobeluk turned on the light. Dirty dishes and coffee mugs lay strewn on the counter next to the sink, and the place smelled of mold, plywood, and Lysol. Tobeluk grabbed as many of the dishes as he could and deposited them in the sink. Two empty bottles of whiskey rested on the messy desk. He snatched them up and threw them in the trash. Then he fired up the Keurig coffeemaker.

"Anyone want a cup?"

"I'd like to get downriver," Gale said, impatiently.

Tobeluk picked up Cassie's missing person report pages that the fax machine had spat on the floor. He sat behind his desk and punched the blinking light on his answering machine.

He lifted the receiver, pressed it to his ear, and moved through the voice mails in silence. When he finished, he hung up, cursed under his breath, and went through Cassie's MPR.

"You don't carry a cell phone?" Trask asked.

"Dropped it in the river last week," Tobeluk said, and then looked to Gale. "So Plant said Cassandra is with her dog?"

"Yes, Maverick, he's a German shepherd."

Tobeluk flipped over the front page of the report and scribbled something on the back. Gale noticed the man's hand shook as he wrote.

"And you have the coordinates where she made that last call?" Tobeluk said.

Emily took out her iPhone, opened Google Maps, and showed Tobeluk the area of Cassie's last known location.

"That's eight miles downriver, we're not going to be able to use the road."

"Why not?"

"Flooded from the rain in the last week, won't be serviceable for at least a couple days." He paused in thought. "That's probably why Cassandra never showed up for work. She's probably stranded down there. Happens a couple times a year during tourist season."

Gale fought the temptation to argue with the VPSO that Cassie had a satellite phone with her—that she could have called someone if she was in trouble—but he knew bringing it up would amount to more time in the office, and less time searching for his daughter.

"Anything else I need to know before we take the boat downriver?" Tobeluk asked.

"No," Gale said. "Not right now."

"Good, let's go get your daughter and her dog."

Chapter 10

FRIGID YUKON WATER splashed Gale in the face and he wiped at his eyes with his forearm. The VPSO's Zodiac boat rose over a large swell of white water and slammed down. Gale loosened his grip on the throttle.

After inflating the Zodiac back in Eagle, Tobeluk's hangover had hit him full bore and the VPSO had retched on the shoreline.

Gale demanded that he drive the boat. Tobeluk didn't argue.

As they jetted down the river, the VPSO sat up front and kept his chin tucked to his chest. Emily and Trask sat behind him and Emily cinched the straps on her life vest and scooted to the middle of the boat's bench, her eyes never leaving Google Maps on her iPhone. An hour into their trip, Emily shouted over the revving motor: "One more mile to the confluence!"

Gale stood tall and let off the motor. The late-morning sun shimmered off the river's silted waters and the sweeping ridges and forests beyond the rocky shoreline. Gale checked to make sure the waterproof rifle cases were still secured below the bench and gunned the motor again.

"There!" Emily said, ten minutes later and pointed ahead where the wide berth of the Yukon split off into a narrow tributary. Gale maneuvered the boat and steered it down the narrow body of water. The current was calmer than the main channel and within five minutes, Emily was indicating the western shoreline where a boulder the size of an automobile sat next to a swirling eddy against the bank.

"GPS says this is where she made the call, Dad."

Gale ran the boat up onshore and cut the engine.

Emily cupped her hands around her mouth, "Cassie!"

Her voice got lost in the sound of flowing water.

Gale grabbed the rifle cases and took out his .300 Winchester Magnum. He loaded the magazine, then chambered a round. Emily and Trask each took their 12-gauge, pump-action shotguns and loaded in rifled-slug and buckshot shells.

Tobeluk stumbled out of the boat, groaning as he clutched his forehead.

"You going to be okay?" Trask asked.

Tobeluk waved him off and fumbled for his own shotgun, a .10-gauge Remington 870.

Emily yelled Cassie's name again.

"Map says the road is a quarter mile from the river. She might not be able to hear us until we're farther inland," Gale said.

The forest looked like a wall of green before them. Gale walked the tight bank searching for an opening in the foliage. He found a game trail slicing through a tangle of willows and called the others over.

The forest floor was soggy, the mud sucking at their boots. Gale led the way. Every dozen yards or so, Emily and Trask would call out Cassie's name and wait for a reply.

None came.

After ten minutes of walking, the forest began to open, blue sky spilled through the canopy, and the sun glinted off an unnatural surface in the distance.

"That's Cassie's truck!" Emily cried.

Gale took another step, circumventing a thicket of brush and stopped in his tracks.

"Oh my God," Emily blurted and tried to get around her father.

"Don't, Emmy!" Gale said, grabbing his daughter by the arm, while staring in disbelief at the sight before them.

What remained of Cassie's red Cabela's tent was strewn about the muddy clearing and across her deflated raft. The nylon and polyester fabric looked like it had done battle with a chainsaw. Food wrappers, punctured cans, and cooking condiments littered the campsite like confetti.

Cassie's Toyota Tundra was parked on the road embankment, its Bridgestone tires sunk in eight inches of mud. The green pickup's tailgate and back cap were wide open—Cassie's purple sleeping bag spilling out of the back.

But what made Gale's heart quake wasn't just the condition of the camp—it was the pancake-sized tracks in the mud.

"CASS—"

Gale covered Emily's mouth with his hand and held it there, her eyes opened wide in confusion. Gale indicated the tracks, and Emily's eyes grew even wider. He slowly released his hand from her mouth and held up a finger for silence.

He unslung his rifle and raised it, his eyes roving the perimeter of the forest for any signs of movement.

"Those are brownie tracks," Tobeluk hissed. "Big brownie tracks."

"Nobody moves," Gale said, thumbing off his rifle's safety. He took a cautious step forward into the demolished campsite. The mud was deeper than in the concealed forest, and he sunk up to the tongue of his boot. He took three more steps and came to the first track and stopped. No water pooled in the deep indentations, or in the four-inch claw marks.

Tobeluk was right. They were grizzly tracks.

Fresh grizzly tracks.

Gale crept sideways and came to the truck's open tailgate. He poked his head inside. Maverick's blankets lay in a clump next to Cassie's sleeping bag. The driver's-side door was unlocked. Cassie's satellite phone and iPhone were on the passenger's seat. Her car keys jutted from the cup holder where she always put them. He let them be and returned to the tracks.

From what Gale could see, the grizzly had entered the camp from the southeast and seemed to have poked its way through the demolished tent, stopping periodically near the opened food wrappers. No crumbs or sign of food lay in the mud. *This wasn't the first animal to come through the camp*, he decided.

Gale followed the tracks as they lumbered to the road and headed north.

"Dad, what's going on?"

"The rain, what day did it start?" Gale asked Tobeluk.

The public safety officer shook his head, his eyes never leaving the destroyed tent. "Um . . . the . . . the morning of the twenty-third?"

Gale's attention returned to the Tundra. The sunken tires in the muddy earth, the raft oars secured to the roof. *Break this down*, Gale thought, trying to keep his mind under control—*the Tundra got stuck in the mud, she might have walked back to Eagle—but why didn't she use the satellite phone to call for help?*

I need to check the phone.

Gale went to the cab of the truck and grabbed the Globalstar satellite phone and tried to turn it on. It was dead, so was the iPhone. He grabbed Cassie's keys, put them in the ignition, and turned the engine over. The satellite phone's charger stuck out of the center console. He plugged the satphone in and a red light appeared on the charging port.

Too dead to make a call.

But why didn't she charge her phone and call out?

"Jim."

Gale stuck his head out of the truck and saw his son-in-law holding Cassie's mud-soaked .375 H&H Magnum rifle in his hands.

"Where did you find that?"

Trask pointed next to the log, near the stone fire pit.

Gale took the gun, dropped the magazine plate, and ran the action. Four bullets hit the mud.

"Hasn't been fired." Gale held Cassie's rifle, staring down at the wrecked tent, and felt a spasm of panic spin up his spine.

"Did a bear?" Emily croaked.

"No," Gale said, pointing to the tracks. "This one was just scavenging."

Gale tried to run through the situations in his head that could explain the state of the camp—maybe Cassie and Maverick had to run from a bear? She could have escaped with her daypack and her pistol. He tried to remember if she had her survival equipment and a small secondary tent with her. Tobeluk knelt then and pushed the remnants of the tent aside, exposing Cassie's daypack.

Other than being covered in mud, the tan Stone Glacier backpack was untouched, a bottle of bear spray strapped to its waist clip. Gale snatched the pack from the VPSO and opened it—Cassie's first aid, flares, and thermal blankets stared up at him.

Tobeluk tugged again at the tent and cursed under his breath.

Cassie's steel-sided food box lay unlocked and open, devoid of anything but a torn-up, plastic Wheat Montana bread loaf wrapper. Tobeluk held the wrapper in his hands. "She left her food box open in her tent."

Gale stared at the box.

"That's not possible," Emily said, finally.

Gale shook his head in disbelief. There was no way Cassie Gale, his daughter, had broken *the* cardinal rule of bear country.

Never leave open food at ground level.

Emily started to cry. "If something got her, we need to find her—she might be hurt somewhere!"

"Jim, we need to call in a search party," Trask said, looking at the radio on Tobeluk's belt. "You can call it in?"

The VPSO shook his head. "We'd have to get closer to town—"

"What about Cassie's satellite phone?" Trask asked.

"We need to get a plane up here," Emily said.

"Everyone just stop!" Gale barked. "Calm down. First things first. Emily give me your phone."

She dug in her pocket and handed him the iPhone. Gale took pictures of the tent, the truck, the grizzly tracks, and the campsite as a whole, then handed it back.

"We'll send those to the troopers so we can get some help. Cassie's satellite phone is charging in the truck; when it turns on, we make the call. Till then, we pull this place apart."

He assigned Trask to the tent, Emily to the perimeter of the campsite, and Tobeluk to walk around the camp in ever-expanding circles.

"If you find anything of interest, holler and we'll all come over. And keep your weapons on you."

"What are you going to do?" Trask asked.

"I'll run down the road and see if there is any sign of her and Maverick trying to get back to Eagle."

Gale slung his rifle over his shoulder and took off. He stayed on the shelf between the muddy road and the tree line. Around every corner he expected to see his daughter sitting on the side of the road anxiously waiting for her father to find her.

Gale trotted on for a couple miles until the searing pain in his hip forced him to stop. He stooped over, gasping. The trees around him creaked and moaned in the soft midday wind.

His mind flashed back on the campsite.

The flayed tent, the ripped apart food wrappers, the discarded rifle.

He started to panic.

Hold it together.

You don't know what's happened.

Remember the promise you made. Nothing would happen to her.

That same voice inside his head then told him to stand, to go back and be strong for his daughter, for his family. This wasn't the time to run away.

This was the time to act.

※※※※※

"We found something," Emily said, as Gale jogged into the campsite.

Trask walked over to his father-in-law and handed him an oddly shaped stainless-steel canister the size of a small thermos. The canister bottlenecked at the top and was open. Gale studied the object.

"What is this?"

"No idea."

"Where'd you find it?"

Trask indicated the mud next to the log.

Gale turned the canister over and looked down the opening, then sniffed it, recoiling immediately. The smell was brutally sharp and chemical.

"Dad, there's something else."

Emily led him to a tall poplar tree standing on the northern perimeter of the campsite. She pointed to a rope hanging over a high branch.

Gale recognized the rope—it was the same type they used at the ranch. One end of the rope was secured around the trunk of the tree, while the other hung over the branch and moved in the wind—its end frayed.

"Cassie *did* hang her food box," Emily said.

Gale stared up at the rope undulating in the wind as Tobeluk entered the camp.

"Anything?" Trask said.

Tobeluk leaned against Cassie's truck and shook his head. "Nothing, you?"

Trask indicated the metallic canister in Gale's hand. "Just this."

The VPSO walked over to them and snatched the canister from Gale. Tobeluk's face turned from confusion to incredulity. "Where was this?"

Trask showed him. "You know what this is?"

The VPSO shook his head, still holding the canister. "No."

Gale's mind spun. None of this was normal. *None of this adds up—where the hell is Cassie? Where the hell is Maverick?*

Gale tried to rein in his thoughts, when a large branch snapped in the forest behind him.

He moved between Emily and the trees.

Another *snap!*

Something was crashing toward them.

Gale drew his pistol.

He could hear the heavy, labored breathing of a large animal—the willows under the poplar swayed and parted.

A glint of brown fur.

Gale wrapped his index finger around the trigger and aimed at the patch of fur with both eyes open.

Chapter 11

A DARK NOSE broke from the willows, followed by a head.

"Maverick!" Gale shouted and lowered his weapon.

The German shepherd stumbled out and collapsed. Gale and Emily ran to him. Maverick whined softly. His fur was matted in filth and dried blood. The dog struggled to his feet. Gale held him down with a gentle hand.

"Mav!" Emily cried, kneeling by the dog, as the others came up behind her.

A deep livid gash scarred Maverick's head from his left eye to the ridge of his nose.

"He needs water."

"Here," Tobeluk said, coming forward with a Nalgene bottle.

Maverick lifted his head, saw the man, and snarled. The dog's body lurched and he tried to regain his feet. Gale held the dog down and ordered Tobeluk to stay back. The VPSO stopped in his tracks.

"He doesn't trust males he doesn't know," Trask said, taking the water bottle and handing it to Gale.

Gale stroked Maverick's fur as the dog began to drink.

"We'll need to carry him. He's limping pretty badly," Gale said, placing his hand on Maverick's rump. The dog yelped in pain.

"It's okay, buddy," Gale said, repositioning himself to look at the shepherd's back right leg. Another deep wound ran down the flank of his thigh. "He needs a vet, that leg might be broken."

Maverick whimpered and looked up at them with forlorn eyes. Gale got a sickening feeling in his stomach. He knew that war dogs—especially German shepherds—were extremely loyal to their handlers. Maverick wouldn't leave Cassie's side unless he absolutely had to, or was forced to.

Gale looked over at the tangle of forest from which Maverick had come and thought that his youngest daughter might be out there somewhere, too, wounded, or worse.

"I have to go in there."

Maverick continued to tremble in Emily's arms.

"Give me twenty minutes," Gale said, then gestured at Tobeluk. "Grab your shotgun, you're coming. Emily, Trask, keep your weapons on you. Fire off a shot if you get into trouble."

"Should I run to the river and see if I can call the troopers?" Emily asked.

Gale stood. "Wait till we get back in case we find something."

Gale moved quickly into the forest with Tobeluk on his heels. Maverick's tracks were easy to discern, and Gale maintained a healthy pace. Tobeluk wheezed and stumbled behind him. After ten minutes they came to a small depression of land where a blowdown tree lay on its side. Gale followed Maverick's tracks into a small nook of the tree's upturned root system.

Gale inched his head inside the hollowed tree. Maverick's paw prints dotted the matted soil.

"He sheltered up here," Gale said, and then he and Tobeluk circled the area for any sign of his daughter.

Tobeluk said, "I've never seen a dog survive in the wilderness that cut up— you think he took on a bear?"

Gale ignored the man and tilted his head back and shouted, "Cassie!"

His voice carried through the trees toward the churning Yukon to their east. He yelled again, his voice grating and strained. He closed his eyes, could hear his heart hammering against his ribcage. The idea of Cassie injured, the idea of Cassie alone in the wilderness consumed his thoughts.

"Wait!" Tobeluk hissed.

Gale's eyes snapped open.

"Did you hear that?"

Gale primed his ears to the sounds of the forest and listened intently, then he heard it—a distant, high-pitched cry.

"There!"

"Shut up!" Gale snapped.

The report of a shotgun blast rippled through the forest.

"Em!" Gale cried out, sprinting up the side of the depression. He held the rifle in front of him like a shield, protecting himself from the low-hanging brush.

He could hear Tobeluk trying to keep up.

Gale burst into the campsite and found his eldest daughter on the ground, holding on to Maverick's limp form. Trask stood over them, his smoking shotgun in his hand.

Emily looked up. "We were checking on the satellite phone and he just started seizing. I can't get him to respond to me!"

Gale got down on all fours and cupped the dog's nose. "He's barely breathing." He lifted Maverick's eyelids and saw his eyeballs swimming in their sockets.

The dog began to shake violently and choke.

"He's going to swallow his tongue."

Tobeluk broke through the tree line, his face soaked in perspiration.

Gale reached into Maverick's mouth and grabbed his tongue, then yelled to Tobeluk, "Is there a vet in Eagle?"

"Yes, horse vet, next to the church."

Maverick's seizing abated and his body went limp.

Gale turned to Trask and said quickly, "Pete, turn off that truck, grab the phones. We're leaving."

Trask did. Gale hefted an unconscious Maverick into his arms and raced to the waiting Zodiac. He placed the dog into the bottom of the boat. Tobeluk and Trask jumped on board and Emily kicked them into the current as she jumped in. Gale gunned the throttle and they tore up the tributary. His attention went from the dog to the wilderness extending in every direction. The sun beat down on the monumental terrain, on the raging river and the small raft.

Emily suddenly lost it, as if the reality of the situation had just clobbered her. She flung herself into her husband's arms, her body lurching with grief.

Tobeluk kept his head down, the mysterious canister in his hands, his eyes glued to it.

"Officer," Gale said over the pulsing motor.

Tobeluk raised his head, his cheeks pale and sweaty.

"It's time to call the troopers; we need a damn search party up here. Now."

Chapter 12

GALE SAT IN the passenger's seat of Tobeluk's Ford Expedition and watched a Cessna 185 Skywagon touch down in front of them and taxi to a stop. A light rain fell and pattered the windshield of the vehicle. Gale opened the door and put on his cowboy hat, still damp from the ride up the Yukon nearly three hours before. He grimaced as the familiar hot poker flash of pain raced from his hip down into his quadricep.

The Cessna's door opened. A portly man in an Alaska State Trooper uniform climbed out and slung a small rucksack and a shotgun over his shoulder. He held a manila folder in his hand.

"Jim Gale?" the trooper said, years of cigarettes on his voice. He gave Gale a grim smile and firm handshake, his eyes resting on Tobeluk in the driver's seat.

"I'm Trooper Glenn Ross; how's the dog doing?"

"He'll be okay. Couple of busted ribs, cut up, dehydrated, and exhausted. My daughter and son-in-law are with him now." Gale indicated the Cessna. "Your pilot coming with us?"

"No," Ross said, walking to the vehicle. "Rutledge needs to refuel before we begin the search." Tobeluk stepped out and Ross placed his pack and shotgun in the man's hands. "Throw my stuff in the back, Max. I'm driving. Sit up front with me, Mr. Gale."

Gale climbed into the passenger's seat. Tobeluk wasn't happy, but he took the back. Ross put the manila folder on the center console and pulled out onto the dirt road heading to Eagle.

The trooper had a bulldog's flattened face: ruddy cheeks behind a handlebar mustache and the faint hint of liver spots patching the tip of his nose. His jowls bounced as they drove down the bumpy road.

"I got a brief look at Cassandra's missing person file on the way up," Ross said, patting the folder. "Sergeant Plant sent me the pictures you took at the campsite. I'll need to get up there and take my own before we get to sweeping the area."

Ross eyed Tobeluk through the rearview mirror. "Meredith said you found some sort of canister and a rifle on the ground?"

Gale dug around in his jacket and took out a Ziploc freezer bag he'd bought at the Eagle Trading Company. In the bag sat the metal canister. He put the contents on the console.

"I don't know what to make of it, smells terrible."

"Anyone handle it?"

"My son-in-law. Me and Officer Tobeluk."

Ross shot Tobeluk a sour look in the rearview mirror, then asked, "And what about her rifle?"

"Hadn't been fired," Gale said.

"And the grizzly tracks, no sign of blood?"

"Rain washed it away if there was any."

"Well, we'll get everyone up there to comb through the area, they know the drill."

Gale eyed the man curiously. "This kind of thing happen a lot?"

Ross flexed his fingers on the steering wheel. "Near Eagle? A few every summer, most of them floating the Yukon on the Circle route. Had a kayaker last year get chased out of his camp by a bear and into the river. He floated for a couple miles, tried walking back to his camp and got lost. Found him a couple days later naked in the woods kissing a tree. Guess he got hungry and started gorging himself on some funny mushrooms. Guy was lucky to be alive."

"What about the others?"

"Lost or body recoveries."

Gale stared hard at the trooper and Ross returned the look, more matter-of-fact and sensible than callous.

"Your daughter is still in the survival window. Rutledge will skim the banks till he's exhausted the effort, and the villagers up here know this place better than anyone." The trooper eyed Tobeluk again in the rearview as he pulled the vehicle into the VPSO Support Office's parking lot. Emily and Trask sat on the front stoop and stood when the vehicle came to a stop. Emily's face was puffy and red.

Three other people stood in the parking lot. They were short—stooped from age and harsh living—their faces resembled cracked leather, deep canyons of worn skin exposed to the Alaskan elements for decades. Two had jet-black hair. The shortest, a woman, had a silver braid that fell down to her lower back. Her face was more shriveled and sun spotted than the others', but her eyes shone brightly, like crystalline blue marbles.

Gale thought the woman could be anywhere between eighty and a hundred years old.

"They came?" Ross said.

"She would only talk with you," Tobeluk said.

"You've even pissed off the elders now?"

"I've really cracked down on the villagers."

"Yeah, I'm sure that's it, and not your constant boozing," Ross said. "Mr. Gale, could you tell everyone to wait inside for me? I need to have a quick word with Officer Tobeluk."

Gale obliged, eyeing the old woman, whose gaze was steady on him as he stepped out of the vehicle and made his way over to Trask and Emily. When he passed the old villagers, he repeated Ross's message.

They stared at him blankly, then the youngest of the men, who looked to be in his sixties, said something quietly to the woman in an odd dialect Gale couldn't place.

The old woman puckered her lips and made a nasally response and shook her head vigorously.

The man translated for her.

"We'll wait," he said, pointing at Ross through the windshield.

Gale collected Trask and Emily and went into the office. Emily grabbed a glass from the kitchenette counter and poured herself water from the tap. Standing at the window, Trask looked outside and spoke softly.

"The veterinarian said Maverick could be released in a couple days. For now they're going to keep him sedated."

"Good, when he wakes, we might need his nose." Gale moved to the window and stood next to his son-in-law as they watched Ross step out of the vehicle. The trooper's face was beet red with anger. When Tobeluk stepped out behind him, he looked like a whipped steer.

Ross went to the elders and led them inside. Tobeluk followed.

Ross took the seat behind Tobeluk's desk in a possessive manner, slapping both the Ziploc with the canister and the manila folder down in front of him.

The small woman took the seat across from him. The two men stood at her shoulders.

"This is Eve Attla," Ross said to the Gales. "And her son, Isaac, and her grandson, John. Eve is the Hän village elder. We'll be coordinating the search for Cassandra with them." Ross looked to Isaac. "How many people would you be able to round up?"

Isaac spoke in the old Athabaskan language to his mother, who spoke back promptly.

"Today? Ten," John said. "Three boats."

Ross turned to Tobeluk. "How many townspeople?"

"Fifteen so far, another four boats."

A pronounced scowl morphed on the old woman's face when Tobeluk spoke. She pointed a knotted finger in his direction and barked at him.

Tobeluk asked, "What's she saying now?"

Isaac put a hand on his mother's shoulder and glared at the VPSO. "She says you are like a raven who attacks his own nest."

"Tell her I'm doing my job."

Eve made a disgusted sound.

"All right, enough," Ross said. He dealt out five black-and-white copies of Cassie's photograph Gale had faxed to the ABI and handed them to the villagers. Mrs. Attla's eyes stayed glued fiercely on Tobeluk.

Ross spent the next fifteen minutes laying out the method in which the search and rescue operation would work. He and Gale would take the Zodiac to Cassie's camp where he would begin doing his initial site work. Two other groups would search around the campsite on foot. Another three boat groups would go north and search the tributaries downriver. A group of four villagers would be dropped off three miles upriver, five miles from the campsite; their task would be to walk the service road until they reached Cassie's truck. Eve's boat would troll the southern shorelines closer to town with John and Isaac.

"Everyone will be equipped with radios," Ross said. "Tobeluk will stay here and man the radio-switchboard; if anyone sees anything of interest, you are to call it in to Tobeluk who will then relay that information to the pilot, who will then relay it to the people on the ground. This is so there won't be overcrowding on the frequency. If need be, he can contact Fairbanks."

"What about me and my husband?" Emily said. "What can we do?"

"You can either come with us, or be an extra set of eyes in the plane with Rutledge."

They chose the plane.

Ross continued, "I know it doesn't have to be said, but I'll say it anyway: everyone moves with a partner, everyone carries a weapon, and each group takes a flare gun." He looked from Tobeluk to Isaac. "When you brief your volunteers, make sure you hammer down that point. I don't want anyone going missing while we're searching for a missing person. If you find Cassandra, send up a flare. If you get lost, send up a flare. And stay off the frequencies, unless you've got something. Clear?"

Everyone nodded.

"Good." Ross looked at his watch. "We've got nine more hours of light to work with, so let's get a move on."

Chapter 13

THE AIR SMELLED like rain and peeled tree bark.

To the east, a billowing dark cloud rumbled over the high terrain and advanced on Cassie's campsite. Gale sat on the Tundra's tailgate and watched Ross as he combed through the scene with a set of latex gloves, carefully moving the debris and carnage of Cassie's supplies before snapping pictures with the Nikon camera hanging from his neck.

The ride downriver had been uneventful and Ross's initial pass of the site had been brief. He had given it a once-over, then had asked to see where Maverick had bedded down. Ross took pictures of the uprooted tree and the area surrounding it.

When they returned to the site, Ross ordered Gale to sit on the tailgate, not wanting to contaminate the site any more than it already had been.

In the distance, the Cessna Skywagon sounded like a buzzing insect. Gale looked skyward, trying to glimpse the small plane through the high canopy.

Ross asked Gale where the mysterious canister had been found, and Ross photographed the area, then took the canister out of the Ziploc and photographed it as well.

He left the tent for last.

Gale watched Ross crouch by the tent. He took pictures of it from all angles, then stroked his bushy mustache in thought.

He called Gale over and grabbed the red Cabela's tent and pulled, spreading it out in front of them.

"What does this look like to you?" Ross said.

"If you're talking about the open food box, there is no way—"

"No, look." The trooper pointed a pudgy finger at a collection of slash marks. "These look like bear claw marks to you?"

Gale scrutinized the slashes. They were mismatched—small, single strokes jutting in every which direction. The slashes looked like the work of a serrated blade rather than a claw.

"If a bear tore this up, we'd see symmetrical slash marks in groups of four or five, I'm not seeing that," Ross said.

Gale pulled at the tent, exposing more surface area. He noted the large, muddy bear prints over the red fabric. Ross was correct, none of the slashes looked like they'd been done by the bear; the bear had just appeared to lumber over it, searching for food.

"I think someone did this with a knife."

"That doesn't make sense," Gale said, shaking his head; he looked at the empty food box, the white rope dangling from the tree. Why would someone slash Cassie's tent and cut down her food box?

Then Gale had a puckering thought.

It was a thought that had teased him earlier in the day. But he had quickly dismissed it. Now looking at the slash marks, it seemed terribly feasible.

"Mr. Gale," Ross said softly, "I need to ask you a difficult question. I refrained from asking it in front of the others, but I think this might be a prudent time. Cassandra—it said in the MPR that she was suicidal in the past?"

Gale gave a small nod.

"Okay," Ross said, quieter, "okay."

"I know what you're thinking, Trooper—that she could have set this up. Made it look like something it wasn't, then went off into the woods to . . ." Gale's voice trailed off, then he shook his head. "But she would never hurt the dog. She would never hurt Maverick. He's her late husband's war dog, her last connection to him. And yes, she had suicidal thoughts, but she was doing so much better . . ."

The silence between the two men turned deafening. Gale began to feel shaky, aware Ross was watching him with quiet curiosity. A short burst of static from the trooper's radio, followed by garbled words, broke the quiet.

Ross kept his gaze on Gale as he keyed his mike. "Repeat that."

The static returned and Ross walked to the perimeter of the campsite, searching for a better signal.

Rutledge's voice crackled. "—Trooper . . . Trooper, do you copy?"

"Copy, go ahead."

"Boat crew six, they've found something."

Ross waved Gale over.

"Who's boat crew six?" Gale asked.

"Attlas."

The radio sputtered again, all static.

Ross said, "We need to move to the river."

They hurried through the brush and stood at the shoreline next to the Zodiac. To their north, they could see the Cessna circling.

The pilot's words came through more clearly.

"They say they got a big grizzly on the shoreline, couple miles south of your position," he said. "It's on something, you want me to do a flyover?"

Ross keyed his mike. "Copy, confirm for flyover."

They watched the plane turn in their direction and zoom overhead and out of sight to the south. The storm to the east was fast approaching; the wind had picked up and a bolt of lightning flashed, followed by a loud clap of thunder.

"Trooper, we got something here—"

Gale felt his legs go weak. Ross turned and pushed the Zodiac into the rushing water, his radio continuing to static and squawk.

"Griz has something—"

"What's the location?" Ross shouted into the mike. He held the raft steady as Gale managed to wade through the water and get aboard.

"Western shoreline, three klicks, yellow jacket—"

"What did he just say?" Gale asked.

Ross held up a finger and tilted his ear to the mike. "Repeat that, pilot, over." More static.

"Shit," Ross said. "Storm is interfering with the comms. Let's go."

"Did he say yellow jacket?" Gale asked.

Ross slammed on the throttle and took off upriver, speaking into the mike, "We're coming to you. Tell the volunteers on the ground to not approach the bear. I repeat, do not approach that bear."

The winds picked up. Then it began to rain, hard.

Ross kept the throttle nailed. They banked out of the small tributary and hit the main channel.

The Cessna appeared in the distance, a speck against the roiling gunmetal clouds and falling rain. Ross released his grip on the throttle a bit and spoke into the radio, "I've got a visual on you. Tell boat six to send up a flare."

"Copy," the pilot crackled.

The Zodiac's motor puttered. The wind howled. The rain lashed them horizontally. Gale held on to his cowboy hat and ducked his head against the onslaught.

After a minute, a spiraling gray smoke column soared out in front of them a mile away before three orange flames mushroomed high in the spitting rain.

"There we go!" Ross shouted and gunned the motor so hard Gale almost fell backward in his seat. Ross took the rapids head on. Gale held on tight to the Zodiac's side lashes and squinted through the pelting squall. The Cessna made a wide swoop and zoomed over them.

The Yukon curved ahead.

Ross stretched the motor to its limit and they whipped around the bend. The far western shoreline came into view. The shore had the shape of a bent elbow. Washed-up logs and river debris littered its sandy beach.

Lightning struck the mountainside behind them. Thunder shook the canyon.

Gale saw the metal dinghy twenty yards from the beach, bobbing up and down over the rushing water. Three figures were in the boat; one was waving to them and pointing to shore. Gale fought to get to his feet for a better view as Ross corrected the Zodiac's path toward the dinghy.

Thunder clapped again, as Gale scanned the sandy riverfront.

Then he saw it. At first he thought he was looking at a big mound of dirt among the downed logs—dark soil pushed onto the beach—but then the mound moved and became a giant head swinging slowly left to right.

"Oh, Jesus, that's a huge bear!" Ross yelled, stalling the motor ten feet from the bank.

Gale stared at the grizzly, its head down fifty yards inland. The dinghy crawled its way over, the small motor struggling against the current. John Attla stood at the boat's bow and shouted, "He's diggin' and eatin' something, we saw a blanket or a jack—"

Gale didn't hear the rest of what the man said. The bear had pawed at the ground, surfacing something bright yellow.

A yellow rain jacket.

Cassie's yellow rain jacket.

The bear flicked the jacket aside, and Gale felt his heart plummet. White bone flecked with pink gore jutted up from the sand—

Something primal escaped Gale's mouth.

Yellow jacket.

Bones.

Cassie!

Gale grabbed the shotgun and was over the Zodiac in an instant. The water was deeper than expected. The current stronger. It grabbed at him, sucked him under. Gale flipped, kicked hard, and thrashed, the glacial water sucking the wind right out of him. He struggled to the surface, gasped for air, his hat ripped from his head.

Muffled by the wind, he barely heard the shouts behind him. Eight feet from the shore, Gale kicked as hard as he could, the shotgun still in his hand. His feet searched for the bottom but couldn't find purchase. Rain hammered the water like machine-gun fire. He knew if he didn't kick now, he'd be swept downriver. He took a deep breath and dove.

Kicking, thrashing as hard as he could, his lungs straining, he willed himself closer, closer to the shore.

His hand hit something—a dead tree—he grasped the soggy branch and pulled himself up, forcing himself up the log. He was up to his waist in the water—three feet from the shore.

Lightning flashed.

Gale flung himself forward and landed in a pile on the shoreline. The current had swept him downriver. The bear raised its gargantuan head, nose twitching in the wind, sensing the presence of a trespasser.

Gale scrambled to his feet, held the shotgun in front of him like a battering ram and charged.

The grizzly stood up on its hind legs, raised up to its full nine feet, then stomped back down over its feast and roared.

Gale didn't care. He ran forward, full of unbridled rage, and matched the bear's roar with one of his own as he raised the shotgun. At twenty-five yards his finger found the trigger and he mashed it . . .

Click!

The shotgun dry-fired in his hands. Gale stumbled in surprise, then aimed and mashed the trigger again.

Click!

The bear reared up over the carcass once more.

Gale dropped the shotgun, backpedaling, stumbling, and fell on his back. His left hand dug into the sand. His boots slid as he tried to get his footing. His right hand strained to release the Colt Anaconda at his hip.

The bear charged.

Twelve hundred pounds of bloodthirsty kinetic energy barreled toward him like a runaway locomotive.

Gale's hand slipped off his holster, and he curled fetal, hands wrapping his neck.

BOOM!

An earth-shattering report cascaded over the shoreline—piercing the ferocious storm.

BOOM!

Five yards from Gale, the bear halted its charge, spun around, and stopped in its tracks, looking unhit. The grizzly's massive head searched for the shots that had come from upriver and close.

Gale followed the bear's line of sight.

A small figure stood obscured in the torrential downpour fifty yards away, a rifle held to the sky. Eve Attla had appeared like a specter, her silver braid flapping in the air like an unruly whip. Her round face remained calm and controlled.

She racked another round and stepped forward with purpose.

BOOM!

The earth shook, the muzzle flashed and bucked in her small hands, sending another bullet to the clouds.

The bear stood its ground and bellowed at the old woman. Gale was so close he could smell the animal's breath of putrid, decaying flesh.

Gale dared not move. His eyes darted from Eve to the bear.

The old woman maintained her steady pace and ran the action of her rifle one last time—and aimed her weapon directly at the bear.

The grizzly growled, deep and guttural, preparing to charge.

PSSSHHH!

A gray cloud erupted over Gale's head and hit the bear squarely in the face. The bear flipped over backward, howling in pain. The gray mist clung to its snout, invaded its eyes.

Ross stepped over Gale, holding a canister of bear spray at arm's length.

"GET UP!" he screamed, hoisting Gale by the back of his shirt.

The bear staggered away and bolted to the forest.

"Are you crazy, old man?!" Ross yelled, grabbing Gale by the collar, and shaking him.

Gale pushed the trooper away and sprinted to the bloody carcass.

A musky, sharp smell hit Gale's nostrils as he stumbled forward, standing over the ghastly scene.

A rib cage stared up at him. A brown hide wrapped partly over it like a tight blanket. Gale's brain tried to register what he was seeing—a black hoof, a set of antlers covered in spruce boughs and sand.

"It's a moose!" Ross shouted behind him. "The bear was eating a little bull!"

Gale was too stunned to feel any sort of relief. The gore-filled pile of sand, roughly the size of an overturned bathtub, was a grizzly burial mound.

Brown bears and grizzlies like to put their kills under dirt, let them rot and ripen before they return for periodic feasts.

Eve Attla picked up the yellow rain jacket from the carnage. She handed it to Gale, its neoprene fabric ripped and sliced at the sleeves. Aged brown bloodstains spotted the crinkled hood.

Ross keyed his mike, alerted the pilot of the discovery, "Get the other boats here, we're going to search the southwestern shorelines."

Gale clutched the jacket, his fingers kneading the bloodstains. "How did her jacket get *upriver?*"

Ross's confused expression showed he had no answer.

The old woman moved past them, her low voice humming in the wind. She seemed to be chanting. Her small frame moved past the burial mound and walked to the forest's edge, where she stood still and closed her eyes. The sound of her chanting intensified.

John and Isaac came up and stopped.

Ross turned to her son and asked, "What's she doing?"

Isaac watched his mother through the pelting rain. Eve's chanting grew louder. It pulsed over the shoreline adding to the cadence of the storm. Her head began to rock back and forth, undulating as if on a swivel.

Then she stopped. Opened her eyes and stepped into the woods where the bear had disappeared.

"Whoa, whoa!" Ross said, as he started to run after her. John held out a hand, stopping the trooper.

"What the hell is she doing?" Ross screamed.

"She sees something."

"Sees something? That's where the bear went!"

"Stay here," Isaac said, and he motioned for John to follow him. Together they disappeared into the thick foliage.

"Goddamn natives," Ross spat, "gonna get themselves killed."

Gale stared down at the jacket in his hands and an idea struck him. He flipped the jacket over and started rummaging through the pockets. Finding a concealed zipper sewn over the left breast, he opened it, and pulled out two white crumpled pieces of paper, still dry from the elements. They were receipts.

"Trooper, look at this."

Ross stepped forward and took the receipts, studied them. The first receipt was from the Northern Breeze Lodge for a one-night stay. The receipt was dated: June 22nd and charged at 7:23 a.m., for eighty-nine Canadian dollars. The other receipt was for two ham sandwiches, charged at 12:13 p.m., the same day at the Eagle Trading Company, in Eagle, Alaska.

"Okay, this will help us with the timeline," Ross said, and went for his mike.

Suddenly, Isaac appeared from the forest, a deadly serious expression on his face. "You both need to come now."

"What in the Christ is going on?" Ross shouted, lowering his hand from his mike, his patience wearing thin.

Less rain penetrated the forest canopy, but a low-hanging fog made the going difficult. Gale kept his attention on the back of Isaac's shirt as the man maneuvered through the forest with the grace of a deer. Gale was trying to wrap his head around the receipts he'd just found when he spotted Eve standing at a break in the woods just ahead. Her body rocked back and forth as she chanted. Her grandson stood next to her.

Isaac stopped behind his mother, motioned for Ross and Gale to do the same.

"Would any of you mind telling me what the hell she's saying?" Ross hissed.

Eve's chanting grew louder.

"This is a dark place. Evil spirits live here," John said, quietly.

"Evil spirits, my ass," Ross said, trying to push by the group.

When Isaac gripped him firmly on the arm, Ross glared at the man's hand.

"Wait," John said. "Let her finish."

His grandmother's body started to shake as her voice reached a crescendo.

Then her chanting ceased and her head slumped. She took a deep shuddering breath, then pointed ahead.

"Kigatilik," she said, in a wavering voice.

John looked at Gale and Ross with sad eyes. "You can go forward."

Gale took an uneasy step. Then another. He clutched Cassie's jacket under his left arm and took his Colt Anaconda out, held it by his side. He moved by low-hanging boughs and stepped into the opening and déjà vu slapped him in the face.

The opening was small, surrounded by ferns. A small green tent lay in ruins in the middle—a food box—its contents opened and strewn. Fresh grizzly tracks punched through the mud.

"Jesus Christ," Ross huffed.

A backpack lay next to a steel-sided rifle case near the demolished tent.

A flash of lightning lit the scene. Thunder broke over them. Gale went to the case, opened it. A .308 Winchester Magnum rifle sat inside; Gale checked the action. A bullet sat in the chamber, four more in the magazine. It hadn't been fired.

Ross grabbed the backpack and peered inside. He took out a fire starter, water filtration tablets, and a quick-dry towel, then his hand stopped on something at the bottom. He looked at it for a moment and something unspeakable came over his face. Gale met his gaze, then Ross slowly pulled out a .357 Colt Python from the backpack.

Cassie's Colt Python.

Gale felt the color drain from his face. He grabbed the pistol and confirmed Cassie's name was engraved on the hilt. He dropped her jacket in the mud and cracked the pistol's six-shot cylinder, letting the bullets fall onto his palm. Four of them were loaded cartridges, the other two were empty shell casings.

Cassie's pistol had been fired. Twice.

Why is her pistol in this backpack three miles upriver?

"Whose . . . whose campsite is this?" Gale asked.

Eve Attla, who had been squatting down over something in the ferns, reached her hand down, and came up with a brown wallet. She gave it to Ross. The trooper opened it, then turned it to show an Oregon driver's license to Gale.

"His name is William French."

Chapter 14

CASSIE'S EYES FLEW open and she sat up, gasping for breath. Her vision swam, a myriad of blotchy greens and blues.

Dizzy, parched, and confused, she sat up on damp earth and put her hand to her forehead in an effort to mitigate her moose-sized headache.

Her tongue felt like a dehydrated slug—sticking to the root of her mouth, a chalky chemical taste in her throat.

As her eyesight normalized and steadied, she realized she was in a heavily wooded area. Lush green ferns wet-kissed her arms, her legs, the sides of her face. Where was she? What was happening? Her brain felt muddied. This wasn't home, this wasn't Montana.

No, she thought. *I went to Alaska—drove north. Stayed at that hotel—the Northern Breeze! The campsite by the river in Eagle. It was nighttime. A loud bright orange flash! And—*

"Maverick!"

It all came back to her and she jumped so fast she nearly fainted. Her body felt weak, depleted, banged up and bruised. She focused on her breathing until she could stand upright and called for Maverick until her voice went hoarse.

There was no sign of the dog.

What had attacked them? She remembered Maverick's high-pitched screams of pain.

She didn't know where she was.

Cassie felt a familiar sensation of panic bubble in her stomach, but she quickly forced it back down as her survival training kicked in.

Remain calm. Take stock of your surroundings. Devise a plan of action.

She started with her body.

Her pants were ripped and filthy. Bruises lined the right side of her legs up to her pelvis. Her tan T-shirt was covered in mud, her right forearm sported a nasty gash that looked like it had been . . .

Stitched?

Cassie blinked, confused. She counted at least twenty black stitches, expertly applied.

How in the hell?

Dread suddenly filled her and she whipped around, scanning the forest. Someone had stitched her up. Someone had put her here. Were they watching her now? Adrenaline elevated her senses and she listened, watched—reacting to every gust of wind, every movement of leaves, every chirp or rustle from a bird.

For ten minutes she didn't move a muscle.

The forest seemed normal, but something was off. The flora: the bushes, the trees seemed *different*.

When Cassie felt satisfied she wasn't being watched, she continued with her checklist. Her body was in good enough shape to walk. Her stomach didn't feel too empty, but, damn, was she thirsty.

She devised a plan.

Find high ground. Then get to civilization. If that's not possible, find water and shelter.

The sun was directly above her; rays of it streaming down between the gaps of leaves. It would be impossible to find her bearings until she found high ground, so she picked a direction and started walking.

Thirty minutes later, she stumbled into a spring that trickled into a small stream. Cassie was so thirsty she dunked her head into the freezing water and gulped until she was satisfied.

The water washed away that nasty chemical taste in her mouth and replenished her body. Almost immediately another memory triggered in her brain—that taste in her mouth—she had tasted it before, back at the campsite, the foul-smelling cloud that enveloped her after Maverick screamed, after the bright orange flash.

Then another memory.

It must have been after the flash.

Much later.

A flicker of consciousness.

It was a sensation of feeling constricted—like she was in a coffin. A mask had been covering her face, it was dark. She hadn't been able to move her arms or legs.

There had been sounds, too.

Loud, thumping sounds, like a helicopter rotor.

Had she been in a helicopter?

Just then she was snapped out of her memory by a faraway buzzing. Cassie looked up through the trees at the clear blue sky and made out a small white dot, almost indiscernible against the glare of the sun.

It wasn't moving like a plane or a bird. It was hovering, then jolting left and right in quick succession.

Cassie squinted at it, trying to make out what it was—when a loud snap of a twig sounded behind her. She turned, peering into the dense vegetation.

Two men stood not twenty feet away.

They were shirtless.

Tattoos covered their bald heads, faces, and chests.

They gazed right at her with hungry eyes and smiling yellow teeth.

One had a knife.

The other started sprinting right for her.

Chapter 15

IF YOU CAN'T run, wait until your attacker is close, use their momentum against them to take them off balance. Then make quick, succinct blows in critical areas until the threat is neutralized.

It was the mantra her father had repeated over and over when teaching Cassie basic self-defense as a young teenager. A mantra that she had repeated to herself various times during her military training. A mantra that reverberated in her head as she backpedaled in surprise and slipped and fell in the ice-cold spring as the tattooed man closed the distance between them.

He splashed into the spring as Cassie crab-walked backward onto dry land. She didn't have time to get to her feet and run, so she let herself fall on her back, her knees and elbows up planklike, waiting.

His hands went for her throat.

Cassie waited until his full body weight rested completely over her.

Then she kicked upward and to her right. The man flopped over, half in, half out of the spring. Cassie got on top of him.

Succinct blows in critical areas until the threat is neutralized.

She balled her fist, cocked her elbow, and delivered a punch in the fleshy part of the man's throat just to the left of the Adam's apple, directly on the carotid. The man's mouth opened and closed, his eyes bulged in surprise, his arms went limp by his side and his eyes fluttered shut.

Cassie spun off the man, found her feet, and immediately twisted her body sideways as a blade slashed by her. The second man had lunged and missed, stumbling into a thicket of brush.

The man wasn't big.

He was skinny actually—malnourished even.

The tattoos on his back, biblical images and foreign symbols, were numerous and crudely done. But Cassie wasn't paying attention to the tattoos; instead she planted her feet and positioned her body for the next attack.

The second man found his balance and turned to face her. The knife glinted in the sun and the man's eyes went skyward, right to where that white, buzzing speck zipped above.

The man licked his lips, and Cassie noticed that even his tongue was tattooed.

Control the blade hand, Cassie thought as the man lunged again. She let the blade come in close to her stomach before she pivoted and grabbed the man's wrist. Her free hand clamped down on his elbow and she used his momentum to spin him while simultaneously twisting the blade hand.

The man bellowed and the knife fell to the ground. Cassie then shifted course, planted a knee behind the man's legs, and tripped him backward.

He fell back and she was on him. She aimed for the throat but the man raised his arm in defense. Cassie's fist glanced off the man's forearm.

She hit him again.

And again.

The man kept his hands over his face and throat.

This one knows how to fight.

Cassie changed tactics—aiming lower, she hit him in the diaphragm. Hard. She heard the breath leave him. He sputtered and gasped like a beached fish.

"Who the hell are you!" Cassie screamed.

She hit him again.

"Why are you attacking me?"

She hit him again, this time in the ribs.

"Where are we? Why are you attacking me!"

A series of words escaped the man's mouth. It definitely wasn't English—it had a Slavic harshness to it.

The man then spat in her face and attempted a punch. Cassie blocked the blow, saw her opening, then delivered a well-timed fist at the man's throat.

The effect was instantaneous.

Cassie got to her feet, shaking, confused. She went for the knife. Held it. It looked new, recently sharpened and perfectly maintained.

The first man still lay unconscious, the second man clutched at his throat. Cassie was having trouble comprehending what had just happened.

The knife trembled in her hand, and before she could run, she heard a loud piercing whistle from above. The whistle grew louder and louder until something landed with a resounding thunk at her feet.

Sticking halfway out of the mud was a stainless steel canister the size of a coffee thermos.

Cassie bent down to examine it when the top of the canister burst open and sprayed a mist of orange in all directions. The familiar foul-smelling chemical cloud engulfed her.

Cassie staggered backward and tried to run but lost her balance and toppled over.

Then all went black.

Chapter 16

GALE WINCED AS he squatted down on the linoleum floor and extended his arm through the open kennel, his hand running from the top of Maverick's head all the way down his back. The sleeping dog's chest rose and fell; the IV line that ran into his leg kept him sedated.

The veterinarian said the dog could leave by tomorrow. The cuts on Maverick's face and leg required stitches and two of his ribs had been cracked. Gale studied the gash on Mav's face—it was the work of a knife, no doubt. Someone had slashed the dog.

Maverick had been protecting Cassie, Gale was sure of it.

Gale rubbed at his bloodshot eyes. It had been nearly forty-eight hours since the encounter with the grizzly. Forty-eight hours since the discovery of Cassie's blood-soaked yellow jacket and William French's campsite.

Gale had barely slept since his arrival in Eagle and his mind was beginning to get sluggish. Gale checked his watch, Petit and Bill Cronin and his men from the Rocking R would be arriving by the evening. After the search team had discovered William French's campsite, Gale had called Montana, knowing that he needed men up here he could trust, men who were willing to do anything to find Cassie.

After the encounter with the grizzly, word had spread fast through Eagle. Suddenly, everyone wanted to help and be a part of the search. After the discovery of Cassie's pistol in William French's backpack, Ross had called Sergeant

Meredith Plant and asked for a criminal case to be opened. This led a press team and television crew to latch on to the story and fly into town.

"Dad, she's here. Plane just landed."

Gale scratched Maverick behind the ear and stood to see Emily and Trask silhouetted in the vet office doorway.

Sergeant Plant had just flown in from Fairbanks to take over the investigation. Ross insisted this case needed the keen eye of a seasoned investigator.

In the time it took Plant to get to Eagle, Ross had organized nearly a hundred townspeople and villagers to search the woods and riverbanks along the Yukon.

All evidence from both campsites had been collected, tagged, and sent to Anchorage for forensic testing—what kind of tests, Gale didn't know; he was hoping to get clarification once he met Plant, especially about the mysterious canister found in Cassie's campsite.

Gale took in Emily and Trask. They both looked haggard. Emily had dark bags under her eyes, and Trask's hair and beard were disheveled.

"How are you two doing?"

"Holding up," Trask said.

"You need sleep, Dad."

Gale waved off Emily's comment and squeezed her shoulder, stepping around them and onto the front deck of the small vet clinic.

It was a beautiful day. Blue sky, and not a cloud in sight. Gale could hear the rumblings of a crowd in the distance. The search and rescue volunteers had been called in for Sergeant Plant's arrival. Gale guessed that most of the volunteers were eating lunch at the supply tent that had been erected in the parking lot of the VPSO's office.

They walked silently down Chamberlain and took a right on Front Street and saw the crowd milling about. Nearly twenty boats, rafts, and dinghies were docked on the shore.

Gale saw the Attlas in the corner of the crowd. John and Isaac were talking to a group of villagers as they ate lunch. Eve sat in a camping chair, and she was staring directly at Gale, expressionless. The day before, he had thanked the woman for warding off the bear on the shoreline and apologized for his rashness.

Eve had just stared into his eyes like she was prodding the darkest depths of his soul. The whole experience had been unnerving. It was like the old woman knew who he really was. Knew his past. Understood his present. And could foresee his future.

Gale peeled his attention from the old woman and saw the Fairbanks news reporter interviewing Trooper Ross by the food tent. Max Tobeluk stood by Ross and looked uncomfortable, sickly and ashen.

A car horn honked over the rumble of the crowd and a truck pulled into the parking lot. A young trooper built like a fly rod got out of the driver's seat and placed his blue Stetson hat over his head and took in the crowd.

A short, blond-haired woman climbed out of the passenger seat and rounded the truck. She had an authoritative air about her: hawkish brown eyes, a sharp nose. She shouldered a travel bag and wore tan cargo pants—a gold badge flashed from her belt next to a holstered Glock. But what really took Gale aback was that the woman was pregnant.

Very pregnant.

This must be Sergeant Plant.

Plant walked through the crowd and caught the attention of Ross who stopped his interview and walked over to her. They talked for a moment, then Ross called the crowd to attention.

He introduced Sergeant Plant and the skinny trooper at her side. His name was Elliot Vance. Vance was also a certified Alaskan bush pilot and had flown Plant from Fairbanks. Vance and the other pilot, Rutledge, would use their planes to aid in the search.

For the next ten minutes, Ross made a show of getting Plant up to speed with the organization of the search. When Ross was done, Plant thanked everyone and applauded their diligence. She then told the crowd that she was heading up a criminal investigation into the disappearances of Cassandra Gale and William French.

When she was done, she pulled a woman from the crowd and together they marched up the stairs into the VPSO's office.

"Should we go talk to her?" Emily asked.

Gale was already moving. He weaved through the volunteers, took the stairs two at a time, and opened the door without knocking.

Sergeant Plant sat at the desk, poring over a stack of papers as the other woman stood opposite her, an uninterested look on her face.

Emily and Trask filed in behind Gale.

Plant looked up. "Ah, you must be Mr. Gale. Good to finally put a face to a name. Please, sit."

The bored-looking woman stepped back as Gale, Emily, and Trask took their seats across from Plant.

Plant indicated the other woman. "This is Sherry Pruitt with the United States Border Patrol. She works the crossing at Little Gold."

Pruitt nodded but didn't say anything.

Plant checked her watch. "Ralph Condon with the Canadian Mounted Police should be here any minute. I contacted the RCMP yesterday and was granted cross-country jurisdiction on this case. Working across country lines can be a hassle. But I've worked with Condon before; he's a good man. Sharp investigator."

Plant was much younger than she had sounded over the phone. Gale had expected someone in their late forties, but Sergeant Plant couldn't be much older than Emily.

Plant said, "I'm really sorry about this whole predicament, but I want you to know we are making headway. Things work a little slower up here, that's all."

"You have a lead?" Gale asked.

"I don't know if I'd call it a lead, maybe a step in the right direction."

Pruitt handed Plant a manila folder and Plant opened it.

Pruitt said, "Cassandra Ann Gale crossed into Alaska on June twenty-second at 9:03 a.m. She was traveling with a canine and another individual, William Edward French."

"She was traveling with William French?" Emily said in disbelief. "Did Cassie look like she was in trouble?"

"On the contrary," Pruitt said, pointing to the manila folder in front of Plant. "We take pictures of each individual and vehicle that crosses. I was the agent on duty at the time. Both French and Cassandra Gale seemed at ease."

Gale studied the black-and-white picture of Cassie and William French in her Tundra. They looked completely normal. Relaxed even.

Gale started in, "What has the ABI got on this French kid?"

"Oregon police sent over his file. Got a DUI ten years back while he was a teenager. That charge was expunged. Other than that, no criminal history. No history of violence. We got in contact with his stepfather. They're estranged, haven't spoken in almost a decade. Stepfather said French was always a bit of a loner."

Gale could see Ross, Tobeluk, and Vance out of the window climbing up the stairs to the VPSO's office as the crowd of volunteers headed back to their boats for the afternoon search. They shuffled inside and both Ross and Vance went straight for the Keurig coffeemaker on the counter. Tobeluk made his way to the back of the room, eyeing Plant nervously.

Agent Pruitt said, "Neither Cassandra Gale nor William French declared their firearms for Canadian transit."

Plant waved away that detail, as she said, "That's not important now—"

"What about the evidence you sent to Anchorage?" Gale asked.

"Forensics are going through the evidence as we speak. They should have their report by morning." Plant cleared her throat, addressed the room. "Okay, everyone is here. Let's begin. As of right now, this missing person case belongs to the Alaska Bureau of Investigation. Due to the nature of the case, I believe this is criminal in nature. So we will tackle it as such."

She reached in her bag, took out a laptop and a stack of papers, and began: "From the receipts found in Cassandra Gale's jacket two days ago, we can ascertain that she stayed the night of June twenty-first at the Northern Breeze Lodge and Smoke House Bar and then crossed the border with William French the morning of the twenty-second. I have contacted the Mountie, Ralph Condon in Dawson, to check on the Northern Breeze to see if William French also stayed there. Cassandra Gale then bought two sandwiches at 12:03 p.m. at the Eagle Trading Company next door. Our last known proof of life was a call made from her Globalstar satellite phone on June twenty-second at 6:32 p.m. I've contacted Globalstar and they've confirmed that the call came from Cassandra Gale's campsite—I've listened to the call and will confirm with the family soon that it is her voice.

"We are looking at a sixty-two-hour window between the time Cassandra made that call until she was expected in Fairbanks on Monday morning for work. Somewhere in the sixty-two-hour window, Cassandra Gale and presumably William French both went missing."

Gale liked the sergeant immediately. She was whip-smart. No nonsense.

"William French is a suspect?" Trask asked.

"Right now everything is on the table," Plant said. "Now, I want to visit both campsites, but until then, let's go over the evidence that is problematic. Cassandra Gale's pistol was found three miles upriver in William French's campsite. Four live bullets were found in the six-shot cylinder along with two empty shell casings. That means that the weapon was presumably fired twice. Bullet trajectory is unknown due to the nature of the environment and the surrounding woods. We need to understand why that gun was in French's backpack.

"The third major piece of evidence that raises questions is the state of both tents found in each campsite." She next mentioned the pictures Ross had taken two days prior of both Cassie's red tent and French's green one. "There is evidence of heavy animal activity in both campsites." She tapped the photographs. "But, and it isn't just me voicing my opinion here, those rips in both tents don't look like the work of an animal. The lab will get back to us with their conclusion. So, if an animal didn't do this, then who did, and why? And lastly, the dog."

She took out a couple of pictures, turned them to show an up-close snapshot of the gash on Maverick's face and leg. Ross had taken the picture at the vet after Maverick had been sedated and stitched. "X-rays say the dog also sustained two cracked ribs, indicating some sort of blunt force trauma."

"What about Cassie's food box?" Emily asked.

Plant arched an eyebrow and Emily explained to her that Cassie would never leave food at ground level in bear country. Plant took note of that.

"And her wallet and passport," Gale added. "All her belongings were left in the campsite but her wallet and passport."

"What does her wallet look like?"

"It's tanned cowhide. Pretty worn, has an etching of a cowboy on the front."

Plant scribbled down those details. When she was done, she took out a photograph of the metal canister from Cassie's campsite. "Then there is this"— she slid the photo to the front of the desk so everyone could see. "The lab will be doing swabs to determine what the hell this thing is. Hopefully, it will lead to something substantial, but I want to make something clear to the family right off the bat. Cassandra could have gone missing up to a week ago. French, too. A week in the Alaskan wilderness is pushing the survival window up to its edge. Now, if we are looking at an abduction, a kidnapping—we're roughly a week behind the captors. That is an incredibly long time. I need to make clear to you how few resources we have up here. My superiors gave me three days in Eagle before I have to go back to Fairbanks—"

"Three days?!" Gale said.

"And I had to fight for those three days, Mr. Gale."

"Why isn't the FBI involved?" Trask asked.

When Ross snorted, Gale turned and saw Ross shaking his head and stirring his coffee. "FBI don't care what happens all the way out here. People go missing in Alaska all the time. They are too wrapped up in dealings in the cities. Big cases."

"He's right, Mr. Gale."

"If this was the Lower 48, there would be full search and rescue teams, at least a dozen cops out looking for my daughter."

"This ain't the Lower 48, Mr. Gale," Ross said, taking a sip of his coffee. "This is Alaska, I've told you that."

Gale gazed out of the window behind Plant. The parking lot of volunteers was now empty, the boats upriver, searching. He felt hopeless as he watched a Canadian Mounted Police vehicle enter the parking lot followed by a big red F-350. The vehicles parked side by side.

"Frankly, Mr. Gale," Plant said, "that search and rescue operation you got going on outside is one of the biggest I've seen in Alaska."

There was a strange coughing noise behind Gale. Everyone turned to see Tobeluk turn beet red; he was staring out of the window at the new arrivals.

"Good, Condon is here," Plant said.

Ralph Condon of the Canadian Mounted Police entered the office first followed by four other people.

A man and a woman roughly Gale's age came in first, followed by a squat redheaded man and a tall burly guy in his early thirties.

Gale noted that the burly guy kept his head low and sported a white splint on his right pinkie finger.

As the group shuffled in, Gale noticed that Tobeluk's hands were shaking. Gale wondered how long the kid had gone without a drink.

"Sergeant Plant," Condon said, "this is Ned and Darlene Voigt. They're the owners of the Northern Breeze just outside of Dawson. And this is Curtis and Jake, two of their workers."

Curtis, the squat redhead, gave a small nod. Jake, the big guy, kept his gaze planted on the floor.

Condon continued, "Ned and Darlene insisted on coming up to Eagle once they heard the news."

Darlene cast sympathetic eyes over the Gale family. "Soon as we heard, we wanted to make sure to offer our help and clear up the air. We're so guilt ridden, honestly—"

"Clear up the air?" Plant said.

"About the little incident that happened last week when Cassie and Billy were staying with us," Darlene said.

This got the whole room's attention.

Gale looked from Darlene, to Jake and Curtis, then to Ned whose crystal blue eyes bore a hole into Tobeluk across the room.

"What happened last week?" Plant asked.

Ned looked away from Tobeluk and said, "There was a bit of an altercation at my establishment between some of my workers and Cassie and Billy." Ned flicked his head to Jake and Curtis. "These two knuckleheads work at my timber site in Clinton Creek. They got in a bar fight with Cassie and Billy. I was in the kitchen and came out when I heard the commotion. By then, Cassie had already ended the fight." He pointed to Jake. "Had Jake here pinned over the bar top by his finger—girl half his size kicked his ass."

Jake kept his eyes down.

"Billy French got a nice shiner on his eye—we offered to comp their stay but both Cassie and Billy refused, so we paid for their meals."

No one said anything for a long moment. Gale's brain began to churn and he got up from his chair, fists clenched. "You two attacked my little girl?"

"We didn't attack her—Jake was just trying to buy her a drink," Curtis stammered.

Jake looked up for the first time, his gaze meeting Gale's. At first, Jake's face was expressionless, then a small, almost imperceptible smile cracked the edges of his lips.

Gale's body moved for him.

"Dad, no!" Emily screamed.

Gale launched forward, his hands gripping the scruff of Jake's shirt, pulling him to the ground. Ned, Ross, and Vance all sprang forward as Gale took Jake to the floor. Gale raised his fist, but it was immediately grabbed by strong arms. Gale felt himself being pulled back.

"What the fuck did you do?!" Gale roared. "What the fuck did you do to my daughter?!"

Chapter 17

"ENOUGH!" PLANT SHOUTED.

Ned, Vance, and Ross had Gale by the shoulders, pinned against the kitchenette. At Plant's instructions they let him go. Trask stood in between his father-in-law and the crew from the Northern Breeze.

"He fucking smiled at me! Did you see it!"

"Dad, stop!"

"I didn't do shit!" Jake sputtered, getting to his feet.

"Everyone calm down!" Ned said.

"ENOUGH!" Plant shouted again, and the room went silent. Plant raised a shaking finger at Condon. "Why the hell wasn't I notified of this altercation at the Northern Breeze?"

Condon, who had taken a backstage role to Gale's outburst, said, "I learned about it three hours ago, Meredith. They offered to come here to tell you personally so I didn't see the harm in waiting until we got here."

"I can vouch for these boys, Sergeant," Ned said. "I already told Condon that after the fight in my bar, I put them on triple shifts at Clinton Creek. They haven't left the timber site until today."

"Can that be proven?" Plant asked.

"I gotta group of men that can attest to that, including myself and Darlene." Plant didn't seem convinced.

"Security cameras at the Clinton Creek site will show they haven't left until today. Those cameras catch everything coming and going down that road, and there's only one road out of there." Ned explained that Clinton Creek was nine miles north of the Northern Breeze and used to be an old gold mining town. Now abandoned, Ned owned the timber rights to the surrounding area.

As Ned finished explaining, Gale caught his eyes floating to the picture of the metal canister on the desk. Ned's eyes hung on it longer than usual.

"Trooper Ross, Trooper Vance. Escort our friends from the Northern Breeze outside. Keep them separated until I can get their statements."

Ross and Vance escorted the four outside.

"Sergeant, can I go as well—I should be aiding in the search," Tobeluk said. He looked nervous.

"Oh, no, Max. You will stay right here until I'm done with you."

Tobeluk shrank back into the corner.

"Agent Pruitt," Plant said, "get all those boys' full names. Run their information through your servers at border patrol, I want to know about every border crossing they've ever made. See if INS can run a full background check as well."

Pruitt said she'd get on it and walked out of the office.

Plant turned her attention to Condon. "Ralph, you should have notified me about this immediately."

"Would it have made a difference?"

"These guys got in a fight with our missing persons—"

"They seemed remorseful, Meredith. They were the ones who wanted to come here. They want to help in the search . . ."

"All of them will need to be interviewed and cross-examined," Plant said, turning to look at Gale, who was still breathing heavily. "Condon, go to Clinton Creek. Take Ross with you. Talk to the workers there. Get the surveillance footage. I want to know for certain that those two never left that camp."

Plant sat back in her chair as Condon left.

"Mr. Gale, I can't begin to understand what you are going through, but I also can't have you acting like this or I'm going to have to remove you from the search. Your rashness with the grizzly bear was one thing, but I can't have you assaulting people."

"That kid knows something, you saw him smile."

"No, Mr. Gale, I didn't see him smile."

"I'm a very good judge of character, Sergeant. I spent a whole career that was dependent on that judgment. That kid is a bad apple."

"And I will talk to each and every one of them. I will get to the bottom of what happened." She paused. "When was the last time any of you slept?"

"Days," Trask said.

"I'd advise everyone to get a couple hours of sleep. I am going to start interviewing those four. When I'm done, I will have Vance come get you so we can go over Cassie's Globalstar call log."

Gale, Trask, and Emily stood up to leave. Tobeluk tried to sneak out, too.

"Not you, Max," Plant said. "You stay right here."

‖‖‖

Gale had booked two rooms at the Eagle Trading Company two days before—right after the encounter with the grizzly—two small rooms that sat on top of the small grocer and offered a view of the Yukon.

Gale's cell chimed and he sat up from his lumpy mattress and officially gave up on sleep. It was a text from Alvin Petit, updating Gale that they were an hour and a half out from Eagle.

Gale decided on a cold shower, then headed outside to pace in the parking lot to think. He was pissed he'd lost his temper earlier. Controlling his emotions when it came to his daughters had always been difficult.

But now with the stress of Cassie's disappearance, it was proving impossible.

His mind flashed back three decades before to the events that were the catalyst of these emotions. To a time of violence and retribution. He always promised himself that he would protect his girls from the truth of those times.

The contents in his back pocket were a reminder of that.

Jake's little smile flooded his mind. *That fucking smile.*

He pictured what it would feel like to wrap his hands around that bastard's neck and squeeze the life out of him.

Cool down, Jim. Cool down.

To the south, Gale caught movement in the back parking lot where Tobeluk's white VPSO vehicle sat. He spied Tobeluk hurrying to the vehicle. The VPSO was in civilian clothing; he carried a backpack over his shoulder, got in the vehicle, and sped away.

Gale was wondering if Sergeant Plant had fired the man when a voice sounded behind him.

"Mr. Gale?"

It was Vance.

The spindly trooper pointed to the VPSO's office. "Plant wants to see you. Where are your daughter and son-in-law?"

"Sleeping. Let them sleep, they can talk to Plant later."

Vance shrugged and led Gale to the office.

They found Sergeant Plant inside. She was sitting behind the desk.

"Come sit down, Mr. Gale. Thank you, Elliot."

Vance ducked out and shut the door.

"What did they say?"

Plant exhaled loudly. "All four of the stories added up. No inconsistencies."

"Someone is lying."

"We will see what Condon and Ross dig up at the timber site. I heard you have some of your own men from Montana driving up today?"

"Men and horses."

"Good, we need the help." Plant eased herself slowly into her seat, keeping one hand over the small of her back and one hand on her stomach.

"How far along are you?"

"Six months if you can believe it. My stomach's so big my husband swears I'm having twins."

"Cassie was a big baby," Gale said. "Over nine pounds."

"That's a big kid; how did her mother feel about it?"

"C-section. Like you, the doctors thought Irina was having twins, too."

"It won't be long before I'm on bed rest." Plant paused for a moment. "Where is their mother if you don't mind me asking?"

"She died when Cassie was one and Emily was three. Car accident."

"I'm sorry to hear that; this was in Montana?"

"We lived abroad back then."

"Abroad?"

"For my work, low-level government job. Pencil pusher, mostly. Met their mother while I was working in Moscow."

This seemed to surprise Plant, and she looked down at her paperwork. "I didn't know that—the girls don't have dual citizenship, do they?"

"No," Gale said, shaking his head. "American citizenship. Both girls were flown back to the States to be born. I like to keep that part of our lives behind us."

"I understand," Plant said, curiosity still burning in her eyes. "I want to play you a recording I was able to obtain from the Globalstar satellite phone service. Cassie's last-known proof of life on June twenty-second."

"I know the one," Gale said, remembering the data call log Trask had pulled up at the ranch. "She was calling Derrick's number."

"I need you to confirm that it's Cassie's voice on the line, do you consent to that?"

"I do."

Plant turned her laptop around so that the screen faced him, then she opened a zip file. "Are you ready, Mr. Gale?"

Gale nodded.

She pressed play.

Chapter 18

CASSIE CAME TO and was met with a light so blinding she immediately clamped her eyes shut.

"It will take a moment for your eyes to adjust," a deep, accented woman's voice uttered.

Cassie kept her eyes closed, noticing the chemical taste was back in her throat.

"Water," she croaked, "I need water."

She heard the sound of water being poured, and a glass being placed in front of her. Cassie squinted and saw the glass on a wooden table; reaching for it, she heard a chain rattle and she realized that she was cuffed to a metal chair. Her ankles and her wrists were secured, but the chain allowed her at least a foot of movement. She grabbed the water and gulped it down.

Her eyes adjusted and she took in the room. It was white walled. One wall had a two-way mirror on it. It reminded Cassie of police interrogation rooms she'd seen on TV shows. A camera with a green blinking light was mounted on the corner of the ceiling.

Cassie put the glass back on the table and finally focused on the woman sitting at the other end. She was heavyset, with a strong jaw and bushy brown eyebrows. Her hair was pulled back in a tight bun and she wore a doctor's white uniform. There was a red binder on the table in front of her.

"How are you feeling?"

"Where am I?"

"At my facility."

Facility? Cassie thought. Her mind went back to the men who had attacked her in the forest, then to the canister and the foul-smelling gas. She was so confused. She shook her head and tears began to fill in her eyes.

"You are disoriented. The drug in your system is a strong sedative derivative. Give it some time."

"My dog. Have you seen my dog? His name is Maverick. I . . . I don't know where he is."

The woman said nothing, her beefy hand caressing a key hanging from around her neck.

Cassie looked back down at her wrists. "Why am I shackled?"

"For your safety."

"I need a phone. I need to call my family."

"I'm afraid that's not possible."

Cassie's head was spinning so badly she shut her eyes again. She couldn't keep her thoughts straight. Bile began to rise in her throat. She leaned over and retched. When Cassie collected herself, she regarded the woman again. "Are you a doctor?"

"A psychologist."

Cassie's eyes went to her stitched arm. "Did you stitch me up?"

"Our resident doctor did. You had a pretty bad gash."

"Those men who attacked me, they're here, too?"

"Not here, no. They are at another facility close by. You are safe here, for the time being."

"Your accent, you're—"

"Russian," the woman said. "My name is Captain Akulina Yermakova. I understand this is confusing, but given your history I thought you'd be responding better." She opened the red binder, began to read out loud. "Cassandra Ann Gale from Lincoln, Montana. Thirty-three years of age. Widowed. United States Army veteran. Communications Specialist. And . . ." Yermakova stopped reading and smiled at Cassie. "A bit of a celebrity."

Celebrity?

"I have to say, we do get our fair share of military trained men at my facility. Special forces types. But never a woman of your pedigree. Third woman to ever graduate from Ranger School, no?"

How does she—

"I've spent the morning reading those press briefings about you. Quite the little scandal you created a couple of years back—advocating for women to be allowed in active combat roles . . ."

Cassie glanced at the pages. She saw lines of data, graphs, readings, and pictures. Pictures of Cassie's wallet, credit cards. Her military ID. Passport. And the pocket-size picture of her Ranger School graduation that she kept in her wallet. Captain Yermakova flipped through the pages and then stopped at a page depicting a brain scan.

"Your fMRI results are very interesting. Our neurologist said your prefrontal cortex and your amygdala responded well to the stress of combat. You usually don't see that, even in combat veterans."

"I'm sorry, I don't know what you're talking about. I think I need to lie down." Cassie suddenly felt incredibly tired and overwhelmed.

Captain Yermakova took a tablet from under the table and slid it to Cassie. The screen showed an aerial view of a forest. The screen flashed and changed and Cassie nearly gasped as she saw a video of herself drinking from the spring before she was attacked. She watched herself rise, spin around. Watched as she was rushed by the first tattooed man, then the second. She watched herself as she subdued them one by one. Watched as the canister flew from the sky, landing at her feet.

Then the screen went black.

Cassie stared at the woman in disbelief, struggling for words. Her vision narrowed, a wave of nausea rocked her, and she lost her grip on the chair.

Yermakova scowled. "Artur needs to knock down your doses. Too much soporifics for someone your size." She looked at the two-way mirror and placed a finger to her ear. "Guards, Artur, get in here!"

Cassie vomited again. The door to the room opened and a string bean of a man entered. He had a square, almost cartoonish face behind black horn-rimmed glasses and wore white scrubs. Behind him, two figures in black combat fatigues entered the room. They wore black helmets and mirrored visors that covered the entirety of their faces.

Yermakova said, "Artur, give the subject another sodium pentothal injection. I have more questions for her. While you're at it, give her an amphetamine cocktail."

A penlight appeared before Cassie's eyes, and the square-faced man checked her pupils; then he shook his head after saying something in Russian.

"What about the scopolamine?" asked Yermakova.

Artur replied in English, "She is too weak, she needs rest. An injection could do her brain irreparable harm. Let the intervening drug do its work."

Yermakova scoffed. "Put her in C-Block and monitor her."

"C-Block, is that necessary?"

"Excuse me?"

Artur bowed his head in defeat and motioned to the black-clad guards who moved to Cassie; unclasping her restraints, they took her under the shoulders and hoisted her to her feet.

"Oh and, Artur, tell Lieutenant Klimentiev in *intelligentsia* to put her profile and her indoc trial online. This princess will cause quite a stir, especially after what she did to those men."

"*Da*, Captain."

Cassie's head drooped and she felt herself being led out of the room.

Chapter 19

CASSIE WOKE ON a dank concrete floor in total blackness.

She perched herself up on an elbow and took a series of deep breaths, try-ing to remember where she was. The drugs in her system were wreaking havoc on her memory and motor functions as well as her concept of time. How long had it been since she and Maverick were attacked at her campsite? How long had it been since the two tattooed men attacked her in the forest? And that woman, Captain Yermakova, how long had it been since she'd sat across from her in that white room? It could have been hours, it could have been days, weeks.

As her eyes adjusted to the darkness, she noticed a blinking green light above her, too high to reach. On all fours, Cassie surveyed her surroundings, crawling, hands stretched out, until she ran into a wall. She didn't have far to go. She was in a small room made of concrete nearly six feet by eight feet.

A loud grating noise clanged in front of her and a door was thrown open. Light poured into the room and Cassie shielded her eyes. Two of the helmeted guards stood beside the door and the tall doctor who Yermakova called Artur ducked into the room. Cassie inched her way to the far wall. Artur looked up at the blinking green light—which Cassie now saw was a camera. He snapped his fingers and the small room erupted in light.

Artur snapped his fingers again and the guards moved around him and grabbed Cassie. She struggled but they hoisted her by the arms, lifting her to her feet; then they held her arms high behind her, causing her torso to bend. The pain was excruciating. They marched her out of the room in this stress position and into a bleak hallway and for the first time, Cassie realized she was wearing a vivid red jumpsuit.

Artur barked something in Russian and the guards stopped and let Cassie stand upright. Artur stood before her, and his cartoonish face seemed almost kind, a caring doctor overseeing his patient. He took the penlight and shined it in her eyes again.

"Pupil dilation normal. How are you feeling? More like yourself, no?"

"More like myself?"

"Clear thoughts? Your body feels healthy?"

Cassie wasn't so sure how to respond. How could she feel normal in this situation?

Artur pointed the penlight on her stitched arm. "Infection looks under control. Antibiotics seem to have worked. Enough time has passed. I'd say Subject 8831 is ready to go down to Red Block."

He nodded to the guards.

Cassie began to protest, but her arms were wrenched back into the air and a blackout bag was thrust over her head. Cassie cried out, thrashing and kicking against the guards. But she was in such a compromising position it was futile. Her shoulders were screaming in agony. The guards led her right, left, right again. She heard the sound of a cage door being thrown open and she was escorted forward then made to stop. Gears rattled and she felt herself descend. They were in an elevator, going down.

When the lift eventually stopped, she was marched forward.

Twenty steps.

Thirty.

A grinding noise sounded in front of her, a heavy door squealing open. Cold air hit Cassie's body as she was escorted into a chilled room. The guards' footsteps echoed. She could hear gurgling water.

Keys jingled and corroded steel moaned against rusted hinges.

Cassie was thrown forward, landing in a heap on a floor of cold concrete, the clang of the door closing behind her, the rattling of keys in a lock.

Cassie ripped the blackout bag from her head and got to her feet.

She was in a cell: iron bars spaced four inches apart surrounded her on all four sides. She determined the cell was at least ten feet by ten feet. An elevated concrete slab sat in its far side. A thin blanket was folded over it. A makeshift bed. To the left of the bed was a small stainless-steel toilet.

She looked around. Counted six cells including her own. They were arranged in a hexagonal pattern around a fountain of spurting water. The fountain's water flowed down into a concrete runnel that spiraled outward and ran through each of the six cells.

The only light source was a single bulb that hung down from an unseen ceiling above the fountain. Cassie couldn't see the ceiling, couldn't see the walls of the great room that she seemed to be in the middle of. It must be big, though, because the noise of the spurting water echoed far and wide.

Movement caught her attention in the cells directly to her left and right. Two figures stood from their own concrete beds, then moved to the bars of their cells—their faces obscured in shadow. Cassie could see they were wearing red jumpsuits, just like her.

The one to her right spoke in an American accent.

"You speak English?"

"Yes."

"American?"

"Yes."

"Where did they grab you?"

"What do you mean?"

"Where were you captured?"

"Just outside of Eagle."

"Eagle?"

"Alaska."

"No shit."

The man stuck his head out of the shadows and Cassie caught sight of the ruggedly handsome face of a man in his forties. His right eye was swollen shut, and he sported a fresh bandage over his left ear.

"What . . . what is going on. Where are we?"

The other man, the man to Cassie's left, laughed out loud, said something in a language Cassie couldn't understand, and moved into the light. This man had long black greasy hair and a ragged beard.

"What's your name?" the first man asked.

"Cassie Gale."

"I'm Paul Brady." He tilted his head toward the wild-haired man. "That's Marko, his English isn't so good."

Brady caught Cassie eyeing the wild-haired man, then her focus went down to the runnel at her feet.

Brady said: "It's safe to drink—you're probably thirsty from the knockout gas."

Cassie knelt down, cupped her hands, and drank from the runnel. When she was done, she stood. "I . . . I don't want to sound like a broken record, but I'm really confused—"

"You don't get to ask the questions, we go first," Marko snapped as he interrupted her.

"Tell us what you know," Brady said.

"What I know?"

"After you were captured, where did you wake up? What happened?"

Cassie shook her head, confused.

"Oh, please," spat Marko. "You must still have some Devil's Breath in your system—answer our questions!"

"Devil's Breath?"

"Scopolamine and sodium pentothal, a cocktail they use on us. Makes us docile, takes away our free will, and acts as a truth serum. A temporary zombification," Brady said, gesturing to Marko. "Those scientists upstairs use it too much on my friend here."

"Enough games, tell us how you got here, tell us what happened," Marko growled.

Cassie sat on the foot of her concrete bed. She recounted how she woke up in the forest, how she was attacked by the tattooed men. How she fought them off, then how a canister had landed at her feet. Sprayed her with that chemical mist.

"The drones," Brady said. "They shoot that stuff from the sky. Knockout gas, God knows what's in it."

Cassie blinked and remembered the buzzing white object that she saw before she was attacked.

"What happened when you woke up at the facility?" Brady asked.

"I . . . I was in a white room. I met that lady—she showed me a video of me fighting those men."

"Captain Yermakova," Marko spat.

"Your indoctrination trial," Brady said. "A test. What did Yermakova say to you?"

Cassie described her brief time in the white room with Yermakova and how she had been too sick to partake in her tests. "I was too tired, then another doctor came in, Arthur or—"

"Artur. The neurologist," Brady said. "Your body must have had a bad reaction to the Devil's Breath."

Cassie described how, minutes ago, she'd woken in a dark room and was then escorted here.

"You're military trained?" Brady asked.

"How did you know that?"

"Most of us are." He flicked his head at Marko. "Marko's Ukrainian army, helicopter pilot. I was in the SEAL Teams. You air force? Navy?"

"Army."

"What did you do in the army?"

"I was a communications specialist, then . . . then I went to Ranger School."

Marko laughed. "A woman Ranger!"

"I'm not a Ranger, I just got my tab." Cassie was used to this type of reaction; she glared at the wild-haired Ukrainian.

"Are you serious?" Brady asked.

"I was the third woman to graduate from Ranger School."

Brady peered forward, squinting in the dull light at Cassie. "Wait a minute—I think I remember reading about you. You were the one who made that fuss with your senator about letting women into active combat."

Marko laughed again. "Real-life GI Jane!"

Cassie glared at him again. She was used to the nickname. Many of the papers and military blogs dubbed her "GI Jane" after Demi Moore's character in the nineties movie of the same title.

"Well, it looks like you are in luck, GI Jane!" Marko said. "You've got your wish."

"What do you mean?"

"You aren't in Kansas anymore, GI Jane!"

"Knock it off, Marko," Brady said.

"No, seriously, what does he mean?"

Brady looked uneasy.

"Will someone tell me what's going on?"

Brady said, "I was picked up in Alaska, too. Just outside of Chicken, about four hundred miles south of Eagle. Maybe a month or two ago. I don't know. But . . . but you might have noticed we aren't in Alaska anymore. You might have noticed everyone in this place is—"

"Russian."

"Yeah," Brady said. "That's the theory. We think we're somewhere in Russia. In some underground facility Yermakova calls Post 866."

Russia. Underground. Cassie took a moment to try to rationalize this. "How is that possible, how can we be in Russia?"

"Because that's where the *sharashkas* are, GI Jane."

"The what?"

"The places of dark rumors, places that don't exist." Marko raised his hands to the sky. "Places like this."

What the hell is this guy talking about? Cassie thought. "What's a sharashka?"

"It is hell, GI Jane. And we are in the seventh circle, right next to Brutus," Marko said, with a sick, almost proud smile on his face.

Cassie suddenly noticed movement in the dark cell next to Brady's. A lump of blankets on the bed that she hadn't noticed before. A figure stirred and lifted its head.

"Aw, sleeping beauty wakes!" Marko said.

Cassie stared at the figure that stood from the bed and limped to the runnel. Matted hair showed in the dim light as the person bent down and drank from the flowing water.

"How are you feeling, pussycat?" Marko teased. "Cat still got your tongue?"

"Marko, stop it," Brady said.

The figure at the runnel continued to drink, acting like he hadn't heard the sneering Ukrainian.

"What?" Marko said to Brady. "He don't talk, all he do is sleep."

"Let him be, Marko."

Cassie got off her bed and made her way to the front of her cell, peering at the man. The mop of hair looked oddly familiar, the scraggly beard—

The figure raised his head and wiped the falling water from a bruised mouth, and a pair of familiar eyes grew wide in recognition.

"Cassie!" the figure croaked.

Cassie felt the breath leave her lungs.

"Billy!"

Chapter 20

GALE TOOK A deep breath and prepared himself for what he was about to hear from Plant's computer. The audio was grainy, then he heard his late son in law's familiar voice.

Hey, this is Derrick. You know what to do. In the meantime, remember: Only dead fish swim with the current.

The voice mail then beeped and there was a moment of silence, followed by Cassie's choking sob.

Derrick, my secret is . . . deep down I know it was my fault. I ignored the signs. I . . . the truth is, I'm not doing better. It's all a sham, I'm not doing better at—

The phone beeped three times and an animatronic voice alerted that the voice mail box was now full.

Plant stopped the recording and Gale felt numb. That was the last thing Cassie had said. She had been lying to them, lying to her family, her therapists, to everyone.

She was still blaming herself.

Tremors of guilt racked Gale. Tears welled in his eyes. His baby girl was suffering.

Plant remained quiet, then said, "Can you verify that was Cassandra on the recording?"

"That was her," Gale said, trying to keep it together. "I know what you're thinking, Ross asked the same question. You think Cassie could have staged this whole thing downriver. That she wanted to make it look like something else, that she ended it elsewhere. But that's impossible, she would *never* hurt Maverick. That dog was the only thing linking her back to Derrick. She would never—"

"I'm not thinking that, Mr. Gale," Plant said. "I think Cassie was going through something terrible, but I don't think this is something she set up. The evidence leads to a possible abduction that was hastily covered up, but not suicide."

Gale dabbed at his eyes, the sound of Cassie's pained voice still ringing in his ears.

Plant said, "You gave me a brief history last week over the phone of what Cassie was going through—about her husband. I thought we could expand on that a little bit. Help me to understand your daughter a bit more." She turned her laptop around so it faced her. "From what I read online, your daughter is an exceptional young woman. The third woman to graduate from Ranger School. That whole political scandal she was embroiled in. Cassie sounds tough."

"Tough doesn't even cut it," Gale said. "She's like no one I've ever met before. She's loving, passionate, disciplined—highly intelligent and determined."

"A woman who can handle herself in any situation."

"For the first ten years of Cassie's life," Gale said, swallowing hard, "I was emotionally absent. Withdrawn. I couldn't come to grips with my wife's death. The ranch hands and Emily took the reins raising Cassie, and I've never forgiven myself for doing that to them. After a while, I pulled myself out of my funk. I realized that I needed to be present in my daughters' lives—I needed to be available. I needed to be a role model."

"From where I'm standing, it looks like you did an amazing job, Mr. Gale. From what I read about that senator in Montana, she used Cassie as a pawn to further an agenda."

"It didn't bother Cassie; she's always had thick skin, just like her mother."

"And what about this year? Tell me what happened with her husband."

Gale shifted in his seat. "My daughter married her childhood sweetheart, Derrick Halpern. He was like a son to me. They married when they were eighteen. He entered the marines right after. Went into Recon. Seven tours overseas over the course of thirteen years. We never saw the signs. He was home on leave last Christmas, deploying again in February. His last tour, so he said. Cassie was already out of the military by then. They spoke of moving up to Alaska. They seemed so happy—Cassie announced she was—"

Gale couldn't get the words out; he just flicked his eyes to Plant's stomach and saw her eyes widen in shock.

"Pregnant?"

"They announced it over Christmas dinner."

Gale felt the tears running down his unshaven face and cleared them with his sleeve.

"A week later, New Year's morning, I was sleeping in when I heard the worst scream I've ever heard in my life. It came from outside. I ran out of the house, through the snow, and found Cassie sitting in front of the barn, screaming at the top of her lungs. The barn door was open. Derrick's body was hanging from the rafters. Cassie miscarried later that day."

Gale saw Plant's features flush.

"A week later, we had Cassie committed to a facility in Missoula. She was on suicide watch for the first month. Doctors let her out in late May. Her therapists said she was doing much better. Ready to start the next chapter of her life. Cassie looked great, she seemed okay—but I guess it was all a lie."

Plant looked like she didn't know what to say, so she stood instead, rounded the desk, leaned on it, and said softly, "I'm going to do whatever I can to find your daughter, Mr. Gale."

"Those people from the Northern Breeze—"

"I can't have you talking with them. Not until we hear back from Condon and Ross. I will question each of them again, multiple times if I have to. But I am going to have to ask you to keep your distance from them. They've checked in at the Eagle Motel down the street. Vance is going to keep an eye on them until Ross gets back so Vance can get his plane in the air."

"What am I supposed to do?"

"I'd suggest you get some more sleep, but let me do my job."

"You've only got three days here, then what?"

"Then I go back to Fairbanks and work it from afar. Work it from different angles if we have to."

Gale didn't like the sound of that, but he was too tired to argue. Petit and Cronin were due to arrive any minute.

Gale thanked Sergeant Plant and headed outside.

||||||||||||||||||||||||||||||||||||||||||||||||||||||||||||||||||||||||||||||||

The high evening sun warmed the top of Gale's head as he wandered up the Yukon's shoreline, parallel to Front Street. His mind kept replaying the hoarse, pained voice of Cassie's voice mail.

How had I not seen how bad she was still hurting?

His cowboy boots punched through the soft sand and crunched over the round pebbles until he realized that he had meandered to the northern perimeter of town. He gazed back at the little forgotten settlement of Eagle and realized that tucked against the tree line, across a wide parking lot, was the Eagle Motel where the crew from the Northern Breeze were staying. Gale walked up to the guardrail separating Front Street from the Yukon's shore, and rested his leg on it to relieve some of the pain from his hip.

He'd seen multiple specialists and they'd all said the same thing: Gale would need a hip replacement within a couple of years. The damage to his pelvis was too severe, the remnants of the bullet had lodged itself deep into the ball and socket joint.

Gale flashed back to the night that the bullet had entered his hip. He remembered how cold it had been in that forest, how far the fall into the river had been, and how damn frigid the water was.

Gale shifted his weight and realized that Trooper Vance was sitting under the Eagle Motel's portico between two of the rooms. Gale squinted—the motel wasn't more than two hundred yards away—and Vance seemed to be too preoccupied with his phone to notice Gale.

Ten seconds later, almost in unison, both of the doors on either side of the trooper opened. Ned and Darlene came out of one door, Curtis and Jake the other. Vance pocketed his phone and stood as the group casually gathered around the trooper. From what Gale could see, Ned was doing all the talking. Gale decided to take his leg off the guardrail and squat down so he wouldn't be caught snooping.

The way Ned spoke to Vance, whether it was his body language or the way Vance seemed to respond to Ned, made Gale believe the Northern Breeze crew knew Vance well.

They talked for a couple more minutes, then Vance hurried to his vehicle and pulled out of the parking lot. But instead of heading south to the VPSO's office on Front Street, the trooper turned west and disappeared into town.

Gale didn't have time to consider the oddity of this behavior, because he was running the logistics in his head on how he could sneak around the motel and talk to Jake and Curtis alone. He knew that this group was lying to the investigators—that thin-lipped smile on Jake's face told Gale everything he needed to know.

Darlene went back to her room and shut the door, Ned said one last thing to Jake and Curtis before they returned to their room and just as Gale was about to jump over the guardrail and circle the motel via the woods, Ned turned abruptly and caught sight of him.

Both stood stock-still for a long moment, two gunslingers about to face off, then Ned turned his attention south, in the direction of the VPSO's office, then north, up Front Street to the access road heading to Cassie's campsite.

Coast clear. Ned made a beeline straight for Gale.

"Shit," Gale muttered, as he straightened himself up. In the old days, he never would have allowed himself to be spotted in such a compromising position.

In the old days, he would have cased out his target for hours, found primary, secondary, and tertiary escape routes as well, then done countersurveillance until he put himself in a viable position to carry out the mission at hand.

Ned Voigt stopped at the edge of Front Street, took a cigarette out, and lit it.

"You know we ain't supposed to be talkin' to each other, Mr. Gale."

"Then why are you?"

"What Plant don't know won't hurt her," Ned said, taking a drag. "And I guess I'd like to take the time to personally apologize, both for what happened at the Northern Breeze and what happened earlier in the office. Once we're cleared, I want your permission to help search for Cassie and Billy."

Gale studied the man, his blue eyes, his silver-streaked hair. He carried himself like someone who was used to being in charge.

When Gale didn't reply, Ned shifted his weight. "Darlene's blaming herself. We were the ones who told Cassie and Billy about those camping spots up north." He pointed a finger to the access road. "It's one of our favorite places, has been for years."

"You told them to come up here?"

"We did. We liked Cassie. That girl of yours has a good head on her shoulders. Not everyone would stand up to someone of Jake's size. Anyway, if we can help, just let us know."

As Ned turned to leave, Gale stopped him, suddenly remembering something from earlier. "Back at the VPSO's office. You seemed to be staring daggers at Max Tobeluk and he seemed to be afraid of you and your group. Why?"

Ned stopped walking and turned with a small scoff. "That boy is nothing but trouble. A drunk. Couple years back he was harassing me and Darlene about camping up here. Eventually, it got so bad we had to get the troopers involved. Vance had to fly up one time to have a talk with him. Everything stopped after that."

Gale recounted the casual interaction he'd just witnessed between the group and Vance.

"You know most of the troopers around here?"

"There's only two of them in this part of eastern Alaska. You spend as much time here as we do, you get to know everyone. Actually, Vance just got word that Sergeant Plant can't find Max Tobeluk."

Gale remembered seeing the VPSO hurrying to his Expedition in the parking lot not an hour before. He told Ned what he'd seen.

"Huh," Ned said, lost in thought.

Belching sounds of diesel engines made Gale turn and look down Front Street where a caravan of familiar black pickup trucks towed horse trailers into town and parked in the Eagle Trading Post parking lot.

Alvin Petit and Bill Cronin had finally arrived.

Gale leaned off the guardrail.

"Your men?" Ned asked.

"My cavalry."

Gale walked away from Ned without another word and headed down Front Street. Petit climbed out of the lead truck with Bill Cronin. At least a dozen of Cronin's men got out of their respective trucks. Gale could even see the Davis brothers.

As Gale got to the parking lot, he turned around and saw that Ned Voigt hadn't moved. The Northern Breeze owner stood implacable, staring at Gale and the new arrivals with his hands on his hips.

In his mind, Gale was forming a plan. Something wasn't ringing true with the Voigts and the boys from the Northern Breeze. They were trying too hard to paint themselves in a positive light. Overextending themselves—being too friendly.

No matter what Condon and Ross found in Clinton Creek, no matter if Sergeant Plant cleared the Northern Breeze crew, Gale decided it was time to take matters into his own hands.

He needed to speak with Curtis and Jake. Alone.

So far, they were the only ones with a motive. Losing a fight to Cassie was enough to seek out revenge. Jake looked like a guy who wouldn't take it lightly getting his ass kicked by a girl.

There was more going on. Jake's thin-lipped smile had proved that.

Cassie had been missing for nearly a week.

It was time to take drastic measures.

Gale greeted the Montanans as best he could under the circumstances, then they all circled around him, soldiers awaiting orders.

"Before we get started," Gale said, "I need something done. A favor. And I need it done quietly."

Chapter 21

"CASSIE! WHAT ARE you doing here?!"

"You two know each other?" Brady asked.

"Oh, now the pussycat talks," Marko said.

"I heard the noises downriver," Billy said, his voice cracking. "I heard the explosions. The gunshots. I didn't know what to do, so I went to the river. I heard screaming. Then . . . then I heard someone coming up behind me. There was a flash of light . . . then I woke up here, in this—"

"Sharashka!" Marko half yelled.

"I'm sorry, Cassie—I tried to do something."

"There's nothing to apologize for," Cassie said, relieved to see a familiar face.

For the next five minutes she told Billy what had happened to her at the campsite right up to the point she was knocked out.

Then Brady piped up. "I had a similar experience."

He detailed how he had left San Diego after a bitter divorce and had driven up to Alaska. "I wanted to get away from it all. I wanted to find the most desolate place I could find and just *live*." He explained that he found a place to camp on the Fortymile River just south of Chicken. On his second night at the campsite he had woken up to a sound, grabbed his rifle thinking it was a grizzly bear, and was met with a vibrant orange light and that terrible-smelling gas. "I woke up at some point later in a box or a bag, it was like a coffin. I couldn't move, my body was paralyzed, then I fell back asleep and woke up in the woods with three men trying to kill me. They were crazed, malnourished—lunatics."

"You were able to escape them?" Cassie asked.

"I killed them," Brady said, solemnly.

Marko laughed.

"That wasn't my experience at all," Billy said. "I woke up in a white room. They injected me with stuff." He showed a series of track marks on the insides of his arms. "They hooked my head up to these machines; the drugs they gave me caused terrible hallucinations, physical pain, my brain felt like it was on fire—"

"That why you no talk?" Marko said. "Because they poke needles in you? Put Devil's Breath in your body?"

"Marko."

"None of you get it," Marko said. "None of you understand."

"Understand what?" Cassie said.

"*History.* This place." He opened his arms to the sky.

"Enlighten us then."

"You know of Aleksandr Solzhenitsyn, no?"

"Yeah," Billy said. "The Russian writer."

"Good job, pussycat. Yes, famous writer. He write about hypocrisy of Soviet state. He lived in gulag. He lived in sharashka. Solzhenitsyn write great books, one called *In the First Circle.* Fictional account of his time in Soviet sharashka. Sharashka is like gulag but nicer. Where scientists, engineers, mathematicians, physicists, and chemists were all sentenced to work for the state. It was where Soviet surveillance technology was created, in a famous sharashka called Marfino, north of Moscow."

"The scientists were prisoners?" Billy asked.

"Yes, but they had it nice. They got food, a bed, their own cell. But they were prisoners, make no mistake."

"Why were they sent there?"

"For their specialties."

Cassie asked, "Then why are we here? I'm not a scientist—"

"We are the lab rats, GI Jane! Solzhenitsyn write that being sentenced to sharashka as scientist was like ascending to the highest and best circle of hell." He pointed to himself. "Us. We are in the seventh circle. Those doctors, Artur—they are in the first circle."

"This is all speculation," Brady said.

"You Americans," Marko spat. "You don't understand Russians like I do. I fight Russians my whole life." Marko paused for a moment. Then his tone got serious. "I was captured a long time ago, after my helicopter crashed in Avdiivka. I've seen many people occupy these cells. I was captured while fighting pro-Russian separatists in Donbass. Growing up, I'd heard the rumors of the secret medical sharashkas where the Soviets put their prisoners. Whispers of secret posts where captured fighters—Westerners, Ukrainians, Zionists—were sent and used like lab rats. This place isn't just a medical sharashka. It is worse. They poke us and prod us—but it is also Yermakova's game."

"A game?"

"Yermakova make us fight in her trials. You want to live, you fight. They record it. Cameras in trees. Cameras in sky—their drones. It is sport for them."

"Sport for who?"

"Ah, that is the billion-dollar question, GI Jane. Who watches us?"

The loud grating noise Cassie heard when she was first escorted into the block reverberated through the darkness.

Marko suddenly went white. He backed into the cell as if the bars were on fire. Cassie looked to Brady and noticed all the blood had drained from his face as well. He started pacing. Murmuring under his breath, running a hand through his hair. "It's too soon."

"What's too soon?" Cassie said.

Loud footfalls started coming toward them out of the darkness.

Captain Yermakova came into the light followed by a dozen guards. She had a nasty smile on her face.

"Regaling them with stories, Marko?"

Marko shrank into his cell. Yermakova walked up to Cassie's cell.

"Congratulations, Subject 8831," she said. "We are going to have a little welcoming party." She motioned to the guards. "Take the Americans."

Cassie saw the other guards descend on Billy's and Brady's cells. Brady got down on his knees and put his hands on his head. Billy followed suit.

Four guards entered Cassie's cell. She watched as Brady and Billy were blindfolded and taken away. Cassie backed away from her guards, searching for a chink in their armor—some way to take advantage of the situation. But the guards were covered entirely by body armor. They grabbed her, forced her down, and a blackout bag was thrown over her head.

Yermakova's voice was near her ear. "Let's see how the little celebrity does in her first *real* trial."

Head yanked down, arms wrenched up behind her, Cassie was marched out of her cell.

She could hear Marko, whooping and hollering behind her. His maniacal voice echoing in the massive cell block:

"WHO IS WATCHING YOU, GI JANE! WHO IS WATCHING YOU!"

Chapter 22

GENERAL VIKTOR ALEKSANDROVICH Sokolov, chief of SVR Line S—the Illegals Directorate in the Russian Foreign Intelligence Service—gazed at the flurry of white snowflakes dotting the illuminated x-ray image on the wall opposite him. The oncologist, a lieutenant in the GRU's Office of Medical Services, sat under the image of Sokolov's chest, his mouth moving slowly, words pouring out, but Sokolov couldn't hear—his eyes were glued to the image. A sense of serenity coursed through Sokolov's veins, a sense of relief, a sense of completion. The small, cold office on the fifteenth floor of the Moscow State University Medical Center somehow began to feel warm, welcoming.

"General?" the oncologist said. "Do you understand what I am telling you?"

The burning in his lungs, the morning coughing fits, the specks of blood in the countless handkerchiefs—the eighty-one-year-old Sokolov snapped back to reality.

"Of course, Doctor—I understand."

The oncologist, a heavyset man in his midfifties, rested his hands on his knees, fingertips nervously caressing his pants—contemplating his next words. But Sokolov waved the man off, he didn't need to hear it, the x-ray showed all he needed to see. It was cancer. Inoperable, untreatable cancer, plain and simple. Lungs, throat, lymph nodes, it didn't matter.

It was a relief.

The oncologist glanced nervously to his nurse as Sokolov grabbed his cane and got to his feet and walked to the door.

"General—there are treatments, aggressive treatments, especially in this day and age."

"I do not care for treatments, Doctor. I have seen the treatments you pump into the veins of your patients. If I am going to die, I am going to die on my own accord, with my dignity intact." Sokolov stepped out of the office and into the sterile marble-floored hallway. His four-man security detail stood at attention and followed the general out of the hospital and to the armored Mercedes waiting in the motorcade in front of the hospital's emergency entrance.

Sokolov gazed up at the gray, gunmetal Moscow skyline as the sun threatened to break through the thick overlaying clouds. It was going to rain. Sokolov could smell it.

He loved the rain. Loved how it cleansed the city. How perfect a day it was for rain. After all, it was a special day, a day to mourn, a day of remembrance.

How fitting to learn of his own demise on this very day.

The same day.

"To the home residence, sir?" Dmitry, his special assistant, asked.

Sokolov kept his gaze on the skyline, his mind dancing with the concept of having a relaxing afternoon in his home library with a chai or a vodka—or even back to Yasenevo to catch up on highly secretive work on the fourth floor. Sokolov breathed in heavily, feeling the weight of the destructive cells in his lungs. No, today was not a day to spend in private, nor was it a day to ruminate in the suffocating offices of Yasenevo—today should be a day of carefree indulgence.

Of entertainment.

He was dying, after all.

What better way to celebrate?

"I wish to visit Lubyanka. I wish to be taken to the *Peshchera*." Sokolov said, climbing into the Mercedes. *I wish to be taken to the Cave.*

|||||||||||||||||||||||||||||||||||||||||||||||||||||||||||||||||||||||||||||||||||

The motorcade, comprising four armored black Land Rovers, two in front, two in back, led Sokolov's black Mercedes through Moscow's crowded streets. Sokolov drank from a glass of vodka and gazed at the gray city that he loved. Moscow—the *Rodina*'s crown jewel—the city that stood impenetrable through the centuries—an industrious monster that stood the trials of time.

In the distance he could see the looming nine-story concrete edifice that once served as the headquarters of the *Komitet Gosudarstvennoy Bezopasnosti*, the KGB. The Lubyanka Building, as it is called, now housed the men and women of the

president's new KGB, the *Federal'naya Sluzbha Bezopasnosti,* the FSB—Russia's Federal Security Service.

The motorcade took the familiar underground entrance, passing half a dozen security checkpoints along the way. Government officials waved them through at the very sight of the Mercedes with the diplomatic state flags and the flashing blue lights. The underground entrance spiraled deeper and deeper under the building until it came to a stop in front of an elevator protected by high-ranking FSB guards. Sokolov stepped out of the Mercedes, handed his glass of vodka to Dmitry, and hobbled to the elevator, placing his right hand outward. One of the FSB guards stepped forward, procured a tablet. Sokolov pressed his palm on the tablet's screen until it vibrated and chimed.

Satisfied, the other FSB guard opened the elevator, Sokolov entered, and the elevator descended. He eyed his aging features in the elevator's mirrored door: his hunched shoulders, his sagging skin drooping under his eyes and cheekbones. His pale complexion made him look like he belonged in an infirmary, but his black eyes—like smoldering coals—still had life in them.

The elevator descended and then the doors whooshed open and Sokolov was met with the familiar, brilliantly lit corridor of black marble that led to a vibrant red door. Two more guards with light machine guns stood before the entrance, both indicating the iris scanner centered in the red door.

The old general eased his right eye to the scanner. A green beam of light flashed over his iris and the door swung open.

It was warm inside. Decadently lit and richly adorned.

Sokolov stood at the elevated entrance to the Russian Federation's most exclusive club.

The *Peshchera.*

The Cave.

The dozen or so men at the various tables, all fingering tumblers of vodka, stopped midconversation to gaze at the old general—the infamous chief of SVR's Line S.

Sokolov paid them no mind. He was used to people staring. Used to powerful men cowering in his presence. It came with his history. Power has a way of making those of lesser stature wilt and shrivel. Even these men, the most powerful men in Russia—the ones staring at him—were all handpicked by the president. Sokolov gazed lazily at the various directors of the government agencies, the ministers, the oligarchs, the fellow generals, the secretaries of the Security Council.

The *siloviki.* The president's inner circle. The old boys' club.

As they stared, Sokolov's gaze went to the familiar screen covering the entirety of the far wall of the lounge. It showed an aerial shot of green forested mountains. Statistics flew down the left side of the screen. The odds. The wagers. The bets.

He was in luck. A trial was about to begin.

Sokolov descended the carpeted steps, choosing his favorite table in the back, where he could observe and watch all.

The *siloviki* returned to their drinks and banter as the bartender arrived at the general's side. Sokolov ordered his usual. A glass of Russo-Baltique. Expense was of no issue down here.

Before the bartender left to fill the order, he deposited the leather-bound dossier in front of the old general.

Sokolov crossed his legs, procured a cigarette, a Black Sobranie—the very tube of tobacco he'd smoked for decades and that had inevitably led him to his current, cancerous situation.

It had been months since Sokolov graced the Cave with his presence. Reluctant to imbibe and consort with the infamous *siloviki*, Sokolov usually preferred the more *hands-on* approach of unwinding—of detuning after a stressful week at work. Though the Cave was macabre in its viewing nature, gambling was never Sokolov's forte. He much preferred his other vices: his drink, his smokes, and his time in the brightly lit cellars of Butyrka or the scarred rooms of Lefortovo, where he could bask in the ecstasy of his favorite pastime.

Pytki. Torture.

Even in *Novorossiya*, the new Russia, a man of Sokolov's stature could indulge in the dark vices of the former Soviet Union without repercussions. But not today.

Participating in *pytki* was physically taxing on the aging, sick general. No, today he would enjoy the morbid viewing in the Cave, relax with a glass or two of Russo-Baltique, and if he was feeling like it, he might even place a rare bet.

Sokolov flipped through the dossier and found the ledger to this evening's trial. It would take place on a mountain slope, heavily forested. He looked over the fractional odds; the trial would consist of three subjects versus six prisoners.

The prisoners were six of the most sadistic men to walk the earth—handpicked from the Federal Governmental Institution—Penal Colony No. 6 in the Orenburg region—the notorious Black Dolphin Prison. Child molesters, murderers, terrorists, cannibals, maniacal serial killers, all facing life sentences—pitted against captured foreigners. These were usually soldiers ripped from some armpit, some hellhole of the world. Syrians, Iraqis, Afghanis—a few Zionists, men with special forces training. The rarest, the most fun, though, for both the viewing pleasure of Sokolov and the *siloviki*, were the captured Westerners.

Sokolov flipped through the pages listing the descriptions of the Black Dolphin prisoners, wondering who the three unfortunate souls pitted against them would be, when he raised an eyebrow.

They were Americans. All three of them.

One was a civilian, a kid. The other, a former Navy SEAL, and the other . . .

A woman.

The bartender deposited a glass of the Russo-Baltique before Sokolov.

"Would you like me to place a bet for you this morning, General?"

Sokolov raised a finger to silence the bartender and read the woman's biography:

> Subject 8831: Name: Cassandra Ann Gale, citizen USA Born 27/1/1986 in Washington, DC, U.S.A. Current Residence, Lincoln, Montana. Widowed. Army Communications Specialist from 2006 to 2015. Resided in Fort Benning from 2015 during which the subject became the THIRD WOMAN to graduate from the United States Army Ranger School. The subject retired from duty in 2017. Subject's husband is DECEASED. Subject 8831 was extracted from Eagle, Alaska, by extraction team KODIAK.

The third woman to graduate from Ranger School, Sokolov thought, impressed.

Surely, Captain Yermakova of the *Glavnoje Razvedyvatel'noje Upravlenije,* the GRU—Russia's Military Intelligence agency—had outdone herself with this Cassandra Ann Gale.

Captain Yermakova, the doughy-faced ogre of the GRU's Science Directorate. A sniveling, Moscow State University–trained pseudo-psychologist, who yearned desperately for the ear of the president. Who would do anything to climb the ranks to get the president's attention, to be the first woman let into the president's inner circle, all because of her macabre medical malpractice.

Sokolov snorted at the preposterousness of Captain Yermakova's unorthodox climb to the top. In the eighties she had been lucky in the USSR's western *rezidenturas,* the Soviet embassies. A seasoned manipulator, one of the GRU's best, she had excelled where others had failed. And she had come up with the outlandish idea to entertain the *siloviki*—to reinstate Post 866—the infamous medical sharashka—for *scientific advancement.*

And *sport.*

The bartender shifted nervously as Sokolov finished skimming through the research the GRU *intelligentsia* had done on Cassandra Gale.

Sokolov picked a standard money line bet.

"A million rubles on the American girl."

The bartender bowed and walked away.

More of the *siloviki* were entering the Cave—undoubtedly aware of the rarity of having not only a woman in the upcoming trial, but a woman with special forces training.

Word traveled fast in the inner circle.

Sokolov scanned the American press clippings attached to the Cassandra Gale file in the dossier, the political scandals—the bigwigs in Washington arguing over whether women should be able to fight in active combat roles—when he flipped to the colored pictures of Cassandra Gale's personal belongings found during her extraction. He viewed her state-issued identification, examining the cowhide wallet, her military identification, passport, social security card, and then a photocopied, wallet-size picture of her in green army fatigues, arm wrapped around a young man, a large German shepherd at their side, held on a leash by a tall, older man wearing a blue shirt—

Sokolov held the glass of Russo-Baltique at the edge of his lips as his arthritic fingers began to shake.

Hundreds of thousands of rubles' worth of premium Russian vodka smashed over the table and landed on the rich red carpeting. The neighboring *siloviki* all turned—watching as a trembling Sokolov nearly fell from his seat. His eyes bore down on the photograph, on the face of the man holding the German shepherd by the leash. The man's square jaw, those piercing blue eyes.

It couldn't be.

It was impossible.

Sokolov felt a burning in his chest, as if his cancer had metastasized tenfold in the last few seconds. Trembling fingers grasped at the page with the photocopied picture. Someone was speaking to him. A voice broke through his own panic and astonishment.

"General? General, are you okay?"

Sokolov looked up at the bartender, trying to find the words, his eyes darting from the bartender, to the *siloviki*, to the screen that was beginning to show the countdown to the trial. Cassandra Gale's picture was plastered on the screen, wagers streaming under her profile.

Memories, dark memories flooded Sokolov's mind—he gazed intently at Cassandra Gale's face and saw the resemblance. It was so obvious. She looked so much like, *him.*

"The trial!" Sokolov gasped. "Stop the damn trial!"

The bartender took a nervous step back, his eyes darting around for help. The *siloviki* sat stock-still in their seats, wondering what had come over the chief of SVR's Line S.

"S-s-stop?" the bartender stammered.

Sokolov had gotten to his feet, one hand on his cane, the other holding the leather-bound dossier. "Get ahold of Captain Yermakova, have her stop the trial at once! It must not begin!"

"Sir, we don't have a direct line to the sharashka, that would be—"

"Kryuchkov!" Sokolov pointed his cane to a rotund, balding man in an FSB dress uniform sitting among the *siloviki* who had turned a deep shade of scarlet at the utterance of his name.

Captain Ivan Mikhailovich Kryuchkov, head of the FSB's Department Fifteen—the FSB liaison to the secret GRU sharashkas, made a gurgling noise and unsteadily found his feet.

"You have the direct line to Captain Yermakova, do you not?" Sokolov snapped. "Your department controls the secure FAPSI line to the Post 866, does it not?"

"I . . . we do. But we can't just—"

"Do not tell me what I can or cannot do!" Sokolov roared, moving to the stairs. His cane pointed again at Kryuchkov. "Where is it? Where is the line to the sharashka!"

"It's upstairs, on the fifth floor."

"Take me to it."

As Kryuchkov weaved his way through the lounge, Sokolov caught sight of the screen on the far wall. He saw the three subjects: Cassandra Ann Gale, the SEAL, and the kid. They were being flown by an Mi-24 helicopter to the wooded hillside. The trial would begin in minutes.

Sokolov needed to hurry.

Chapter 23

THEY HAD BEEN escorted out of Red Block and into what Cassie had determined was some sort of prep room.

Each of the Americans had been stripped naked and re-dressed in green combat fatigues by the guards.

Captain Yermakova had been in the room. She'd looked giddy as she gazed down at her tablet. After they were dressed, black bracelets were secured around their left wrists.

"This is how we monitor you," Yermakova said. "GPS, heartbeat. We track everything for our experiments. Don't try to run. There is nowhere to go. Don't try to take off the bracelet, it's tamper proof."

Artur, the neurologist, had then entered the room and rechecked the bracelets; when he was finished, he gave Yermakova the go-ahead.

They were cuffed again. Blackout bags were placed over their heads and they were escorted out of the room. Cassie had tried to remember how many steps they had taken, how many direction changes, but it proved impossible. After what had felt like forever, they were marched outside.

She could feel the sun warming up her blackout hood as the whine and rotor thump of a helicopter blocked out all other sound.

They rode in the helicopter for a long time before they landed, then were stress marched for two hundred steps and made to sit down, back to back.

Yermakova spoke: "Your restraints will electronically unlock themselves. Then the trial will begin. Your only goal is to survive."

After the helicopter had taken back off, Cassie felt her handcuffs click open.

She wriggled out of them and took the blackout hood off her head. Brady and Billy did the same. Brady was already on his feet, walking toward the base of a large tree.

Cassie took in her surroundings. They were on a heavily wooded mountainside—a jagged cliff to their right and a steep embankment of downed trees to their left.

"We're in luck." Brady returned from the base of the tree and held three old wood-stocked rifles. "Mosin-Nagant M1944s, two bullets in each." Brady handed one of the rifles to Cassie. She checked the safety, ran the action, and examined the magazine. Brady was right, two bullets.

"I've never been given a gun before. They usually only arm me with a knife," Brady said.

"What do you think it means?"

"That whatever we're up against isn't going to be easy. Six bullets total means there are probably at least six of those psychos out there hunting us. Maybe more. I don't know, I've only experienced my trials alone." He walked over to Billy, who was still sitting, and handed him his rifle. Billy took it without looking up at Brady.

"How many trials have you been in?" Cassie asked.

"This will be my sixth including indoc," Brady said, offering a hand to Billy. "C'mon, kid, we need to get moving."

Billy didn't react to the hand, just muttered something under his breath.

"What's that?"

"Bad-Luck-Billy," Billy said, then looked up. "That's what my friends called me back home. I find myself in the worst situations. I'm not military trained, how am I supposed to survive this?"

"You are going to survive by listening to me and Brady. We're lucky we got a SEAL with us," Cassie said. She smiled and looked over at Brady, who shifted uncomfortably. "You know how to shoot a rifle, Billy, you know how to hunt, just do what we say when we say it and you'll be fine. I promise."

Billy didn't look assured as he gazed down at the antique rifle in his hands.

"C'mon, we'll get through this, then we'll figure out a way out of here."

Cassie helped Billy to his feet.

Brady squinted at the sky. "They have eyes everywhere. Drones. Cameras in the trees. You'll see some, no doubt. Don't pay them any mind, just focus on getting through the trial alive."

They devised a plan.

They would head uphill, try to find an opening where they could survey the land, then either take the offensive or the defensive based on their findings. Brady suggested they walk with Billy in between them as they headed uphill so Billy could cool his nerves.

It took them nearly thirty minutes to summit the mountain. The peak was covered in jagged rocks. Brady had them move slowly out of the forest and onto the rocks near a large boulder.

"Keep low and don't skyline yourself."

Cassie looked out at the vast expanse of wilderness below. Mountain ranges interspersed by deep green valleys. In the distance, she could make out white-capped volcanoes and a wide river stretching into the horizon.

"This is all new," Brady said, shaking his head. "I've never seen any of this before."

Cassie looked up and could see three drones—mere specks in the sky zipping about. "What's the plan?"

Billy was lying down behind the big boulder. Brady, still looking out at the wilderness, didn't seem to hear.

Cassie wished they had been given something to eat or drink. She wished she had never gone to Alaska, wished Derrick were still alive. Her thoughts floated to that day in January when she'd woken early and walked to the barn. She remembered how loud she screamed, how she had fallen into the snow. How her father had sprinted out of the house and grabbed hold of her.

Cassie was thrust out of her memory when she caught movement in the forest below.

She grabbed Brady by the arm and was about to alert him to the movement when the loud whip-crack of a bullet whizzed over their heads.

Chapter 24

CAPTAIN KRYUCHKOV OF FSB's Department Fifteen led General Sokolov out of the Cave and back into the elevator. Taking a key from his pocket, Kryuchkov inserted the key into the elevator's control pad and punched in the button for Lubyanka's fifth floor, all the while clocking the general's demeanor in his peripheral vision.

The old man was shaking. The leather dossier in his gnarled hand tapped violently against his leg.

When the elevator dinged and stopped at the fifth floor, Kryuchkov nearly leapt into the hallway. "I can't guarantee we will be able to contact Captain Yermakova in time. The trial has already started, the multilevel encryption from Moscow to the sharashka could take minutes—the satellite that receives and transfers the encrypted FAPSI line—"

Sokolov exited the lift and rounded on Kryuchkov. Kryuchkov stiffened, seeing the intense fury building in the old man. Like everyone in the federal and foreign intelligence communities, Kryuchkov had heard the rumors about the chief of SVR's Line S. The time he had spent in the KGB, the elite assassination squads he trained and ran to this day. Men with no names, a highly secretive unit of dedicated SVR operators who specialized in deep penetration, sabotage, and black work. All under the command of the old man standing before him.

If the rumors were true, which Kryuchkov believed they were, General

Viktor Aleksandrovich Sokolov and his team of elite killers were responsible for the Federation's most high-level assassinations to date: Litvinenko, Politkovskaya, Golubev, and Puncher.

The old general had written the book on modern Russian espionage and counterespionage, holding the USSR's and now the Federation's deepest, darkest secrets. He was, after all, the one who controlled the *illegals* who penetrated the West.

Illegals were Russian spies with civilian covers, living normal lives, who were trained to handle assets behind enemy lines. The identities of these *illegals* were strictly limited to the men and women of SVR's Line S and, of course, the president.

That being said, it wasn't necessarily Sokolov's history and stature in the Foreign Intelligence Service that frightened Kryuchkov the most. Nor was it Sokolov's legendary rage, or his knack for violence and brutality. It was Sokolov's close relationship to the most powerful man in all of Russia that truly made Kryuchkov quiver.

Sokolov's relationship with the president.

Like everyone in the intelligence communities, Kryuchkov had heard the rumors of Sokolov's past, how, after he had lost his own son, he had shaped a then young president—a nobody KGB agent in an East German posting—to climb the ranks to become the feared and cunning leader he was today.

It was common knowledge that the president called Sokolov *Dyadya Viktor*. Uncle Viktor. And that Sokolov called him *plemyannik*. Nephew.

Kryuchkov shuddered to think what Sokolov was capable of and then stammered, "I-I-I will take you to the phone."

He led the old general down another hall of broad maroon carpeting. Hurrying, Kryuchkov opened a door labeled V561 and kept the door open for the general.

An FSB guard snapped to attention next to a small table with a glossy black telephone.

"This line leads directly to the sharashka," Kryuchkov said.

"It's clean?"

"Completely. No prying ears—our most encrypted, it might take a few minutes, like I said."

"Both of you out," Sokolov snapped.

The guard moved out instantly, but Kryuchkov stood implacable. "My duty, General—is to bear witness to every conversation held over this line. I wouldn't be doing my job unless I adhere to the rules. I am supposed to be the link between Department Fifteen and the GRU sharashkas."

Sokolov held the receiver to his ear. A ringing sounded on the other line.

He lowered the receiver to his shoulder, glaring at Kryuchkov. "Tread wisely out of the room, Captain. The FSB has no business listening in on SVR Line S dealings—especially this one."

Captain Kryuchkov remained still so Sokolov continued.

"Or shall I call the Senate Building—maybe I should discuss this impropriety with my *plemyannik*?"

Kryuchkov's eyes widened in horror while Sokolov kept his face neutral.

The phone continued to ring.

Kryuchkov considered his options for another beat and then bowed out of the room and shut the door.

After a tense minute, the deep, irritated voice of Captain Akulina Yermakova sounded over the line. Sokolov kept his voice calm and his hands steady as he peered down at the photocopied picture of the man in the blue shirt holding the dog by the leash.

"This is General Viktor Sokolov; do you know who I am?"

Captain Yermakova's voice turned from annoyed, to frightened, "Yes, of course, General. I know who you are."

"The girl in your trial, Cassandra Gale. She must be pulled from it immediately and housed somewhere safe until I get there."

"Get here, General? The trial has already started, the subject is currently engaged in— "

"STOP THE TRIAL!" Sokolov roared. "Stop it now! If anything happens to the subject, I will see to it personally that those responsible will spend the rest of their miserable lives in the basements of Butyrka!"

"General, I—"

"This is above your stupid game, Yermakova. This isn't entertainment. Not anymore!"

"I can't just stop the trial—there are current experiments being run on the subjects. Plus, the *siloviki* have already placed their bets, the money is already in a GRU-handled escrow."

"I don't give a shit about your fraudulent experiments. I don't give a damn about *siloviki* money!"

Yermakova started to argue again but Sokolov cut her off.

"This matter concerning Cassandra Gale is reserved for me and goes to the highest level of government—" Sokolov made an almost imperceptible sucking noise; the rising tide of vexation was building in his chest and making him go almost apoplectic.

"Captain," Sokolov said. "You know who I am. You know I am not a man to cross. Now, you either stop the trial or shall I get the president to contact you personally?"

"*Nyet*. That will not be necessary. I . . . I will do what I can to stop it."

"Do more," Sokolov snapped. "I will stay on the line until it is done."

"*Da*, General. Of course."

Sokolov gazed back down at the photocopied picture of Cassandra Gale and the man holding the dog and felt a rage he hadn't experienced in decades.

Chapter 25

CAPTAIN AKULINA PETROVNA Yermakova stood in the sharashka's control room overlooking the ten-foot LED monitors broadcasting in real time, the live feed from the trial, and put down the black receiver on the table.

The dozens of drone operators, technicians, and scientists in the sharashka's control room all stared at her. Flashes of fighting on the screens behind them were left unnoticed. Captain Yermakova looked over the crowd for a moment, trying to rationalize the conversation that had just occurred over the line.

General Viktor Sokolov, the feared chief of SVR's Line S, had just demanded a trial be stopped. Never in the history of the modern sharashka had this ever occurred. The general must have gone through FSB's Department Fifteen, through Captain Kryuchkov—that incompetent fool—to get to the FAPSI line.

Yermakova weighed her options. On the screens she could see the Americans had just been engaged by the prisoners. If she were to stop the trial, all the *siloviki's* money would have to be returned, their entertainment for the day ruined.

What would that do to her reputation?

Would it hurt her chances of being the first woman ever let into the inner circle? This whole sharashka—this source of entertainment, this grand experiment—was meant to propel her upward. To show the Moscow elite that she was capable, that she was worthy.

Then there were the medical experiments she would have to consider. She glanced at another workstation where Artur was hovering over a screen. The screen provided all the statistics from the prisoners and the Americans. Heart rate, blood pressure, hormonal stress level readouts. If the trial would have to come to an end, Artur's data would be skewed, ruined—

Yermakova looked at the head drone operator, a GRU lieutenant. "Shut it down, Gregory."

The GRU lieutenant's eyes grew wide. "How, ma'am?"

"I don't care," Yermakova said. "Use the gas. Get a team down there now. Two teams. Their sole objective is to secure Subject 8831. That Cassandra Gale girl."

Artur looked up from his screen, protesting, "You will be ruining the whole experiment!"

And be a complete embarrassment, Yermakova thought.

The results would be void. Tens of millions of rubles returned, all because General Viktor Sokolov had ordered it. She pointed a finger at the GRU lieutenant piloting the primary drone system.

"Cut the live feed to the Cave. Do it now, then gas them. Gas them all."

|||||||||||||||||||||||||||||||||||||||||||||||||||||||||||||||||||||||||||||||||||

A barrage of bullets cut through the air, snapping off the rocks as Brady threw his whole body weight onto Cassie and Billy, sending them face first in a small depression behind the large boulder.

"Stay low!" Brady screamed.

Cassie got to her hands and knees, making sure to keep her profile low. Never before had she been actually fired upon. She'd been through countless live-fire drills but had never been victim to someone actually trying to kill her. Strangely enough, she felt incredibly calm.

Her training told her that they needed to return fire immediately. The first minute of a firefight was the most important and fire superiority needed to be established ASAP.

Brady rose to her level behind the boulder.

"We're screwed if we stay here!" Cassie said.

"We've got the uphill advantage and don't have enough ammo to establish a base fire to keep them suppressed!" Brady yelled, as more automatic gunfire pummeled over them. Whoever was shooting had modern guns and lots of ammo. They were severely outnumbered. "How many did you see?"

Cassie flashed on the movement in the woods before all hell had broken loose. "Five, maybe six."

The bullets suddenly ceased and they could hear yelling below.

"They're coming close," Brady said. "We've got to pick them off, create a lane, and then make a break for it. You ready to run, kid?"

Billy was curled up in the fetal position at their feet. Cassie gave Brady an uncertain look, then movement broke over Brady's shoulder. A large tattooed figure rounded the boulder, a machine gun in hand. He was pointing the weapon at the trio.

Cassie didn't have time to think. She raised her weapon over Brady's shoulder and fired.

She ran the action and fired again.

Both shots found their mark in the man's chest. He dropped his weapon, and looked down at the gaping wounds in his chest before he folded to the ground. Brady whipped around, wide-eyed and scampered for the dead man's machine gun. It was an AKM, an old Soviet assault rifle; he checked the magazine—half full. He nodded in appreciation to Cassie.

Cassie held the rifle she had just killed the man with, looking down at it in wonder.

She had just killed someone.

She didn't have much time to think because Billy was pulling at her pant leg, shouting something. Brady stood, aiming over Cassie's head. She turned around and saw three more men. They had scaled the rock field to their left and had popped up nearly fifty yards away.

Weapons began to bark from three directions.

Fire erupted from Brady's muzzle. He ducked and bullets ricocheted everywhere. Cassie scrambled for Brady's neglected Mosin-Nagant M1944 at his feet. She grabbed it, and then caught movement from above.

Another two men.

They had circumvented the mountaintop and come over the other side.

They were sitting ducks. They were surrounded.

Cassie raised Brady's weapon and fired.

Missed.

She ran the action, aimed, and fired again. One of the men stumbled. She dropped the weapon, grabbed Billy's rifle. Two shots left. Meanwhile Brady was firing back at the men to their left.

Cassie raised Billy's weapon, took aim when something hot seared through her left arm. The force of the blow spun her, and she landed on Billy.

The sound of gunfire consumed all. Brady was yelling. Billy was screaming—she heard Brady's gun *click*—empty.

Cassie sat stunned, looking down at her arm. A small red hole showed in her left bicep, blood was oozing out of it. Then Brady's alarmed face was in front of her own. He was yelling, tugging at her shirt, trying to get her to stand.

Then all at once, she heard the sounds of a high-pitched whistle. Then another, and another.

Cassie and Brady looked to the sky.

The gunfire ceased.

White contrails arced over them. The whistling grew louder. The contrails turned and headed straight for them.

Cassie could see at least half a dozen of the white streaking lines.

Brady started pulling at her again. Billy got up when two of the metal canisters punched into the rocks just feet away.

Cassie stared down at the canisters as if in a trance. In the distance, she thought she could hear the sounds of helicopters.

Cassie watched as Brady reached down, grabbed one of the canisters, and threw it down the mountain.

But before he could grab the second one, it blinked red and opened.

The orange cloud exploded in front of them.

Cassie didn't try to fight it.

She inhaled and felt something in her head loosen. Her body slumped and the world around her fell away.

Chapter 26

CAPTAIN YERMAKOVA WATCHED via the aerial drone feed as Subject 8831 lost consciousness among the other Americans. According to her health monitor bracelet, the woman's vitals were becoming erratic.

"She's been shot," Artur said, his face angry, pinched.

"I can see that; prep your lab for surgery," Yermakova replied, and Artur ran out of the room. On the screens, the military helicopter was swooping down over Subject 8831's position. Yermakova keyed the microphone on the control console to talk directly to her guards in the chopper. "Subject 8831 is to be taken first. Team Two can come back for the others."

She got a confirmation from her guards in the chopper and then had the drone operator pull back in a wide shot over the mountaintop. Two Black Dolphin prisoners lay dead, the other four unconscious from the heavy doses of knockout gas that had been rained down on them. A wave of relief spread over Yermakova as she watched Subject 8831 being lifted into the helicopter.

"ETA twenty-two minutes," a guard said over her mike.

"Copy that."

Yermakova looked out over the control room and cursed under her breath for what the general had made her do. The glossy black phone that connected the sharashka to Lubyanka still lay with the receiver resting on the table. The last thing she wanted to do was talk to Viktor Sokolov, but she knew she didn't have a choice. Yermakova had only heard rumors of what this place used to be during the days of the Soviet Union. Rumors of what the KGB used it for, what Viktor Sokolov and his late son had used it for.

She knew that as soon as she picked up that phone she would be victim to Viktor Sokolov's world.

Why the senile old man was so interested in Subject 8831 Yermakova could only guess, but she knew that whatever the reason was, she was now complicit. She took a step toward the phone and then envisioned herself walking out of the control room and straight to her executive living quarters. Drawing a warm bath, turning on some Bach, and relaxing with a glass of red wine before dealing with the general. Or maybe she could call her colleagues in Moscow about the motives of the old *generalnyi*.

Nyet.

That would be suicide. The general had eyes and ears everywhere. He had moles and resources so vast it would be a mistake to go behind his back.

If Yermakova wanted to get out of this godforsaken place in the next year or two, she would play the game the way it was meant to be played.

Kiss their asses. And be granted admission into their inner circle.

Her career flashed before her eyes. A young GRU intelligence officer stationed in the West. She thought of all the assets she had run over a decorated twenty-nine-year career. LIPSKI in Washington, ICARUS in New York. Her times in the *rezidenturas* had been paramount in establishing a name for herself in Moscow. But it wasn't until KODIAK walked through the embassy doors in Ottawa that Yermakova really made a name for herself. KODIAK was her baby, an asset so valuable in seizing Western military *intelligentsia* that Moscow had given her a promotion just for running him. She had run KODIAK for years and gathered more than valuable intelligence. When it was time for KODIAK to retire—she had offered him a lucrative deal to work for her in her new position.

The offer was to move KODIAK somewhere desolate so he could build an extraction team for the revamped sharashka.

It frightened her that KODIAK had extracted Subject 8831 and would now be in the cross hairs of General Sokolov.

KODIAK was hers. KODIAK's team was hers.

She would protect them by whatever means necessary.

She grabbed the black receiver of the FAPSI line and envisioned herself in two years' time in a luxurious Black Sea *dacha*. If all went to plan with this sharashka, if she pleased the *siloviki* and the president, her future would be beyond bright.

She heard the general breathing on the other line and tried speaking with confidence. "General Sokolov, the trial has been stopped. Subject 8831 is safe and on her way to the sharashka for medical attention."

Yermakova felt a sick sense of foreboding as she spoke into the phone. Bigger things were at play now and she felt like a pawn on a chessboard.

A cog in a defective machine.

It wasn't a feeling she enjoyed.

General Sokolov's arm was growing numb from keeping the phone pressed to his ear for so long. He listened to Captain Yermakova's deep voice come over the other line.

Cassandra Gale was safe.

He felt himself relax.

"What is going on, General? Why was I made to stop the trial?"

Sokolov chuckled, caressing the photocopied picture in the dossier with his finger. "You have Cassandra Gale's file in front of you, do you not?"

"I do."

"The picture found in her wallet?"

"*Da.*"

"You see the man holding the dog? The man with the blue shirt—what was GRU *intelligentsia* able to find on this man?"

"What does he have to do with anything?"

"He has to do with everything!" Sokolov snarled, picking up the photo and waving it in front of him as if Yermakova could see it. "I want your GRU *intelligentsia* to find out everything they can about this man. I want to know who he is, what his relationship to Subject 8831 is. I want you to find out if he is looking for her!"

"Looking for her? How could I possibly find that out?"

"Your dossier stated that she was picked up by your extraction team, KODIAK. Is that correct?"

"*Da.*"

"Ask KODIAK if they have had contact with this man. Your team is to drop everything and focus their efforts on this task, is that understood?"

"*Da, Generalnyi.*"

"You will have until the end of the day to send your report to Captain Kryuchkov before it is to be reviewed at the Senate Building."

"*The S-Senate Building?*" Yermakova stammered, knowing full well who would be reading the report. "I cannot guarantee if it is possible to get into contact with KODIAK in such a short amount of time. I don't know if my *intelligentsia* department will be able to pinpoint what you desire—that could take days!"

"Then maybe I will have an SVR team take over, maybe I will inform the president that Captain Yermakova is no longer of any use to us. That her games are of no use to the *siloviki*—that the sharashka's macabre games are not—"

"*Nyet*, that will not be necessary! I will get my team on it immediately. I will establish contact with KODIAK and a report will be sent to Kryuchkov this evening. We will determine who this man is."

Sokolov gave Yermakova the exact time her report was due before hanging up and exiting the room.

In the hall, a sweating Kryuchkov was pacing in front of the startled FSB guard who snapped to attention as soon as Sokolov emerged from the room.

Sokolov felt charged. He checked his watch, remembering the heavy clouds over Moscow, the undeniable smell of imminent rain. Traffic heading north would be a disaster this time of day. Driving was out of the question; he needed something faster.

"Kryuchkov, notify your director. Tell him we will be using his helicopter. It still sits on the roof, does it not?"

"I assume it does—"

"Then get it ready."

Kryuchkov barked the order to the FSB guard who saluted and tore off down the hallway.

"And where are you going, General?"

"*We* are going to see my nephew. *We* are going to see the president."

‖‖‖

Captain Yermakova stood in stunned silence, the FAPSI line still pressed to her ear. She could feel the technicians, the drone operators, all staring at her as she tried to wrap her head around the conversation that had just taken place.

How the hell was she going to find that man in the picture in such short time? How could she guarantee that she could even get ahold of KODIAK? Her GRU *intelligentsia* team was one of the best in the whole Federation, but what Sokolov was demanding could prove impossible.

Lieutenant Klimentiev, the head of her GRU *intelligentsia*, stood expectantly from his station.

Yermakova knew she had to maintain an air of confidence, so she put the receiver back on the FAPSI line, held up the photocopied picture of the man, and began to shout orders. The man's face was to be run through every GRU, FSB, and even SVR facial recognition database they had. Everything they could find on Subject 8831 and her family was to be dug up and put into a report. She told them the time constraint, told them the stakes, and listened and watched as everyone in the room tensed.

They understood how serious this was.

This was going straight to the president.

Everyone jumped to work, then Yermakova called over Klimentiev. As he hurried to her, Yermakova gazed back at the aerial footage of the helicopter transporting Subject 8831 back to the sharashka.

Who the hell was this Cassandra Gale?

Who the hell was that man in the picture?

And why was General Viktor Sokolov so interested in them?

Klimentiev snapped to attention. She rounded on him. "Get me a secure line to KODIAK straightaway. Today is not a day to play games."

Chapter 27

NED VOIGT ROSE out of bed, walked to the bathroom, and splashed cold water on his face. He gazed at himself in the mirror and tried to remain calm. Staying asleep had proven impossible not because of the uncomfortable bed, or the rattling radiator in the old motel room, but because his mind couldn't stop going over what a colossal, fucked-up situation he and his team were in.

Ned checked his wristwatch, it was nearly two in the morning. Trooper Ross and Ralph Condon should have been back from Clinton Creek by now. He'd tipped off his men that they were arriving and what kind of questions they were going to be asked. He had them double-check that the surveillance footage from the last week wouldn't show any incriminating evidence of Jake's and Curtis's actions, or his own for that matter.

His men had insisted the footage would show nothing and that they'd all have their stories straight.

It was what they were paid to do, after all.

But that wasn't the main reason why Ned couldn't sleep. It was a sense of failure that kept gnawing at him. For eleven years, he and Darlene had been running their extraction team in this desolate part of the world. His men came and went, like any organization, but never before had they experienced a hiccup like this.

Hell, he thought, *it wasn't a hiccup. It was a complete clusterfuck.*

Picking up and *extracting* loners from the woods wasn't exactly rocket science, so how the hell had this blown up so magnificently?

Well, he knew the answer.

It was all because of one person.

Max *fucking* Tobeluk.

The VPSO had been on his payroll for years with the simple job of keeping his damn mouth shut and turning a blind eye to the dealings of Ned and his team.

For years, Tobeluk had done just that. He'd taken his money and never made a peep. Until this spring—when the little bastard had come knocking on Ned's door, demanding not only pay raise, but also insisting that he participate in the extractions. Tobeluk had warned Ned that if he refused to let him join the team, he was going to sing like a bird to the authorities.

Ned should have listened to his gut then and there. He should have shot the VPSO and thrown his body in the river. But Ned needed a man on the west side of the border, so he gave Tobeluk a bump in pay and let him do cleanup on the campsites.

And what had Tobeluk done?

He screwed it up.

And now he was gone.

Max Tobeluk, the witless wonder, had escaped under their very noses.

Ned knew only he could make all of this right.

The day before, when Mountie Ralph Condon had come to the logging site asking about Cassandra Gale's and William French's stay at the Northern Breeze, Ned knew something had gone spectacularly wrong. He'd asked Condon delicate and concerned questions—found out that Cassie and Billy were both missing and that the ABI had opened a criminal investigation and had instructed Condon to dig into the Northern Breeze.

Ned knew not to lie. Well, not to lie *too* much.

The best lies were the ones that were closest to the truth.

Ned understood that the fight between Jake, Billy, and Cassie would get out sooner or later if the patrons in the Northern Breeze were questioned. So he'd had no choice but to tell Condon about the altercation.

Before Condon had time to grow suspicious, Ned had called in Jake and Curtis from the field. He'd told Condon the two boys were on his shit list and were working triple shifts until Ned deemed them worthy to take up their regular schedules.

Condon seemed to take him at his word, but Ned knew that the buck wasn't going to stop there. The ABI could be meticulous. Ned needed to get in front of this and find out as much as he could in order to gain some semblance of control.

He'd offered to take Curtis, Jake, and Darlene to Eagle to help out in the search.

Condon had agreed.

As they drove, Ned raged at Curtis and Jake in the back seat. Ned was terrified of the unknown more than anything. Terrified what the ABI had discovered. He cursed Jake for his impetuousness at the bar, cursed Curtis for egging it on.

By the time they arrived in Eagle, he'd calmed down significantly, but that went out the window when he saw Tobeluk in the VPSO's office and a picture of the "knockout" canister on the desk. Right then and there, Ned knew that the little prick had messed up royally.

"Ned, honey, what are you doing?" Darlene came into the bathroom, clearing the tired from her eyes. She wrapped her arms around her husband. Their eyes met in the mirror. "What are you worried about?"

"You know what I'm worried about."

"The workers in Clinton Creek won't say anything. The surveillance footage won't show anything. There's no hard evidence against us. Vance has seen Sergeant Plant's report. We're in the clear."

Trooper Elliot Vance was one of Ned's best men. A damn fine soldier for Ned and a damn fine pilot. When Vance wasn't working his day job, he was flying the captured subjects to the rendezvous points in his AST plane. It was perfect cover.

"I'm worried about Tobeluk and what he could tell the authorities."

"What could he say? He doesn't know—"

"He knows enough. He knows we take people. It would be enough to put us away for life. Enough to end this whole operation."

"We've planned for that."

In fact, they *had* planned for this. Deep down Ned knew that they were too old to be living this kind of life. But he was addicted to the money, addicted to the adrenaline of it all. It made him feel young. But in reality, they had enough money stashed away, they could live anywhere they pleased, be anyone they wanted to be. Then why was he so hesitant to walk away from it all?

If he was being totally honest with himself, it wasn't just the money, and the adrenaline—it was the *power* he was truly addicted to.

He'd been an agent of a foreign government for the better part of his life. First spying for the Soviets while he worked for the Canadian Maritime Command, then as the Soviet Union fell, he continued his spying with the same GRU handler.

The cash had been great, the expensive vacations, the hunting trips . . .

As his navy career ended, his handler approached him with a new job opportunity. The money would be exceptional, the operations thrilling. She'd promised him he would be in charge of recruiting his own team and even given the liberty to pick a predetermined destination to begin *extracting*.

They had picked Dawson due to its proximity to the US border, and the number of drifters heading into Alaska. Plus, Ned loved the fishing, camping, and hunting that the region offered. And, in the off-season, when the snow closed the area for half the year, Ned and Darlene could travel wherever they pleased.

It had been a hell of an eleven years. Ned had lost count how many people they had extracted for the Russians.

Hundreds?

God only knew what they did to them in Russia.

"What are you so afraid of, Ned? If Tobeluk starts blabbing, we send out our distress signal and we follow the extraction procedure. Just you and me, like we always planned."

Like always, Darlene was acting sensibly.

"And if Yermakova doesn't let us leave?"

"You know we've taken precautions for every eventuality."

"I hope it doesn't come to that."

"Then hope that Vance can find Tobeluk before the *real* authorities find him. What orders did you give him?"

"Vance? To find Tobeluk and silence him."

"Then that is what will happen."

"We've been too greedy, Darlene. We've been extracting too many people. Calling too much attention to ourselves. It's my fault. I let Tobeluk in. I let that drunk do a cleanup on the two subjects—what the hell was he thinking, putting Cassandra Gale's pistol in French's backpack? Slicing the damn tents like that, and the knockout canister? He made both campsites look like a damn circus!"

"It was a miscalculation."

"I'm an idiot for giving him so much responsibility."

Suddenly, a shrill beeping sounded from the bedroom. Ned nearly lost his footing.

The beeping hit a crescendo and then stopped.

Darlene moved first and Ned followed her into the bedroom. He peered at his day bag sitting next to the minifridge. Darlene dug her hand into the bag and pulled out the black tablet.

Thoughts swirled in Ned's mind. This wasn't normal. This certainly wasn't normal. Yermakova would only make contact if something had gone seriously wrong.

Ned reached for the tablet and held it like a fragile stick of dynamite.

Placing his right hand over the tablet's screen, he felt the warmness of the scanner flit under his palm and fingers. The screen blinked green. Ned removed his hand and adjusted the tablet so its camera lens could scan his face. After that was accepted, he typed in the necessary passcodes known only to him.

That was the point of this operation. Knowledge had to be compartmented.

Ned was the true agent on the ground, known to the Russians by the cryptonym: KODIAK.

In his team, Darlene was second-in-command. But the others—the others he paid: Jake, Curtis, Vance, and Tobeluk—they only knew so much. They had no idea where Ned sent the subjects, no idea who Ned worked for, and no idea that Russia was footing the bill.

Ned finally accessed the secure message and instantly felt confused.

"What does it say?"

Ned turned the tablet so Darlene could read before the message would self-erase.

URGENT: Whereabouts and Identity of this INDIVIDUAL needed. Asking KODIAK for any information. Reply IMMEDIATELY.

Below the message was a family picture where James Gale was holding Cassandra Gale's German shepherd. James Gale's face was circled in red ink. It looked to be some sort of military graduation.

"They're interested in the father?" Darlene asked. "Why would they care?"

"I don't know."

"Do you think they know about the search? That the Alaskan authorities have gotten involved? They couldn't have seen it on the news, could they?"

"Again, Darlene. I don't know."

"What are you going to reply?"

Ned typed:

INDIVIDUAL is JAMES GALE, the subject's father. Individual's whereabouts: Eagle, Alaska, at time of message. Individual is searching for the subject.

Ned hit send and watched the message encrypt itself and disappear from the screen. A minute later, another message arrived.

Send PHOTOGRAPHIC proof of JAMES GALE—IMMEDIATELY.

"How are we going to do that, Ned? It's the middle of the night."

Ned shook his head; he was thinking. He knew that the wording, IMMEDIATELY, to his GRU handler actually meant *immediately*.

As in now.

This moment.

Drop everything and act.

Ned replied that he got the message, then handed the tablet over to Darlene for safekeeping. He hated that thing; modern-day SIGINT intelligence perturbed him. When he was spying for the Soviets, he much preferred the HUMINT meet and greets with Yermakova. It seemed much more secure. Face-to-face. There was a tradecraft to it all. An excitement. This new technology scared him, mostly because he didn't understand how it all worked. How could he know it wouldn't be hacked or intercepted?

"The Gales are staying above the Eagle Trading Company, right?"

"Yes."

"Then we wake them, tell them something to get them outside. I'll make something up, you take the camera and get a picture of the father. I'll try to get him under a light."

"We should wake Jake and Curtis. Curtis is much better with this kind of stuff. He can use his camera with the 800 mm lens."

"Fine," Ned said. "I'll go get them."

Ned threw on his jacket and stepped into the brisk June air and knocked on Jake and Curtis's door. He was surprised to find it slightly ajar. Ned walked inside. The room was a mess. The TV was on the floor, the blankets all over the place. He checked the closet, the bathroom.

Jake and Curtis were gone!

Ned ran back into his room. Darlene was tying her hair in a bun and saw the fear on her husband's face.

"They're gone!"

"What do you mean they're gone?"

Darlene ran out and inspected the room herself.

"It was him," Darlene said. "Him and his men that arrived this evening."

Of course it was James Gale and those cowboys from Montana who must be behind this disappearing act. Cassandra Gale's quick-tempered father had suspected Jake and Curtis from the get-go.

"What do we do?" Darlene asked.

Ned walked out of Jake and Curtis's room and stared at the light glowing from inside of the VPSO's office down near the shoreline. Sergeant Plant was surely in there, still awake.

"We're going to do what we've been doing all along. Keep our friends close and our enemies closer."

Chapter 28

GALE BREATHED IN the cool night air and looked at the stars glinting like white pinpricks on a black tapestry. The wind rustled the bushes and leaves of the trees around Cassie's campsite, and Gale tried to focus on his breathing.

To focus on what he was about to do.

Maverick whined at his side and Gale put a protective hand over the dog's head. He had taken Maverick from the veterinarian clinic earlier in the evening and had driven the dog up to Cassie's campsite. They'd spent the better part of the night trolling around the adjoining woods, Gale allowing the dog to sniff out anything the searchers might have missed. Then they'd moved down to William French's campsite and done the same thing. At both campsites, Maverick sniffed the perimeter and then led Gale straight to the Yukon's shoreline.

They'd found nothing new.

At one a.m., just as the sun had been setting, Gale received word from Petit and Bill Cronin that they had succeeded doing the favor Gale had asked of them and were on their way to Cassie's campsite.

He checked his watch. It was just after two a.m., and his usual razor-sharp mind was beginning to feel sluggish from sleep deprivation. It had been days since he'd slept more than an hour at a time. He hoped Trask and Emily were able to get the much-needed rest they both deserved.

It's better they sleep and stay out of this.

He walked over to the pickup truck Bill Cronin had lent him and turned on the headlights.

The high beams flooded the area as Gale heard the rumble of diesel motors coming up the access road.

Gale took Maverick by his lead and made sure that the dog's collar was secured around his neck.

The plan called for Maverick to not cause bodily harm.

He needed to see the dog's reaction and the reaction of the men witnessing the dog.

That would show the truth.

Petit and the Davis brothers drove into the campsite first, followed by Cronin.

Gale watched Petit exit the truck, load a clump of Copenhagen in his mouth, and nod at his boss.

Gale nodded back. Petit was wearing a pistol on his hip and had a double-barrel shotgun hanging from a shoulder sling. Gale had insisted that everyone be armed. It added to the intimidation factor. Gale fingered the hilt of his Colt Anaconda as Bill Cronin and three of his men dragged two bound figures from the back of their vehicle.

"Drop them, here," Gale said, pointing in front of him.

As Cronin's men dragged Jake and Curtis into the light, Gale watched Maverick's ears perk up. The dog reared, lunging forward, but Gale yanked at the dog's lead. Maverick snarled, spittle and foam flying from his mouth. Gale let Maverick rage as Jake and Curtis were placed five feet away.

They squirmed and looked terrified.

The Montanans created a semicircle around the scene.

Gale said, "Maverick, down."

Maverick suddenly stopped barking and sat down at Gale's side in a sphinx position.

"Bill," Gale said, "take your men and head back to town. Take the Davis brothers with you. Alvin, stay with me."

Cronin collected his men and drove away without a word. When the sound of the trucks dissipated in the cool night air, Petit moved forward and removed the gags from both Jake's and Curtis's mouths.

"What the hell are you doing, man!" Curtis yelled. "You can't do this! It's kidnapping!"

"We're not kidnapping you," Gale said. "We're borrowing you, so we can have a discussion."

"When Ned finds out—"

"He isn't going to find out," Gale said, and he tugged on Maverick's lead. The dog stood and Gale led him in a slow circle around the two men. "You boys familiar with war dogs? This here is Maverick, he's a retired marine. Served three tours with my late son-in-law in Afghanistan. I'd introduce you two to him, but it seems you've already met."

Gale stopped Maverick so the dog was right behind Curtis and Jake. He could almost smell the fear emanating off them.

"While Maverick might be getting old, his mind is still sharp. He listens to his alpha and obeys his every command." Gale led the dog and had him sit four feet in front of Jake and Curtis. "After Maverick was discharged from service, we took him in. Even went to Germany for two weeks so we could be trained in handling such a dog. There are two people left on this earth who Maverick will take orders from. One of them is me, and the other is my daughter Cassie."

Gale let her name hang in the air. Both Curtis and Jake had their eyes planted on the ground. Maverick began to snarl again.

"Maverick doesn't seem to like you two. Any idea why that is?"

Both men shook their heads forcefully.

"Hmm," Gale said. "Maverick is usually a sweetheart when he's not working. For him to have such a visceral reaction to you two is . . . alarming."

"What are you trying to say, man?" Jake said.

"I'm going to ask a series of questions and you two are going to give me answers, got it?"

Petit walked behind Gale, cradling his shotgun.

Gale said, "Did you two or your crew have anything to do with the disappearance of my daughter?"

Both of them shook their heads.

"Did either of you hurt my dog?"

More shaking of heads.

"It would take quite a person to get the best of Maverick. That dog has over three hundred pounds of bite pressure and he can run like a freight train."

"We didn't hurt your damn dog or your daughter, man!" Jake yelled. "You're fucking crazy. We didn't do shit!"

Gale looked up at Petit. "You find anything in their rooms?"

"Just this," Petit said and tossed Gale a white iPhone. "Go in his videos; dumbass doesn't even have it password protected."

Gale caught the iPhone, swiped it open, found an open video.

Curtis whimpered.

Gale looked at him. "This phone yours?"

Curtis didn't say anything but his eyes told Gale everything that he needed to know.

Gale pressed play and he watched as the video focused in on a man wearing red flannel approaching a bar. Gale recognized the man as Jake. Jake leaned against the bar and began talking to a woman that Gale recognized as Cassie.

Gale felt a familiar feeling of anger ripple through him. Sounds of men snickering came from the phone as Gale continued to watch. Then he saw that the other patron sitting next to Cassie was William French. He watched French stand, get sucker-punched by Jake, then watched Cassie jump to her feet, grab Jake by the finger, and slam him over the bar top. The video cut out as Ned ran out of the kitchen.

Gale threw the phone back to Petit, then squatted down in front of Jake and looked him directly in the eyes. "Earlier, back in the VPSO's office. You smiled at me. Why did you do that?"

"I didn't fucking smile at you."

Gale grabbed Jake roughly by his shirt collar and shook him. "Is it because you did something to my daughter? Is it because you knew where she was camping? Maybe you wanted to get back at her for kicking your ass; pride is a delicate thing. Maybe you convinced some of your boys to drive up here and settle the score with Cassie and French—"

"We were at the logging site all week, man!" Curtis sputtered. "Ned was punishing us for the fight!"

"I don't believe you," Gale said, and released Jake. "Maverick, heel!" The dog sprang forward and landed in the same sphinx position at Gale's side. "You two must take me for a fool. Some senile old man who's losing his grip. But let me tell you something, you two are fucking with the wrong old man." Gale's hand went to his holster.

Maverick growled, and Petit said, "Jim."

Gale continued, inching his face closer to theirs, "You don't know what I'm capable of when push comes to shove. If I find out that either of you—"

"Jim!"

"What!" Gale snapped, turning to Petit.

"Someone's coming."

Gale turned his attention to the access road and could hear the sound of vehicles heading toward them. At first he thought it was Cronin returning, but it sounded like multiple engines.

Gale said, "Alvin, you sure nobody saw you guys?"

"Thought so, we moved quietly in and out."

Gale swore and grabbed Maverick and had the dog sit farther away from the men. "Untie them," Gale ordered.

Petit descended on Jake and Curtis and cut their restraints. The two men got to their feet and rubbed at their wrists.

"You're all so screwed, man," Jake said, smiling.

Gale licked his lips as four vehicles flew into the campsite. The first two trucks were Cronin's and Petit's. The last two were an AST vehicle, then Ned Voigt's red F-350.

Bill Cronin climbed out of his truck. "Sorry, Jim. They caught us just down the road."

Sergeant Plant, Trooper Ross, and Mountie Condon flew out of the AST vehicle. Plant marched into the light while Ned and Darlene stayed in the shadows.

Plant roared, "What the hell is going on here?!"

She had her hand on her service weapon, Ross coming up behind her as she stared at Jake and Curtis, then at Gale and Maverick.

"We were just having a little chat," Gale said.

"Don't insult my intelligence, Mr. Gale. I saw the state of their motel room."

"They kidnapped us—" Curtis said.

"They know something they aren't telling us, Sergeant," Gale said. "This whole Northern Breeze crew isn't telling us something; my dog reacted—"

Sergeant Plant scoffed, kept her hand on her service weapon. "They're not telling you anything because they didn't do anything." She pointed a finger at Ross and Condon. "These two just got back from Clinton Creek. They talked to all the workers, viewed all the security footage. These two never left the site until today."

"They're lying."

Plant took out a pair of handcuffs. "Turn around, Mr. Gale."

Gale saw Petit and Bill Cronin step forward, even Maverick growled. Gale put up a hand to stop his men and silence the dog.

"Mr. Gale, I'm taking you and your men into custody."

"On what charges?"

"Let's see: breaking and entering. Kidnapping—"

"I acted alone."

"We'll see about that," Plant said, grabbing Gale's wrist.

"Now, hold on a second," Ned said, stepping into the light. "I think we're overreacting a bit."

"Ned, they ripped us out of our beds! They kidnapped us!"

"Shut your mouth, Curtis!" Ned snapped.

Maverick started growling again as Ned approached. He stopped walking when he realized it.

"Ain't no need to put Mr. Gale in cuffs, Sergeant—we aren't gonna be pressing charges."

"Ned—" Jake said.

Ned turned viciously to the two. "We aren't pressing charges, ain't that right, boys?"

Both Jake and Curtis stared at the man coolly—then after a tense moment said, "That's right."

"Good. Mr. Gale here has been under an incredible amount of stress. If it was me in his position and you two knuckleheads got in a fight with my daughter—I'd be doing the same thing. Hell, I'd probably done worse." Ned kicked Curtis in the boot. "You two idiots get in the damn truck."

After they sulked to the truck and shut the doors, Ned walked to Gale, extended a hand. "I'm willing to let bygones be bygones if you're willing to."

Gale stared down at the hand, then to Plant who still held the handcuffs.

"Sergeant?" Ned asked, knowing she was the only one with the power to bless this turn of events.

Plant sighed. "Fine."

Gale reluctantly took Ned's hand.

Ned held Gale's hand firm when Gale tried to release his grip. "Since my crew is cleared, let us help with the search."

Gale squinted in the harsh headlights, trying to read the unreadable man in front of him. After a moment, Gale said, "Sure, you can help."

"Then let's head back and get some much-needed shut-eye."

As everyone walked back to their vehicles, Gale grabbed Maverick's lead and walked over to Petit's truck.

Good, let them stay, Gale thought—he'd seen what he'd needed to see. Maverick had a visceral reaction to Jake, Curtis, and Ned. They had something to do with Cassie's disappearance, Gale was willing to put his life on it. A dog with Maverick's training and intelligence wouldn't steer him away from the truth. The Northern Breeze crew was dirty—and he was going to prove it.

Gale was so consumed in his thoughts that he didn't notice Darlene snap a picture of him from her phone as he climbed into the truck.

All Gale was thinking about was his next move.

Chapter 29

A HARSH RAIN pelted the side of the FSB's AgustaWestland AW139 helicopter as it soared over the dull gray, sopping wet streets of Moscow toward the Kremlin.

General Sokolov had received word ten minutes prior that the president had been briefed of his upcoming arrival. The general turned his attention from the window to the frightened-looking Captain Kryuchkov cowering in the large club chair across from him.

What a fool, Sokolov thought, looking at the diminutive Kryuchkov. Everyone associated with the new sharashka—the *siloviki*, the idiots in FSB's Department Fifteen, the GRU *intelligentsia*. Fools. All of them.

The infamous sharashka—Post 866—used to be a place of legend. A crowning achievement of the *Rodina* and her many exploits. Now, it was an embarrassment.

Sokolov yearned for the old days of the Soviet Union as he looked back out the window while the chopper roared over the Moskva River, back over Moscow State University, where he had stood only hours before. In the distance he could see St. Basil's Cathedral, Red Square, the Gates of the Kremlin. As his eyes flitted over the rain-soaked, multicolored rising spires, he realized he was flying near Bolshoy Deviatinsky Pereulok, Number Eight.

The United States Embassy.

For more than fifty years, Sokolov had actively fought against the lecherous Americans arrogantly residing in his beloved Moscow. Fought against them at home as a high-ranking member of the KGB and abroad as a general in the SVR. The massive compound below represented all that he hated in the world—the Western powers; their unabashed treachery, their greed. He audibly snarled down at the compound as he remembered what the Americans had taken from him.

What the man in the picture had taken from him.

Minutes later, the helicopter circled over St. Basil's and Lenin's Tomb before turning and zipping over Borovitskaya Tower and into the Kremlin grounds. The helicopter rotors thumped through the onslaught of rain, flew low over the green-domed Senate Building, and landed on the executive helipad.

The doors were thrown open by Kremlin guards, black umbrellas opening for the general.

Sokolov used his cane to hit Kryuchkov in the shin. "Has KODIAK contacted Yermakova with any news yet?"

Kryuchkov fumbled with the secure tablet on his lap. "Not yet, General."

The guards escorted them into the Senate Building and past the various security checkpoints. There was no need for the metal detectors, the x-ray machines, or the bomb-sniffing dogs to pay any mind to Sokolov. The old general had not been subjected to such security measures in the Kremlin for decades.

A presidential aide met them in the great reception hall, motioning them to a side door leading to a vaulted ceiling anteroom where five men stood waiting.

Sokolov scowled as he recognized the men. The SBP, the Presidential Security Service. The president's personal bodyguards—a secret branch within the FSO, the Federal Protective Service, a descendant branch from the Ninth Chief Directorate of the KGB. The leader of the group, a man Sokolov recognized, raised a hand to frisk the old general.

"Don't you dare touch me, Sergei Antonov," Sokolov snapped. "This fool can take the honors."

Sokolov pointed his cane at Kryuchkov who had turned that deep shade of scarlet again.

"General," the aide said in an even-toned voice, "the president would like to welcome you." The aide bowed slightly, his arms gesturing to the massive twin doors of the president's office.

Kryuchkov got the hint that he would not be invited into the office, at least not yet, and a look of relief swept over him as he finished being frisked and took a seat on a plush leather couch in the anteroom.

Sokolov held the leather-bound dossier in front of him as he hobbled through the double doors into the president's office.

The narrow room was dim like it always was. Dark paneled wainscoting ran its length, interspersed by bookshelves. A diamond chandelier in the low ceiling caught the light from the small lamp sitting on the unremarkable wooden desk at the end of the room. And behind the desk, standing as still as a statue, was the president of the Russian Federation.

Sokolov walked forward and gazed into the cunning eyes of President Vladimir Vladimirovich Putin.

"Mr. President."

Putin smiled his notoriously rare smile and rounded the desk, taking Sokolov by the elbow and helping the old general to the cushioned seat before the desk.

"*Dyadya*," Putin said. "If you told me earlier you were coming, I'd have your favorite dishes prepared in the kitchens."

Sokolov coughed and tried to catch his breath, ever aware of the cool, calculating eyes of his protégé, of the man he considered his kin, the man who saw everything and never missed a beat.

"Never mind that, something pressing has happened."

Putin's lips pursed. He went behind the desk and sat down.

"I am aware."

Sokolov blanched; had Yermakova notified the Kremlin about the happenings at the sharashka? Had she gotten a direct line to the Kremlin without going through Kryuchkov?

"How did you find out?"

"Because I spoke to your doctor at the university."

Sokolov shook his head in disgust. "Never you mind that, that's not important—it's something else entirely."

"He said you are refusing treatment."

"I'm refusing to let them poison me. I'm refusing to let them shrivel me up like a prune with their radiation. If I am going to die, I will go on my terms. That is my decision. Not yours, and not some doctor at the university. It's inconsequential." Sokolov let out a series of violent coughs, more blood spotting his handkerchief.

"Then why have you come, Viktor?"

"You know what day it is, do you not?"

"Of course I know what day it is."

"Then you did not forget?"

"How could I have forgotten, *dyadya*?" Putin said, delicately. "Your son was like a brother to me. I could never forget Evgeny."

"He would have been fifty-eight today, Vladimir Vladimirovich."

"That is why you have come all this way, to reminisce?"

"No. Something miraculous has happened, something serendipitous." Sokolov threw the leather dossier on the desk, opened it, and tore out the photocopied image of the man holding the dog next to Cassandra Gale. He pointed to the man's face and then turned the photograph so it faced the president. "Do you recognize him?"

Sokolov licked his lips in anticipation, watching as Putin's cold eyes squinted in concentration.

"I do not."

Sokolov was taken aback. His protégé was not only one of the top political minds in the world, but he was primally so—instinctive and brutal, strong and complex—but he also had the gift of a photographic mind.

"Take another look."

Putin did, then his eyes snapped open in recognition. "Impossible."

Suddenly, there was a sharp knock at the door and Sergei Antonov, the head of Putin's security, opened the door and Kryuchkov entered.

"Mr. President—General. Captain Yermakova has sent her report."

Putin stood, confused, an emotion not usually shown on his stern face.

"Bring it to me," Sokolov snapped, indicating Kryuchkov's tablet.

Kryuchkov moved forward and handed the tablet to Sokolov before the old general ordered him back out of the room.

When the door shut, Putin said, "What the hell is going on, Viktor?"

Sokolov wasn't listening; his eyes grew wider and wider as he read.

"Viktor!"

Sokolov looked up with a devilish expression on his face. "We've found him, Vladimir Vladimirovich. A GRU asset team has located him; he's in Alaska looking for his daughter."

"What are you talking about, *dyadya*?"

"We have his daughter. We have Robert Gaines's daughter, and now we can have him."

Chapter 30

GENERAL SOKOLOV TURNED the tablet and showed a perplexed Putin the new picture of Robert Gaines, his features older, his face unshaven and lit by a brilliant light.

"Tell me what is going on, Viktor."

General Sokolov explained the dealings in the Cave earlier that day. How he had seen the photograph in the dossier and how the trial had been stopped.

Putin snatched the tablet and read Yermakova's report twice through. After he was done, he put the tablet down and didn't speak.

Sokolov grew impatient.

"Vladimir Vladimirovich—"

"Robert Gaines died in that river thirty years ago. I saw the shot myself. We scoured the whole river bottom for days. The surrounding woods."

"The body was never found."

"Nobody could have survived that fall, not with that kind of bullet wound."

"He's alive—"

Putin got to his feet and walked to the small single window that overlooked the Senate Square.

"The Americans changed his name to James Gale," Sokolov said. "Hid him and his daughters in the middle of nowhere. KODIAK is with him as we speak."

"Yes, Viktor, I read the report!"

"On the day of Evgeny's birthday. It's beyond poetic."

"It's a disaster," Putin said, turning from the window.

The smile on Sokolov's face faded.

"A disaster? It's a miracle. A coincidence beyond rationality. The same sharashka that Robert Gaines tried to expose—the same very one he tried to infiltrate—now his own daughter is there! And we know where *he* is—"

"What do you want, Viktor?" Putin said, angrily.

Sokolov sat back and studied the president. He hadn't seen his protégé this upset in years. The usually cool, calm, collected Putin was now turning red in the face. Sokolov knew a nerve had been prodded, a chord struck. Sokolov understood that if he was going to get what he wanted he needed to be tactful. He needed to play with the one weakness the president had. He needed to manipulate that weakness.

"You know what I want, *plemyannik*. This is as much of an embarrassment for you as it is for me." Sokolov enunciated the word *embarrassment*. The president's greatest fear: embarrassing himself and in turn embarrassing the Motherland.

Sokolov continued: "A large part of your meteoric rise in the KGB was due to that operation targeting Robert Gaines—the operation against the Americans. You think if it wasn't for me that you'd be sitting here today? Who plucked you out of your East German post?"

Putin remained silent, his eyes giving away nothing.

"Your success that night—the hunt for Robert Gaines—was what got you through the necessary doors to propel yourself to the top. You know I opened those doors, don't you?"

"I know, *dyadya*," Putin whispered.

"So, tell me, Vladimir Vladimirovich. How does it feel to know you failed? That you failed me? That you've failed Evgeny? What will the intelligence communities say if they find out that Robert Gaines is alive and well? How will that make you look?"

Putin's eyes finally opened wide. "Careful how you speak to me, *dyadya*."

Sokolov smiled to himself; he had the president exactly where he wanted him. Sokolov patted the photocopied image of Robert Gaines with his family. "Then let us make this right. Nobody outside of our little circle needs to know about this—we can keep that under lock and key. We will deal with this internally. Quietly. You know the *embarrassment* Robert Gaines has caused you. The pain he has inflicted on me and my family. I am dying, Vladimir Vladimirovich. My days are numbered. Let me seek my revenge, let me avenge my son's death!"

"And what do you plan on doing, *dyadya*? Go to the United States by yourself? You are an old man!"

"No. I am going to bring him here. I am going to bring Robert Gaines here and return the favor—I will make him watch just like he made me watch!"

Putin slapped his desk with such force the lamp nearly teetered to the floor. "Listen to yourself. You are not making sense!"

"No, *you* are not making sense!"

"You should be thinking about finding your replacement for Line S, retiring to your *dacha*—dying in peace, not worrying about something that happened three decades ago!"

"There is only one way I can die in peace."

"You are going to let this KODIAK extract Robert Gaines?" Putin was yelling now. "Who is KODIAK anyway?"

"GRU-run assets. Captain Yermakova's. Husband and wife team. Sold Canadian PACOM intelligence to us since the eighties. A walk-in at the *rezidentura* in Ottawa. Yermakova has handled them since. The husband was a lieutenant for the Royal Canadian Navy who wasn't getting the promotions he wanted so he decided to spy for us."

"And now KODIAK works extraction for GRU sharashkas?"

"In their retirement, yes. Yermakova pays well, as you know."

"Yermakova and her games," Putin said, shaking his head.

"You allowed those games."

"For morale, for entertainment for the *siloviki*!"

"She has made a mockery of the great post. That sharashka was our Mauthausen. Our best were there. Our training grounds. Our place of scientific advancement. Now it is an embarrassment!"

"So you want me to allow KODIAK to go after one of the most effective CIA operators in the world to settle *your* score?"

"*Our* score! Don't forget, Vladimir Vladimirovich, it was the men you led who were supposed to kill him. And no, I would never let some GRU team do SVR's work. Let me send in my elite SVR Spetsnaz *Vympel* Group. Let me and my son's creation bring back Robert Gaines!"

"Enough with your poetic justice!" Putin roared. "I loved Evgeny like a brother, *dyadya*, you know that. But what you are asking is too much."

"My Vympels can intercept within—"

"No, Viktor! You have the daughter. She is yours. You are not to do anything with Robert Gaines. I don't want to hear any more on the subject." Putin walked past Sokolov and headed for the door. "You can choose the *dacha* of your liking. You will receive the best medical staff the Federation can provide to make you comfortable in your final days. But you will leave Robert Gaines alone."

Sokolov stood, fury building in his chest. He grabbed the dossier and the tablet from Putin's desk and limped to the door, stopping before him.

Putin said, "You have a month to find your replacement. I want your resignation on my desk by then."

"*Da*, Mr. President. Very well."

Sokolov walked out of the presidential office, past Kryuchkov, past the body guards and into the cream-colored hallway of the Senate Building.

Da, Mr. President. But this isn't your call. It is mine.

|||||||||||||||||||||||||||||||||||||||||||||||||||||||||||||||||||||||||||||||||||||||

Sokolov sat in his home study overlooking the rain-soaked skyline of Moscow to the south. The sun had just fallen under the horizon and made the city look like it had been painted in streaks of differing shades of charcoal.

The old general was still fuming over his contemptuous treatment by the president. Ice clinked against the crystal tumbler of vodka as he brought it to his lips.

Vladimir Putin didn't understand the pain Sokolov had to endure over the last thirty years. The pain brought upon him by Robert Gaines.

He set the crystal tumbler on the table next to his most cherished picture of his son.

His dear Evgeny.

The last of the Sokolov bloodline.

The picture had been taken when Evgeny was twenty-one, the day he was indoctrinated into the KGB Intelligence Services.

Viktor remembered that day like it was yesterday.

He looked at the young handsome face of his son wearing his KGB garb; the boy would have been fifty-eight today. He would have probably been married, had children, maybe even grandchildren.

Instead, Sokolov's dear Evgeny was just an attractive face encompassed by an ornate gold picture frame.

"General, we've received word."

Sokolov returned to reality and waved Dmitry, his special assistant, into his study.

"All three Vympel teams have landed in Vladivostok"—Vladivostok, the Federation's southeasternmost naval base. "They can intercept the target within forty-eight hours."

"I want two teams on the primary target. Team Three will extract the second daughter, the other one in the picture."

"General?"

Sokolov smiled. KODIAK's report stated that Robert Gaines was with his eldest daughter searching for Cassandra. Sokolov remembered the young girls that night in Paris when he'd had the Gaines family within his grasp.

"I want the pair. Gaines and both his daughters."

"Do you want KODIAK made aware of the Vympel's presence, General?"

Sokolov paused, running his tongue around the front of his stained teeth. "Alert Yermakova that KODIAK may assist in the extractions, but then they must be dealt with. There are to be no loose ends."

"Sir?"

Sokolov turned to face Dmitry. "KODIAK is to be eliminated once the Vympels have secured the targets."

"*Da*, General. *Of course.*"

"And what have you told Yasenevo?"

"We have alerted the directorship and told them you will be taking a week off while you recover from an illness. They understand, of course."

Sokolov growled. Showing weakness of any kind to his comrades was strictly forbidden in Sokolov's mind. He shuddered to think what they were saying about his failing health behind his back. He wondered what plans those power-hungry bureaucrats had in store for him once they learned he would be surrendering his position.

"And the Kremlin?"

"We have sent them word that you would be flying to your *dacha* tonight for some much needed rest. A plane and a decoy with a security entourage have already been sent. When we receive word that the targets have been secured, we will get you out of the city and to the sharashka. We have a jet on standby."

Sokolov nodded and sent the man from the study. Forty-eight hours until his men made the intercept. How would he spend his time in the interim? Certainly he would be too excited to keep his mind at ease.

No.

He would spend the next day catching up on some sleep so he could stay sharp. Then he would have to prepare for what awaited him. He would have to practice, refine his skills.

Chapter 31

SERGEANT MEREDITH PLANT put her hand over her bulging belly and felt the baby kick. It was occurring more frequently as the pregnancy entered the third trimester but it still weirded her out. No matter how many baby books she read, how many birthing classes she took, or how many YouTube videos she watched about expectant mothers, it was always strange for her to think that there was a little human growing inside of her.

She and her husband, Marcus, had decided on waiting until the birth to know the baby's sex. Well, it was more of Marcus's idea—Plant had actually wanted to know. It seemed logical to know. How would they know which type of clothes to buy? What color to paint the baby's room? But Marcus insisted; he loved uncertainty—while Plant was the polar opposite. Maybe it came with the job. She spent her days sifting through mounds of evidence, examining, cross-examining—trying to obtain hard facts and proof.

But like most of her days in the Alaska Bureau of Investigation, facts could be scarce, proof even scarcer, and finding cold hard evidence was usually non-existent, especially when it came to finding missing persons.

The ABI was still a small branch of law enforcement in a state that could physically cover almost a third of the Lower 48 in physical size alone. Plant and her coworkers were overworked and understaffed, their caseloads monstrous. Earlier in the day, she'd received word from her lieutenant that six more missing person reports had been filed in her jurisdiction in the three days she'd been gone.

Six more MPRs that would probably never be closed.

Drifters, thrill seekers, or end of the roaders who slipped between the cracks of society and would never be heard from again.

Plant's phone vibrated; she reached into her pocket and checked it. It was a text from Marcus, wondering if she would make it home in time for dinner that night.

She sighed and gazed out the window of the VPSO's office at the dwindling volunteer crowd on the waterfront. They'd started three days ago with almost a hundred boots on the ground. Everyone had been so eager to search for Cassandra Gale and William French. Now, the white food tent sat deserted, the boats moored at the docks, gone.

She would be leaving Eagle in two hours with Trooper Ross. The bush pilot, Rutledge, who had flown Ross in from Tok, said that he could fly Ross to Tok and then Plant back to Fairbanks. Trooper Vance would have done it, but he had prescheduled time off in Anchorage for the next couple days to visit family.

Plant was dreading the meeting that was scheduled to begin in ten minutes. The lab back in Anchorage had come back with inconclusive results on the evidence from the campsites. Cassandra Gale's .357 pistol had been too contaminated with prints to give a definitive conclusion on who had handled the weapon. They'd pulled Cassie's prints from it, James Gale's prints, Ross's prints as well as Tobeluk's, all of whom were already documented to have handled the weapon. Interestingly enough, William French's prints had not been on the gun, but again, that brought more questions than answers. There was a litany of various circumstances that could have led to that gun being in that bag. But no proof.

Cassandra Gale's coat and the mysterious canister came back inconclusive as well. The blood on the jacket had been animal blood, not human. And the canister was still a mystery. The lab technicians suggested they send it down to their parent lab in Dallas, Texas, for further tests. Plant had given them the green light to do that earlier in the day.

The only piece of evidence that came back conclusive was the condition of the tents in both campsites. The lab determined without a shadow of a doubt that the tents had been ripped by a serrated blade, not by animal claws.

The question was why?

Plant had interviewed close to thirty people in the town and village of Eagle.

She'd interviewed the grocer at the trading post who had sold Cassandra the sandwiches, and anyone who had seen Cassie's green Tundra enter the town.

Nothing came of it.

Plant herself had spent the better part of a day in each of the campsites and pored over the evidence at night. She'd searched and re-searched Cassandra's green Tundra a dozen times and pulled no valuable evidence or incriminating fingerprints.

Then there was the security footage pulled from Clinton Creek as well as all the interviews she'd conducted with Ned's logging crew. She had gone across the border with Condon to interview patrons at the Northern Breeze. All stories corroborated with one another.

Nothing new kicked up.

Everything cleared Ned, Darlene, Curtis, and Jake.

Condon had done his due diligence, and even Sherry Pruitt had done a fantastic job pulling up criminal history of the Northern Breeze crew as well as their border crossing records. Everyone's criminal histories were squeaky clean. Jake and Curtis hadn't crossed into Alaska in over a year and Ned and Darlene did so only every so often to camp in the region.

They were clean even though James Gale was convinced of their guilt.

Plant didn't know what to think of James Gale. He was a whole other story, the reason she was dreading this meeting. She would have to tell him it was all over. That she was leaving, that Ross and Vance were leaving. If he wanted to continue the search, he'd have to do so out of his own pocket.

It broke her heart. It really did.

Even after everything that James Gale had done—his aggressiveness and rash decision-making—Plant really felt for the guy. It was evident how much he loved his daughter and how far he was willing to push the envelope to get her back. Over the course of the last few days, he'd made noise about wanting to get the FBI involved.

She surmised that he would soon head down to Anchorage and try.

Vance's Cessna buzzed in low over the Yukon River, heading for the airport. It would be another ten minutes before he got here. Soon, the Attlas' dinghy pulled into the docks followed by the crew from the Northern Breeze.

This whole investigation was winding down, the doors were closing. This case would just be another thrown in the stack of unsolvables along with thousands of others. She wouldn't tell James Gale that of course. She'd tell him what she told all the grieving family members of the missing. That the case would remain open and worked on by a team in Fairbanks.

It was a half-truth.

The case would remain open, and a team would be assigned to it, but, unless more evidence appeared, the case would remain stagnant.

There was one aspect to all this that still nagged at her and would certainly cause headaches when she returned to Fairbanks. And that was Max Tobeluk, the VPSO.

Max Tobeluk was gone, and like it or not, Plant felt somewhat relieved. She had chewed him out rather harshly a few days before for his drinking and general insubordination. But what had the guy expected? He had a drinking problem and a problem with authority.

When they searched his house after he took his VPSO vehicle and fled, they found the place a sty with most of his personal belongings gone.

Plant registered the VPSO's vehicle missing, and even had one of her guys try to locate Tobeluk's location via his cell phone but he must have ditched it.

Oh well, Plant thought. The vehicle would turn up eventually and Tobeluk would probably turn up, too. Most likely in a hovel in some faraway village. He'd be arrested, stripped of his titles, and charged.

But that was the AST's problem now, not hers.

Her problem was telling James Gale and his family that the ABI could no longer stay in Eagle looking for Cassandra.

Sometimes, more often than not, this was a thankless job.

Ten minutes later when everyone assembled out in the VPSO parking lot, Plant thanked everyone for their help. She apologized that she would have to be leaving and told the Gales what she hoped to accomplish in regard to the case when she returned to Fairbanks.

Surprisingly, the Gale family took the news in stride.

After Plant finished her speech, James Gale walked up and thanked her.

"I've decided to go to Anchorage," Gale said. "I'm going to talk to the FBI."

This didn't surprise Plant. Usually after families had exhausted their own resources and the resources of the local authorities in search of their missing, they'd want to reach out to the feds.

Plant blamed it on the movies. The FBI were always the heroes, the men and women you turned to as a last resort.

She didn't have the heart to tell Gale that it would be a dead end.

"I can make copies of what I have and fax it to their Anchorage office," Plant said. "When are you thinking of going?"

"Whenever I can get a pilot to fly me down there."

"Vance said he was heading to Anchorage tonight, didn't he?" Ned said, over-hearing their conversation.

Vance, who had been talking to Ross, perked up at the mention of his name.

"That's right," Plant said. "Elliot, would that be all right if you took Mr. Gale with you to Anchorage?"

"Sure, I don't see why not."

Gale thanked the trooper, then thanked Plant again for her help and went back to Emily and Peter Trask.

Plant again felt sorry for them. Emily Gale's face was red and puffy—she looked like a woman at the end of her rope—and that wild-looking husband of hers looked like he could fall asleep standing up. Plant checked her watch and gestured to Ross.

"Almost ready to go, Glenn?"

"Rutledge said we need to leave soon, there's a bit of a storm getting into Fairbanks tonight that he wants to beat."

Plant said her personal good-byes to Ned, Darlene, Ned's men, and the Attlas before following Ross to his truck and heading out of Eagle.

She gazed at the bloated brown water of the Yukon and wondered when she'd be here again, when the next unfortunate soul would go missing in this forgotten place.

Ned Voigt watched Trooper Ross and Sergeant Plant drive out of Eagle and felt like a weight had been lifted from his shoulders. Not a massive weight, though; there was still plenty to worry about.

The most urgent matter was that James Gale was now traveling to Anchorage. Yermakova needed to be contacted about this change of plans immediately.

For the last two days, she'd insisted on updates every two hours of Gale's whereabouts.

That meant that Ned had to keep the secure tablet on him at all times as he aided in the search. It also meant that he, Darlene, Jake, or Curtis had to be in some sort of close proximity to Gale at all times. That hadn't been tricky, though; it was as if the Gale patriarch *wanted* to be around them.

The man obviously still suspected Ned and his crew.

Two aspects of this whole debacle that still irked Ned were that Tobeluk seemed to have vanished from the face of the earth and that Yermakova had notified him that another team was being sent to Eagle.

Another team.

This of course made Ned incredibly nervous, so much so that he and Darlene had nearly fled on their own the night before. When he asked Yermakova to elaborate, she had been sparse in her reply, other than saying Ned's group would be *acting in a supporting role* with the new team.

It was Darlene who'd persuaded him to stay and wait it out. She reasoned if things went south, they'd demand to be extracted with this new team and start a new life somewhere else.

Somewhere warm.

But still, Ned wasn't sharing his wife's relaxed attitude. He was feeling uneasy about the whole damn situation.

Elliot Vance approached Ned as the Gales walked to the shoreline. Vance kept his voice low. "You okay with me taking him to Anchorage, boss?"

Ned hadn't told Vance anything about the new interest in Gale.

Ned said quietly, "I'm going to need you to keep your burner phone on you. I want developments every two hours on James Gale's location; is that going to be possible?"

"I got a family thing in Anchorage."

"Cancel it. I'll triple your rate for the time you're there."

"What's the sudden interest in the old man?"

Ned flirted with the idea of telling Vance that a new team was being flown in, but decided against it. It was need to know. And Vance didn't need to know. "Can you do what I'm asking?"

"Sure, boss."

"Good. I want to know where he stays, where he eats, where he shits. You get the point?"

Vance said he did and walked to his motel to collect his stuff.

Ned made eye contact with Darlene, then both of them gazed out at James Gale who was walking to the shoreline with Emily and her husband.

Surely, it wasn't going to end well for this family. Not with all the attention Yermakova was affording them.

Ned needed to get back to the room and update her on the latest developments, then go over their escape plan if things went south.

<hr>

"And what should *we* do, Dad?" Emily said, huddling under the massive arm of her husband.

"Continue the search with Petit and Cronin. I shouldn't be gone more than a day or two. Make sure Maverick is healing okay."

"The search is done, Dad. What do you think we're going to find that we haven't found already? What's the point of being here if there is nothing to find? We should come with you to Anchorage."

"No, I want you here—it's too much to ask Trooper Vance to take all of us in his plane. Help Petit and Bill—"

"They don't need my help, Dad," Emily said, with a tone of finality. She ducked under her husband's large arm and stormed off back to her room.

Gale looked at his son-in-law. "You watch over her while I'm gone, Pete."

"I will, Jim," Peter Trask said, quietly.

Gale sighed as he looked back to the parking lot where Petit, Bill, and his men were gathered. Beyond them were the Attlas and the Northern Breeze crew.

Gale waved over Petit and Cronin. When they got to the shoreline, Gale said, "I want you two to do something for me while I'm gone."

"Anything," Petit said.

"I want some eyes on the Northern Breeze for the next few days. Maybe have a couple of your boys that you trust cross the border and hang out. I want to know if anything unusual springs up."

"Still don't trust them?"

"Not a chance."

"You got it, Jim."

"You think the FBI will be able to do anything?" Bill asked.

"Probably not, but what other choice do I have?"

An hour later, Gale was sitting in the passenger seat of Vance's Cessna, gazing down at the little township of Eagle, and battling a feeling of failure.

For the first time since Dennis Price called him six days before, Gale began to come to grips with the fact that he might never see Cassie again.

The contents in his back pocket seemed to burn through his jeans. He knew if the FBI was a dead end, he always had the possibility of opening that envelope and calling for help.

If everything failed, he would make that call.

He would make the damn call.

Chapter 32

GENERAL SOKOLOV LOVED having the light so bright that he could see everything: the fascia, the microfascia, the tendons, the ligaments, every popped artery and vein, every drilled kneecap and elbow. He loved seeing it all, but especially he loved when *they* could see it.

Sokolov felt more alive than he had in decades. So much so that it had been almost impossible for him to sleep over the last forty-eight hours.

Tonight—to squelch his excitement—he'd had his men drive him to Butyrka Prison in the Tverskoy District in central Moscow.

Other than Lefortovo, Butyrka was Sokolov's favorite place to indulge in his favorite pastime: *wet work*.

While the cellars of Lefortovo offered the sterile, white-tiled rooms that resembled his late *babushka*'s bathroom, Butyrka was different. It still had that old Soviet quality about it: The plumbing was the same from the twenties, the walls made of plastered concrete, etched with the nail marks of centuries of desperate prisoners. The cells were freezing and smelled like piss and shit. If the walls could talk, they'd speak of Mayakovsky, Dzerzhinsky, Solzhenitsyn, and Bauman. Traitors, betrayers, collaborators, and backstabbers.

How many had died in these cells? In these basements?

It was impossible to know.

Nearly ten years before, it had been General Viktor Sokolov who had advised the president to make an example of the degenerate and dissident lawyer Sergei Magnitsky who dared go against the Russian government. The little twerp had accused the state of kleptocracy, large-scale fraud and theft. Magnitsky lasted 358 days in Butyrka and died from torture and lack of medical care.

A pity. Well, not really.

International backlash did follow, then the Magnitsky Act was passed— punishing the *Rodina*.

No problem, though; that act would soon be squashed under the Motherland's might.

Sokolov put the power drill on the long metal table and wiped the gore from his surgical apron. The naked man cuffed to the steel chair in the middle of the concrete room had passed out. Urine ran down his bleeding legs and pooled at his feet.

Sokolov had requested this dissident journalist specifically from the *undesirable cells*.

To the rest of the world, the unconscious man had already died from a fire in his apartment two months before. A gas leak. A subsequent explosion. The man's charred body was found in the rubble, two of his back molars discovered untouched. Sokolov's elite team, the Vympels, had done the dirty work. The charred body had come from a dead *refusenik* from Lefortovo, the molars pulled from this very journalist during his first hour in Butyrka and planted amid the rubble of his scorched apartment.

No one would ever know the truth.

Sokolov smiled, grateful that there were still some of the old Soviet qualities about *Novorossiya*, New Russia. As mad as he was at his *plemyannik*, Sokolov was still grateful that Putin allowed this type of unrestricted wet work. It made Russia strong—just like the days of the USSR.

In the decade that followed the collapse of the Soviet Union, the *Rodina* had stumbled from grace. The Russian bear, once a superpower, had fallen asleep.

Slowly, Sokolov's *plemyannik* had awoken that bear. Prodding her awake, returning her to glory.

Sokolov felt awake, too, as he looked down at the cauterized nubs of green and black flesh that had once been the journalist's traitorous fingers.

The man wouldn't survive the night without medical attention.

Sokolov ran his hand over the various syringes, his twisted fingers dancing over the multicolored liquids resting in the vials. He would take all this to the sharashka. He would torture Robert Gaines and his daughters in ways that hadn't been seen since Lenin and Stalin.

He grabbed a syringe filled with an amphetamine derivative and plunged the needle into the man's quadricep. Instantly, the journalist opened his eyes and screamed. Screamed at his nubby fingers, the fingers that would never write such slanderous articles again. Screamed at the holes drilled into his elbows and kneecaps.

A loud knock sounded at the door and Sokolov cursed, turning to see Dmitry step into the room holding a tablet. "General, a development with KODIAK."

"Well, spit it out!"

"Robert Gaines has moved. KODIAK has said he is heading to Anchorage to meet with the FBI."

"How far out are the Vympels?"

"They can make contact with a KODIAK asset named WHISKEY outside of Anchorage within hours."

"Does KODIAK have an asset watching Gaines?"

"Yes, Gaines is currently at a hotel."

"Good. Tell the Vympel commander he has a green light. Where is the other daughter?"

"Currently in Eagle being monitored by KODIAK himself."

"Send Vympel Team Three to rendezvous with KODIAK in Eagle. They will take the daughter."

"Of course."

"Contact a member of the *siloviki*, one we trust; we need a jet. I don't want the Vympels using the normal extraction methods with Gaines, it will take too long. Get a jet into Alaska now, have it waiting. They fly back to the Motherland in that."

"What about the daughter?"

"The submarine will work just fine with her. I want a couple days with Gaines before I start on his girls."

Dmitry bowed and made to leave.

"One more thing," Sokolov said. "Ready *my* jet. As soon as we hear from the Vympels that Gaines is captured, I want to fly to the sharashka."

Dmitry bowed and hurried out of the room. Sokolov smiled with deep satisfaction.

He had a little treat in store for Gaines and his daughters, but first he needed to take care of this scurrilous traitor. Sokolov grabbed a fresh pickax from the table and held it in front of the trembling journalist before bringing it high and swinging it into the man's abdomen.

Chapter 33

THE *LADY ALAINA*, a fifty-foot oceangoing power troller, swayed in the brackish waters twenty nautical miles southwest of Anchorage in the Cook Inlet. Pavel Andreev Nakov, a fifty-five-year-old Bulgarian native and the *Alaina*'s captain, stood on the stern of his ship and checked his watch.

He'd made sure, almost fifteen minutes prior, that the cargo netting was secured off the starboard side of the vessel, that his trolling equipment was up and stored away properly, and that he had turned off his GPS as well as all other electronics on the ship.

Nakov hadn't told anyone about his late-night jaunt onto the ocean and he was certain he hadn't been seen leaving the marina.

But still, he was on edge.

Nakov had come to the United States nearly fifteen years prior on a visa to work during the Alaska fishing seasons. Business had been good, and after four years of frugal spending and constant saving, he'd been able to put a down payment on the troller, naming it after his late wife.

The power troller had been purchased because of its efficiency in the Bering and its ability to sustain a crew large enough to turn a profit. But the investment had proved disastrous.

The *Lady Alaina* ended up being difficult to maintain—a fifty-foot power troller needed constant repairs. It proved even more difficult to find a hardworking, reliable crew.

Soon, Nakov realized he was mounting up serious debt. He'd sold his small house, rented a dumpy apartment, and sold his truck and some of his most valuable possessions. But the bills kept stacking up. He even tried selling the *Alaina*, but her value had plummeted in the recession.

At his wits' end, Nakov found himself frequenting every dive bar in town, trying to drink his misgivings away, until one night, seven years before, he was approached by a man who would change his life forever.

The man was an affable sort, a Canadian who owned a hotel and bar up in the Yukon and had spent the better part of his life in the Royal Canadian Navy trolling the Bering Sea. They'd connected over the shared interests in fishing and boats—so much so that the Canadian had insisted on buying the captain's drinks for the rest of the night.

As two beers turned into eight, the captain told the stranger of his financial woes.

The stranger listened intently. As beer turned to liquor, the stranger became more and more interested in the *Lady Alaina*, and he had insisted on seeing the boat for himself that very night.

Nakov, piss drunk, agreed.

After buying a bottle of whiskey from the bartender, they walked down to the marina and onto the *Alaina*. As they drank into the night, Nakov showed the stranger all that needed repair: the nets, the outrigger, even the engine.

As the night grew older and the last drops of whiskey had been consumed, the pleasant Canadian offered the captain an opportunity of a lifetime.

At first, Nakov couldn't believe his ears.

"I work in the export business," the Canadian said. "The export of valuable cargo, and I need someone of your skill set and resources to help me."

"What do you export?"

"It would be better if you didn't know."

"Could you tell me *who* you export to?"

Again, the Canadian couldn't give him an answer. "Listen. Your job will be simple. Every week or so in the summer months, a package will be delivered to your ship. You will be a carrier, an intermediary to get that package from point A to point B."

The Canadian detailed how he would give Nakov a set of coordinates in the Bering.

"Once you reach point B, another carrier will pick up the package from you."

Nakov had been skeptical, but that was until he heard what he'd be given in return.

"You will receive ten thousand dollars in cash for each delivery."

Nakov had been shocked, even more shocked as the Canadian pulled out a stack of hundred-dollar bills and said, "This is a ten-thousand-dollar advance to show my good faith."

Nakov stared down at the money in disbelief and took the cash. Over the next hour, the Canadian laid out the rest of the rules.

"You will work alone, always. You will never tell anybody about the job. As for the cargo boxes, you will never look inside. If you break any of those rules, your position in my enterprise will be terminated. Do you understand?"

The Bulgarian agreed fervently.

Next, the Canadian gave him a BlackBerry. "This is how I will contact you. You will receive the dates and coordinates for each of your drops. This phone is secure, but still, you will never use my name. Nor discuss operational dealings over the phone. I will *never* call, only text." He detailed the code words and phrases to use instead. "I will go by KODIAK, and you will go by WHISKEY."

As the sun started to rise, KODIAK rose from his seat and shook WHISKEY's hand. "Expect a text soon."

Two days later, a message came over the BlackBerry with a set of coordinates and a time.

That night, Nakov walked onto the *Alaina* to find a coffin-sized black box in the hull of his ship. Remembering KODIAK's words, he left the box alone and drove to the designated coordinates given to him. Nakov had been both terrified and excited as he dropped anchor and threw the cargo netting over the starboard side of the ship as he'd been instructed.

Ten minutes after his arrival, bubbles erupted from the sea next to the *Alaina* and a submersible the size of a small whale broke the surface. A hatch opened from the top of the submarine. Two figures wearing shiny black rubber diving suits materialized from the craft, jumped into the water, climbed the cargo netting, and boarded the *Alaina*.

Without so much as a word, the men walked belowdecks, grabbed the coffinlike box, wrapped it in a black neoprene sleeve, took it back to the submersible, and disappeared.

When Nakov returned to land later that night, he docked the *Alaina* and walked home to find ten thousand dollars of crisp one-hundred-dollar bills sitting on his kitchen table.

For the next seven summers, the Bulgarian had worked with KODIAK the same way.

Every time, except tonight.

Early that evening, Nakov's BlackBerry rang for the first time ever.

Startled, he answered the phone, hearing KODIAK's voice on the other line telling him that he had an urgent request for that very night. It would be double the rate—and the captain would be *picking up* instead of delivering.

Nakov had been ecstatic—growing accustomed to his newfound wealth, he knew he couldn't say no to *another* twenty grand.

He agreed without reluctance, but as he took the *Alaina* out that night, he began to regret the decision.

The pickup point was farther out than usual: nearly twenty miles. And as he anchored at the preselected coordinates, dropped the cargo netting, and waited, he couldn't help but wonder *what* he was picking up.

As twenty minutes turned into thirty, Nakov shifted nervously and gazed down at the water trying to glimpse the familiar convex hump of the submersible breaking the surface—but it never came.

Instead, something odd happened.

As Nakov was about to raise anchor, he saw a small black balloon breach the water and bob to the surface.

Followed by another.

Soon, a dozen of these black balloons bobbed in the water and the captain realized that they weren't balloons after all.

They were heads.

Black diver masks and rebreathers concealed the faces. The figures swam for the cargo netting draped over the ship.

As they broke free of the water and climbed aboard, hoisting large waterproof duffels with them, one of the figures took off his mask and hood and asked in a thick Russian accent, "Are you WHISKEY?"

The man asking the question had a shaved head and a large scar extending down the left side of his face.

"I am."

"How unfortunate."

Before Nakov could react, the man with the scar took a pistol from his waistband, aimed it at the Bulgarian's forehead, and pulled the trigger.

Chapter 34

JAMES GALE SIPPED on gas station coffee and checked his phone as he climbed into the taxi outside his hotel. It was 8:55 a.m., and his head was throbbing from too much caffeine and too little sleep.

As Gale gave the driver the address to the Anchorage FBI building, he relaxed into his seat and thought back to the evening before when Trooper Vance had flown him to Anchorage and driven him to the hotel in the city. Vance had said it was decently priced considering it was located in the middle of downtown and had even checked himself into a room, not wanting to burden his grandparents, whom he had flown down to spend time with.

The flight in Vance's Cessna went by without a hitch and Gale learned a bit more about the young law enforcement officer. Vance was one year shy of thirty and had been working for the Alaskan State Troopers for more than five years. He'd explained to Gale that getting his pilot's license had made sense given the thousands of square miles in his jurisdiction. Gale liked the kid and had almost been sad when the plane landed in Anchorage.

Vance promised he'd try to drop by after Gale visited with the FBI and wished him luck.

As the cab pulled onto one of Anchorage's main drags, Gale sent Petit and Emily a text asking them for any updates, then pocketed his phone and sighed, his eyes instinctually checking the cab's rearview and side mirrors.

Gale saw them instantly.

Two black vans.

Vans he could have sworn he saw parked across the street from his hotel were now three and six cars behind him. Gale watched them as they kept their distance.

Maybe he was just paranoid due to his lack of sleep. But, for five minutes, he kept his eye on them until the cab turned off the busy street and parked in front of the FBI building.

The vans didn't follow.

Gale relaxed, paid his fare, stepped out in front of the building, and checked his surroundings. Chain-owned restaurants and some mom-and-pop stores were opening their businesses across the street. A few cars were parked on the street in front of them—all normal.

He entered the FBI building and spoke to the receptionist, who escorted him into a corner office belonging to Special Agent Burke, the FBI agent Sergeant Plant had gotten him in touch with.

Burke was a tall man of roughly forty. He sported a crew cut of salt-and-pepper hair and wore a cheap black suit. Burke didn't stand when Gale entered the room, but instead looked at his watch and said, "The ABI sent over their report. Earl has it—he deals with the missing person cases here."

Burke spoke as if he thought Gale knew what he was talking about.

"Earl?" Gale asked.

"Earl Marks, I'll take you to him."

Burke led Gale to an elevator, and when the doors shut and they began to descend, Burke said, "Earl's a bit of an eccentric. Been around forever. Technically, he retired a decade ago, but like a lot of career feds, he has a narrow scope of interest and found sitting at home watching *The Price Is Right* to be a bore."

"He's still an agent?"

"Still on FBI payroll, but more of a paid volunteer with high-level security access."

"What does he do, exactly?"

"I'm sure he'll tell you all about it."

The elevator dinged and Burke led Gale down a dim hallway to a nondescript door. Burke put his hand on the handle.

"When you're done, have Earl escort you back upstairs."

"You're not going in?"

"No time. You want to talk to the FBI's expert on missing persons in Alaska, you talk to Earl Marks." Burke opened the door, motioned for Gale to step through, and shut the door behind him.

Loud classical music assaulted Gale's ears. The room was lit with bright fluorescents, exposing stacks upon stacks of filing cabinets, documents, and boxes.

A narrow path presented itself through the clutter. Gale moved cautiously forward. The music reached a deafening crescendo as the pathway spilled out into a larger, open area where Gale stopped and took in a strange sight.

An enormous topographic map of Alaska nearly twenty-feet high and at least thirty feet wide covered the back wall directly in front of him. Tens of thousands of colored tacks were stuck to the map, most of them clustered in and around a large triangle made of red string.

Floor-to-ceiling bookcases covered the adjacent walls. On the right-hand side, a sliding library ladder hung from a track that went around the room. In the middle of the open space was a long metal desk, nearly twelve feet in length, covered in a haphazard array of computer monitors, empty coffee mugs, papers, binders, and folders. Another small table rested under an antique turntable, amplifier, and two speakers. A record spun under a worn stylus.

A door next to the small kitchenette opened. A hefty, bespectacled man with a white beard and a shiny bald head shuffled into the room. His belly threatened to spill out between red suspenders and a stained white shirt.

Earl Marks put most of his weight on a wooden cane as he limped toward the turntable and lifted the stylus from the record. Then, as if he hadn't noticed Gale standing in the room, he plopped down heavily in his desk chair, adjusted his glasses, and studied his computer monitor with a squint.

Gale cleared his throat. "Excuse me, I'm—"

"I know who you are, Mr. Gale."

"Sergeant Meredith Plant said she sent over my daughter's MPR?"

"She's sixteen hundred and forty-six."

"Come again?"

"She's the sixteen hundred and forty-sixth person to have gone missing this year. That's up nineteen-point-three percent from this time last year and I'm only counting the MPRs that were filed. All of those missing have been in the triangle."

Gale was caught off guard by the bluntness this man was affording him. "The triangle?"

Earl looked at Gale, then at the map, before raising his cane and pointing at the high tip of the red-string triangle. "From Alaska's most northern township, up there in Barrow and all the way south to Anchorage and over east to Juneau, is a landmass nearly the size of Texas that accounts for more missing persons than anywhere else in the United States, nearly three thousand a year. These tacks symbolize each person missing since I started keeping track in eighty-eight."

Earl explained that the colors corresponded to the decade the person went missing. Green was the eighties, blue the nineties, yellow the two thousands, and finally orange, the two thousand tens.

He used a laser pointer to point north of Eagle along the Yukon River. "These two tacks represent your daughter and William French. Both in the triangle, both within a landscape so large and vast it's easy to disappear."

"How many of these people were found?"

"These are the ones that weren't. Those gone above the sixtieth parallel north latitudinal line have a way of never being found; they just seem to disappear without a trace."

"You attribute these disappearances to the wilderness?"

Earl laughed. "If I attributed them to the wilderness, I wouldn't be down here. Some of them, yes, of course. The majority, even. I've lived here nearly my whole life, seen born-and-raised Alaskans, tough men and women, die from the elements right outside their front doors."

"You said nearly three thousand people go missing up here a year? This should be a national emergency, the FBI should have a task force of fifty agents on this."

"The FBI doesn't care about people getting lost off the grid. It's not illegal to intentionally go missing. They don't have to contact friends or family if they don't want to and we're not going to make them."

"But you're doing something."

Earl sighed. "Mr. Gale, my little brother Nicholas vanished near Nome twenty-five years ago. I have access to databases—records that require high-level security clearances—but at the end of the day it all comes back to nothing, a big fat goose egg." Earl made a fist to prove his point. "Since 9/11 the FBI in Alaska, due to our proximity to China, Russia, and North Korea, pools most of its resources into antiterrorism operations: intel gathering and worst-case scenario prep. The remaining resources are focused on big-city crime."

Earl leaned forward. "I've got to be clear with you, Mr. Gale. I've seen hundreds of family members walk through that door and stand right where you're standing. Hundreds of families the troopers and the ABI were unable to help. The fact you had such an extensive search party looking for William French and your daughter is unheard of. The fact that an ABI investigator flew to Eagle was miraculous."

"I keep hearing that. But I still need to find my daughter."

Earl nodded. "Last night when the ABI sent over Cassandra's and French's MPRs, I spent a couple of hours going through them and noticed something." He grabbed a stuffed folder and opened it, took out two pictures, and slapped them on his desk.

Gale moved forward and recognized the pictures Ross had taken of both Cassie's and William French's tents.

"I read the crime lab's report, Mr. Gale. And they're right—no bear or animal did that. These were done by a human, with a serrated blade." Earl got slowly to his feet, walked to a filing cabinet, and pulled an orange folder from inside. He walked back to his desk, fished through the folder, and took out another picture, presenting it to Gale.

The picture showed a navy blue tent, strewn across a small rock bed. The blue fabric was ripped just like Cassie's and French's.

Earl said, "A little over a month ago, troopers photographed this on the Fortymile River just south of the town of Chicken. Did this ever come up in conversation with the AST or the ABI?"

"No," Gale said, confused.

"I was afraid of that."

"What do you mean?"

Earl opened the orange file. "In late May, a woman in California filed a missing person report after her ex-husband failed to touch base with either her or their children. Ex-husband's name was Paul Brady, disappeared a few hundred miles as the crow flies from where your daughter went missing. Tent ripped the same way—"

"The troopers knew about this?"

"They did. What's also interesting is that not only were the tents ripped in the same fashion, but Paul Brady was also ex-military like your daughter. Former Navy SEAL." Earl read from the report: "Paul Brady, forty-one years old, divorced, two kids. He took 9/11 personally when his mother died in the second tower. Enlisted in the navy two days after. Graduated BUD/S then was selected to operate with SEAL Team Two out of Virginia. Nearly a half dozen deployments in the Middle East. Retired from the navy a couple years ago to spend some more time with his family in San Diego. Did contract work on the Mexi-Cali border. Wife filed for divorce couple years ago. Brady struggled with alcohol. Ex-wife took the house, the kids, and moved in with a high-end realtor in Los Angeles."

"And Brady hasn't been found?"

"Not a trace. But now I think we have a link."

"The tents?"

"The tents and the fact that both Brady and Cassandra were military trained," Earl said, pointing to a stack of more orange files on his desk. "There's a pattern I'm seeing all over the place within the triangle. A pattern both Director Hughes and that dolt Special Agent Burke think is hogwash." He pointed the laser pointer at Eagle. "There are various areas in the triangle where a large amount of the missing are ex-military men and women. Areas like Eagle."

"Alaska's a tough place, it attracts tough people."

"Of course, but in the last decade my data has been showing anomalies. Hundreds of the missing are veterans. This wasn't the case a decade before, or the one before that."

"What do you attribute it to?"

"It's obvious, isn't it?"

Gale raised an eyebrow.

Earl said, "They're being taken, scooped up. That's my theory anyway. And until last night, I didn't think it could be proven."

"The ripped tents?"

"Not just the tents, Mr. Gale. It's the authorities whose jurisdiction those tents were found in. The Alaska state trooper who photographed Paul Brady's demolished campsite. The Alaska state trooper who aided in the search and subsequent investigation of your daughter."

"Ross?"

"No."

"Who then?"

"Trooper Elliot Vance."

Chapter 35

"VANCE?"

"He was the lead investigator on the Paul Brady case. He's been the officer in charge of nearly four hundred MPRs since being assigned to D-detachment in the town of Northway Junction. Just shy of one hundred of those missing were military trained. Correct me if I'm wrong, Mr. Gale. You said Elliot Vance never mentioned the Paul Brady case or his ripped tent?"

"Never."

"And it was never brought to Meredith Plant's attention?"

"Not that I know of."

Vance had seen Paul Brady's campsite, the ripped tents, and said nothing? Almost a hundred ex-military personnel had gone missing in his jurisdiction in four years? This whole time, Gale had been focused on the crew from the Northern Breeze.

The Northern Breeze!

Gale flashed on the scene he'd witnessed: Vance talking to Ned and the others in front of the Eagle Motel.

"The Northern Breeze—Ned and Darlene Voigt," Gale said. "Have you heard of them?"

"Should I have?"

Gale detailed how Cassie and William French stayed at the Northern Breeze, detailed the bar fight. He told Earl how the Northern Breeze crew aided in the search, and how Gale had been suspicious of them from the get-go.

Earl squinted down at Cassie's MPR. "They *were* cleared by the ABI and the Mounties?"

"Yes. Any way to tell if more of the missing stayed at the Northern Breeze?"

Earl ran a hand through his white beard. "I can check. I'll cross-reference with those missing in the area. See if I can pull credit card statements—it might be difficult. A lot of the paperwork isn't digitized."

"If Paul Brady stayed at the Northern Breeze—"

"That would be something. I'll get on the horn with the RCMP after I go through Brady's credit card records."

"And if he paid cash?"

"Then we're out of luck."

Gale took his cell phone out, tried to find Sergeant Plant's number.

"That won't work down here, Mr. Gale. You'll have to go upstairs."

"I need to alert Sergeant Plant about Trooper Vance and Brady."

Earl scrunched his face. "Hold up about Vance. It wouldn't be wise to accuse a law enforcement officer about something like this until we have definitive proof. Tell her about the Paul Brady tent; tell her I'll fax over the file immediately."

Gale turned to leave, but then remembered something. "The metal canister that was found in Cassie's campsite, have you seen anything like it before?"

Earl sifted through Cassie's file and took out Ross's picture of the canister. He squinted at the image, then frowned. "No, I can't say that I have."

"Not in any of the missing person cases?"

"Not that I recall. Why the interest?"

Gale didn't really have a reply, other than the fact that the strange object didn't sit right with him. He was about to tell the FBI man about the sharp odor that emanated from the canister when Earl got up from his seat and walked up to him.

Earl looked like he was struggling to say something. "I've been with the bureau for a long time, Mr. Gale. Last night when Plant sent me Cassie's MPR and said you were coming, I did a little investigation of my own on you. I have access to some DoD and NSA servers as well as level-five clearance in the FBI databases"—Earl shifted uncomfortably—"I looked you up, Mr. Gale, after I looked up Cassandra."

Gale kept his face impassive.

"I know a doctored identity when I see one. There's only one organization that has the ability to do that. I don't know who you really are, and frankly, I don't care. But it looks like you have friends in high places, higher than the FBI. If things go south, if this turns into a shit show, I'd suggest you call those friends."

Gale stared at the old man, his eyes never wavering, and said, "I need to call Plant."

And left.

||||||||||||||||||||||||||||||||||||||||||||||||||||||||||||||||||||||||||||||||||||||||||

Gale tried getting reception in the elevator, and when that failed, the lobby, only to be disappointed again. He walked outside and stood in front of the building, holding his cell to the sky, trying to obtain enough service to make the call.

He finally got service on the sidewalk outside and dialed Plant. Straight to voice mail. He gave her a brief overview of his discussion with Earl Marks regarding Paul Brady's tent. He said nothing about Vance, just to call him back immediately.

When he hung up, he dialed Emily; as he looked up the road, he nearly froze as he spotted a black van parked across from a Subway.

Maybe it had just been a coincidence. Maybe he was just being paranoid.

No.

Something was off. This was one of the vans from before—tailing his taxi from the hotel.

Holding his phone to his ear, Gale walked south down the street and stood in front of an insurance building, using its reflective windows to clock the black van to the north.

Emily's phone went straight to voice mail.

So did Petit's.

Why the hell weren't they answering?

He'd just had that thought when he saw two telephone workers round the corner from the south. Alarm bells started chiming in Gale's brain.

The van to the north started its engine. Using the window as a mirror, Gale estimated that he was a good two hundred yards from the front entrance of the FBI building.

There was no one else on the sidewalks, no cars driving up and down the road. Something was wrong, very wrong. Gale wished he had his pistol, but he'd left it in the hotel room.

He shot a furtive glance at the telephone workers, both in blue jumpsuits and white hard hats. Fifty yards away. They each held a toolbox, but their jumpsuits were too clean. Their hardhats too white. Their boots weren't scuffed and dirty, they were pristine, shiny—

As Gale wondered if the FBI building had security cameras that would reach his side of the street, a motor roared and tires squealed. A second black van peeled around the street from the south and came to a screeching stop behind him. Gale turned around just in time to see Elliot Vance jump out of the van.

"Mr. Gale!" Vance said.

"You sonofabitch—"

The telephone workers had dropped their toolboxes, pistols now in their hands.

Five men spilled out behind Vance wearing black jumpsuits and ski masks. Gale put his weight on the balls of his feet and dropped his center of mass. The first man grabbed him by the elbow, Gale leaned forward, countered, and threw him down to the sidewalk. But the other men were already on him.

An aerosol canister was thrust into his face and orange mist exploded from the cap. Gale gasped as he breathed in the noxious chemical and immediately lost his footing, his balance, and all motor functions.

The last thing he remembered was being hoisted off his feet and into the back of the van.

Chapter 36

SOMETHING WAS WRONG.

Ned Voigt could sense it like a deer could sense a predator. That's what he felt like now as he stood in the Jack Wade airfield, holding the tablet, staring south into the deep blue morning sky. Darlene stood next to him, her face placid, but her slight fidgeting told him that she was inwardly worried. And she had every right to be. These were uncharted waters for both of them.

Jake and Curtis had helped them clear their little makeshift runway beyond the old slow-motion gold dredge—the runway they constructed to extract their victims to Anchorage before the long trip to Russia.

Ned still had no idea how Yermakova transported the victims to another continent. He'd wondered for years, but after a while he realized it was better he not know. It was better to drop it and just do his job. The KODIAK team was only responsible for getting the subjects to WHISKEY.

For nearly eleven years, Ned felt like he had been an expert trapeze artist doing a high-risk tightrope act. For eleven years, he'd never fallen. Never so much as faltered on the high line.

Now, he felt like he was taking a swan dive into the ground.

"How long are we supposed to wait?" Jake said.

"As long as we have to," Ned growled, his attention still on the skyline.

"And who are these guys?" Curtis asked.

"Another team sent to help us."

"Help us do what?"

"That is need to know. And you don't need to know."

Thing was, Ned didn't really know what was going to happen, just that he was assisting another team in a supporting role. He honestly thought that when James Gale and Vance went to Anchorage he and his team would be in the clear. But Yermakova's message the night before said otherwise.

This had prompted wild speculation between Ned and Darlene. If James Gale was gone, why would this new team still come to Eagle? Would they insist on taking Emily Gale and her husband? Would there be a kill team to take out Ned's team? There was no way of knowing, so Ned and Darlene hoped for the best and prepared for the worst.

Their get-out bags were packed, their money secured, their new identities ready to go. If this new team insisted on taking Emily Gale and Peter Trask, both Ned and Darlene would assist them and then order this new team to extract them from the country.

At least that was the plan.

Now, if this new team was sent to *take out* Ned and his crew, they were ready for that, too.

Jake and Curtis both had semiautomatic rifles and backup weapons. Ned had his tactical shotgun and Darlene her rifle.

Plus, they had enough knockout gas loaded in the canisters at their feet to take out a pride of angry lions. If this team had the wrong intentions, they were going to be in for a bad time. Ned took a deep breath, trying to calm his nerves. He thought over every fuckup he had been responsible for.

Max Tobeluk was first on his list.

The little shit was still MIA.

He'd had Curtis and Jake out all night looking for him.

At this point it didn't matter; Ned knew he was either going to be leaving the continent by the end of the day or be dead.

"I think I hear it," Darlene said, breaking Ned from his thoughts.

Ned strained his ears and heard the light buzzing of an aircraft approaching.

"Should we smoke them as soon as they land?" Jake asked.

"You will do nothing unless I give the order, is that clear?"

He almost felt bad keeping Curtis and Jake in the dark. He liked the boys, they were good workers and ruthless extractors. No matter what happened today, nothing would turn out well for them. He and Darlene would never take them out of the country, they would either be dead or on their own.

The plane came into view, a 172 Cessna. A bigger plane than Vance flew. It came in low, landed smoothly in the tall grass, and taxied over to them.

Ned gripped his shotgun and raised his other hand. He could see the pilot raise a hand in acknowledgment, then the engine cut and the side doors opened.

Three men wearing black combat fatigues spilled out. They carried large duffels. Ned felt uneasy. They looked like soldiers. Hardened soldiers. The pilot got out and joined his men. The tallest man marched up to Ned.

"State your call sign," the man asked in a thick accent.

Ned cleared his throat, then, trying to keep the fear from his voice, replied, "KODIAK."

The man took in Ned and his group, then reached into his jacket and for a moment Ned thought he was taking out a gun. Instead, he came out with a tablet similar to Ned's. The man fidgeted with the tablet, then turned it, showing a picture of Emily Gale.

Ned felt himself relax. These men weren't here to kill them—they wanted the girl.

"You know her location?"

"We do."

"Good, take us to her."

||||||||||||||||||||||||||||||||||||||||||||||||||||||||||||||||||||||||||||||||

EAGLE, ALASKA
Tuesday, July 2nd, 8:43 a.m.

Peter Trask felt worthless.

He'd been married to Emily Gale for less than a year, and in that time—while their relationship had never been stronger—the events of the last year had been the hardest he'd ever had to endure in his whole life.

He'd watched from what felt like the sidelines as his new brother-in-law took his own life. Watched how Cassie had lost the baby, and then how Cassie almost lost herself.

Now she *was* lost and would probably never be found again.

He looked over at Emily, the person he adored most in the world, and put his arm around her as they sat on the Yukon's shoreline with Maverick.

They'd all woken early after a late night out searching with Petit and the Cronin boys; Emily had insisted on going to the riverbank. She said she needed to talk with him.

This worried Trask. For the last week, his wife had been a wreck. Trask didn't blame her—he didn't know what he would do in her situation. Emily always felt like she had to be the protector in the family. The glue that holds the foundation in place. But that foundation had crumbled and the glue wouldn't bind.

"What did you want to talk to me about?"

Emily wiped at her eyes with her sleeve. "You don't have to stay here if you don't want to. I feel like I've dragged you into this crazy family and you're just watching it self-destruct. I'd understand if you wanted to leave."

Trask let go of his wife and stared at her incredulously.

"Why would you think I'd want to leave?"

Emily was crying now. "Because, I feel like I've upended your life. I made you move to Montana after Derrick killed himself. I made you walk away from your career—"

"I chose to move, Em. There was nowhere else I wanted to be."

"I know you hate the ranch—"

"I don't hate the ranch, it's just different. I would follow you anywhere. You know that." He took her hand, held up her ring finger where the diamond band caught the reflection of the sun. "When I married you, I swore to remain by you, in sickness and in health. When I married you, your family became *my* family. I'm not going anywhere, Em."

Emily threw her arms around her husband and sobbed into his neck. "She's gone, isn't she, Pete? My little sister's gone . . ."

"No, she's not, Em. We don't know where she is, but she's alive. I can feel it." Truth was, Trask actually did believe that Cassie was still alive. He'd only known his sister-in-law for a few years, but in that time, he'd come to the conclusion that she was unlike any other person he'd ever met. He'd known a lot of tough people in his life. Having grown up in Texas as the youngest of four boys, Peter Trask had a childhood that revolved around one thing: football.

He'd gotten a full ride to play for the University of Utah, only to be injured his junior year. Eventually, he went to physical therapy school and worked for the team. In the football world, he'd met some physically and mentally tough individuals. Men who went on to play for the NFL. Men who had Super Bowl rings.

But he'd never met anyone as tough as Cassandra Gale.

She was hard to describe. She wasn't macho, or domineering, or even intimidating. But she had this quiet energy about her. When she put her mind to something—she just did it. She was sharp, keen, and intelligent.

Emily was different. She was a people pleaser—she cared deeply what other people thought about her, which made her more of an emotionally intelligent person than her younger sister. Cassie was headstrong. Calm under pressure. That is why her disappearance was so odd.

Trask held Emily close as she continued to cry into his shoulder. He watched the river water lap gently on the shore, watched Maverick's chest slowly rise and fall as he slept on the sand in front of them. Trask didn't know what else he could do to help. Didn't know what good the Cronin boys or even that old cantankerous bastard Alvin Petit could do with the horses. Cassie wasn't in those woods—he just hoped that Jim would be able to get the FBI involved.

Trask noticed that Maverick's ears perked up and he raised his head, looking upriver. Following the dog's gaze, he saw John Attla running down the shoreline from the village toward them.

"Em," Trask said and pointed at Attla. Emily wiped her eyes and stood.

John stopped in front of them. "I need you to come with me."

"What is it?" Emily said, alarmed.

"My grandmother has sent me out to find you. Please, come quick." He turned and started hurrying back upstream without waiting for a reply.

Emily and Trask shot each other furtive glances, then grabbed Maverick and followed the man.

They jogged up the shoreline until they got to the edge of the village.

John turned abruptly into the woods and led them on a small path.

As soon as they entered the woods, John skirted around a corner and stopped before a small enclave, a hut of sorts, supported by small logs and wrapped in what looked like deer or elk hide.

Odd-smelling smoke rose from the dwelling's makeshift chimney. Trask wondered if this was some sort of sweat lodge. John reached for the flap in the hide and opened a small slit.

"She's inside."

Trask was hesitant, but Emily took Maverick by the lead and went in before Trask could stop her. Trask reluctantly followed, ducking under the flap, and was instantly met with a sharp-smelling purple smoke.

Trask and Emily both coughed, and Maverick began to growl.

Trask rubbed at his watering eyes and gasped at the sight before him.

Eve Attla sat next to a small fire in the middle of the hut; she wore a bearskin cape that was draped over her shoulders, and eagle feathers poked out of her silvery hair. She was chanting in a low hum, rocking back and forth as a mysterious herb burned over the fire.

But that wasn't what had startled Trask.

What made his mouth drop was the figure gagged and bound behind her.

The VPSO.

Max Tobeluk.

Chapter 37

"WHAT THE HELL is going on?" Trask said, backing away from Eve.

Maverick growled at Tobeluk, who seemed to not notice that anyone had entered the sweat lodge. His eyes had a glazed-over, bloodshot appearance to them. Drool had slopped out of his gagged mouth and pooled in the dirt below. He lay on his side, his bound ankles and wrists almost touching.

Eve continued to chant.

John said, "We found him last night trying to get into his house. We had someone staking it out in case he came back."

"Why would you have someone watching his house?"

"Because Max is a vile person. He poisons our people."

"What do you mean poisons?"

"Alcohol is illegal in the villages in Alaska. Max is supposed to enforce that rule. But he is the person who brings in and sells the alcohol. It has ruined our village."

"Why didn't you tell this to Trooper Ross or Sergeant Plant?" Emily asked.

"Because they don't know us or respect us. They will just send another corrupt VPSO. We will deal with Tobeluk ourselves."

"Why did you bring us here?" Trask asked, feeling more and more uncomfortable.

John squatted down, picked up the mysterious herb simmering over the fire. "This is an indigenous herb only found in this part of Alaska. When it is inhaled in great quantities, it is said to show you the truth. You come face-to-face with your own inner spirit and the spirits around you. Last night, Tobeluk participated in this ritual."

"You drugged him?" Emily said.

"We cleansed him," John replied. "And he told us everything."

Eve suddenly stopped chanting and her eyes focused on the group.

"Wake him, Grandmother."

Eve stood, took out a small leather pouch, and procured another herb. She mashed the herb in her hands, rubbing it profusely, then crouched down and blew the herb into Tobeluk's face. The VPSO coughed and his eyes immediately bolted open. Eve took the gag from his mouth.

He struggled, then let out a gurgling whimper at the sight of the group.

Eve said something in her native tongue, and John translated, "Tell them, Max. Cleanse your soul and tell them what the spirits told you to say. Tell them what you did."

"Water," Tobeluk croaked.

Eve grabbed a water pouch and poured some into the man's mouth. When he was satisfied, he sat up.

"Tell them, Max," John repeated.

Tobeluk choked out a sputtering cry, "They, they took her!"

"Who took her, Max," John said, forcefully.

"They did—we did."

"What are you talking about?" Emily said.

"Ned and his people—me. We were all in on it. We took your sister and that kid. We hurt the dog."

"Where did you take them?" Emily demanded.

"I don't know, I was just paid to do cleanup on the campsites. Make it look like an accident."

There was a collective silence in the sweat lodge.

"Where did they take Cassie?" Trask asked.

"I don't know," Tobeluk sputtered. "I honestly don't know. They just kidnap people from the woods. Make it look like they just wandered off, or a grizzly got 'em."

"You were the one who tore up the tents—put the food canister on the ground?"

Tobeluk nodded.

"You put Cassie's gun in French's backpack?" Trask asked

"Yes. And her yellow coat over the moose kill."

"Why?"

"I was drinking, I thought I could make it look like that kid was in on it. Nobody even investigates these cases up here—"

"How did you take them?" Emily asked.

Tobeluk sniffled. "At night. Ned has this gas, they call it knockout gas. It's in a canister. Like the one you found. I forgot to clean it up. They shoot the canister out of this projectile launcher. Jake, Curtis, and Ned use them while Darlene drives the Zodiac up the river from Clinton Creek. I pick everything up in the morning and make it look like something it's not."

"How did Maverick get that scar on his face?"

"He attacked Curtis and Jake. Jake shot a canister at the charging dog. Hit him in the ribs, then Jake slashed him with his knife. I think he thought the dog was dead," Tobeluk said, looking fearfully at Maverick.

"And once my sister was passed out, where did they take her?"

"The same place they took William French. Upriver to Eagle, then drove them to the airfield in Jack Wade."

"There is no airfield in Jack Wade," John said.

"They made one, behind the gold dredge. A long clear-cut. Most of their equipment is in the garages at Jack Wade. Open them, find out."

"And they flew them somewhere. Who flies them?" Emily asked.

Tobeluk looked nervous. "They're gonna kill me."

"Who flies them, Max?" John said. "Cleanse yourself."

"Vance."

Trask was shocked. "Trooper Vance?"

"He's on Ned's payroll. That's all I know, I swear. I've only known about this for a couple of years. This was the first year I actually helped them, I swear to God."

Trask didn't know what to say; he looked at his wife, saw the astonishment in her eyes.

"You don't know where they take them?"

"No idea. Ned doesn't tell me anything. He just gives me whiskey or money as payment."

"And then you sell that whiskey to the villagers," John said.

"What about Ross, or Sergeant Plant? Are any of them in on it?" Emily asked.

"I don't think so."

Emily turned to Trask. "We need to tell my dad this immediately. We need to call Plant."

Trask reached for his phone. There was no service.

"We gotta get back to the town," Emily said, then gestured to John. "What will you do with him?"

"He will stay here."

Emily grabbed Trask by the elbow. "Let's hurry."

|||||||||||||||||||||||||||||||||||||||||||||||||||||||||||||||||||||||||||||||

As instructed, Ned had brought two vehicles to the airstrip. One for the new team and the other for him and his crew.

Ned drove his red Ford F-350 behind the black Chevy usually parked in the storage garage in Jack Wade. The Russians drove the Chevy. Ned followed as best he could.

"Why do those guys sound Russian, Ned?" Curtis asked when they were a mile outside of Eagle.

"We working with Russians, Ned?" Jake said.

"Shut up, both of you," Darlene snapped.

"We taking that Gale bitch?" Jake said. "I call shooting the dog."

"You do nothing unless I say so," Ned growled.

"And you do what the Ruskies say?" Jake asked.

Ned flexed his knuckles on the steering wheel as the Chevy with the Russians came to a stop on the road just outside of Eagle. One of them climbed out and tapped on Ned's window. Ned rolled it down and was given a flip phone.

"You go in, locate subject. Then call. We extract her."

Ned grabbed the phone and pocketed it, trying to figure out when a good time would be to ask if he and Darlene could be extracted with them. He'd have to do it out of earshot of Jake and Curtis.

"Like I said earlier, the girl is probably at her motel."

"Make sure. Then call."

The Russian walked away and Ned cursed, rolled up his window, and pulled back onto the road, heading into town.

"If they ain't at the motel, they're probably out with the Montana hicks," Curtis said.

Ned scanned the roads, knowing that Curtis was probably right. He turned left on Front Street, parallel with the shoreline, the VPSO's office in the distance.

"Wait! Ned, there they are!" Jake yelled.

Ned slammed on the brakes, his head darting around wildly—he caught movement on the shoreline, saw Emily Gale running with her husband and the dog toward town. They stopped abruptly when they saw Ned's truck skid to a halt.

They were easily a hundred yards away, but their body language was clear: they were scared shitless at the sight of his truck. Ned watched them backpedal and turn toward the village.

"They know something's up!" Curtis yelled.

"No shit!" Ned roared and fumbled for the phone, pressed the speed dial, while throwing the truck in reverse. There was a click on the other line.

"Got 'em on the shoreline, they spooked when they saw us. They're running east toward the village."

He didn't wait for a reply, snapped the phone shut, and grabbed his knockout gas canister from beneath his seat.

"Everyone out!"

"It's broad daylight, Ned. We can't do this now!" Curtis said.

"We don't have a choice. Everyone out!"

|||||||||||||||||||||||||||||||||||||||||||||||||||||||||||||||||||||||||||||||||||||||||||

Adrenaline thumped through Trask as he ran, arms pumping, legs straining to keep up with Emily and Maverick. He looked over his shoulder and saw Ned's red truck reverse and then come to another stop. He saw Jake and Curtis fly out of the back of the truck. They had guns.

"Run faster!" Trask screamed. "They're armed!"

Emily tripped on a piece of driftwood and Trask scooped her up, looking back again as Ned, Curtis, Jake, and Darlene cleared the guardrail and landed on the shore.

Panicked, Trask tried to find the trail leading to the sweat lodge—but the bushy forest looked the same. He looked for smoke, but couldn't spot any.

"Where the hell is the trailhead?!"

"I don't know!" Trask looked around frantically. Ned and his crew were two hundred yards away and closing. He considered running into the river with Mav and Emily, but what would that do? It would take them right by the Northern Breeze crew. They'd be floating ducks.

"We make for the village and hide," Trask decided and they took off again.

Trask remembered what Jim had said to him before leaving for Anchorage.

You watch over her, Pete.

They rounded the shoreline's curve and saw squalid cabins and run-down lean-tos sitting interspersed in the woods. The Northern Breeze crew still hadn't rounded the bend behind them. Trask did a three-sixty looking for a place to go, when a dark figure materialized out from the trees and onto the shore.

Another followed.

Then another.

A fourth figure came out behind them. They were all dressed in dark clothing, black ski masks over their faces, and all had assault rifles that were aimed directly at them.

Maverick growled, moving in front of Trask. Trask grabbed Emily, putting himself between her and the men. They were thirty yards away and closing. Trask kept backpedaling, pushing Emily toward the river.

Emily was screaming but Trask wasn't registering.

Then he caught movement to his right.

Ned Voigt and his crew rounded the bend and something loud *popped.*

Then another, *pop, pop!*

Trask felt something icy-hot pierce his abdomen. Then again through his chest. He looked down, surprised, and saw blood rose-budding beneath his shirt.

Maverick exploded forward, leaping on the man closest to them.

Trask grasped at his chest and felt his knees buckle.

There were more popping noises, and a loud yelp. Emily's face was in front of his, her hands covered in his blood. She looked terrified.

Trask felt himself fall forward, his face landing on the sandy shore. He tried to get up, tried to get to his feet, but he felt so tired. He turned ever so slightly just in time to see two of the men grab his wife and spray an orange mist into her face.

Trask tried to call out, but his vocal cords were clogged with blood.

He shifted again, this time on his back, and coughed. His eyes flickered on the impossibly blue sky above him and heard his father-in-law's voice reverberate over and over in his head before all went dark.

You watch over her while I'm gone, Pete.

You watch over her.

Chapter 38

"OH MAN, WE'RE so screwed!" Curtis screamed from the front passenger's seat of Ned's truck as Jake drove like a bat out of hell down the road toward Jack Wade.

"What the hell was that!" Jake yelled, gas pedal to the floor. "I thought we were supposed to do that quietly!"

Minutes before, Ned and his crew had witnessed those Russian bastards murder Peter Trask and the dog in broad daylight on the shoreline and capture Emily Gale. Ned had been flabbergasted by the brazenness of the attack. When the bullets stopped flying, the four Russians told them to hurry back to Jack Wade, but Ned must have been in shock because he hadn't been able to move his body. It had been Curtis and Jake who had grabbed him and Darlene and ran with them back to the truck.

As Jake had climbed behind the wheel and tore out of town after the Russians, Ned had noticed that the firefight on the riverbank had caught the attention of the whole place. The residents of Eagle had pooled on Front Street and had certainly seen Ned, Darlene, Curtis, and Jake make their escape.

"They all fucking saw us, Ned!" Curtis said.

"I know they saw us, Curtis!"

"We're so fucked!"

Jake kept the black Chevy in view ahead, Ned knowing full well that Emily Gale was unconscious in the Chevy's truck bed.

When they were nearly five minutes away from the Jack Wade landing strip,

Ned had a disturbing realization. The Russians in the Chevy had no reason to keep them alive. Their plane was too small to take everyone out of the region.

KODIAK was compromised *and* expendable.

Ned decided that he wouldn't let Jake stop at Jack Wade—he wouldn't even ask for an extraction. They would hit the Taylor Highway, turn east, and the four of them would ditch the truck before the border crossing, go into the woods, cross into Canada on foot, then he and Darlene would secure their get-out bags and disappear.

The only problem was Jake and Curtis. They would want to run with them.

Ned glanced at Darlene and could tell she was thinking the same thing. Ned wondered if he had the guts to shoot Jake and Curtis in cold blood.

If it meant he and Darlene could make a safe escape—he wouldn't have a choice. They needed to close all loose ends. That only left Vance.

But it would be too risky to go after Vance at this point. Their only option would be to shoot Jake and Curtis then get the hell out of Dodge.

Ned saw the slow-motion gold dredge in the distance, then saw the Russians' brake lights suddenly illuminate. The truck came to a grinding halt and turned broadside, blocking the road.

It was everything Jake could do to stop his own truck in time. He slammed on the brakes and swerved, before coming to a stop.

Two of the Russians jumped out, their weapons raised.

Ned knew what was coming and barely had time to react. He grabbed Darlene and threw her to the floor, covering her body with his own as a barrage of bullets peppered the truck.

Chapter 39

SOMEWHERE OUTSIDE OF ANCHORAGE

JIM GALE'S TOES tingled awake, followed by his legs, his torso, and his chest and arms. Then his eyelids fluttered. He was on his side, his head bouncing off a cold metal floorboard, something sticky and wet adhering to his face.

Crude voices were talking around him over the sound of an engine.

Then he remembered. The men had gassed him and must have thrown him into the van. He surmised he was still in the back of that van.

He dared not open his eyes, not now. He took a quick mental stock of his body, moving his limbs slowly. His wrists were zip-tied in front of him, and tape was over his mouth, but his ankles and legs were free. That meant they were going to move him and they wanted him to walk.

That was good.

That's when he would make his move.

He concentrated over the roaring engine.

Four voices, low murmurs, not speaking English, but—

Russian. They were speaking Russian.

He focused his hearing. His kidnappers were talking about another captured subject in Eagle, how two other teams were exfiltrating the subject through the secondary extraction route in Anchorage.

Gale fought the urge to open his eyes, to leap up, disarm, and kill everyone who had taken him captive, but it was better for them to think he was still knocked out.

He went over the attack in his head: The two men in the telephone repair uniforms with the guns, the five men in black, the driver, and Vance. Eight men—professionals, obviously—and Vance. That meant nine men, nine captors. Those were *not* good odds.

He listened to the low voices, determined they were in front of the van and decided to open his eyes slightly to take in his surroundings.

He opened his left eye and recoiled.

The wetness he was feeling on the side of his face was blood, oozing blood. The blood dripped from a ghastly bullet wound between the eyes of a very dead Trooper Elliot Vance, his mouth open, slack-jawed in muted surprise.

Gale cautiously looked around and saw an open black duffel next to Vance's body. Black masks and tubing poked out of the bag and Gale instantly recognized the objects as rebreathers, apparatuses—used by divers or special operators—that absorb CO_2 and convert it into breathable oxygen.

The van began to slow. He snapped his eyes shut and the van stopped. Doors opened and closed. He heard the back door open. Someone grabbed him by the shirt collar and slapped him across the face. Gale opened his eyes.

A man in a black ski mask knelt over him.

"*A ty govorish' po russki?*" the man asked. Do you speak Russian?

Gale didn't say anything. He was noting the three other men standing at the door. In the distance he could hear the intense whine of a jet engine. The air was salty and humid. They must be near the ocean.

Gale was ripped from the back of the van, and forced to stand, as they tore the tape from his mouth. He looked around, saw they were on a black runway. A sleek-looking jet sat a hundred feet away.

The man repeated his question, then spat, "*Konechno, u vas.*" Of course you do.

The man wrenched his ski mask from his head. His scalp was shaven, his face blocky, a giant scar running down the length of it.

Scarface took a tablet from his tactical vest, snapped a series of pictures of Gale, then said, "We have your bitch daughters, you will see them soon. It will be family reunion."

Gale felt terror consume him; he balled his fists and shot his arms up, striking the man in the nose. Blood spurted out, but the man didn't react. He just wiped the blood on his sleeve and then struck Gale across the face.

"You hit hard for old man," Scarface said. Then he leaned forward and whispered in his ear, "Don't you, Mr. Gaines?"

Gale couldn't help himself, his eyes widened in horror. This was impossible, how did they—

"Where the hell are my daughters?!" Gale roared and tried to fight off the men, but they held him tight.

Scarface smiled and took a syringe from his pocket, yellow liquid floating in the vial.

"We have long trip ahead of us. This will help you relax."

The man thrust the needle into Gale's neck and depressed the plunger. Gale yelled. Scarface grabbed him by the back of the head. "Viktor Sokolov is looking forward to seeing you at the sharashka."

Gale clutched at the man and felt his limbs grow heavy. The drug acted fast, making his world tilt.

Three of the men dragged him toward the plane and Scarface poured gasoline in the van and lit a match.

Flames engulfed the black van as Gale struggled for consciousness.

Viktor Sokolov.

The sharashka.

His past had come for him.

Everything he'd feared, everything he had run from had come for him.

They had his daughters.

Now they had him.

Chapter 40

THE DRUG IN his system kept Gale conscious but his body was sluggish, his muscles so heavy he could barely lift a finger, let alone keep his head upright.

He was placed into a white-leather sequined captain's chair in the back of the ornately styled private jet; with his head lolling over his chest, he was doing everything he could just to stay awake. Scarface barked orders to the other three men and a scared-looking captain who scurried into the cockpit. Gale willed himself to keep his eyes open.

He envisioned Cassie's face. She needed him. Emily needed him.

He couldn't let these men take him. His odds were better now, only five, including the pilot, to contend with; the others must have been left behind.

Scarface glanced at his tablet. "Team Three has secured the subject and are rendezvousing with Team Two for secondary extraction. It's time to go."

Gale noticed that the men each had a holstered pistol in their tactical vests.

MP-443 Grachs—a classic Russian special forces weapon—a Spetsnaz weapon. Semiautomatic, effective at close range with an eighteen-round magazine.

How the hell did they find me? How do they know who I really am?

The name the man had whispered in his ear, a name he hadn't heard in nearly three decades.

Viktor Sokolov.

Gale's eyes flashed on that fateful night thirty years before. The night that changed everything. *The night Viktor Sokolov—*

The jet engines whined loudly, and the plane lurched forward. The men took their seats in front of Gale, paying him no attention.

Gale knew that this plane could not get to its destination, or he would be a dead man; Cassie and Emily would be dead too.

He knew what Sokolov was capable of. He knew what Sokolov would do to him and his family.

The plane turned on the runway, and Gale fought for control of his head, fought to look out the window. Outside he could see the ocean. He determined he was somewhere southeast of Anchorage, past Alyeska, Portage, or even Whittier. Or maybe he was north of the city, there was really no way to tell. The engines roared. He was pressed into the back of his seat as the plane barreled down the tarmac, into the air, and out over the ocean.

Scarface turned around in his seat and checked on Gale as they ascended. The operator to Gale's right took off his ski mask and rubbed at his scalp. Gale immediately clocked the pistol hanging from the man's tactical harness, dangling under his armpit. It was literally two feet away, just across the aisle.

If only Gale could move his body.

He shut his eyes, trying to regain control of his faculties.

Seconds passed. Minutes—yet the drug held him like a vise.

Focus, dammit!

His mind zeroed in on the pistol.

More minutes passed, and Gale felt the jet level out. He strained his eyes to see outside the window—they weren't that high up. Maybe seventeen thousand feet. He wondered why they were flying so low—was it to stay out of radar? No, radar could pick them up at this altitude. From what little he knew about flying—having gotten his pilot license nearly two decades before—radar had trouble picking up a plane's transponder under a thousand feet and over fifty thousand feet. Out of the window he saw a small island to his left, its rolling green hills a stark contrast to a sea of blue. A brown landing strip bisected the island, which looked deserted and uninhabited.

It was now or never. Gale had to act.

He'd need adrenaline to counteract the drug.

He focused on the rage he'd felt thirty years ago. What Viktor Sokolov had done to him, what Sokolov had done to his wife, his asset—the family Sokolov murdered like animals—what Sokolov had intended to do to his daughters.

Move, dammit!

Gale felt that rage grow, proliferating from somewhere deep within—he willed the control of his arms, his legs!

Move!

His fists balled, his arms twitched, and his legs jolted.

He already mapped out the next ten seconds—they'd made a huge mistake by zip-tying his wrists in front of him.

His focus narrowed to the task at hand—his rage kicking his adrenals into overdrive—overtaking the effects of the sedative.

Gale's eyes snapped open and his hands flew in the direction of the Russian's gun. He snatched the pistol before the man could react, flicked off the safety, racked the slide, and put two in the side of the man's head.

The noise was deafening, the man's head snapped sideways. On his feet now, Gale fired two precise shots into the skulls of the other two men.

Scarface jumped to his feet, standing in front of the cockpit door, his AK-15 assault rifle in hand, aiming at Gale.

Gale fired.

Scarface jumped out of the way—Gale's bullet punched through the cockpit door and the plane immediately jolted to the left—sending Gale back into his seat—he ducked, making himself small on the ground.

Scarface returned fire, a volley of bullets pierced the window above Gale's head. A great sucking noise erupted in the cabin and a hole the size of a basketball appeared where the window had been. Gale plastered himself on the floor as bullets punched through the floorboard, the walls, and seats.

Alarms blared, as the plane rattled violently and pitched downward.

Face to the ground, Gale peered down the cabin, under the seats, and saw Scarface's boots. Gale aimed. Fired.

The Russian screamed and hit the ground, Gale fired again, two in the chest, one in the head. Clambering to his feet, fighting the centrifugal forces of the diving plane, Gale made it to Scarface's dead body. He unsheathed his tactical knife from the Russian's belt and cut his zip ties, then wrenched open the cockpit door and felt a wave of dread overtake him.

The captain sat in one of two seats, slouched over the control wheel, a gaping bullet wound in his neck—Gale's rogue bullet. The control console featured four computer screens, all flashing like broken Christmas tree lights.

A paralyzing moment passed as Gale supported himself against the cockpit's doorframe and dropped the Russian's pistol. He'd been trained to fly small airplanes—single-engine aircrafts—but this jet looked as complicated as driving a Formula-1 race car.

Gale heard another alarm blare—the fuel gauge—and watched the altimeter drop faster. He yanked the dead pilot out of the seat and dragged him back into the cabin, then flung himself into the captain's seat and buckled himself in.

Numbers flew across the screens, and the control wheel in front of him shook violently. He pulled on the captain's headset. Out of the front windows, he could see the ocean coming closer. The altimeter read just above fifteen thousand feet.

Gale tried to remember the universal emergency frequency his instructors had him memorize back in flight school. Was it 121.7 or 121.5?

He spun the red frequency dial in the middle of the console, tuned it to 121.5, and pulled back the control wheel as far back as possible, all the while keying his mike on the headset and screaming, "MAYDAY, MAYDAY."

Hoping to God someone would answer.

En Route Air Traffic Controller Andrew Martin of the flight service station in Juneau poked his head above his computer monitor and peered out over his cubicle to make sure his supervisor, Boyd Jenkins, had left the small control room for lunch.

Sure enough, Jenkins was gone.

Andrew sat back down in his chair, reached a hand into his desk drawer, and pulled out a small bag of pretzels. It was strictly forbidden to eat while on shift, and if caught, he would be fired on the spot. But it had been a boring morning, both for radar readings in southeast Alaska and for monitoring the emergency frequency.

Plus, Andrew Martin was starving.

He'd slept through his morning alarm and had missed breakfast and had to drive like a madman to the FSS to make his shift on time.

Jenkins wasn't thrilled when he showed up ten minutes late, but Andrew made up for it by covering Jenkins's lunch hour. He knew Jenkins liked taking long lunches. And by long lunches, he meant Jenkins liked to chain-smoke cigarettes behind the building.

Andrew took a handful of pretzels from the bag and stuffed them into his mouth, before his attention turned back to the radar screen.

The monitor showed the radar readout that covered the southern tip of the Chugach National Forest and the eight hundred square miles of 3-D airspace over the Gulf of Alaska. As a civilian en route air traffic controller, it was Andrew's job to watch and communicate with aircrafts via the push-to-talk radiotelephony unit at his station if the need ever arose.

It rarely did.

Actually, it never did.

This was a boring job in a boring part of the world and Andrew knew it. At thirty-one years old, Andrew had gotten his air traffic control license with subqualifications in the disciplines of en route control (both radar and nonradar), and approach radar, and aerodrome with the intention of getting a cushy job at the Anchorage airport. It had always been his dream, but his OJTI, his on-the-job training instructor, had been a hard-ass in Anchorage, and Andrew had failed the training. His dream of one day working in an aerodrome at a major airport crumbled. Hence the reason he was stuck in a dusty control room in the Juneau FSS manning the civilian emergency frequency away from all the real action.

Andrew gazed down at the registered flights that were supposed to cross into his airspace over the course of his shift. A private prop was scheduled to pass through in an hour on its way to Seward and a 737 out of Anchorage would be heading through in two hours on its way to Seattle.

A boring afternoon.

Andrew was about to grab another handful of pretzels when a crackling urgent voice cut over the emergency frequency line.

"MAYDAY! MAYDAY!"

Andrew nearly jumped out of his chair in surprise. He keyed the push-to-talk button on his headset, and in a higher voice than usual said, "This is the Juneau flight service station—"

"MAYDAY!"

The problem with the push-to-talk radiotelephony units was that only one transmission could be made on a frequency at a time. That was why air controllers and pilots adhered to a strict code of communication while talking to each other.

Andrew waited for the emergency frequency line to go quiet, then repeated, "This is the Juneau Flight Service, please state your emergency."

"My damn plane is going down, I'm losing fuel, and I don't know how to fly the damn thing!"

Andrew sat there for a paralyzing moment, and then nearly laughed at the absurdity coming over the frequency. Was someone screwing with him? Was this a joke?

"—GODDAMMIT CAN YOU HEAR ME?!"

The terror in the voice made Andrew Martin realize that this was no prank. Andrew sat forward, his eyes flying over his blank radar screen.

"I can hear you! Please state your location and tail number. You are not coming up on my radar!"

"I don't know my damn tail number! Everyone on board is dead and I'm trying to fly a jet that's dipping into the ocean!"

It took a moment to process what the man on the emergency frequency just said. *Everyone on board is dead?*

"I need instructions on how to fly this damn thing!"

Andrew, his mouth agape, stared at his radar readout. There was still no aircraft showing in his airspace. Surely, the US Navy and Coast Guard would be picking up this transmission. Their communication lines were much more sophisticated than any civilian instruments—but still, if this man was telling the truth, Andrew would need to alert them immediately.

Andrew took out his iPhone and called Jenkins who answered on the first ring.

He gave him sparse details of what was happening and told him to get back immediately and that both the Coast Guard and Joint Base Elmendorf-Richardson in Anchorage needed to be contacted at once.

He could tell Jenkins was flabbergasted on the other line and Andrew could almost envision him stomping out his cigarette and his rotund frame sprinting back into the building.

As Jenkins hung up, Andrew thumbed the headset mike again, "Okay, sir. I need you to tell me what kind of aircraft you are flying so I can help you."

॥॥॥

Gale had no idea what type of jet he was attempting to fly. His arms strained as he fought to keep the control wheel pulled back and the plane flying as level as possible. He was halfway succeeding. The plane was still losing altitude, but at a much slower rate than before. The altimeter showed he was still above thirteen thousand feet.

"I told you, I don't know what type of plane I'm in. I barely know how to fly and this cockpit looks like something out of Star Wars."

"Look for a flight manual in the cockpit. It will be a big binder."

Gale looked around the cockpit and didn't see anything.

"It will usually be under the captain's seat or between the seats."

Gale looked down to his right and saw the spine of a thick blue binder wedged between the two pilot seats. He picked it up and flipped to the first page of the manual. "It says it's a Gulfstream G650!"

There was static over the line.

Gale yelled, "HELLO?"

"One second, sir!"

Gale swore out loud, wondering what was wrong.

॥॥॥

Andrew muted his headset as Boyd Jenkins ran into the room. "I alerted Elmendorf—what's going on?" Jenkins stopped behind Andrew's workstation, trying to catch his breath.

"Do you know anyone who knows how to fly a Gulfstream G650?"

Jenkins turned pale. "That's what this guy is flying?"

The Gulfstream G650 was a modern marvel in the realm of private aircrafts. With the price tag of sixty-five million dollars, the G650 had a seven-thousand-mile range, could fly up to six hundred miles an hour, and required specialized and experienced pilots behind the controls.

"HELLO?!"

Andrew turned to his boss. "Would anyone upstairs know how to fly one of these?"

Jenkins shook his head. "I need to get in contact with Elmendorf again. The military is going to have to take over."

As Jenkins started hurrying away, Andrew stood and yelled, "What am I supposed to tell him?"

"Try to get him flying in a straight line. Find his altitude, his speed, get him using his flaps. Elmendorf is going to have to figure out where the hell he is and why we can't find him on radar!"

Chapter 41

COLONEL RICHARD C. Wallinger closed his weekly PACOM intelligence briefing and leaned back in his chair, daydreaming about his upcoming day off. He envisioned himself taking his Cessna out and exploring the Kachemak Bay State Park south of Anchorage. It had been almost a month since the colonel had had a day off and he was feeling the itch to decompress.

As the commander of Third Wing at Joint Base Elmendorf-Richardson, or JBER, Colonel Richard C. Wallinger was one of the highest-ranked air force officers on base. His office, which sat in the base's main compound, was large and lavish—appropriate for a man that held such power.

Most of his colleagues would have been miffed if they were assigned to this desolate corner of the world, but not Wallinger. He was done with the high-stress environment of deployment, of the crazy hustle and bustle of an overwrought base.

JBER offered a repose to a colonel who fought his way to the top, and to Wallinger, this assignment as commander of Third Wing was the top. Compared to his time overseas, he was now a man in control, a commander virtually left alone by his superiors.

So it was a surprise to Wallinger when his office door burst open and General William Bressant barged in followed by a slew of aides.

Wallinger jumped to his feet and saluted the general—the highest-ranking officer at JBER—and wondered what could have caused the broad-shouldered behemoth of a man to muscle in unannounced.

"What can I do for you, General Bressant?"

"Colonel Wallinger," Bressant said. "We've got a situation. Your expertise is needed in CAOC"—the Combined Air Operations Center—"a vehicle's waiting outside."

Before Wallinger could reply, the general turned on his heel and hurried out.

After a moment of stunned silence, Wallinger caught up to the general in the hallway.

Without stopping, Bressant said, "A few minutes ago we received a call from a civilian air traffic control supervisor out of a flight service station in Juneau. They received a distress call over the civilian emergency frequency." Bressant walked outside and climbed into the back of a jeep. Wallinger climbed in next to him, and Bressant ordered the driver to step on it.

Bressant continued, "Control said they were talking to a man who was piloting a G650 who didn't know how to fly the damn thing. He said there were casualties on board. Supposedly, the aircraft is severely damaged and going down."

"Where is the aircraft?"

"That's the problem. It's not showing up on radar. Pilot thinks he's over the gulf, but he's losing fuel quickly and needs instructions on how to land."

Wallinger suddenly understood why he was summoned. He was familiar with Gulfstream jets. Years ago, he'd worked as a military liaison to the Gulfstream company and even test-piloted various engine systems for them. That's why he was summoned: he knew how to fly the G650; they wanted him to help the pilot land that plane.

Wallinger said, "What is the navy doing to find the plane?"

"They've got three naval vessels using their high-tech radar searching for it now."

"Why did the Juneau traffic control pick up this distress call and not the navy?"

"Unclear."

"Is the navy speaking to the pilot?"

The jeep stopped in front of the CAOC building and the general climbed out. "No, that responsibility will fall on you."

Wallinger swallowed hard, but he was up for any challenge. "Are we viewing this as a possible threat, General?"

"A jet is traveling without its transponder on, we've got a man in the cockpit who can't pilot it, you're damn right we're viewing this as a threat. Our F-22 Raptors will be launched to intercept as soon as we locate. Then you're the one who will help that sonofabitch land, do you think you can do that?"

||||||||||||||||||||||||||||||||||||||||||||||||||||||||||||||||||||||||||||||||

The Juneau air control operator who had now introduced himself to Gale as "Andrew" was in the middle of instructing him on how to engage his wing flaps when a powerful voice overtook the emergency frequency.

"JBER to unidentified aircraft. This is Colonel Wallinger of the United States Air Force, do you copy?"

Gale, who had been keeping the control wheel steady for the last twelve minutes as Andrew ran him through basic diagnostic and instrument checks, said, "I copy, Colonel."

"State your name and the nature of your emergency, pilot."

Gale swallowed. "My name is James Gale; I already explained to the—"

"Explain it to *me*, Mr. Gale. All we know here is that a Gulfstream G650 is somewhere over the Gulf of Alaska and it is not showing up on radar and there are casualties on board."

That was pretty much the gist, Gale thought, but added, "I was kidnapped in Anchorage, brought on a jet by my assailants and was able to fight them off. Now I'm the sole survivor. The plane is losing fuel and altitude and there is a hole in the fuselage."

"The plane was still at a reasonably low altitude when the fuselage was compromised?"

"Correct, the plane was still flying low even fifteen minutes after takeoff."

"And where did you take off?"

"That I don't know. I was hoping you could figure it out for me."

"Were there any identifiable landmarks you saw, any landmarks you see now?"

Gale flashed back to seeing the small island with the landing strip they'd flown by right before his assault on the Russians. He told the colonel about the island, and then the colonel had Gale read off his ground speed, altitude, and magnetic heading as well as tell him about any alarms the systems on the jet were reporting.

After two minutes, the colonel alerted Gale that a navy vessel had located the jet.

"We're sending two F-22 Raptors to intercept. They will be at your location in five minutes."

"Intercept?"

"Standard operating procedure. They will piggyback with you back to land. They're a precaution and our eyes in the sky, do you copy that?"

Gale said he did, but didn't like the idea of jets with missile capabilities hanging too close to him.

"Colonel," Gale said. "I'm not sure how I am going to be able to land this thing, I've only been trained to fly single engines."

"You let me worry about that, Mr. Gale."

||||||||||||||||||||||||||||||||||||||||||||||||||||||||||||||||||||||||||||||||||||||||||||||||||

Wallinger stared at the bright monitors on the wall in the CAOC room and watched as a green blinking dot showed up almost one hundred nautical miles southwest of Middleton Island in the Gulf of Alaska. The navy had found the plane.

Bressant stood next to him and put down a phone. "F-22s just took off, intercept will be in four minutes."

In all his years in the air force, abroad and at home, this was truly one of the most peculiar events of Wallinger's career. He couldn't believe he was about to instruct a man who barely knew how to fly a prop plane to now land a G650 with a compromised fuselage.

But the longer Wallinger thought about it, the more he recognized that he was truly the right man for the job. The colonel had clocked more than a thousand hours in Gulfstreams over the years and could fly one with his eyes closed.

Wallinger muted his headset and announced to the room of military air traffic controllers and technicians: "I want a list of potential places to land away from the civilian population that are safely within the bounds of the G650's leaking fuel supply. Account that the G650 needs a landing strip distance of six thousand feet." He then turned to Bressant and asked, "Has the Coast Guard been notified?"

Being at the top of the food chain at JBER, General Bressant was not used to a subordinate running the show, especially a colonel. But Bressant was an adaptable man; he understood the fog of battle, understood that in dire situations it was best to let the right man take the helm and lead.

Bressant hung up a phone on the control board after conferring with the Coast Guard. "They're ready. They just need to know where the G650 plans on landing."

A controller to Wallinger's left stood up. "Sir, I crunched the numbers; we only have one option and it'll be cutting it close. With the limited fuel, the aircraft will never make it back to the mainland. It's going to have to land on Middleton Island."

"You're sure?" Wallinger asked.

"Positive."

Two other controllers confirmed the math.

"But there's a small problem," the controller said. "Middleton's runway is only four thousand feet long. The G650 needs at least—"

"Six thousand."

"Yes, sir."

Wallinger swore and tried to figure out what he was going to say to James Gale.

"Mr. Gale, do you remember what I told you about the reverse thrusters and wing flaps?"

"I do."

Wallinger rubbed at his brow. "You're going to land on that island you saw. I'm going to need you to turn the plane around and then you are going to listen to me very carefully."

||||||||||||||||||||||||||||||||||||||||||||||||||||||||||||||||||||||||||||||||||

Gale was starting to feel fatigued. His adrenaline rush was wearing off, and his arms burned while he tried to keep the compromised jet from losing more altitude.

He glanced at his altimeter: seven thousand feet and dropping.

He hoped to God this Colonel Wallinger knew what he was doing when suddenly he heard what sounded like a rocket blow by him. The G650 wavered slightly as two lightning-fast gray masses shot by Gale and then banked around for another flyby.

"We've received word the F-22s made intercept?"

"Jesus Christ!" Gale bellowed, not believing the speed of the jets.

"They're going to come up beside you and then lead you back toward the island, do you copy?"

Gale said that he did. Thirty seconds later the F-22s slowed to either side of him.

"Move the control wheel to the right, Mr. Gale. Then ease the power lever like I told you and follow the F-22s."

Gale watched as the jet to his right tipped sideways and veered out of sight. Gale took a deep breath and followed.

"Now the power lever, just a little bit."

Gale eased the power lever forward and kept the control wheel cocked to the right until the lead F-22 appeared back in his sight line, then Gale leveled the plane back out.

Six thousand feet.

"Good job, Mr. Gale."

"Am I going to have enough fuel to get to the island?" Gale asked, noticing that his fuel gauge was dangerously redlining.

"You're one hundred and fifty nautical miles out. You'll make it. No more throttle, we'll keep the speed low and start engaging those flaps."

|||||||||||||||||||||||||||||||||||||||||||||||||||||||||||||||||||||||||||||||||||

General Bressant muted Wallinger's headset for him. Bressant said, "Coast Guard is thirty minutes out from Middleton. What are your ideas on landing this thing?"

Wallinger thought for a minute. It was good that the G650 would virtually have no fuel by the time it got to Middleton, meaning the jet would be lighter and easier to stop on the short runway. Plus, less fuel meant less chance of an explosion in the event of a crash. As for the landing, the G650's autopilot had automatically disabled itself with the loss in cabin pressure due to the hole in the fuselage.

But Wallinger thought he had a way for James Gale to land the jet. "The G650's autopilot can be engaged for landings. The computer is sophisticated enough. The pilot will just have to be able to engage it when he gets to one thousand feet."

"And if the autopilot can't be turned on?"

"Then he'll have to land the jet himself."

|||||||||||||||||||||||||||||||||||||||||||||||||||||||||||||||||||||||||||||||||||

Fifteen minutes passed with Wallinger instructing Gale on how to lower the landing gears and how to land the jet in case the autopilot failed. As the plane limped to three thousand feet, Wallinger had Gale deploy the landing gears in an attempt to create more drag and slow the G650.

It worked, and nearly twenty miles in the distance, Gale could see the brown-and-green hump of Middleton Island coming out of the seemingly endless blue waters.

Gale shot a furtive glance to the F-22s at his flanks. He knew his fate would be decided in a matter of minutes, because the autopilot would either engage or it wouldn't. If it didn't?

Gale tried not to think about that, but it was impossible. If he crashed this damn jet and died, both Cassie and Emily would meet an excruciating death at the hands of Viktor Sokolov. Gale flashed back to that dreary Moscow night a lifetime before—when he'd found Sokolov's victim outside the US Embassy. Then his mind flashed to that day on the Finnish-Soviet border, the ambush—the bodies falling, the pictures he found pinned to the bodies. Then his mind wandered to Paris—what Sokolov had done to Gale's late wife, Irina—what Sokolov had intended to do to his young daughters.

No matter what happened, dead or alive, Gale wouldn't let Cassie and Emily die at the hands of that monster.

The odds of him landing this plane were slim; he knew the landing strip was too short. He knew even if he survived the initial landing, that the plane would surely continue off the tarmac and into the field beyond, or potentially off the island and into the ocean. Gale made a decision.

"Colonel, are you there?"

"I'm here, Mr. Gale."

"How many people are listening to this frequency?"

"Just us, Mr. Gale. And my colleagues in the room with me."

"You trust them?"

"With my life. Why?"

"If this ends badly, I need you to get in touch with someone."

"This won't end badly, Mr. Gale."

"Just listen to me." For the next minute, Gale told the colonel who he needed to contact, what had happened, and what to do in the event of his death.

Gale could hear the disbelief in the colonel's voice when he finally replied, "I . . . I will Mr. Gale. I will make sure they are contacted."

The jet dropped below two thousand feet, Middleton Island growing bigger and bigger. Gale felt like he was just on top of the waves; he tested the flaps again and looked down at the brakes and buttons he would have to press if the auto-pilot wouldn't engage.

At fifteen hundred feet, the F-22s peeled away, leaving Gale alone in the cockpit with only Wallinger's voice.

"Are you ready, Mr. Gale? Do you have any questions before you engage the autopilot?"

"No."

Twelve hundred feet.

Perspiration poured down Gale's face and he eased the plane to a thousand feet. Middleton Island was less than two miles ahead. The landing strip was a long brown stain.

"Engage now!"

Gale pressed the autopilot button hoping to God this sixty-five-million-dollar hunk of metal was up for the challenge.

Five seconds passed.

Ten.

Seven hundred feet.

One mile away.

"It's not engaging."

He heard the colonel swear over the frequency, then his voice became sharp and urgent.

"Okay, no problem, Mr. Gale, I'm going to coach you through this." Wallinger led him through which buttons to press, which switches to flick, and how to compress the brakes one last time.

Three hundred feet.

Gale flew over Middleton's shore, the runway just ahead.

"Flaps! Flaps! Slow the jet!"

Gale triggered the flaps and the jet tilted.

Two hundred feet.

One hundred.

Fifty.

Twenty-five.

The front wheels smacked onto the runway and the plane bounced.

"BRAKES!"

Gale smashed on the brakes, did exactly what the colonel had told him to do, but the plane was going too fast, it was tilted too far to the left side.

Gale put all his weight onto the brakes. Metal crunched as the port wing collided with the tarmac—the momentum turned the plane to the right side and Gale felt himself go weightless as the jet pitched into the air.

He closed his eyes, covered his face, and was blasted with the loudest noise he'd ever heard.

※※※※※※

Wallinger glanced over at General Bressant. The big general had his eyes glued to the screens on the wall.

A controller stood. "F-22s are reporting a crash landing."

Wallinger said, "How far out is Coast Guard?"

"Fifteen minutes, sir."

General Bressant took off his headset, handed it to Wallinger, said, "I need to contact the Northern Unified Command immediately."

"Sir?"

Bressant leaned in close to Wallinger. "If one iota of what that pilot said was true, we've got a problem. A big problem. I've got to follow protocol on this one."

The general rushed out of the room.

Wallinger turned back to the screens. "Any sign of life on that island?"

※※※※※※

Gale's face was warm.

Sunlight streamed through the cockpit's spider-webbed window. He blinked, took in the erratic beams of light flooding through. The headset had been thrown from his head, lying in pieces by his feet, and the cockpit's contents were strewn about.

Gale unlatched himself from the seat and slowly got to his feet. His head hurt, his vision was blurry.

Taking a moment to steady himself, he went into the cabin. The place looked like a bomb had gone off. The dead Russians and the pilot lay like rag dolls over the seats. One was propped up against the wall: it was Scarface.

Gale stood over the man, bent down, and grabbed the black tablet in its Velcro holder from Scarface's tactical vest. As he went for it, he noticed a satellite phone was strapped next to the tablet. Gale snatched both items and planned on using them when he got out of the wreckage, but first he needed to do something.

Gale took off Scarface's tactical vest and threw it aside, then he grabbed the dead man's undershirt and took that off as well.

Scarface's chest showed a myriad of scars and battle wounds; clearly he was a seasoned soldier. But Gale wasn't looking for scars. He raised the dead man's right arm, exposing the inside of his right bicep.

And there it was, the confirmation Gale needed.

The small, almost imperceptible, "*V*" tattoo. The tattoo etched on every KGB and now SVR Vympel Group operator in the world. Russia's most deadly covert assassins. *Viktor Sokolov's most deadly assassins.*

After all these years, Sokolov is still alive and these men are still operational.

Gale let Scarface's arm drop and he walked over to the door, pulling on the red emergency release lever. After a moment of struggling, the door blew open. Gale jumped onto a patch of dirt and hobbled away from the wreckage.

He tried turning on the tablet first, but nothing happened. Next, he went for the satellite phone, which chimed on immediately.

He punched in Emily's phone number. Straight to voice mail. Same with Trask's. Gale started feeling sick to his stomach. He called Petit's number and the old cowboy answered immediately.

"Alvin, it's Jim—"

"Jim, oh Jesus, something's happened." For the next minute Gale listened to his old friend's frantic voice on the other line. When Gale eventually hung up, he found himself on his knees.

Gale dropped the phone and took in the wreckage. The G650 was missing both its wings and horizontal stabilizers. The fuselage looked like a crumpled tin can and small electrical fires blossomed from numerous holes in the galley. Gale determined the plane had skidded and tumbled a good thousand feet beyond the runway after the crash.

Rotors thumped in the distance and Gale could see a red blur of a Coast Guard helicopter on the horizon.

He had a couple minutes before they got here.

They have Cassie.

They have Emily.

Trask is—

Gale reached into his back pocket and took out the folded envelope he'd taken from the green lockbox underneath the floorboard in his office.

What lies ahead can't be done alone.

His fingers trembled as he unfolded the envelope and took out the contents.

The horrid photographs gazed up at him; they were just as he remembered them. The cruelty of the pictures and what they symbolized. What they led Gale to do.

He sat down in the grass, looked at the photographs for another moment, and then put them back in the envelope, leaving only the worn, bone-white card. He flipped the card over and gazed down at the phone number scrawled in pen on the back.

After thirty years of escaping his past, it was time to confront it head on.

It was time for James Gale to die.

And Robert Gaines to live again.

He dialed the number on the satellite phone, pressed it to his ear. As it rang, the Coast Guard helicopter got closer.

The roar of the two F-22s cracked like thunder in the distance.

When the ringing stopped, he heard a click, and then the familiar animatronic woman's voice say:

"Station. State your call sign."

"This is PEGASUS. I need to speak to Susan Carter and Prescott McGavran. Tell them it's about Striker. Tell them Robert Gaines is blown."

Gale talked for thirty more seconds and then hung up just as the Coast Guard helicopter touched down on the field next to the crash site.

He lay down in the tall grass and stared up at the blue sky, his eyes misting over—hoping to God someone from his old life would answer his cry for help.

Chapter 42

IT HAD BEEN a hell of a day for Susan Carter and it was only going to get worse.

The sixty-six-year-old Tennessee native stood in her office on the seventh floor of the old CIA headquarters building and took a swig of expensive sour mash from a tumbler as she gazed out over the Potomac River in the distance, her mind reeling from the call she'd received on a burner phone from Prescott McGavran nearly thirty minutes before.

Susan, turn on the news to the footage of the plane crash in Alaska. It's concerning Striker and PEGASUS. Meet me in the executive SCIF in forty-five minutes. Speak to no one until we talk.

As the director of the Central Intelligence Agency, Susan Carter was not a woman who was easily rattled, but the surprise call had shaken her to her very core.

She turned from the window and stared across her office at the flat-screen on the wall where a news anchor talked over a live feed of a plane crash on Middleton Island just off the coast of Alaska. So far, local authorities were reporting *multiple deaths* and *one survivor*. The aerial footage showed the crumpled features of a Gulfstream jet, rescue crews, and an FBI team surveying the wreckage.

What the hell is going on? What does this crash have to do with Striker? What does this crash have to do with PEGASUS? The man has been dead for over thirty years.

Deep in thought, Carter traversed her office, downing the rest of the bour-
bon. It had been over three decades since she'd heard the cryptonym PEGASUS.
Over thirty years since she and her old boss Prescott McGavran, the legendary
spymaster and former Moscow Chief of Station, had run their deadly agent in
the Moscow streets.

Eight months before, Susan Bradford Carter had been appointed by the
young new president, William McClintock, to be the first woman to head the
CIA. The president—a former marine himself—liked what he saw in Carter, especially when it came to her views on foreign policy. Due to the decades Carter
spent abroad at the behest of the United States government, she understood the
world much differently than the pencil-pushing bureaucrats in Langley. She understood the nuances of the United States' enemies: China, Russia, North Korea,
and of course those thugs in office in Iran. Not to mention the hornet's nest that
was the Middle East and the proliferation of ISIS in Africa and Southeast Asia.

President McClintock became a fan of Carter after her first interview for
the D/CIA position. Carter, the then deputy director of counterintelligence, had
detailed to McClintock how China needed to be strictly monitored, how Russia
couldn't get away meddling in US affairs and that their dictator, Vladimir Putin,
only understood one language, and that was force. After she had mapped out how
the CIA would deal with the rising terrorism and tyranny abroad, McClintock
appointed her to the position and three weeks later, Susan Bradford Carter was
confirmed by a majority vote in the Senate—designating her to the coveted role
of D/CIA.

With the proverbial glass ceiling shattered at her feet, Susan Carter, nick-
named the *Ice Queen* by her subordinates, began her aggressive foreign intelligence campaign.

So far, it was going splendidly.

That was until Prescott McGavran's alarming message came over her burner
phone thirty minutes before.

A knock on the door tore Carter's attention from the news as her special
assistant, Jack Crowley, poked his head into her office. "Ma'am, I know you said
you didn't want to be disturbed—"

"Is my detail ready to take me to the SCIF?"

SCIF was the acronym for a Secret Compartmented Information Facility, a
secure room where secret information could be passed along without having to
worry about electronic surveillance or data leakages.

"Almost, ma'am, but the associate director of military affairs, Werner Monroe, is outside trying to see you."

"I'm not speaking to anyone."

As she said it, Werner Monroe pushed past Jack Crowley and barged into

Carter's office. The AD/MA's face was flushed with stress. He held up a USB in his hand.

"Ma'am," Monroe said, "we've got a big problem that requires your immediate attention." His eyes flicked to the television. "The Northern Unified Command has been calling me nonstop to get ahold of you. There is a situation in Alaska."

Carter steadied herself against her desk, McGavran's words reverberating in her head.

PEGASUS. Striker. Speak to no one until we talk.

She had ten minutes until she would meet the old spymaster in the SCIF and she didn't intend on speaking to Monroe, but the panicked look on the AD/MA's face made her relent. She ordered Crowley outside and shut the door.

"What is it?"

"Ma'am, the Northern Unified Command has received a recording from a general at JBER in Anchorage. The recording came from a pilot aboard a private jet"—Monroe indicated the crash on TV—"that jet."

"And why does this concern me. Shouldn't that be the FBI's problem?"

"That's the thing, ma'am, before that plane crashed, the pilot asked to get a message to you," Monroe said, putting the USB on her desk.

"I'm sure there are a lot of quacks out there trying to get ahold of me, Monroe."

"Ma'am, the pilot says he's an old agent of ours. Robert Gaines."

"Robert Gaines is dead," Carter said, trying to keep her voice restrained, but knowing the cat was out of the bag.

"I know that, ma'am. I checked—"

"Thank you, Werner," Carter said, grabbing the USB. "Wait outside."

Carter waited until the door closed, put the USB into her computer, and opened the encrypted zip file. Blood was starting to pound in her ears, as the fear of what she might hear on the audio bubbled up within her. Her finger hovered over her track pad for a moment, then she pressed play. A crackling of static sounded, followed by the voice of a man she thought dead long ago.

"Just listen to me, Colonel. I need you to get a message to Prescott McGavran and Susan Carter at the Central Intelligence Agency. Tell them it's about the Striker program. Tell them that it's their old agent, Robert Gaines, tell them I've been compromised. That PEGASUS has been compromised. Viktor Sokolov and his SVR Vympels have found me. Tell them that the Russians have been kidnapping Americans off American soil and that they took my daughters. Tell them that they are taking them to the sharashka. Tell them if they don't do something, Viktor Sokolov will kill them."

Carter stared at her computer, Robert Gaines's words detonating in her head like fireworks.

All these years Prescott McGavran had been lying to her. The deception was incalculable. Robert Gaines was alive! But not only that, he'd brought the darkest chapter of Susan Carter's professional career back to light. For a full minute, Carter sat in disbelief at her desk and wondered how Prescott McGavran, a *now* low-ranking analyst within OREA, the Office of Russian and European Analysis, had known so quickly about Robert Gaines. Had he hacked into some military channel and heard this before her? Or had PEGASUS contacted him directly as well?

Carter snatched the USB from her computer and marched out of her office. Crowley jumped up from his desk, his phone pressed to his shoulder. "Ma'am, DNI Nagle is trying to get ahold of you."

Monroe, his own encrypted cell phone against his ear, cupped a hand over the receiver. "I've got the office of the SecDef asking for you, ma'am."

The cat is surely out of the bag.

Carter stopped in the middle of the room. "Tell each of them I will speak to them in thirty minutes." Fast-walking out of the reception room and into the hallway, she told her security detail to follow her into the private elevator reserved solely for her and pushed a button for the fifth-level basement.

As the elevator descended, she clutched the USB tight in her hands and closed her eyes, trying to compartmentalize all that was going on. As the elevator reached its destination, the doors opened, and she walked down the sterile white hallway to a door that led to the CIA's executive SCIF. She scanned herself in and told her security detail to wait in the hall. Stepping inside, she saw the hunched figure of Prescott McGavran waiting for her at the table in the long white room.

Carter wasted no time sealing the airtight doors. When the SCIF pressurized, she sat at the table across from the old man.

Prescott McGavran wore a tweed jacket and pushed his bifocals up along his long crooked nose, his white hair combed perfectly over his head. A steel-plated briefcase was handcuffed to his left wrist, which sat on the table between them. "Madam Director—"

"Oh cut the crap, Prescott. Just what in the name of Christ is going on?!"

Chapter 43

A SHARP, STABBING pain ricocheted down Cassie's left arm and thrust her out of a deep, dreamless sleep. She sat up abruptly and grasped at her upper arm, which was covered with heavy bandages. IV lines ran out of each of her forearms and she realized she was sitting on a gurney in a room that looked like a mad scientist's laboratory.

A computer monitor flashed from a table across from her, displaying a 3-D rendering of a human brain that constantly changed color. It took a moment for Cassie to realize that dozens of wires and electrodes hung down from her scalp.

"Don't touch them!" Artur ordered, turning away from the computer monitor; his face sported a deep five o'clock shadow. He moved to her and forced her hand away from the throng of wires she had attempted to wrench from her head. "How is the pain?"

Suddenly, it all came back to her. The trial. The firefight on the mountaintop. Billy cowering behind the large boulder and Brady firing at the prisoners. Cassie remembered the searing pain of a bullet entering and exiting her arm, then she remembered being surrounded before the drones had fired down upon them with the knockout gas.

"It hurts."

"I can fix that," Artur said, grabbing a syringe and injecting it into her IV line. "You just tell me if you need any more."

Cassie immediately felt a warm wave flood over her body and she relaxed. Artur stood over her and gently put a hand on her forearm.

"*Bez prikosnoveniy!*" No touching, a voice shouted. A black-clad, armored guard came into Cassie's field of view, grabbed Artur by the shoulder, and shoved him away. Artur pointed a finger at the guard's Kevlar vest and spat at him in Russian, making the guard retreat toward the door.

"Where are Billy and Brady?"

"Red Block," Artur said, returning back to the computer monitor that showed the 3-D image of the brain.

"Are they okay?"

"They're fine. You're lucky the bullet didn't nick your brachial artery. Another centimeter to the left and you would have bled out."

Cassie sighed and relaxed even more as the drug fully took hold. She smiled with the euphoria it brought and then began to take in the room. It was unlike any other room she'd seen in the facility so far. It was cluttered, filled with sophisticated-looking lab equipment. Pictures of the human brain covered the walls. A futuristic chemistry setup took up a massive workbench, and behind the workbench, Cassie could make out a small nook that housed a bunk.

"This is where you live?"

"Most of the time," Artur said, without turning around. "I prefer it over the residential rooms. Nobody bothers me here."

Cassie contemplated the guard that stood blocking the door, his blacked-out visor reflecting the gadgets and gizmos in the room. The guard tilted his chin up toward the ceiling and then directed his gaze at Cassie. It was the first time she had seen a vulnerable space in the guards' protective attire—they usually wore a Kevlar neck wrap and sported a weapon, a Taser or a nightstick. "He doesn't bother you?"

Artur turned. "Who, him? No."

"Does he always watch you like this?"

"Only if a subject is in the lab."

"Can he understand us?"

"The guards only understand Russian and their thinking is limited to orders given to them by Captain Yermakova through her earpiece comm link."

Cassie studied the guard. "They don't ever rebel?"

"Their brains have been surgically and chemically castrated. The connectivity of their frontal and parietal lobes to that of their basal ganglias are completely altered."

"They're lobotomized?"

"It's much more sophisticated than that. Their motor functions remain intact, but they have no sense of free will."

"How can you be so sure of that?"

"Because I both invented and carried out the procedure on each and every one of them."

Another wave of euphoria cascaded through Cassie's body as she tried to understand what Artur had just said. The drug flowing through her veins felt unlike anything she'd ever experienced before. She'd been given opioids by an army doctor once after she'd broken her ankle. The opioids had made her feel groggy, but this drug was different. "What did you give me?"

Artur swiveled in his chair, offering a faint hint of a smile. "You like it?"

"Very much."

"It's a little cocktail I constructed—an opioid derivative that activates all the pleasure centers of the brain but doesn't affect the prefrontal cortex. Meaning you still have your faculties—you feel clearheaded do you not?"

"I feel amazing." And Cassie did. Her mind wasn't foggy in the least; in fact, she felt razor sharp. "You know your chemistry."

"My father was the brilliant chemist. It's just a hobby of mine." The scientist seemed oddly eager to talk, and with the clearness of the drug coursing through Cassie's veins, a plan began to form in her mind.

"Is that my brain?" Cassie asked, pointing at the computer monitor.

"It is."

"In real time?"

"Yes."

"Why are you studying it?"

"I'm accumulating data for my research."

Cassie thought back to when she was in the brightly lit room with Yermakova after her first encounter with the two tattooed men. She remembered Yermakova talking about her fMRI results—that Cassie's brain was a bit of an anomaly—she decided to go with this. "When I was first brought here, Captain Yermakova said my brain responded well to the stress of combat. What did she mean?"

"Ah," Artur said. "Most people who go through highly stressful situations, like combat for instance, become victim to changes in their brain chemistry. Certain parts of the brain get overwhelmed, and other parts have to overcompensate. Every brain has different neural pathways, so every brain reacts differently to stressful stimuli."

Cassie tried to recall her sophomore-year biology class. "Like fight or flight?"

"Exactly."

"And that's what you study? Why some people fight and some flee?"

"It is a component of my studies, yes, but not the main component."

Cassie could see that Artur was dying to talk about his work so she kept prodding. "What are you trying to achieve?"

Artur took a proud breath. "The state has provided me with an inimitable environment not seen anywhere else in the world. An environment where I can study human beings under the pressures of live combat. At this facility I can study the subjects far away from the concerns of ethical, legal, and social impacts that would otherwise hinder my research in a modern society. Because of that, I have achieved more here in a decade than most scientists could possibly achieve in five lifetimes. Just look what I've done with the guards." Artur walked back to his desk, collected his tablet, and returned to his chair. "Your file says you lost your husband to suicide, correct?"

"Yes."

"He was a veteran, multiple deployments to the Middle East. He suffered from PTSD?"

Cassie suddenly felt a wave of emotion and her throat constricted. She nodded her head.

"Yes, a most unfortunate silent killer. And also why I was sent here."

"To study PTSD?"

"To wipe it out entirely. To make sure no Russian soldier, no person who ever falls victim to neurological trauma ever has to go through what your husband went through." He pointed to his computer monitor. "I've studied *thousands* of subjects at this facility. From psychopaths to the average Joe—as you Americans say. I've been able to map their brains before they've entered their trials and have been able to study their brains after. Over time, I've spotted recurring patterns in a subject's response to stress. Through neuroimaging and neurointervention I've been able to dampen the negative effects of PTSD in suffering subjects, and I'm currently on the precipice of total and complete eradication."

"Neurointervention? You give them drugs?"

"Think back to your last trial, you killed a man, did you not?"

"Yes."

"And what did you feel?"

"Nothing, but I didn't have the time to think."

"And how is your mind responding to it now?"

Cassie scrunched her eyes and tried to understand what Artur was saying. Honestly, she still hadn't had the time to think about the fact that she had killed someone. "I . . . I don't know."

Artur indicated the live 3-D rendition of Cassie's brain. "From the time you came here, even before I stitched up your arm, I conducted tests and mapped out your brain. After your indoctrination trial with the two prisoners, you were mapped again. There were no neural changes whatsoever."

"What does that mean? I'm a psychopath?"

"Far from it, actually. You exhibit none of the traits of a psychopath or even a sociopath—you display, in what we call in the world of neuroscience—guarded higher-brain functions. Your ventromedial prefrontal cortex, your amygdala, and your hippocampus all work the way they should during fight-or-flight stimulation, but unlike the vast majority of the population, those parts of your brain are able to return unchanged to an *unstressful state* much faster than normal."

"I am like this naturally?"

"No, you've been given the *intervening drug*."

"When?" Cassie asked, shocked.

"When you first arrived here. Your results are showing promise."

"So I won't get PTSD?"

"It's hard to say. It will take many more trials to get a legitimate data sample."

Cassie looked down at her injured arm and thought for a moment and then said, "But what about Yermakova's game? Doesn't that disrupt your data samples? The subjects must die in the trials all the time, there is no way to control what happens out there."

"I am not a fan of Yermakova's game. It is no secret, but it was the deal I had to accept when I was sent to this place."

"So what? You have a problem with Yermakova's game, but you don't have a problem with injecting humans with chemicals and sending them against their will to die? You don't have a problem lobotomizing these guards?"

Artur tilted his head. "I am a scientist, Subject 8831. I am also a prisoner at this facility just like you, but that doesn't mean I am not a human being. I am making the most of my situation. I have the opportunity to change the world. I have the opportunity to save millions."

"You are a *brainwashed* prisoner," Cassie said, pointing at the guard. "You've created the guards. The very thing that watches you and holds you captive. If that's not brainwashed, I don't know what is."

Artur tensed; Cassie had obviously struck a nerve. "Miss Gale, since I was thirteen I was taken from my family to be educated and controlled by the state. My existence has been confined to one sharashka or another, the only link to my family are these letters." Artur placed a heavy hand on a mound of letters sitting on his desk. "Years ago, the state offered me a deal: cure PTSD and get my freedom back. Here I have a goal, here I have a drive to succeed, a drive to get out of this place and back to my mother and sisters."

Cassie gazed at the troubled scientist, whose hand still remained on the stack of letters. Cassie said, "You have been a prisoner your whole life and you've never tried to escape? You've never tried to fight your way out, get back to your family?"

"Of course I have!" Artur snapped. "When I was a boy I tried to escape every week, but I never made it off sharashka grounds. The state sees everything, Miss Gale."

Since the beginning of their conversation, Cassie had been casing the room for the next component of her plan. She'd noted the surgical equipment on the tray, two arm's lengths away from her gurney, especially the surgical knife. But one thing she also noticed was the lack of cameras in the laboratory.

"The state doesn't watch you in here, do they?"

"No, here I have my privacy. A certain level of trust has been established between myself and Yermakova. Occasionally my minder watches me." He flicked his head toward the unarmed guard.

The minder you created, Cassie thought, but said, "So Yermakova doesn't completely trust you."

"I don't hold it against her. There is an old Russian saying: *Trust but verify.*"

Cassie thought about that for a long moment, then went back to something Artur had said earlier. "What about your father?"

"What about him?"

"You said he was a chemist; was he also a prisoner of the state?"

"At Marfino, yes."

"And what does he think about his son being a prisoner at Yermakova's facility?"

"My father died when I was a boy, an explosion in his lab."

"I'm sure he would be sad that his son had to live out a worse existence than him. Why was he able to have a family and not you?"

"Enough!" Artur spat and stood. "We've talked too much." He walked over to Cassie, pulled the wires and electrodes from her head and took out the IVs.

When his face got close enough, Cassie whispered, "Help me get out of this place."

"There is no getting out of this place, Subject 8831."

Artur motioned to the guard, barking something in Russian. The guard approached Cassie and dragged her onto her feet. Cassie pretended as if her legs couldn't hold her weight and stumbled forward, landing over the surgical tray. Fingers folding around the surgical knife, she spun lightning fast, sunk the razor-sharp blade deep into the fleshy part of the guard's unprotected neck, and sliced sideways.

Hot, crimson blood erupted from under his helmet and the guard grabbed at his throat and stumbled back, knocking over a surprised Artur. Cassie moved fast, grabbing Artur by the scruff of his lab coat.

The guard's legs kicked violently then stopped moving.

Cassie brought Artur in close. "We're underground, right? You're going to show me a way to the surface. I'm getting the hell out of here."

Chapter 44

"I THINK WE might have a problem, Susan," McGavran said.

"No shit we have a problem! I just heard a dead man's voice spilling compartmented secrets to an air force colonel in Alaska, for Christ's sake!"

The old spymaster gazed at Carter from behind his bifocals as he reached into his tweed jacket and pulled out a microcassette player. He placed it on the table next to the steel briefcase and arched a bushy eyebrow. "Excuse me?"

"Robert Gaines is alive! PEGASUS is alive?!"

"He is," McGavran said. "What do you mean you heard him spilling compartmented secrets?"

Through gritted teeth, Carter explained that the Northern Unified Command had given her AD/MS Werner Monroe a USB of Robert Gaines's distress call addressed to them. She held up the USB for McGavran to see. "You have ten seconds to explain what the hell is going on, Prescott, or so help me God."

"What would you like me to explain first, Susan?"

"Let's start with how Robert Gaines is still alive! Then maybe you can explain to me what the hell is going on in Alaska."

"Robert is alive because of me. He is alive because I hid him and his family after the events in Moscow. I gave his family a new life. New names and a fresh start."

"Why?!"

"You know why."

"Robert Gaines has a star on the memorial wall upstairs. He died in the Khimki Forest!"

"That's what everyone was led to believe."

"Then what the hell happened in '87?"

"For now that is not important. We need to focus on what is happening at this very moment." McGavran fingered the microcassette player. "At 1400 hours eastern time, I received a call on an old encrypted analogue line known only to me and Robert Gaines. I set up this line as a direct mode of communication if Robert ever needed to get in contact with me. For over thirty years that line was silent. That was, until this afternoon."

McGavran pressed play on the ancient microcassette player and Carter heard Robert Gaines's voice again:

> *"This is PEGASUS. I need to speak with Susan Carter and Prescott McGavran. Tell them it's about Striker. Tell them Robert Gaines is blown. Viktor Sokolov found me. Russian Foreign Intelligence found me. Vympel teams kidnapped my daughters. They're taking them to the sharashka . . . I need help, dammit . . . there was a plane crash off the coast of Alaska, I'm the sole survivor. I'll likely be taken into federal custody in Anchorage. I repeat, I need help. I need to speak with Susan Carter and Prescott McGavran."*

The message was nearly identical to the message Susan Carter had heard on the USB. For thirty seconds, the director of the CIA stared down at the microcassette player. Then she said, "Sokolov. The sharashka, do you think he's talking about—"

"Post 866."

"Can any of this be confirmed?"

"I recently got off the phone with Jim Brower at the FBI's Foreign Counterintelligence Division. He spoke to the director of counterterrorism at the bureau who confirmed that a private jet crashed on Middleton Island off the coast of Alaska this morning. Five dead, one survivor. The pilot was identified as James Gale."

"His alias?"

"Yes."

"And is he in federal custody?"

"He was treated for injuries in Anchorage, and yes, he's currently in federal custody at the FBI's office in Anchorage and I've been unable to get in contact with him. An FBI counterintelligence team led by Jim Brower as well as a counterterrorism unit is en route to Anchorage as we speak. Turns out the plane that Robert crashed was flying east over the Gulf of Alaska and had no tail number, no transponder, or black box, and according to FBI special agents on scene, there were weapons and devices on board that suggest the deceased were all foreign operators."

"They died from the crash?"

"Bullet wounds."

"Robert's work?"

"Does that surprise you?"

"No. Have the deceased been confirmed as SVR Vympels?"

"They all had the tattoo. I spoke with a contact in the NSA; the feds have run facial recognition software on them—two of the dead came up as matches on the Interpol database. These guys are tied to black operations in Syria, assassinations in Israel and Chechnya. Known SVR Vympels."

Carter took another long moment to think everything through. She felt betrayed by her old friend, the man who had taught her the art of tradecraft, the man she looked up to.

Robert Gaines died over thirty years ago. I grieved for him, I grieved for his late wife, and now after everything that had happened, he's alive.

And not only alive, he was supposedly in a hell of a mess with one of the most dangerous men in the world. *Viktor Sokolov. Vladimir Putin's mentor.*

Every cell in Carter's body screamed at her to force McGavran to tell her everything that had transpired in Moscow but that would have to wait.

"If what Robert Gaines is saying is true, that means—"

"It means that Russians are operating on United States soil."

"That's an act of war."

"It is."

Carter cursed. "How did they find Robert in Alaska of all places?"

"Brower also notified me of another unfortunate incident. A shooting in the township of Eagle in northeast Alaska this morning. Turns out, Robert's youngest daughter, Cassandra, went missing in that area last week. I believe he was looking for her."

"You think the shooting and the plane crash are connected?"

"The FBI is in the process of connecting those dots. But we do know that his eldest daughter, Emily, is now missing and his son-in-law is in critical condition in Fairbanks. That has been confirmed."

"Jesus."

McGavran tapped the steel briefcase with his fingers. "Susan, I believe Robert's message was right on the money. There is no reason for him to lie, and I don't believe this is an isolated incident. I believe the Russians have been taking Americans from US soil for a while now, just like the rumors swirling in the Soviet days. Considering the events that transpired today, I'd say there is enough evidence now to support my theory."

Carter took in the OREA analyst and shook her head in disbelief. Prescott McGavran should have had a spectacular career given his skill set in the field, but it had all fallen apart after the Striker program debacle. While Susan Carter had escaped with her career intact, Prescott McGavran had been fired from his role as Moscow Chief of Station and was subsequently demoted to headquarters to work a desk job for the rest of his career.

"What are you talking about, *your theory?*"

McGavran's fingers drummed the briefcase again, and for the first time, Carter sensed anxiety in the old man.

"What's in that briefcase, Prescott?"

"A pet project of sorts."

"What sort of pet project?"

"After the Striker program was abolished, I continued its OVERDRIVE case file on my own."

Carter's eyes grew wide in disbelief. The Striker program they ran in the eighties was a clandestine operation to find Post 866, the rumored medical sharashka run by General Viktor Sokolov and his son, Evgeny. The program was established by President Reagan after various foreign sources provided intelligence that the Soviets had a secret installation that experimented on Americans, mostly soldiers captured in war zones and sold to the Soviets.

Striker had been established by the Reagan administration as a *cutout* CIA program because of its sensitivity. It was an off-the-books operation; no State, no Justice, or oversight committees. The money to run the operation was siphoned through offshore proxies and the only individuals who knew of its existence were Reagan's inner circle and the CIA agents running it. Textbook for plausible deniability.

All the HUMINT and SIGINT intelligence gathered by the Striker program was consolidated into a compartmented case file, code-named OVERDRIVE. During the six years that Striker was operational, Prescott McGavran and Susan Carter updated the White House personally on the OVERDRIVE case file. And while the location of Post 866 had nearly been discovered, it had all fallen apart in the winter of 1987.

"The OVERDRIVE case file was destroyed, Prescott. Reagan saw to that personally."

"I know."

"So excuse me if I'm a bit lost. But *how* exactly did you continue OVERDRIVE on your own?"

"I made a copy before I was demoted. After the winter of 1987, I thought I was done in the agency. The fact that Director Casey gave me a desk job in OREA, where I had access to Russian intelligence, was a blessing. Yes, I would never be officially operational again, but given the resources I still had, I felt like I owed it to those who were killed."

"You ran a private investigation behind the agency's back?!"

"For thirty years, yes," McGavran said. "I couldn't let it go, Susan. After I hid Robert, after what the KGB did to those families, after we got so close to finding the sharashka, after everything that happened—"

"You understand what will happen to you if this gets out, don't you?"

"Of course," McGavran said. "I will lose my job and almost certainly be investigated and probably indicted for using CIA resources for my own personal gain. That being said, I think you should see what I have gathered. If what Robert said was true, if Sokolov and his Vympels have kidnapped his daughters and are taking them to the post, I believe you should look at the contents of my updated OVERDRIVE case file."

"Why?"

"Because I believe I might have finally located Post 866 and you are not going to believe what the Russians are doing there."

Thirty minutes later, after McGavran finished his detailing of the OVERDRIVE case file, Carter stared at him, dumbstruck. "Why wasn't this brought to my attention sooner, Prescott?!"

"Because until I heard Robert's distress call, I was gathering evidence based on speculation. Now we have a firsthand account."

"You firmly believe Post 866 is located at these coordinates on the Kamchatka Peninsula, at this old Soviet missile silo, the location you've dubbed in OVERDRIVE as Site X?"

"Without a doubt."

"If I take this to the National Security Council, they are going to ask for more proof. They are going to want *concrete* evidence that the Gaines girls are at Site X."

"Then I suggest we give them that concrete evidence."

"How?"

"Look at the patterns I've detailed in OVERDRIVE. Somehow the Russians bring Americans across the Bering and into the Kamchatka Peninsula. We don't know the exact mode of transportation, but we do know about the increase in activity at the Russian-owned Gazprom oil rig off the coast of the peninsula."

"You mean the Russian stealth helicopters?"

McGavran took the specific paper from OVERDRIVE and placed it before Carter. "Precisely. Somehow, the Russians get their victims across the Bering. It could be by boat or even by submarine, I don't know. What I do know is that I have imagery of Russian stealth helicopters arriving at the Gazprom oil rig. I have imagery of them picking up packages and then flying to Site X, before returning to Vladivostok. Emily Gale was abducted eight hours ago, if we put our spy satellites on the Gazprom oil rig and Site X, I'd be willing to bet we'd see a stealth helicopter arrive at the rig, then fly to Site X. It could be in a couple hours, or it could be a couple days, but I guarantee that's what we'll find."

"Do you know what that would cost, Prescott?"

"Don't patronize me, Susan. I understand the nuances of satellite telemetry. I also know that someone in your position could order that, no questions asked. Go talk to the geospatial and imagery directors in analytics—they can get the Keyhole images we need."

Carter wasn't convinced. "But we still wouldn't be able to determine if Emily Gale was on that stealth helicopter. For us to intervene, we'd have to have definitive proof."

"Ah," McGavran said, looking pleased with himself. "I have a plan for that, too, but we'd need to get Robert to DC as soon as possible. I don't think it'll be hard to persuade Robert, but the president and the National Security Council will be a different story."

"Bring Robert to DC?"

"Of course. His presence will be crucial in persuading the powers that be that we need to take direct action."

For the next fifteen minutes, McGavran detailed his plan to Carter. When he was done, Carter sat silent for a long beat and then stood, heading for the door.

"Where are you going?" McGavran asked, loading the papers back into the OVERDRIVE case, before following her out of the SCIF and into the hallway.

The basement hallway was flooded with Carter's security detail and members of her staff. Jack Crowley, her special assistant, ran forward. "Ma'am, DNI Nagle is ordering you to contact him, the chief of staff is calling for an emergency meeting at the White House—"

"Chairman Bridgewater is asking to speak with you, ma'am," Monroe half shouted.

Carter motioned for McGavran to unlock OVERDRIVE from his wrist. He took off the cuff and handed both the keys and briefcase to Carter. "Crowley, give me your hand."

The flustered special assistant raised his arm in confusion and Carter locked the briefcase to his wrist, then said, "Monroe, I want you to get me a direct line to General Bridgewater, now."

"What about DNI Nagle?" Crowley asked.

"Nagle can wait. After I speak to Bridgewater, get ahold of Director Connelly at the FBI." Carter turned to McGavran. "You are going to go to Andrews Air Force Base."

"Why?"

"Because I want *you* to be the first person Robert sees when he lands. Go with him to the Hoover Building."

"You're going through with it?"

"He's crucial for your plan, is he not?"

McGavran nodded.

"I'll convince Connelly that Robert needs to be in DC."

"How will you pull that off?"

"You let me deal with that," Carter said, turning and fast-walking to the elevator.

"What about the satellites?" McGavran shouted after her.

Carter pivoted and faced the old spymaster. "I am going to speak with the directors in analytics now."

Chapter 45

GALE STARED AT the two-way mirror in the small interrogation room at the FBI's Anchorage building and tried rubbing the soreness out of his wrists. The handcuffs that had been slapped on him were too tight, but he had yet to find an agent to loosen them.

After Gale had called the secure line to his past life, he'd sat down in the tall grass and broken down. Within minutes, the Coast Guard had arrived and flown him to Alaska Regional where he was examined, treated, and then released to the FBI.

Special Agent Burke was the agent in charge, and together with a slew of other agents, Gale had been taken back to the Anchorage FBI building, the same building he was talking to Earl Marks in not nine hours before.

Gale had bombarded Burke with questions of what had happened in Eagle. During Gale's conversation with Petit before the Coast Guard had arrived, Petit had told him that Trask and Maverick had been shot and Ned's crew and a group of men had reportedly abducted Emily.

Burke was reluctant to share information, but he said there was an FBI team on the ground investigating the events in Eagle as they spoke.

Burke was completely in over his head.

The whole Anchorage office was.

After an hour of trying to get answers out of Gale, Burke was called out of the interrogation room for a couple of minutes. He soon came back in.

"Mr. Gale," Burke said, "I've received word that our DC office is sending a QRT up here to take over this investigation." Gale knew that QRT was an acronym for the FBI's Quick Response Team that dealt with the investigations after a terrorist attack.

Good, Gale thought. *Finally some competent people on this.*

"I am flying to Middleton Island to meet the QRT. I've also been ordered to keep you here until agents from DC arrive. I'm leaving Earl Marks here to watch over you."

That had been three hours ago, and since then Gale had not seen a single agent, let alone Earl Marks.

Gale bided his time, going over everything that had transpired in the last week. His mind kept going over what Scarface had said that very morning.

Viktor Sokolov is looking forward to seeing you at the sharashka.

Then his mind floated to the conversation he'd had with Petit after the plane crash. Gale wondered where the old cowboy was now, how Trask and Maverick were doing. Surely, the FBI had leads on the Vympels operating in Eagle. Surely, they'd been able to track down the Northern Breeze crew.

He spent his time either staring at the two-way mirror that made up the left side wall or into the lens of the dated security camera that blinked green from its perch in the corner of the ceiling.

He watched the blinking light on the camera, counting the seconds between each blink, hoping that his emergency call to Langley had reached its desired target when the green light suddenly stopped blinking entirely.

Gale frowned and shot a glance to the two-way mirror, just as the door opened and Earl Marks came in and shut the door behind him.

He held two steaming cups of coffee and placed one before Gale as he sat down opposite him. Only then did Gale realize that Earl also held a series of orange folders under his arm.

Gale's eyes shot to the camera.

"Don't worry," Earl said. "We're not being watched. Everyone has been running around like chickens with their heads chopped off. We've got some time."

"You cut the video feed?"

"And made sure nobody was behind that glass."

"Why?"

"To talk."

"What the hell is happening in Eagle?"

"The FBI is investigating a shooting and kidnapping."

"Any leads on Emily?"

"Not yet."

"What about my son-in-law, Peter Trask?"

"Your son-in-law is currently in emergency surgery in Fairbanks. They're talking about life-flighting him to Anchorage."

"What about what we talked about this morning? The Vance lead, the Northern Breeze—did the FBI find the van with Vance's body? What about getting security footage of my kidnapping?"

"They've got the footage but aren't letting anybody see it. They did disclose that they found Vance's body," Earl said, "at an airfield outside of Whittier. The van was torched, like you said it would be."

"And what about the Voigts and their crew?"

"They are keeping information tight, but I was able to learn that two people were found dead in a truck just outside of Jack Wade. They have not been able to identify the bodies."

"Ned and Darlene?"

Earl shook his head. "Two males."

"What else have you found out?"

"Remember the picture of the canister you showed me? The one found in Cassie's campsite?"

"I do."

"The FBI have found an abandoned Chevy truck, burned like the van we found Vance in, in Jack Wade next to an old gold dredge. The dredge had a locked garage connected to it. The FBI opened it and found dozens of those canisters loaded with some sort of unidentified propellant. Inside the garage were also these strange black bags we've been unable to identify."

"A stash. Probably Ned and Darlene's."

"It looks like it."

"How did they know to look inside?"

"They've taken into custody the Eagle VPSO, a man named—"

"Max Tobeluk."

"Yes," Earl said. "This VPSO led them to the garage in Jack Wade and then to a makeshift airstrip behind the gold dredge."

"They must have used the airstrip to fly Emily out. Have they been able to identify any planes coming out of the area?"

"No, but all major airports in Alaska are on shutdown. Only a small plane would have been able to take off from the little landing strip. Air traffic control is working overtime, but it'll be like finding a needle in a haystack especially since there are thousands of landing strips in Alaska."

Gale thought back to his own abduction. Why hadn't the Vympels waited for their other team with Emily to show up? When Gale was grabbed and shoved into the van, he had counted eight men, plus Vance. Only four of those men got onto the jet. So where were the other four? Had they waited for the other Vympel team to meet with them, then had they gotten on another plane?

Gale voiced this concern to Earl. "Have there been any other planes, any jets that have taken off this afternoon from Alaskan airspace?"

"Not that we know of," Earl said. "After your crash, the navy has been taking severe precautions in surveying both the Gulf and the Bering with their radar. Nothing of note has showed up. Just a—"

"Just a what?"

Earl leaned forward, his big belly bumping into the table. "A dock manager reported a boat missing from his marina. A fifty-foot power troller, called the *Lady Alaina*. Its captain is also missing."

"Is that rare?"

"Supposedly, yes. The Coast Guard enforces strict rules on both captains and dock managers to keep a log of their schedules. The *Lady Alaina* was supposedly seen leaving the harbor last night and never returned—no paperwork was ever in the books for the troller to leave the marina."

"Has the FBI looked into this?"

"They currently are."

Gale motioned to the orange files Earl had brought in. "What did you want to talk with me about?"

"I'd like to continue the conversation we had this morning. I want you to know that I did find Paul Brady's credit card statements for the week before he disappeared in Chicken."

"And?"

"Paul Brady *did* stay at the Northern Breeze a couple days before he disappeared. And that's not all, I cross-checked over six hundred missing person reports that were filed in that region in the last five years and found that nearly sixty of those persons had passed through the Northern Breeze—and these were the ones I've been able to track through credit card statements."

"How many of those MPRs were investigated by Trooper Vance?"

"Thirty-eight."

"How was this not caught before?"

"You have to understand that there have been nearly twenty thousand MPRs filed in Alaska in the last decade."

"So what now?"

Earl shifted in his seat. "From what I've been able to find, the Voigts purchased the Northern Breeze Lodge and Smoke House Bar roughly eleven years ago. So far, I've only been able to cross-reference five years of MPRs that coincide with the missing who had stayed at the Northern Breeze."

"So the Voigts could have kidnapped over a hundred people?"

"Probably more than that, Mr. Gale. Again, we are only seeing those who have a digital credit card trail linking them to the Northern Breeze. Most likely *many* more people have fallen victim to Ned and Darlene Voigt."

"How many do you estimate?"

"I'd put my estimation between two hundred and four hundred."

"Jesus."

"The only question is, where are these people being taken?"

Gale shuddered. Could it really be true that Viktor Sokolov and the Russians had taken up to four hundred American citizens to the sharashka? Were the Vympels assisting with the kidnappings each and every time?

"Have you given this information to your superiors?"

"I have, yes, but with everything going on, I'm not sure how seriously they are taking it." Earl was quiet for a moment. "Those men on the airplane, they weren't Americans, were they?"

"Correct."

"They were Russians?"

Gale looked up and met eyes with Earl. "How did you know?"

"Our agents on scene in Middleton called in the QRT right after they secured the scene. The weapons, the AK-15s they found are notoriously used by Russian Special Operations Forces. The technology found, the tablets they had on them, were encrypted, but our tech guys were already able to find that they were using a Tor network connecting back to Russia."

Gale nodded.

Earl said carefully, "You know more than you are letting on, Mr. Gale. Burke said that they took a satellite phone and a tablet from you after the crash. You called a number, a number that has since been disconnected. Who were you calling?"

"I was calling the only two people on earth who could possibly help me get my daughters back."

Suddenly, there was the sound of footsteps from the hallway. Gale glanced up and saw the camera was blinking green again. The door to the interrogation room burst open and an incredibly tall man entered the room followed by agents wearing blue FBI field jackets.

The tall man flashed a badge indicating he was with the bureau. "What is going on here?"

Earl closed the orange files and put them under his arm. "I am the agent in charge of watching this man in custody and who might you be?"

"My name is Special Agent Jim Brower with the FBI's Foreign Counterintelligence Division."

"The FCI? What's your business?"

Brower produced a sheet of paper from his jacket pocket and handed it to Earl.

"I've been ordered to escort this man to JBER and take him by flight to Washington, DC."

Gale nearly jumped out of his chair. "No! I need to stay here."

Brower ignored Gale. Earl, who was still squinting at the sheet of paper Brower had handed him, said, "This says that FBI director Connelly has ordered Robert Gaines to the FBI offices in DC. Who is Robert Gaines?"

Gale suddenly felt hopeful; his distress calls must have worked. Susan Carter or Prescott McGavran must have gotten his messages. "I'm Robert Gaines."

Brower put his badge back into his jacket pocket and gave a look like he knew *exactly* who Gale was. He indicated for his agents to take Gale.

Gale said, "Wait a minute; have you spoken to Susan Carter or Prescott McGavran?"

Brower didn't reply.

"You're not really taking me to the FBI offices in DC, are you? You're taking me to them."

"I've been instructed by Director Connelly to take you to DC—"

"Then you need to take him as well," Gale said, indicating Earl Marks. "McGavran and Susan Carter need to hear what this man has to say. He is crucial to all of this. He is the one who records the missing up here. He has evidence that my daughters are not the only ones who have been taken. Please, call whoever you need to call, but this man needs to come with us."

"I have my orders to escort only you."

"Special Agent Brower," Earl said. "Mr. Gale is right. If I could just speak with you for a moment, I could clear a few things up." Earl marched out of the room, and Brower reluctantly followed.

Five minutes later, Brower came back into the room followed by Earl, who held a large cardboard box in his arms. Brower said, "You got your wish, let's go."

They were escorted outside to a caravan of black SUVs and Gale was pressed between two burly agents in the back of one SUV while Earl and Brower sat in the bench seats in front of him.

They made it to JBER in ten minutes and parked in a hangar next to a busy runway. Gale was taken out of the SUV and was told to stay put.

A green military jeep pulled up to the hangar and two high-ranking officials climbed out of the back.

The bigger of the two marched up to the group. "Special Agent Brower? I'm General Bressant, this here is Colonel Wallinger," he said as he pointed to the serious-looking man standing next to him.

Gale looked up when he heard Wallinger's name and the two locked eyes.

"I can't imagine what you boys are going through, today," Bressant said. "But we're here to help in any way we can. When I got the call from Chairman Bridgewater that an escort plane was coming in from Nevada and needed to take precious cargo to DC, I had no idea we'd be in for such a treat."

"I would like to thank the air force for supplying the plane to the FBI, sir," Brower said.

Bressant looked at Gale for a long moment. "Well, it looks like larger things are at play. Larger than I could begin to understand." He jacked a thumb over his shoulder. "Plane's this way, follow me."

The agents marched Gale out of the hangar and hooked a right. The loud whine of a jet engine consumed the group and Gale nearly gasped when he looked out to see one of the sleekest-looking jets he'd ever laid eyes on.

"The Lockheed YF-8," Bressant bellowed over the sound of the roaring engine. "Technically, it doesn't exist, but it'll get you from Anchorage to DC in under two hours."

Chapter 46

SOKOLOV SCREAMED IN rage and threw his glass of vodka at Dmitry, hitting the man square in the face, making him drop his tablet and yelp in pain.

"What do you mean, Robert Gaines has escaped! They made it on to the plane, did they not?!"

Dmitry wiped the vodka from his watering eyes and leaned against a plush leather captain's chair within the private jet that was escorting them all to Vladivostok—Russia's easternmost military base.

According to the in-flight map on the backs of the luxury seats, they were forty minutes from their destination. They had been in the air for nearly nine hours from the time they'd left Moscow, and Sokolov was getting angry, drunk, and impatient.

Sokolov grabbed Dmitry. "What the hell happened? I thought Teams One and Two secured Robert Gaines and Team One had boarded their flight with him!"

"They did!" Dmitry yelped. "Right after we got confirmation that they secured the target, there was a plane crash! The American press is reporting that there is only one survivor."

"Is Robert Gaines the survivor?"

"I don't know!"

Sokolov pushed Dmitry to the floor, then used his cane to beat the seat next to him in fury. The rest of Sokolov's detail sat in the front cabin of the plane, all staring fearfully at their boss. This would certainly complicate things. It wouldn't be long before the Americans would be able to identify the dead Vympel operators for who they really were. And only a matter of time before the information would reach President Putin.

"How can we determine if it was Robert Gaines who survived?"

Dmitry got slowly to his knees. "I can reach out to our assets within their FBI to try to get the name of the survivor."

"Do it." Sokolov breathed like a bull and waited for his rage to subside as he watched Dmitry poke away frantically at his tablet. After Sokolov caught his breath, he said, "And what about Team Three? Were they able to accomplish their mission?"

Dmitry nodded furiously. "Team Three successfully captured their target and eliminated KODIAK. They rendezvoused with Team Two and are currently en route to the sharashka."

"How far out?"

"Roughly thirty hours."

"Thirty hours!" Sokolov spat. "Alert them to take measures to speed that up! I want the second Gaines daughter at the sharashka by the time we arrive. Surely, even those idiots in the GRU have measures to expedite a subject!"

Dmitry nodded furiously again and kept tapping away on his tablet.

"How long until we are at the sharashka?" Sokolov asked.

"Another half hour to Vladivostok. Then we will switch jets and head to Petropavlovsk-Kamchatskiy. Once there, it is an hour via the helicopter to the sharashka. Roughly four hours, General."

"Contact Captain Yermakova. Alert her of my arrival time and that of the expedited Gaines girl. Tell her that her GRU team is to use whatever means necessary to get the daughter to the sharashka as quickly as possible."

"*Da*, General!"

Sokolov slumped back into his seat. Robert Gaines had eluded him again. His plan to torture his daughters in front of him just like Gaines had done to him all those years ago with his dear Evgeny was now squandered.

Sokolov would just have to play with the cards he'd been dealt; he'd have to cash in on his consolation prize.

He still had the daughters.

He could still get his revenge.

A memory crept up in his mind. An event that he had almost forgot. He thought of that traitorous scientist who had almost blown the lid off Post 866 those many years ago.

He remembered the pictures Evgeny had taken.

The pictures.

That's what Sokolov would do.

He would take pictures of the daughters as they participated in his torture techniques. He would take pictures and then he would send them to Robert Gaines.

That would be his revenge.

. How did those Americans say it?

A dish best served cold.

Chapter 47

CAPTAIN YERMAKOVA CLOSED her eyes and sighed deeply as the hot water and the scent of lavender relaxed her hectic mind. Mozart's Fifth Symphony played in the background of the elaborately decorated bathroom in her executive living quarters deep within the sharashka.

When she had gotten permission to rebuild Post 866 and turn it into a place for science and sport, she had also decided that the place needed some sprucing up.

When the president had given the green light to reconstruct the sharashka, Yermakova had insisted on taking *siloviki* funds to create a lavish executive wing just in case any of the *siloviki* wanted to visit—or maybe even the president himself.

In the eleven years since the completion of the new Post 866, only a dozen of the *siloviki* had ever visited, and even fewer had participated in what the sharashka had to offer. At first, many of the *siloviki* had been more than enamored enough to try their luck against a Black Dolphin prisoner, or even a captured soldier from the West.

In the beginning it was a big hit. Hunting another human being was all the talk among those in Putin's inner circle, but once one of them (a coal minister) had been killed in a trial, the others had simply lost interest and focused on gambling from a safe distance.

Their loss, Yermakova thought as she breathed in the lavender scent and relaxed even more. Without the *siloviki* coming in and out of the sharashka, Yermakova got to take full advantage of the "executive wing." Its decadence rivaled that of the Kremlin and she got to enjoy it all to herself. Truly, she would miss it when Putin welcomed her into his inner circle, but surely, once she was a member of the *siloviki*, she would become more than accustomed to extravagance.

That was, if she could survive the visit of General Viktor Sokolov.

It was Sokolov's message nearly three hours before that had caused Yermakova to go into a tailspin of stress and anxiety from which she sought refuge in the hot water of her gold-winged bathtub.

Viktor Sokolov and his men had alerted her that they were nearly four hours away from the sharashka at the time, and that an SVR Vympel team was en route via a GRU submarine in the Bering Sea carrying an unknown subject for the general.

Sokolov's message had been explicit: do whatever is necessary to get the Vympel teams and the captured subject to the sharashka as fast as possible.

It had sent Yermakova into a frenzy. How was she able to contact the submarine in the Bering? And who was this mysterious subject?

Yermakova had immediately begun to worry about KODIAK and had tried contacting them three times to no avail.

She knew all this had something to do with Subject 8831 and that picture Sokolov had obsessed over.

She hoped that KODIAK was safe, but her intuition said that something had gone terribly wrong. People simply disappeared around Viktor Sokolov. All the stories she'd heard of what happened in Post 866 when the old general ran the place: all the experiments, the human testing, the genetic modifications.

Luckily, she had been able to get ahold of the submarine carrying the mysterious subject and scramble a stealth helicopter to intercept as they surfaced in the Bering. The subject would be brought to the Gazprom oil rig off the peninsula to refuel and make the last hump back to the post.

If everything went according to plan, the mysterious subject and Sokolov's Vympels would arrive exactly an hour after the old general landed at Post 866.

Yermakova intended to stay in the bathtub as long as she could before Sokolov arrived. She needed time to relax. She still had the urge to call the Kremlin and ask what in the hell was going on with Sokolov. But in the end she resisted. Sokolov had threatened the wrath of the president twice while they had spoken. Surely, President Putin was aware of General Sokolov's arrival—she just hoped the old general would understand that this place wasn't his anymore.

This was *her* post, not his.

She would just as much rather blow the place than let Viktor Sokolov take over. She fingered the key that hung around her neck, wondering if Subject 8831 was awake yet in Artur's laboratory. She had ordered one of the guards to watch over Artur as he performed surgery on the bullet wound on Cassandra Gale's arm. It's not that she didn't trust the scientist—he was as submissive as they come—but Cassandra Gale was undoubtedly a dangerous prisoner. One that needed extra monitoring.

Yermakova took a deep breath and let her head sink below the bathwater, willing her tense muscles to relax. She intended to stay like that for thirty seconds but was jolted out of her meditative state by a shrill alarm.

Water splashed out of the tub as Yermakova sat bolt upright and gasped for air. The lights in her bathroom had dimmed, replaced with red strobes from the facility's alarm system.

She had barely enough time to register what was happening when two guards rushed into the room.

"What the hell is going on?!" Yermakova shouted, stepping out of the tub and throwing on a robe.

One of the guards handed her a tablet. "Breach in the emergency stairwell!"

Yermakova grabbed the tablet and stared down at the screen showing a live feed of the emergency staircase heading toward the surface. It showed one of her black-clad guards shoving Artur up the stairs at knifepoint. Perplexed, Yermakova zoomed in on the pair. She saw how the guard's armor looked too big for the small figure wearing it, how the visored helmet had trouble staying on—

Cassandra Gale!

"Initiate a complete lockdown of the facility and gas the stairwell!"

Yermakova stripped her robe in front of the men and dressed as they initiated the lockdown. "I want two dozen men to secure that landing. Another dozen with me above ground!"

Grabbing a gas mask from a cabinet, she followed the guards out of her suite and ran toward the elevator.

Chapter 48

THE GUARD'S BULKY helmet wobbled over Cassie's head and threatened to fall off entirely. She breathed heavily, her warm breath fogging the visor, but she held the knife at Artur's back and kept forcing him farther up the staircase.

Ten minutes before, after killing the guard and holding Artur at knifepoint, she'd changed into the dead man's black, hefty uniform and forced Artur to change into clean, blood-free lab clothes. Artur, in a panic, had pleaded with her not to attempt an escape, but Cassie was hearing none of it. He might have been a brilliant scientist, but he was also a brainwashed fool. She'd left the guard in the laboratory in a pool of blood and, holding the knife, had Artur lock the room behind them, threatening him that if he made any attempt to thwart her escape she'd carve out his left kidney.

"You are making a big mistake," Artur had whispered as they left the lab, walking down a narrow hallway toward an elevator. "There are security measures in place so nobody can reach the top of the facility."

"Bullshit!" Cassie said, as they made it to an elevator door.

"No, you don't understand. There is only one lift that can take you to the top and it is heavily guarded."

"If there is a lift, then there also must be an emergency staircase," she said, pressing the blade a bit farther into the small of his back. "Correct?"

"*Da*, but it won't work."

"I don't really have a choice."

The elevator dinged and they got inside. Artur pushed the button for the main level and the elevator began to rise.

When the doors opened, Artur walked out into a large circular room with a high ceiling. The gigantic room was busy with people: uniformed men, women, and black-clad guards. Artur marched across the room with Cassie in tow, making sure to give the scientist enough distance ahead of her so as to not arouse suspicion. They walked to the opposite side of the circular room, through a door, and down a deserted hallway. The place was like a maze and all the signs on the doors were in Russian. Cassie made a mental map of their route in her head. Finally, Artur stopped in front of a red door with an electronic keypad.

"This is it."

"Scan us in."

"They will know as soon as I do. I'll be flagged. There are cameras in the stairwell, sensors!"

"Then we will go quickly."

Artur fumbled for his keycard and placed it in front of the sensor and it blinked green and Cassie shoved him through the door and forced him to run up the spiraling staircase.

"This will never work!" Artur kept gasping. "Please, just turn back!"

"Shut up!" Cassie growled. It had been a rash decision and she knew it, but she had seen an opening and taken it. It wouldn't be long before the dead guard's body was discovered in the lab. Her only goal was to get out of the facility and to ground level. From there she would take her chances in the woods. The guard's gas mask that hung from her baggy pants thudded against her leg with each stair climbed. The drones outside would shoot the canisters of knockout gas down at her, but the mask would protect her.

The stairs continued to spiral and her legs began to burn. The grated steps clanged with each hurried footfall as she counted twenty revolutions.

Thirty.

Looking up, she could see a ceiling not ten rotations above, a circular hatch showing in the dim light.

We're gonna make it!

"Move!" she shouted, just as a blaring alarm sounded. What light was in the stairwell instantly shut off, replaced by red strobes. The wailing of the alarm grew louder.

"HURRY!"

They climbed two more revolutions before she heard a hiss and the smell of the familiar knockout gas being deployed into the stairwell.

"NO!" Artur wailed and turned around to face Cassie, his face lined with fear.

Cassie pushed him in the chest and the scientist landed butt first on the grated stairs. She threw the guard's helmet from her head and it careened down the staircase. Fumbling with the gas mask, she secured it to her face just as the noxious orange cloud surrounded them.

The scientist was panicked, trying to simultaneously hold his breath and wrench Cassie's mask from her face. She held the man down with her leg and watched as he finally gulped in the knockout gas. His eyes momentarily bulged, then he lost consciousness.

Cassie gripped her knife and then saw movement through the grates in the stairs far below.

Guards. Lots of them.

She looked up at the hatch, five flights above her.

Cassie moved, leaping up the stairs, two at a time. Reaching the hatch in thirty seconds, she sheathed the surgical knife in the guard's tactical vest. Her gloved hands gripping the turn wheel, she heaved with all her might, but it wouldn't budge.

Cassie released her grip and looked down the stairwell. There were at least two dozen guards thundering up under her.

I have less than a minute.

Panic began to settle in and she turned back to the hatch. Images of Derrick flooded her mind. Their wedding, their honeymoon—all those times she'd greeted him on the tarmacs after his long deployments—him sweeping her into his arms. She thought of her father, her sister, Maverick, the ranch, and of course the moment she'd found out that she was pregnant.

All that had been taken away from me.

And now she was going to die in this godforsaken place. The unfairness of it all released something primal within her and in one last colossal yank, she screamed with all the pent-up rage she could muster and felt the turn wheel give and blow open.

Fresh air blew down on to her as natural light flooded over her body. For a moment, overwhelming relief washed over her, but it was soon squashed by dread.

Daylight was momentarily blotted out as gloved hands grabbed her by the hair and pulled her out of the stairwell. Her gas mask was dislodged from her face, and her fingers tried to find the hilt of her knife but it was too late. More hands grabbed her by the arms and she was tossed onto the dirt.

A half-dozen guards pinned her to the ground as she struggled, kicking wildly. Eventually she was overpowered, her face pressed into the ground, her wrists bound behind her back.

Then she was flipped over. Heaving like a cornered animal, she squinted into the bright daylight. A brawny figure stood over her, then bent down and grabbed her by the hair again, dragging her through the dirt.

"Idiot girl!" Yermakova screamed, tugging up so violently on Cassie's hair she had no choice but to get on her knees.

Yermakova, her hair dripping wet, stood in front of Cassie and backhanded her so hard that Cassie fell to the ground again. Yermakova's boot connected with Cassie's stomach and she felt the breath escape her. "Look around you!"

Cassie sputtered and feared she might throw up.

"LOOK AROUND YOU!"

Cassie opened her eyes. Yermakova stood in front of her, her face purple with rage. At least three dozen guards stood nearby. Cassie took in her surroundings, realizing they were on top of a very tall, very steep mountain. The circular hatch sat open to her left. Twenty yards behind the hatch was what looked like a concrete entranceway expertly constructed into the rock slab of the mountaintop. The concrete door was open and showed what appeared to be a large elevator dock inside.

"WHAT DO YOU SEE?!"

Cassie's gaze peeled away from the open concrete elevator to the vastness of the scenery around her. They were so high up, Cassie could look down at the immense, sprawling wilderness in all directions. A half-dozen snow-capped volcanoes protruded from the untamed earth. It looked like it never ended.

"Wilderness," Cassie let out. "I see wilderness."

"That's right!" Yermakova thundered. "Immeasurable wilderness." Walking behind Cassie, she gripped her hair and pulled back so Cassie was looking at the deep blue sky; the drones zipped above like angry birds of prey. "There is nowhere for you to run, stupid girl. Nowhere for you to hide! You will die here, do you understand?"

"Yes." How could she have been so foolish? How could she have been so impulsive? She would never see her family again. She would die without them ever knowing what happened to her.

The thought made Cassie's heart thump wildly in her chest.

The thumping grew louder until it was the only thing she could hear, then a great shadow passed overhead and an ungodly wind beat down on the mountaintop.

Cassie looked up to see an enormous military helicopter settle down a hundred yards away on a landing pad she hadn't noticed before. Cassie squinted and saw that behind the landing pad sat two other helicopters shrouded under camouflaged military netting.

A half-dozen figures exited the newly arrived chopper and made their way to her. As they marched forward, Cassie spotted that the group was surrounding a frail figure walking with the assistance of a cane.

The rotor wash died as the group approached. Yermakova and the guards snapped to attention, their focus on the frail figure.

He was wearing a pressed green military uniform; countless medals hung from his chest. The man leaned over Cassie, a wicked smile on his face. An arthritic, liver-spotted index finger found the bottom of her chin and lifted it slightly.

"Ah, Cassandra Gaines," the man said, "how long it has been."

Chapter 49

IT HAD TAKEN Susan Carter nearly two hours to prep, plan, and execute everything that needed to be done before she walked into the White House to deliver the news.

Her first call had been to her friend General Paul Bridgewater, the chairman of the Joint Chiefs of Staff, who had heard Robert Gaines's recording through the Northern Unified Command.

Carter, who had been marching down the marble halls of Langley, her secure cell phone to her ear, had asked General Bridgewater to order a specific, and expedient, mode of transportation to JBER to pick up Robert Gaines and bring him to DC. The gruff marine said he'd get it done and alerted Carter that he was currently en route to the White House at the command of the president's chief of staff, Morgan Fray—who had ordered an emergency meeting for select members of the National Security Council.

Her next call had been to her counterpart over at the FBI, Director Stuart Connelly.

Director Connelly had told Carter that he had also been summoned to the White House and that he had just heard the USB recording after it had been kicked down to him by the director of national intelligence, Ralph Nagle.

"I'm being asked why a dead CIA agent crashed a jet with five suspected Russian operators on board, Susan," Connelly had said. "They're asking questions I can't answer!"

"It will all be explained," Carter said. "I need to put some things into motion before I get to the White House and I have a favor to ask of you." She'd detailed to Connelly how General Bridgewater was sending a high-speed military jet to JBER. "I need you to tell your men in Anchorage to get Robert Gaines on that jet. We need him in Washington."

"Susan—"

"Stuart, he will remain in FBI custody, but I need that man in DC. Have him flown into Andrews. Your agents can escort him to the Hoover Building. I need him close, do you understand?"

Connelly reluctantly agreed. "I'll have Jim Brower bring him here personally."

"Thank you, Stuart."

"Susan, what the hell is going on?"

"I'll brief everyone at the White House."

"Secretary Macy and DNI Nagle are in full meltdown mode. They're going nuts because you aren't answering their calls. They're asking for your head."

"They're always asking for my head, Stuart."

Carter had hung up and then worked on getting McGavran transportation to Andrews. After the old spymaster had left, she marched to her office where the geospatial and imagery directors stood waiting for her. The meeting had been brief and she kept the details of what she wanted to a bare minimum.

After she had given them the two desired geographical coordinates Prescott McGavran had discussed with her, the directors said they'd report back their findings as soon as possible.

When her motorcade got to 1600 Pennsylvania Avenue, Carter entered through the West Wing entrance with Jack Crowley in tow. After passing through the various Secret Service checkpoints, Carter and Crowley walked past the Roosevelt Room, rounded the corner, and were met by the White House chief of staff, Morgan Fray.

The man's squirrelly build and bald head reminded Carter of Mr. Magoo.

"You have some nerve, Susan," Fray snapped, clearly irritated. "We've been waiting for almost an hour—"

"Where is the president?" Carter said.

"Coming back from Geneva, he'll be landing in an hour."

"Has he been briefed?"

"Of course he's been briefed."

"Then let's begin." Carter marched around the chief of staff and into the Cabinet Room, where Secretary of Defense Alan Macy and Director of National Intelligence Ralph Nagle were in a heated argument in the corner. General Bridgewater sat at the head of the table, flanked by a man in uniform that Carter didn't recognize and the national security adviser, Thomas Bowman.

FBI director Connelly was talking with his aides farther down the table and stood when Carter and Crowley entered the room followed by Fray.

"Gentlemen," Carter said, standing at the edge of the mahogany table, "I apologize for my tardiness, but there were certain things that needed to be done before I arrived." She nodded in appreciation to Bridgewater and Connelly.

DNI Ralph Nagle pointed an accusatory finger in Carter's direction. "This is not how things work around here; if my office calls your office, you respond immediately, do you understand me?"

"That goes for my office, too," interjected Secretary of Defense Macy.

General Bridgewater's booming voice cut over the squabbling men, "Gentlemen, enough! Director Carter is here now, so let's get on with it."

It was more than apparent that both Nagle and Macy despised Carter and her role at the CIA. They had strongly disagreed with President McClintock's decision to appoint her as D/CIA and made their stance on it ever apparent.

"Before we begin," Carter started, "I'm going to have to ask all aides and nonessential staff to leave the room."

As the staffers got up to leave, Carter stopped her special assistant, Jack Crowley, and unlocked the OVERDRIVE case file from his wrist, placing the steel briefcase on the table.

When the room was secure and everyone had taken their seats, Carter began: "Approximately three hours ago, I received a recording through my associate director of military affairs and I assume each of you have already heard the contents of this recording?"

The room nodded in unison.

"I will say now, for the record, that I was just as surprised at the contents of that recording as you all must be."

"Is any of this true?" Thomas Bowman asked, holding up a transcript of the recording.

"You will have to be more specific."

"This nutjob, the one who crashed the plane. He's saying he's a former agent of the CIA?"

Nagle interjected, "My sources in the CIA said Robert Gaines died in the late eighties!"

"I thought the same thing until a few hours ago," Carter said. "But it is confirmed. The man who crashed the jet on Middleton Island is Robert Gaines, and I can confirm that he was an agent of the CIA."

A rumbling of dissent came over the Cabinet Room.

"And what about everything else that this Gaines fella said?" Macy asked. "He's claiming there are Russian operators kidnapping Americans on US soil."

"As of now, that's what it looks like. Director Connelly can probably paint us a better picture of what's been happening on the ground."

The attention in the room shifted to Connelly. "Thank you, Director Carter. As all of you know, the pilot who crashed the G650 on Middleton Island has been identified as James Gale. His fingerprints have been entered into our databases and have come up as a match for Robert Gaines, a man who Director Carter has just confirmed was an agent of the CIA. I received my last briefing twenty minutes ago from my men in Anchorage. Five bodies were recovered from the crash site and taken to Anchorage where federal agents working with the NSA identified two of the men via facial recognition as known SVR Vympel operators. Our counterterrorism task force has reported that certain 'suspicious' technology has also been found in the wreckage."

"What type of technology?" asked Bridgewater.

"That is currently under investigation, but our experts believe, due to the specific security on the devices, that they're encrypted through a Tor network. Our experts have backtraced their VPNs and are linking them to Russia. As far as the weapons we've found on board, they're all synonymous with those used by Russian Special Forces."

"Let's go back to the plane," said Bowman. "Are there any records of the jet entering US airspace?"

"Negative. There have been no recorded G650s entering Alaska nor any G650s registered in any of the air traffic control systems in that part of the world. For now, we are going to have to assume that the jet entered the United States illegally and undetected."

"How is that possible?" exclaimed Nagle.

"It's more than possible," Bridgewater grunted. "It's rare for naval radar to provide constant surveillance in such a desolate region, especially over the Bering Sea. Without a working transponder, planes can virtually slip in and out of US airspace undetected; they'd just need a place to land."

"And we've located that place," Connelly confirmed. "My agents have found a private airstrip near Whittier, Alaska, where we believe the plane took off before the crash."

"And how do you know that?" Macy asked.

"We've been working in coordination with military air traffic control for possible flight patterns the plane might have taken. Once we surmised the jet could have taken off from Whittier, I had a task force look into it. There they found a burned-out van near the tarmac with one dead body. An Alaskan state trooper named Elliot Vance who Robert Gaines claims participated in his abduction."

"Did the aircraft have a tail number or a flight plan?"

"Negative, but we've located a manufacturer's serial number on the jet. We are currently working with the Gulfstream company to determine who purchased the aircraft."

Bowman piped up, "Do we believe the incident in Eagle is connected to the plane crash?"

Connelly sighed. "Yes. My agents in Eagle are working with the local authorities as we speak. According to them, at approximately 9:14 a.m., local time, gunfire was reported outside of the village. Eyewitnesses have corroborated that roughly eight individuals engaged in a firefight that led to the abduction of one individual. That individual has been identified as Emily Gale of Lincoln, Montana."

"Robert Gaines's daughter?" Bridgewater asked.

"Yes. I can also report that another man was shot and is in critical condition at a hospital in Fairbanks and two other bodies have been found south of Eagle near an abandoned mining town called Jack Wade."

"Have the bodies been identified?"

"All we know is that they're Canadian citizens, two males, but my agents have confirmed that the cause of death of the two individuals were due to multiple gunshot wounds and the two vehicles found on scene were both registered to another Canadian citizen, Ned Voigt. We are currently working with the Royal Canadian Mounted Police and Border Patrol to get more information."

"Two vehicles?" Carter asked.

"Correct," replied Connelly. "Another vehicle was found scorched farther down the road next to a series of abandoned garages. They have also found a makeshift landing strip not far away in the woods."

"Another plane took off from the area?"

"We believe that is how they escaped the region, yes. As of a few hours ago, the governor of Alaska has grounded all civilian planes in the state. Canadian authorities have also grounded all civilian air travel in northwestern Canada."

"What are the odds of finding that plane?"

"Slim to none. We don't know what type of plane we are looking for and have no idea where it was going. The length of the landing strip suggests only a small plane could have taken off on such a short runway. But considering that the witnesses say they saw eight individuals kidnapping Emily Gale, and two of those individuals are dead, we have to assume the plane would have to be big enough to carry seven individuals."

"What if they didn't escape by plane?" Carter asked.

"Border Patrol has closed the borders heading into Canada, and authorities in a five-hundred-mile radius are doing individual car searches."

"Has there been any other evidence to suggest that the plane crash and the incident in Eagle are related?" Carter asked.

"Yes. A piece of technology was found next to the two deceased that is similar to the technology found on the downed G650. Also, at the time of the FBI's arrival into Eagle we have taken into custody a thirty-three-year-old male, a village public safety officer who we believe was linked to the attack. This individual tipped off our agents to a stash of weaponry locked in a garage near the makeshift airfield."

"What type of weaponry?" Macy asked.

Connelly opened a binder in front of him and took out a series of photographs and passed them around. "The agents have found a supply of canisters with a foreign chemical agent inside. The chemical contents are currently being investigated."

"This man in custody, the village public safety officer, has he provided any more information?" asked Carter.

"Negative. But he is being transported to Anchorage as we speak."

Macy asked, "Director Connelly, you stated that the two deceased Canadian citizens had in their possession the same type of Russian technology as found on the crashed jet?"

"Yes."

"But we don't know if the other individuals who took Emily Gale were American, Canadian, or even Russian? We don't really know anything about them."

"We know that at least two of the individuals who took Emily Gale were Canadian citizens and that the vehicles they were using to transport her to Jack Wade were registered to a third Canadian citizen, Ned Voigt. We have not been able to locate Ned Voigt but we are working on it. As for the others, you are correct; they could be anyone—Canadian, Russian, or American—but I'd put my money on Russian."

"If they were Russian operators, just like the ones on the plane," Macy said, "could these Canadians be working with them? Could they be some sort of sleeper cell?"

"All options are on the table, but we haven't been able to verify that."

"This stinks like shit," Bridgewater said. "What else does the FBI know?"

Connelly let out a long exasperated breath. "We can confirm that the survivor of the plane crash, Robert Gaines, was kidnapped outside the FBI offices at 9:24 a.m., Alaskan time. Surveillance cameras caught the abduction and can confirm that at least nine men in two black vans took Robert Gaines in Anchorage this morning and drove off. One of those vehicles has been identified as the burned-out van in Whittier, the other van has been found south of Anchorage on a dirt road next to the ocean. Burned as well."

"What does the press know?" asked Nagle.

"They're reporting the incident in Eagle and the plane crash. We're withholding information until we know more."

"All right, thank you, Director Connelly," Bowman said, and turned to Carter. "Your turn, Director Carter. I want to go back to the contents of Robert Gaines's recording. Surely, you'll be able to clear some of this up for us, starting with a name that Robert Gaines mentioned." He started flipping through his notes. "Viktor Sokolov. Do you mind telling us who that is?"

Carter leaned forward in her chair. "General Viktor Aleksandrovich Sokolov is a chief within the Russian Foreign Intelligence Service, the SVR. Our intelligence sources believe he leads the SVR's Line S, their Illegals Directorate. He runs spies for the Russian Federation as well as all their black work and is believed to be one of the principal decision makers for nearly all Russian covert operations abroad. You've all heard of Litvinenko, Politkovskaya, or Golubev? Any big assassination linked with Russia most definitely has Sokolov's prints on it."

"Wait a minute," Nagle interjected. "Is this the same guy close to Putin?"

"Yes, Sokolov is usually credited as the puppet master behind Putin's rise to power; they are very close."

Carter's attention went to Morgan Fray, who rubbed his bald head as he read the file in front of him. "What the hell is a Vympel?"

Carter was about to respond when the man in the military uniform next to Bridgewater spoke up. "A Vympel is a clandestine Russian Spetsnaz unit that specializes in high-level assassinations and black work. They're Russian-trained operators very similar to the CIA's paramilitary and work under the direction of the FSB and the SVR."

Carter finally figured out where she recognized the man in uniform and cursed herself for not recognizing him right away. It was the newly appointed JSOC commander, Scott R. Spear, a former Navy SEAL DEVGRU commander who had recently been named to lead the Joint Special Operations Command. Spear was a legend in the SEAL Teams and had been an obvious choice to lead JSOC.

"General Sokolov created the Vympel Group during his KGB years and we believe he still runs an elite Vympel unit that works under the jurisdiction of the SVR," Carter said.

"I don't get it," Nagle noted. "How would Robert Gaines know all this? How does he know it was Sokolov and his Vympels who kidnapped his daughters? Does Robert Gaines have history with Sokolov?"

Carter chose her words carefully. "Yes, Robert Gaines does have a history with General Sokolov."

Nagle glanced down at his notes. "Does it have to do with the Striker program?"

"What is the Striker program?" asked Macy.

"And what the hell is a sharashka?" Bowman interjected.

Carter could see all the men hunched over their transcripts of Robert's distress call to JBER. She knew she needed to tread softly here on forward if McGavran's plan was going to be successful.

"And what the hell is in that briefcase?" Nagle asked, pointing at the steel briefcase containing the OVERDRIVE case file.

Before Carter could field any of the questions, Fray's secure BlackBerry chimed. "POTUS has just landed in DC. Secret Service has alerted me that he's just boarded Marine One and is currently en route to the White House. We can expect him on the South Lawn in ten minutes."

Thank God, Carter thought. "I suggest we take this downstairs to the Situation Room and wait until the president gets here."

"Why?" snapped Nagle.

Carter patted the OVERDRIVE case file. "Because I don't trust the security of the Cabinet Room, and what I am about to divulge is highly compartmented and cannot be subjected to leaks of any kind."

Chapter 50

TWELVE MINUTES LATER, President William McClintock entered the Situation Room and took his seat at the head of the table. At thirty-nine years old, McClintock was the youngest ever person to serve in the United States' highest office. A former marine and senator from Ohio, William McClintock secured his presidency by connecting to the American people in a truthful and brutally honest manner. Gone was the chaos of the last administration, gone were their lies and deceit.

McClintock had run on transparency and youthful determination to get the country back on track, to be a force for good abroad and at home.

After the president told everyone to sit, he took in the room, eyes giving away nothing. "I spoke with FBI deputy director Smith on the way over here and I listened to the recording—how certain can we be that these were Russian agents acting on United States soil?" The question was directed at DNI Nagle.

Nagle cleared his throat. "Sir, the evidence is overwhelming. Using NSA facial recognition software linked to Interpol, we've been able to identify two of the deceased. Both of them are known Russian operators who've been photographed by Mossad around the time of high-level assassinations in Europe and the Middle East. They've also been linked to Russian operations in Syria."

McClintock steepled his fingers so the tips rested under his chin. "As of now, we believe that these men were attempting to kidnap this Robert Gaines?"

Connelly spoke up. "Yes, sir. And we believe that they succeeded in kidnapping his daughters." Connelly briefed the president on what had happened in Eagle, as well as recounting what the FBI discovered on Middleton Island and confirming Robert Gaines's identity. "Director Carter has made the necessary arrangements to get Robert Gaines to DC."

"Why?" asked the president, looking at Carter.

Carter cleared her throat. "Sir, the situation surrounding Robert Gaines is a delicate one. It will be the responsibility of my agency to vet and investigate his claims in person. Due to his sensitive history, and the stakes surrounding this situation, I will interview him personally."

The president didn't say anything for a long moment, then looked down at his intelligence report. "Director Carter, I understand that you've had a long and illustrious career at the CIA. You probably know secrets that we at this table probably couldn't comprehend. But to understand this whole situation properly, I am going to have to ask you to tell us everything you know about Robert Gaines and this General Sokolov."

Carter moved her hand off the briefcase, retrieved the keys from her pocket, and took out the OVERDRIVE case file. "I'll start with the Striker program, sir." Carter cleared her throat again. "In 1981, at the beginning of the Reagan administration, the Central Intelligence Agency received viable intelligence from both assets and agents behind the Iron Curtain that the Soviets had been, and currently were, taking Westerners—Americans—into the Soviet Union and performing medical experiments on them at secret instillations known as sharashkas.

"From what we know, the Soviets were trying to create the *perfect soldier* as well as have the captured Americans *teach* potential Soviet spies the nuances of American life so they could later come to the United States and spy for the Soviets under total disguise. While the latter has never been confirmed, the former has.

"When my old boss, Prescott McGavran, former Moscow Chief of Station, obtained that information through three valuable assets on the ground—scientists who had been prisoners at one of these rumored sharashkas—he immediately sought the guidance of William J. Casey, the man chosen by Reagan to lead the CIA.

"As you can imagine, Casey was disturbed by the intelligence, and looking to revamp the CIA after its tumultuous years in the seventies, he wanted to make his mark and rebuild our covert paramilitary so we could stand a chance against our enemies abroad. I don't have to tell you, Mr. President, what Reagan was up against in the 1980s with Iran, the Soviet Union, and the Middle East. Terrorism was flourishing and the United States was getting crushed. So Casey and Reagan's inner circle created the National Security Planning Group, or NSPG, thus giving presidential authority to implement and oversee covert action against terrorist organizations."

"This was the birth child of Reagan's *preemptive neutralization program*?" Sec-Def Macy asked.

"Yes," Carter replied. "Reagan's assassination program. His covert *hidden hand*. Officially, the program wasn't installed until April 3, 1984, when President Reagan signed National Security Decision Directive 138, authorizing the CIA to develop capabilities for the preemptive neutralization of anti-American terrorist groups that plan, support, or conduct hostile terrorist acts against US citizens, interests, and property overseas. But while not made *legal* until 1984, the CIA had already begun training and implementing our assassins abroad years before that."

The president said, "And I take it that Striker was part of his preemptive neutralization program and this Robert Gaines was one of these assassins?"

"Yes, sir. The Striker program was formed in late 1981 and was headed by Prescott McGavran and myself. We took our orders straight from Casey and the NSPG. In the beginning, Striker was a covert intelligence gathering operation with the goal of finding the medical sharashka in question, which became known to us as Post 866."

"And General Viktor Sokolov? What does Gaines have to do with him?"

"Gaines was already a CIA paramilitary operator when he came on my radar. He was one of the original Delta Force boys who caught the attention of Bill Casey and Prescott McGavran. Gaines was an unconventional warfare expert, an elite commando who was chosen with a group of others to be taught the ins and outs of spycraft at the Farm. He excelled with languages, he blended in everywhere, and after succeeding in various clandestine missions abroad, he was selected to be our man on the ground in Moscow starting in 1983, under the guise of a lowly state diplomat. In the four years that Prescott McGavran and I ran Robert Gaines, he started a family and carried out numerous operations before it all came to a head in 1985 when Robert made contact with a high-level Soviet scientist. The scientist claimed he could give us information on Post 866 and the man who ran it, KGB general Viktor Aleksandrovich Sokolov, the then chief of the KGB's Department S."

Carter paused, collecting her thoughts, then went on, "This scientist, code-named BLUEMAN, almost led us to Post 866, giving us invaluable information along the way about what was going on inside, as detailed in this case file"—she tapped the stack of papers—"code-named OVERDRIVE.

"BLUEMAN wanted a deal; he'd give us information and the location of Post 866 in exchange for the CIA helping his family defect to the West. Unfortunately, that never occurred. In late 1986, we'd set BLUEMAN up with a tracking beacon as he was flown back to the sharashka, but we lost the signal somewhere over the Kamchatka Peninsula. A day later, Evgeny Sokolov, General Sokolov's son, a rising star in the KGB—and also the cofounder of the KGB's Vympel Group—was seen dumping the body of BLUEMAN on the street outside the United States Embassy in Moscow and flipping off our security cameras. It was a 'fuck you' to our country, agents, and our program. When Robert Gaines tried getting BLUE-MAN's family out of the USSR later that day, they had already disappeared."

Carter explained that Reagan, Casey, and the NSPG gave the green light for the Striker program to kill or capture Evgeny Sokolov, claiming his actions fell under Directive 138. Gaines and McGavran found him hiding in Helsinki and took him to a CIA black site in Poland. The interrogation techniques that were carried out on Evgeny Sokolov weren't enough to get all the information they wanted. After days of this information extraction, General Sokolov reached out to the CIA and offered an exchange. BLUEMAN's family for Evgeny Sokolov.

"The NSPG was against the trade from the start," Carter said. "Evgeny Sokolov was too valuable to us, but Gaines told McGavran to convince them otherwise. Gaines had made a promise to BLUEMAN that he would protect his family and bring them to the West. A week later, on the Finnish-Soviet border, the exchange was made.

"On the way to the exchange, I received intelligence of a potential KGB hit on Robert Gaines's family while they were in hiding under CIA protection in Paris. It was my decision to send a backup team to protect them. It was also my decision not to alert Robert to the threat on his family before the exchange was made. I wanted him focused on the task at hand."

A long silence followed, and then the president broke it. "What happened?"

"It was a foggy day that was ripe for an ambush, sir. As we released Evgeny Sokolov and he made his way across the border bridge to his countrymen, BLUE-MAN's wife and two girls made their way to us. When they were just feet away, the Soviets took them out. Robert was first to the bodies. As the Soviets retreated safely with Evgeny in their possession, we found that BLUEMAN's family had photographs pinned to their coats—pictures of Robert Gaines's family—his wife, his two young girls.

"At the same time, General Sokolov was carrying out the hit on Gaines's family personally. He shot Robert's wife, Irina, and had almost succeeded in killing his young daughters before my action team was able to chase him off. Irina Gaines died from a traumatic head wound five days later, stateside."

The room went graveyard quiet. Carter went on: "After Irina died, Robert wanted answers. He blamed me for not alerting him about the threat to his family. While Gaines was being debriefed in Washington, he'd begged Director Casey to let him seek retribution, but Casey felt Gaines was too emotionally compromised. He ordered Gaines to remain in DC while he sent McGavran and myself back to Moscow to continue the Striker program. Days after we returned, we received word that Robert had left his daughters in Washington with a family friend and disappeared. Two weeks later, in January of 1987, bodies of known KGB members that were close to the Sokolovs started showing up dead all over Moscow. It didn't take a genius to figure out who was behind the assassinations. During 'bloody January' as we have come to call it, nearly twenty bodies showed up in the snowy Moscow streets. They were well-orchestrated, professional assassinations. I knew Robert was behind it, I just didn't know that my boss, Prescott McGavran, was helping him.

"On January 25, 1987, the Soviets confirmed that Evgeny Sokolov was found dead at his family's *dacha* in the Khimki Forest outside of Moscow and the body of Robert Gaines was found in a river five miles away . . . Casey called us back to DC at once. During our debriefing, Prescott McGavran admitted to helping Robert Gaines with the assassinations.

"Reagan ordered the Striker program to be shut down indefinitely and for the OVERDRIVE case file to be destroyed. Everything that we worked on was gone. Instead of firing McGavran, he was given a desk job at Langley, and I was sent back to resume my role as deputy chief of station, Moscow. Until four hours ago, I had always assumed Robert Gaines was dead, and that his children were raised by family friends."

"So Robert Gaines did kill Evgeny Sokolov?" the president asked.

"The Soviets claimed Gaines tortured Evgeny to death. But we never saw Evgeny's body, so we could never confirm it."

"And what about Gaines's body, what was the Soviet's excuse for not handing it over to us?"

"The KGB said Gaines's body 'disappeared' before it got to Moscow."

"Who hid Gaines?" Nagle asked. "Who got him his new identity?"

"Prescott McGavran. He admitted it to me before I got here. Gaines survived somehow, but I don't know the full story."

"Jesus Christ," General Bridgewater breathed.

"You said the OVERDRIVE case file was destroyed. If that is true, what the hell is this?" Chief of Staff Fray asked, pointing at the stack of papers in front of Carter.

Carter explained to the group that McGavran had made a copy. And that from his position in the Office of Russian and European Analysis at Langley, he'd continued his search for Post 866—that he had been updating OVERDRIVE by himself, without the oversight of the CIA for more than thirty years. "And that is what I wish to explain next."

Carter opened the OVERDRIVE case file to the pages that McGavran had marked for her in the SCIF and began telling the most powerful men in the United States what it contained.

Thirty minutes later, when she'd concluded with the contents in the case file,

President William McClintock stood up from his chair so fast it rolled back and hit the wall behind him. He paced around the Situation Room and then pointed a finger at Carter. "So this suspected location of the sharashka, this Site X, it's in an old Soviet missile silo?"

"Yes, sir. In the late sixties, the CIA obtained the locations and schematics of various nuclear silos in the USSR. This was one of them."

"And the schematics of the silo are sound? We know what it looks like inside?"

"We have the layout of what the silo looked like in the late sixties, sir. According-ing to OVERDRIVE, there was a vast amount of construction on Site X starting twelve years ago. If you want a more in-depth analysis, you would have to consult Prescott McGavran." Carter let the name linger in the air, throwing it out like bait, hoping the president would bite—it was essential if McGavran's plan was going to work.

"And where is Prescott McGavran?"

"He's at Andrews, sir. Picking up Robert Gaines."

The president thought for a moment. "I want both of them brought here. I want to hear everything from their mouths." Turning to Macy, the president said, "And get the Russian ambassador on the phone. This shit with the Russians might have slid with the previous administration, but it won't slide with mine."

"Sir," Carter said, "I would not recommend that. Tipping off the Russians that we know about their botched job to take Robert Gaines would be a mistake. For now, let them believe we're ignorant."

"I agree with Director Carter," Bridgewater said.

"Fine." McClintock motioned to Bridgewater and JSOC commander Spear. "In one hour, I want a full action plan laid out before me on how to handle this militarily. Commander Spear, which JSOC unit would you suggest?"

The coolheaded JSOC commander looked straight at the president of the United States. "I'd suggest the SEAL DEVGRU squadron that covers the re-gion. Blue Squadron, the Pirates. They're currently on standby at Dam Neck in Virginia Beach."

"Good, make the call, and draw up an action plan on Site X. We reconvene back here in one hour."

Chapter 51

GALE HAD NEVER been in a jet as fast as the Lockheed YF-8. It had taken them under two hours to make the jump from Anchorage to Andrews Air Force Base, just outside of DC.

Gale had sat, handcuffed and secured to his seat between two counterterrorism FBI agents. Special Agent Brower and Earl Marks had sat across from them in the small cargo hold being used as a makeshift passenger cabin. The plane had been too noisy to talk, and the agents hadn't given Gale a headset, just earmuffs, so communication between the men had been impossible.

Earlier, Brower had told him that he was going to be taken to the Hoover Building in Washington for an interrogation, but Gale suspected that something else was afoot. There was no way the CIA would let that happen, not with his past. He didn't know if Prescott McGavran was still working at the CIA, or if the old man was even alive. Susan Carter, on the other hand, was a different story. Gale had always tried to stay away from the news as much as possible. He found it generally enraging and time consuming, but he also paid enough attention to know that Susan Carter had been appointed as director of the CIA.

An old anger bubbled up inside Gale as he thought back to Carter's decision not to alert him of the KGB threat on his family all those years ago. Deep down, Gale still blamed Carter for the death of his beloved Irina. If Gale had known about the threat, he could have done something. He could have saved Irina and stopped Viktor Sokolov.

As the Lockheed YF-8 landed at Andrews, the two agents to his right and left unclasped his restraints and stood him up. Earl scooped up the box of documents he'd taken from his office in Anchorage and gave Gale an uneasy look.

The door to the Lockheed's side cabin opened and Gale was led down a set of stairs that had been pushed up to the jet. Instantly, Washington, DC's muggy, hot summer air assaulted him.

The place was surrounded with military personnel, black SUVs, and agents dressed in dark tactical getups.

As Gale's feet touched the tarmac, he watched as the back door to one of the SUVs opened. A familiar man stepped out and approached Special Agent Brower.

The man still wore his signature tweed jacket, but his face was more withered, his once-black hair now a brilliant shade of white, and he sported glasses that rested over his hawkish nose—

Prescott McGavran walked around Brower and stopped. Gale could see the emotion on the old spymaster's face.

"Hello, Robert."

"Been a long time, Prescott." Gale looked back to the Lockheed YF-8. "Your idea?"

"Susan's."

Gale tensed at the mention of her name.

Prescott said, "You've caused quite a stir in Washington, Robert."

"Carter's letting the FBI handle me? I didn't know the agency had gone soft."

Prescott chuckled. "Actually, your presence is requested at the White House. The president has ordered us there personally."

Gale chewed that over for a few seconds and pointed at Earl. "This is Earl Marks. He's coming with me. He knows more about what's happening in Alaska than anyone."

"Hello, Prescott," Earl said.

"Agent Marks, it's been a while."

Gale turned to Earl in surprise. "You two know each other?"

"Prescott and I have been in contact with each other for the last two decades or so. He seemed to have had an interest in the missing in Alaska."

"Why didn't you tell me?"

"The relationship I have with Earl has nothing to do with you, Robert. I've requested his services a handful of times over the years. Now, if you don't mind, we need to hurry."

Susan Carter made it a point to stay away from the men she'd just briefed in the Situation Room. After everyone had exited, Carter had secured OVERDRIVE to her wrist and walked back into the basement hallway and grabbed her special assistant, Jack Crowley, leading him to a corner where they couldn't be overheard.

"Have the satellite analysts gotten back to us?"

Crowley, going through his secure phone, said, "Yes, they've sent over two encrypted files about thirty minutes ago. Do you want to see them?"

"Yes," Carter said, grabbing the phone and directing Crowley to turn around.

She opened the first file and typed in the necessary passwords to access the series of Keyhole, or highly secretive spy satellite, photographs she had ordered to be taken from the CIA's KH-11 surveillance satellites.

The first series of photographs came up on the screen and Carter read the intelligence notes provided by the analysts. Relief spread over her body as she swiped through the pictures and read the reports below them. She opened the second file and felt a sense of elation and justification but also a sense of fear.

The old spymaster had been right.

A slew of Secret Service agents rounded the corner followed by President McClintock and Morgan Fray and led them into the Situation Room. Carter glanced down at her watch, surprised that the last hour had flown by so quickly.

She closed the files on Crowley's secure phone and pocketed it as the rest of the men filed into the Situation Room. General Bridgewater and Commander Spear went in last.

As Carter marched back down the hall, a second group of Secret Service agents rounded the corner, escorting three men.

One of the men was Prescott McGavran, the other an older gentleman with a large gut, the third—

Carter felt as if a lead weight had dropped into her stomach, and her hand shook as it gripped the brass handle of the Situation Room. She looked into the eyes of the man she had betrayed, of the man she had thought dead thirty years before.

"Hello, Robert."

Chapter 52

THE PAIN IN Cassie's shoulders was searing and electric.

The cuffs cutting into her wrists had caused her fingers to go numb ages ago. She didn't know how long she had been in this painful position. Hours? Days?

After her escape attempt, the old man in the Russian military uniform had ordered both his men and Yermakova's to ready the *interrogation room*. A foul, sour-smelling blackout bag had been forced over Cassie's head as she was marched back into the underground facility and into a room that reeked so badly of ammonia it cut through the putrid smells of the blackout hood.

She had been forced to kneel on a frigid tile floor, her wrists cuffed and wrenched behind her back. Soon after, she felt a metal clasp hook to her cuffs—then the sound of a chain rattled and a ratchet cranked. Cassie's wrists had been forced higher and higher behind her until she was forced to stand—but the winch continued to whir, and her shoulders were stretched up behind her in the most unnatural position until she was completely off the floor and hanging.

Cassie moaned as she felt a blast of cold air hit her body and realized that she wasn't wearing the guard's uniform anymore.

Suddenly, the blackout hood was whisked off her head and she sputtered at the sight before her.

Fastened to three chairs were three familiar figures. Marko sat in the middle, a filthy hospital smock covering his body. His greasy black hair fell around his shoulders as blood dripped from a cut on his puffy lips. To either side of him sat the equally disheveled figures of Paul Brady and Billy French.

All three men were fastened to the chairs, their limbs anchored by tight wires.

"*Vy govorite po-russki?*" an excited voice asked to Cassie's left. Do you speak Russian?

Cassie cocked her head and saw the old man who had exited the helicopter. He'd changed out of his military uniform and was now wearing a stained cowhide apron with the Soviet hammer and sickle emblazoned on the front. His hands were covered in blue surgical gloves as he sharpened a curved blade on a whetstone.

"What?" Cassie sputtered.

"Your mother was Russian but you never learned the language?"

Behind the man was a long, stainless-steel table with dozens of instruments of torture: knives in varying lengths, axes, picks, and prods. A small chainsaw sat on the edge next to a series of multicolored syringes and vials.

Cassie took in the white-tiled room. It was circular and reminded her of an old operating theater.

A pair of rubber soles squeaked behind her and the ashen faces of Artur and Captain Yermakova appeared.

Billy whimpered behind his gag, and Cassie could see a stream of yellow urine begin to flow down his bruised leg.

The old man smiled and said something to Artur and Yermakova in Russian, and they immediately headed toward the far wall of the room. Then the old man stood in front of Cassie. "Do you know who I am?"

Cassie shook her head.

"You don't remember me? You were quite young, no? My name is General Viktor Aleksandrovich Sokolov. I am a chief in the *Sluzhba vneshney razvedki*, the SVR. Welcome to my old post, Cassandra Gaines."

Cassie didn't say anything, instead she just stared at the man, trying to figure out what the hell he was saying.

We've met before?

Why had he called me Cassandra Gaines?

The man held the sharp, curved blade up to Cassie's cheek and slowly caressed it.

"Oh, how much you look like him. I can't believe I didn't recognize you from the picture in your file. You both have the same eyes. Pity he won't be able to see your fate today." Sokolov traced the blade down Cassie's chin, down her throat, and then to her straining right shoulder and added pressure.

Cassie grimaced in pain as hot blood poured out of the wound and dripped onto the floor. Sokolov then made his way behind Marko, Brady, and Billy. He placed a hand on Billy's shoulder. "I thought we could invite your friends to watch and participate in this little party of ours. I hope you don't mind?"

"Don't you dare hurt them."

Sokolov laughed. "Or what? You don't seem in a position to be making demands." Suddenly, he grabbed Billy by the hair, wrenched his head back, and brought the curved knife to his throat.

"NO!" Cassie screamed. "STOP IT! DON'T HURT HIM!"

Sokolov laughed and retracted the blade.

"Why are you doing this? What do you want?!" Cassie sobbed.

"I want to hurt you, Cassandra Gaines. I want to hurt you just as your father hurt my son!"

"What are you talking about?!"

"He never told you?" Sokolov asked, his face contorting in mock surprise. "Of course he didn't. Robert Gaines would never have the decency to be held accountable for his actions."

"My father's name is James Gale, not—"

"So he lies to you more." Sokolov walked back to Cassie. "He never told you who he was?"

Utterly confused, Cassie shook her head, wondering what this maniac was talking about.

"He never spoke about his old job? His time in Moscow? What he was?"

"He . . . he was a diplomat—"

Sokolov laughed harder, shaking his head then turning suddenly serious. "Oh no, Cassandra . . . He wasn't a diplomat. Your father was a killer. A hunter, a monster." Sokolov raised his arms in the air. "Do you know he was trying to find this place? Did you know he was trying to find what my son and I created? What a coincidence you ended up here."

Something chirped and Yermakova fumbled with her tablet, before saying something to Sokolov in Russian. A wide smile appeared on his face.

"Do you remember that night in Paris, my dear? You were such a little girl, as was your sister. Do you remember the night your mother died?"

"My mother died in a car crash."

"Another lie, told to you by your disingenuous father. No, your mother died from a bullet to the head, fired from *my* gun. You were there, my dear, as was your sister. It was a dark, snowy night, your mother hid both of you in a bedroom closet. Your sister was crying like a stuck pig—screaming for her mother when I put a bullet in Irina's head. I was going to kill all of you—ship you back piece by piece to your father, but I was interrupted. I will not be interrupted again. I will finish what I started in Paris."

A loud knock on the door reverberated through the small room and three guards entered, carrying a limp figure with a blackout hood over its head. They dropped the figure before Cassie.

"Our final guest has arrived," cried Sokolov and lifted the blackout bag.

Overwhelming dread consumed Cassie as Emily Gale blinked and squinted up at her sister.

"Cassie!"

Chapter 53

"ARE THEY HERE?" the president asked, as Susan Carter entered the Situation Room after her awkward encounter with Robert Gaines. She shut the door behind her.

"Yes, Mr. President."

"Good, sit, I'll call him in shortly." McClintock motioned to Connelly, asking, "Any updates?"

"Yes, sir," Connelly replied, opening a file. "Max Tobeluk, the Eagle village public safety officer has just told one of our counterterrorism agents that two Canadian citizens, Ned and Darlene Voigt, are responsible for the abduction of numerous individuals and that the two deceased men found near Jack Wade worked for the Voigts. We are currently working with the RCMP to search their places of residence across the border."

"What else?"

"Tobeluk claims that he was only a cleanup man for the kidnappers. But he did give us some new information, something he overheard the Voigts saying before, that they deliver the victims to someone named 'Whiskey' in Anchorage."

"Whiskey?" replied the chief of staff, Morgan Fray.

"Most likely a code name," Carter said.

"We are following up on a couple leads." Connelly gave details of the missing fishing boat, the *Lady Alaina*, and the missing Bulgarian captain who had disappeared the night before the Gaineses' kidnappings. "Navy and Coast Guard are searching the Bering and the Cook Inlet as we speak. The FBI is trying to get a warrant for the missing captain's house."

"Good," McClintock replied. "General Bridgewater, Commander Spear, what have you got for me?"

"Sir," Bridgewater said, "JSOC has the Blue Squadron SEAL Team ready at Dam Neck. They are on standby and ready if need be." He pointed to the large television screen on the wall behind the president. "The commander of Blue Squadron is Seamus Cafferty. He is currently awaiting via videoconference if we need him."

"Thank you, General. Okay, send in Prescott McGavran and Robert Gaines."

<hr/>

This wasn't the first time that Gale had been in the Situation Room. Nearly thirty-five years ago, the old director of the CIA, William J. Casey, had him sit in on an operation during the Reagan administration. Gale's role had been as an adviser to a clandestine operation the CIA was trying to pull off against one of Muammar Gaddafi's Libyan assassination teams.

Gale was escorted into the room now with McGavran and Earl Marks and cuffed to a chair by two Secret Service agents. Earl and McGavran stood behind him. The first thing Gale thought when he looked around the room with the low ceiling, the television screens, and the rich oak wainscoting was that everyone looked to be his age, everyone except the man directly opposite him, who looked much younger in person than he did on TV.

The president of the United States sat in his high-winged leather chair and took in Gale. Farther down the table to his left, he saw Susan Carter avoiding his gaze, a metal briefcase in front of her.

"Which one of you is Prescott McGavran?" the president asked.

"I am, sir."

"Director Carter has just briefed us on your OVERDRIVE case file. I want you to tell us how sound this new intelligence is. How certain are you of the location of Site X?"

Gale frowned at the mention of OVERDRIVE and immediately turned his head to look at the old spymaster.

OVERDRIVE still exists?

"As I told Director Carter, I'd stake my life on it, sir. I believe Site X is indeed in the old Soviet missile silo. Given the Keyhole images, plus the HUMINT and SIGINT intelligence documented in OVERDRIVE about the shipment of drones north out of Petropavlovsk-Kamchatskiy with the specialized chemical cannons, it is safe to say that we know the location of Post 866."

Gale nearly jumped out of his seat. "You've found it?"

"Quiet, Mr. Gaines," the president snapped, turning his attention back to McGavran. "In your report, you said that you believe that the activity at the FSB's Lubyanka Building in Moscow is correlated to the increase of drone activity around Site X."

"Yes, sir. That has been documented on twelve occasions by both surveillance outside the Lubyanka Building, as well as Keyhole surveillance of Site X. As I stated in OVERDRIVE, it is my conclusion that the *siloviki* watch from a highly fortified lounge deep under the FSB building the dealings of *trials* at Site X. The intelligence on that is sound, sir."

"But this is all speculation," said Morgan Fray. "How am I the only one here who doesn't see any definitive proof? OVERDRIVE is just some half-cocked intelligence report from a renegade CIA agent!"

"I'd have to agree with Fray, sir," DNI Nagle said. "This is purely speculation. In no way do we have *any* concrete evidence that Americans are being taken to this facility. The Russians could be doing any number of things at Site X."

McGavran didn't back down. "Sir, I disagree. The intelligence I have gathered in regard to the activity off the east coast of the Kamchatka Peninsula at the Gazprom oil rig, as well as the shipments coming out of Vladivostok to Petropavlovsk-Kamchatskiy and then north toward Site X, strongly repudiates that claim. If you take another look at OVERDRIVE, you would see that."

"But it still doesn't say for *certain* that Americans are being taken in those stealth helicopters," said Fray. "You can't prove that."

"Sir, if I may," Carter said, turning her chair toward the president. "At 1700, after I was first briefed on OVERDRIVE by Prescott McGavran, I spoke to my satellite directors at Langley. Given the patterns illustrated in OVERDRIVE in relation to the Russian-owned Gazprom oil rig in the Bering, I thought it was prudent to aim a series of our spy satellites at the Gazprom oil rig in question as well as over Site X."

Carter opened the message on the computer screen in front of her and transferred the images to the big screen behind McClintock. "According to witnesses in Eagle, Emily Gale was kidnapped around 9:23 a.m., Alaska time. That would mean the men who captured her got to Jack Wade around 10 a.m. Considering it would take a prop plane nearly two hours to get to Anchorage, or any of the coastal towns in Alaska—we can deduce they hit the water by boat or even aircraft by noon. According to the FBI, all planes were grounded by that time and the navy was searching the Bering with radar."

"You're saying they took a speedboat to Russia?" Fray said sarcastically.

"No," Carter said, "I'm saying they could have used multiple modes of transportation. Possibly that missing fishing boat to get off the coast and out to sea, but then they could have used anything."

"Where are you going with this, Director Carter?" the president asked.

"Sir, we don't know for certain how the Russians transport Americans across the Bering." Carter put a slide of the satellite imagery up on the big screen. "But I can tell you that approximately one hour and twenty minutes ago, one of our satellites looking at the Russian Gazprom oil rig just off the Kamchatka Peninsula picked up a Kamov Ka-82K Russian stealth helicopter landing on the rig. The helicopter came in from the east, sir. Shortly after, we believe that the Kamov refueled and then flew directly west in the direction of Site X."

Carter flipped to another picture. "This was taken nearly three hours ago over Site X." The picture showed a topographic view of a mountaintop where two large helicopters sat under camouflaged netting and an even larger helicopter sat unobscured on the peak. "The unobscured helicopter is an AgustaWestland AW101, which arrived at Site X from Petropavlovsk-Kamchatskiy." She clicked another slide. It showed two unobscured helicopters parked on the peak of Site X. "Thirty minutes ago, the Kamov Ka-82K from the Gazprom oil rig arrived at Site X. Take note that a group of individuals can be seen carrying something through the concrete bunker doors."

The room went deathly silent for a long moment. Gale gazed from the screen to the president of the United States.

"Still doesn't explain how that stealth helicopter was able to fly across the Bering undetected by our navy," muttered Fray.

"It's called a stealth helicopter for a reason," grunted Bridgewater. "And Director Carter might be correct; maybe they used a different mode of transportation to cross and the stealth helicopter picked them up halfway."

"Like a boat?"

"Or a submarine," Gale said. "When I was captured by the Russians, I heard them say that two other teams were rendezvousing together with the captured subject in Eagle—they said they would take the secondary extraction route out of Anchorage and that it would take longer. I also noticed that my captors all had rebreathers with them. Correct me if I'm wrong, but from the limited intelligence I've seen so far, it strongly suggests that the Russians are taking Americans to Site X and from what the Vympel operators told me before they got me on that plane—"

"What exactly did they tell you?" asked Carter.

"They said: Viktor Sokolov is looking forward to seeing me at the sharashka. That they had my daughters and it would be a family reunion." Gale watched as Carter took a deep breath, then he said, "My daughters are there"—he pointed to the screen. "Viktor Sokolov has them. The Russians have been taking Americans for decades. Torturing them. And now we know where they do it."

"We don't know that for sure," said Fray.

"What more evidence would you need?" Gale yelled. "Would you like Russian foreign intelligence to drop a pin? Maybe they can send you a picture of my daughters while they are at it."

"Enough," the president said calmly. For a long moment the president said nothing, then he began to shake his head. "I think my chief of staff is correct, we can't prove that your daughters are at Site X. I cannot in good faith send American operators on a mission like this, given the lack of intelligence."

"Sir," Commander Spear said. "After listening to the contents of OVER-DRIVE and looking at these satellite images of Site X, I can say in confidence that I've sent men into battle on far less intelligence."

"But we're not talking about sending men into Pakistan, Commander. We are talking about sending operators into the land of a global superpower—Russia for God's sake. That is an act of war."

"With all due respect, Mr. President," Spear said, "that didn't stop the Russians from operating on US soil. Those men in Alaska have been identified as Russians. Russians are kidnapping our citizens. It is the consensus of both myself and General Bridgewater that JSOC has the capability to infiltrate and rescue any Americans within Site X under Article 51 of the United Nation's Charter."

Article 51 was a nation's inherent right of self-defense.

The president took in the JSOC commander for a long moment.

"You're not really considering this, are you, sir?" Fray asked, always thinking of the political ramifications of the president's actions. "It would be a suicide mission that would result in an international crisis. If it went south, it would ruin this administration."

McClintock continued to think.

"Sir," Gale said, "if you don't send in the United States military, I am going to go in anyway."

Fray laughed. "You think we're just going to let you go to Russia? You're a loose cannon. We heard what you did in Moscow; you should be in a cell in Leavenworth!"

Gale shot the man a serious look. "My actions in Moscow were warranted. President Reagan and Director Casey gave McGavran and me permission under Directive 138 to go after Sokolov and the men working with him. Those assassinations were sanctioned and legal."

"Is that true?" asked Carter, looking at McGavran.

The old spymaster nodded.

"Then why were you demoted?"

"I wasn't. I persuaded Bill Casey to put me at OREA—so I could keep looking for the sharashka."

"So Casey was a trigger-happy lunatic. No surprise there," muttered Fray.

"You weren't there. You weren't on the ground. If this administration decides to throw me in Leavenworth, so be it," Gale said. "But help me get my daughters first. They are innocent Americans who have been captured by a foreign state."

The president shook his head. "I can't in good faith order Americans to execute such an operation—even if it falls under Article 51."

"Excuse me, Mr. President," Earl Marks said, introducing himself and putting his box of research onto the oval table. "Sir, it wouldn't just be saving the Gale daughters. It would be saving the hundreds, if not thousands of American souls who were lost at Site X over the decades." He opened the box and plopped dozens of the MPRs representing the missing who had stayed through the Northern Breeze only to disappear days later. He started reading off the names of individuals who vanished in the Alaskan wilderness. The last folder in the pile, he held up, and read off the name: "Paul Brady, sir. Retired Navy SEAL. Went missing six weeks ago, after staying at the Northern Breeze—he was last seen near a town called Chicken."

Gale watched as both Spear and Bridgewater snapped their attention to Earl.

Earl continued: "He might still be alive, sir. Max Tobeluk confirmed to the FBI that Brady was picked up by Ned Voigt and his crew. Paul Brady might still be at Site X, sir."

The expression that crossed Commander Spear's face was visceral and the president nearly winced as he caught the commander's stare.

"Let me go in, sir," Gale said.

The president shook his head again. "My chief of staff is right. We do not have complete verification that Americans are at Site X. Until there is proof, I will not send our operators onto Russian soil. The risks are too high."

"Sir," Carter said, "what if we could get verification? Would you send the SEALs in then?"

"What do you have in mind, Director Carter?"

"Due to some technological advances in the recent years, I think we might have a way to get a camera into Site X to verify the possible American prisoners."

"And how would we go about that?"

McGavran cleared his throat. "We give Robert his wish. We send *him* to Site X."

Chapter 54

"*SUKA!*" BITCH! SOKOLOV yelled, slamming his cane into the small of Emily's back as she let out a wail of pain.

Cassie flailed from her compromised position in the air, the sight of Emily completely breaking her.

Emily sobbed uncontrollably, a maelstrom of tears, snot, and drool falling down her trembling face.

Sokolov glared at Cassie. "How does it feel? How does it feel to know there is nothing you can do to save your sister's life?"

"Cassie, where are we?" Emily whimpered. "What's going on?"

"I am righting a wrong!" Sokolov said. "I am seeking retribution for the sins of your father. I am showing Cassandra what it feels like to have the one you love suffer at your feet!"

"If you touch her again, I will kill you!" Cassie screamed.

"You mean like this?" Sokolov raised his cane and brought it down over the back of Emily's head. *Thwack!* The impact of the cane made a sickening noise, and Emily buckled to the ground, moaned, and became still.

"EM!"

"Stop it!" Billy yelled from his seat.

Cassie looked up to Billy secured to his chair, both Marko and Brady looking at him with expressions of caution on their faces.

"Yeah," Billy continued, "I'm talking to you, you sick fuck! You want to pick on someone, pick on me!"

"Billy—" Brady whispered.

"No," Billy said. "I can't just sit here and let this happen. I'm done with this. I'm done with this place. I'm done with being your little lab rat. I'm done with your experiments and your sick sport!"

Sokolov smiled. "There is always a *geroy*, a hero."

The old general looked at his Vympels, then to Captain Yermakova and Artur, seeing if they thought Billy's outburst was as funny as he thought it was. But both Yermakova and Artur looked like they were about to be sick while the four Vympels in the room grinned with amusement. Sokolov hobbled in front of Billy. "I read your file, William French. You are an outcast, a coward, an unremarkable person. A forgettable human being, no? I heard that you cried like a baby when you were put into Yermakova's trials. Yet you stand up for Cassandra, why?"

Cassie made eye contact with Billy and mouthed, *Don't*.

Billy remained stoic and kept his chin high.

Sokolov pointed down to the puddle of urine at Billy's feet. "Here is what I think, William French. You are scared. People lose control of their faculties when they are afraid, no? I've seen it many times. Brave men, when confronted with the inevitable, are not able to control their terror. But now, in the face of death, you are trying to stick up for Cassandra."

Billy glanced again at Cassie who shook her head, pleading with her eyes for Billy not to talk.

"It's because you love her, no? It's because you *love* Cassandra."

Billy swallowed hard.

"You love her, so you will stick up for her. Let me tell you something, William French, I know exactly how you feel. I loved my son more than anything. I watched him die at my feet. I watched him suffer like an animal at the hands of a monster!" Sokolov pointed his cane at Cassie. "Her father tortured and murdered my son in front of me while I pleaded for him to stop. I begged him. I said, take me, not him! I watched the person I loved most in this world be slaughtered at my feet."

Sokolov lifted Billy's head and snapped at Artur, pointing to the table holding the syringes. "Give him a double dose of amphetamines. I don't want him passing out."

Artur took a reluctant step forward and grabbed a milky syringe and approached Billy. Artur lifted the sleeve of Billy's smock and injected the needle into his arm. Billy's eyes immediately grew wide, his pupils dilating. His muscles spasmed slightly, his arms and legs flexing against the cables holding him down.

Sokolov pointed to Emily's limp figure on the ground. "Give her a dose, too; I want her awake for this!"

Artur returned to the table, grabbed another syringe, and injected Emily. She shuddered awake.

Sokolov grabbed the curved blade and told two of his Vympels to release Billy from his chair and stand him up.

On trembling legs, Billy swayed in the middle of the room.

"Take two steps forward," Sokolov ordered.

Billy took two wobbly steps and stopped.

Then, handing the curved knife to one of his Vympels, Sokolov said, "January 27, 1987. Your father marched my son in front of me, just like William French is standing before you now. My Evgeny was sick, beaten and bruised, hypothermic and extremely ill. Your father had stripped him of his clothing, marched him through the snowy wilderness before bringing him to my *dacha*. As my son fought to stay alive, your father placed him in front of me and immobilized him." Sokolov snapped his fingers and the Vympel operator holding the curved knife bent behind Billy and in one fluid motion sliced through both Achilles tendons.

Billy's screams of surprise and anguish echoed through the room. He fell, flopping around like a fish out of water.

Both Marko and Brady jerked in their chairs.

Sokolov grabbed the knife, making eye contact with Cassie.

"And as my son struggled in front of me, your father grabbed him, just like I am grabbing William, and sliced his throat."

The glint of the curved blade flashed in a fluid arc across Billy's throat. The surprised look on his face, and the flow of crimson falling down his dirty hospital gown made Cassie scream louder than she'd ever screamed before. The screams filled the room as Billy collapsed to the floor.

The memory of finding Derrick hanging from the barn scaffolding last January filled her mind. It was all too much. The agony was so acute she vomited on the floor. The room began to swim so fast that she hadn't seen Captain Yermakova cover her mouth and dart out of the room. Hadn't seen Artur backpedal so his back was plastered to the wall in surprise.

Cassie's shock and revulsion was so traumatizing that she hadn't heard Sokolov break out in a coughing fit. Hadn't seen the old general fall to one knee, blood dotting the palm of his hand as he lifted it from his mouth.

Cassie just wanted all this to end.

|||||||||||||||||||||||||||||||||||||||||||||||||||||||||||||||||||||||||||

General Sokolov felt like his lungs were on fire as he collapsed to the floor, coughing forcefully into his hand.

"Are you all right, General?" asked Dmitry, grasping him by the elbow, as two of the Vympels helped him to his feet.

Cassandra Gaines's screams filled the room, making Sokolov's nausea worse.

"When was the last time you've slept, General?"

Sokolov pointed a finger at Cassie. "Will someone shut her up!"

A Vympel operator grabbed a leather gag from the metal table and secured it over Cassie's mouth.

Sokolov breathed in deeply, trying to catch his balance. His body felt off, weak and exhausted. Maybe he *should* take a break; it had been days since he'd slept. Pointing to William French's body, he said, "Clean this up. Find Yermakova, tell her I will use her residence for the time being."

Dmitry asked, "What do you want to do with the prisoners?"

Sokolov, hobbling out of the room, stopped. "Return them to their cells." Then he looked to Artur and said, "Go with them. Make sure they are cared for. I want them healthy when we reconvene."

Chapter 55

GALE STOOD OVER the hospital bed in the Anchorage Regional ICU and put a hand on Peter Trask's bandaged forearm. His son-in-law lay unconscious, a breathing tube down his throat, his chest rising slowly up and down. Trask's head and beard had been shaved in Fairbanks after he'd been life-flighted out of Eagle.

Supposedly, after the firefight on the Yukon shoreline, Alvin Petit and the Rockin' R boys had found Trask lying next to the river. Two bullet wounds had pierced his massive body; one in the right side of his chest, the other in his abdomen. Maverick had already succumbed to his injuries by the time Petit and Cronin's men got to his side.

Gale looked up from Trask's damaged form and felt his eyes mist over, remembering what he'd said before he'd left for Anchorage.

You watch over her while I'm gone, Pete.

Gale stifled a sob. "You did your best, son."

Outside in the hallway, Alvin Petit and Bill Cronin talked to a doctor. Behind them, Gale could see the handful of military personnel that had been ordered to escort Gale back to Anchorage.

After Susan Carter and McGavran pitched their plan to the president about Gale infiltrating the sharashka, the president had ordered Gale and Blue Squadron to JBER, where, with the help of a CIA special task force, they were going to prep him for his upcoming mission, which had been dubbed Operation SLEEPING BEAR.

Carter's main argument in persuading the president to agree to her plan had been based on the fact that he, James Gale, would be entering Russia as a citizen of the United States looking for his daughter, and not an individual associated with the US military or intelligence services.

The proposal was to have Gale enter the premises of Site X rigged with the CIA's most state-of-the-art video- and audio-capturing devices. Once Gale was close to Site X, his goal would be to infiltrate the sharashka by any means necessary, including getting captured.

The CIA would retrofit Gale with the audio and visual transponders that would be live-feeding back to Langley, JSOC Command, and the Situation Room where the president and the selected staff from the National Security Council would watch. Once the council got definitive proof that Americans were being held in the sharashka, Commander Spear would take over from JSOC Command in Fort Bragg and order the NSWDG, or Naval Special Warfare Development Group, to send in the SEALs.

In the halls outside the Situation Room, Gale had stopped Carter to thank her.

"After everything that has happened, Robert, it's the least I can do."

When the Lockheed YF-8 landed back in JBER, Gale met the DEVGRU Blue Squadron commander, Seamus Cafferty, as well as his assault troops who had flown in from Dam Neck.

When JSOC and CIA personnel briefed Cafferty and his lieutenant commander, Craig Anderson, about the upcoming mission, they'd initially been taken aback that Gale was to go in alone.

"It's a suicide mission," Anderson stated flatly to Spear through the video comm linking the Situation Room and Fort Bragg to the briefing room in JBER. "We can't guarantee we can get every American out. We don't know how many personnel the Russians have in that facility."

It was one of the senior enlisted SEALs, a thirty-seven-year-old chief petty officer from Missoula, Montana, who spoke up first. "They're saying they got a SEAL down there and who knows how many Americans. I say we get in the middle of it and sort this out ourselves. The Russians have one of our own; it should be our job to get him back." The senior enlisted man gestured to Gale across the briefing room. "From one Montanan to another, first round of beer is on you when we get back."

After Cafferty drew up a rough outline of the mission plan with his command master chief, he allowed the other senior enlisted SEALs and officers in his squadron to "murder board" or "critically review" their operational analysis.

Once the SEALs questioned, scrutinized, and then agreed upon their methods of operation, Susan Carter's CIA task force took over, retrofitting Gale with the high-tech equipment needed to verify American proof of life within the sharashka.

Gale had been apprehensive about taking an audio and video transponder with him into the sharashka given the fact that it was a transponder that had blown BLUEMAN's cover all those years ago.

But as the CIA team showed Gale the nearly invisible video-capturing contact lenses that would relay, in real time, everything Gale would see, he'd been impressed.

While the contact lenses eased Gale's nerves, it was the nano-microphone and communications transponder that really surprised him.

One of the CIA techs held up an almost imperceptible skin-colored fleck and placed it on Gale's Adam's apple. "This nano-microphone is impervious to detection. They can hold you up to any sort of scanner and this baby won't show, same with the contacts and this." The tech held up a small red-and-white capsule. "This is how we track you, as well as communicate." The tech opened the capsule and a miniature tick-shaped device fell on his hand. "This is the latest in nano-robotic technology. This little guy is untraceable, and after it's swallowed, will latch on to the wall of your stomach."

"How am I supposed to communicate through something in my stomach?"

"You won't be able to communicate directly to us, but we will be able to communicate with you." The tech explained that once the nanobot was latched to Gale's stomach lining, it would vibrate based on what the CIA was trying to tell him. "One jolt from the nanobot means we've got confirmation from the president to send in the SEALs. It will take them exactly thirty-eight minutes once leaving their takeoff point from a navy aircraft carrier in the Bering, one hundred and forty miles from Site X." The tech explained that JSOC wanted the SEALs as close to the peninsula as possible, but still in international waters, so as to not alert the Russians of their presence.

"Three jolts mean that the rescue mission has been aborted and you're on your own," Spear added.

"Fair enough."

That had been two hours before Gale stood over Trask.

After Gale had been fully briefed and the brass felt confident on getting him into the Kamchatka Peninsula via a HAHO jump, a High Altitude High Opening descent from a military aircraft, they'd allowed him to leave the base and see his son-in-law who had just been life-flighted from Fairbanks.

As Gale stood over Trask, he'd thought over all the events in his life that had brought him to this terrible moment. Gale knew his odds of success on this mission were incredibly low. But he didn't care. Viktor Sokolov had taken his wife from him—he wasn't going to let him take his girls, too.

Looking down at his watch, he saw it was time to head back to JBER.

"You stay strong, Pete. When you wake up, we'll all be here."

Chapter 56

EXACTLY THIRTY-SIX HOURS after Gale crash-landed the G650 on Middleton Island, the MC-130 Combat Talon II took off from JBER with Gale and the SEALs in the cargo hold.

The mission was designed so that Gale would dive out of the MC-130 on the border of the Kamchatka Peninsula in the middle of the moonless night, allowing him to parachute into Site X undetected.

Gale tried his best to get some shut-eye as the MC-130 flew east over the Aleutian Chain—the Alaskan Islands that stretched across the Bering Sea into Russian territory. For four hours they flew, until reaching Attu Station, Alaska's most westerly island nearly three hundred miles from the eastern shores of the Kamchatka Peninsula, and almost three hundred sixty miles from Site X.

As the MC-130 landed to refuel and drop the SEALs at Attu, Gale exited the plane and made his way to a small building near the landing strip where the CIA task force would give him his last briefing. As Gale moved with the SEALs to the building, which served as an FOB, or forward operating base, he looked over at the flurry of activity near the western end of the landing strip. Four sleek military helicopters sat idly while a group of mechanics worked on the birds.

"The 160th SOAR are going to be taking us in. The Night Stalkers, best pilots in the world. Coupla' those guys flew us in during the Bin Laden raid," the SEAL chief petty officer from Montana said as they walked into the FOB.

Inside, the CIA's task force had set up a multitude of equipment: computer screens and small satellite dishes sat on tables, next to high-tech comm links used to keep contact between Gale, JSOC Command, Langley, and the White House.

The SEALs watched intently as the CIA tech inserted the visual-capturing lenses onto Gale's irises as well as the microphone placed on his throat and the nanobot that would latch on to his stomach lining.

After the CIA group confirmed that everything was in working order, they let Commander Cafferty and his SEALs help Gale put on his gear. He was given dark op cammies with a corresponding Kevlar vest and bulletproof plates. His face and neck were painted black and dark green, the same color as the bump helmet that was fitted to his head.

"Since your audio and visual will be feeding through your eyes and throat, there is no need to set you up with any cameras, but you'll obviously want a pair of these," Cafferty said, securing a pair of four-tubed quad NODs—high-tech night-vision devices—to Gale's helmet. Next, Gale was given a GPS unit with a built-in altimeter that was secured to his wrist, as well as a black parachute bag and oxygen mask for his HAHO jump.

"You ever make a jump like this, old man?" asked the chief petty officer from Montana.

"Unlike you frogmen, us Delta boys learn to fly before we learn to swim. I was doing HAHO jumps before you were even born, son."

The SEAL smiled. "And when was your last jump?"

"Before you were born."

That got a laugh from all the SEALs except Cafferty, who had finished cinching Gale's weapons of choice, a Delta 1911 pistol and an HK 416, into Gale's belt and parachute rig.

Even though Gale was trying to give off the appearance of being cool, calm, and collected in front of the younger SEALs, internally he was second-guessing both the HAHO jump and his mission into Site X. Mostly, he was worried about his hip not being able to take the parachute landing. It had been nearly three decades since he'd jumped out of an airplane. He hoped to God that his body would hold up.

"Let's go over this again," Cafferty said. "Once we get the green light to come get you, that thing in your stomach will buzz you once. That means it will take us thirty-eight minutes from the moment we take off from the navy carrier to the time we land on target and come knocking on your door. CIA will be tracking you via your iris video feed. So what you see, they see. Good luck."

"Thank you, Commander."

Ten minutes later, Gale walked out of the FOB and across the tarmac to the now refueled MC-130. After the SEALs loaded into the four UH-70s, Gale watched as they lifted off the tarmac and headed east toward the navy carrier waiting for them outside the peninsula.

"You ready?" an airman from the Twenty-Fourth Special Tactics Squadron, STS, asked, coming out of the MC-130.

"As much as I'll ever be."

Five minutes later, Gale double-checked his kit and then leaned back in his seat as the plane took off from Attu Station and headed toward the Kamchatka Peninsula before banking north. During the flight he repetitively kept going through his parachute emergency procedures until he got the two-minute warning signal and stood. Cinching the oxygen mask over his face, Gale rechecked his altimeter and GPS: the small LED display determined he was just under thirty thousand feet and roughly fifty-eight miles due east from Site X.

After the one-minute warning, the back of the MC-130 opened and the noise became deafening. Gale began the breathing sequences necessary for a HAHO jump, and for a split second, fear shot up his throat. Was he up for the challenge?

As the STS airman counted down from five with his hand, Gale pushed all that self-doubt aside.

Walking forward, arms and legs outstretched, he jumped and felt himself go weightless.

Chapter 57

"CASSIE, YOU NEED to get up!" Brady hissed.

Knees pressed against her chest, Cassie sat on the concrete bed in her cell in Red Block, staring through the darkness, only cognizant of the bubbling of the fountain and the sound of the water moving through the runnel. She hadn't moved in hours, as the image of Billy bleeding out in front of her held her paralyzed.

She heard Brady whisper, "You're her sister, make her talk."

"Cass . . ." Emily's small voice said. "Cassie, are you okay?"

"Let her be," Artur said, tersely. The scientist had come down into Red Block some time ago to treat the prisoners and was currently running an IV into Emily's arm. "She's in shock."

"Now is not the time to be in shock!" Brady said. "We can't continue like this. We won't survive another session in that room." He shot a searing look at Artur. "Give her something—we need her clearheaded!"

"And why would I do that—"

Cassie shut her eyes, not hearing Brady's retort to Artur's remark. She was trying to get rid of the image of Billy dying on the floor. She thought of Derrick— is this how he felt after witnessing so many traumatic events?

Thinking back to what Artur had said in his lab earlier about her having received the intervening drug to prevent a response like this—*is the drug intervention not working?*

If she had the drug in her system, how come she felt like this?

"GI Jane," Marko said, standing in his cell. "We need you to answer us . . . I know you are in pain, but we need your help."

Cassie sat up slowly and took in the half glow of the cellblock. Brady and Artur were still squabbling as the scientist continued to run an IV line into Emily's arm.

"It's not working," Cassie said.

"What's not working, GI Jane?" Marko asked.

Cassie looked at Artur, who had stopped arguing with Brady. "Those drugs you've given me, your PTSD drug."

"You haven't received a dosage in nearly forty-eight hours," Artur said. "It has to be administered every twenty-four hours, you've missed your window."

"Then give me some."

"It doesn't work like that," Artur said. "You've experienced trauma in between doses."

"Cass," Emily said. "Who was that man? Why was he saying those things about Dad?"

Cassie walked to the bars and stared at her older sister. She'd been thinking over everything the general had accused her father of. "I don't know, Em." Deep down, though, Cassie knew it was true. Her father had always been a complicated man, an enigma of sorts. But a CIA assassin? A murderer? Her mind went back to what Sokolov said about the death of her mother.

But my mother died in a car crash!

"Listen," Brady said. "We need to have a plan. The general could take us up there at any moment. We need to find a way to fight back."

"There is nothing we can do," Cassie said. "There are too many of them. We are going to die here."

"I will not accept that," Brady said. "We owe it to Billy. You saw how sick Yermakova looked when Sokolov killed him. We can get her on our side!" Brady motioned to Artur. "You can help us. I saw you in there, too; you looked like you were going to faint."

"Subject 8831 is correct," Artur said. "You will die here. There is nothing I can do."

Marko banged a fist against his bars. "You are not just a prisoner here. You have the power to help us!"

"I shouldn't be talking to you," Artur said.

"But you are!" Marko yelled. "You once told me you knew this facility better than anyone. You told me that you *do* have some control!"

Artur shook his head.

Marko spat out his words. "You do! It's why I am alive; you're keeping me alive for a reason!"

"What are you talking about?" asked Brady.

"He knows I am helicopter pilot! He keeps me alive because I am helicopter pilot. I haven't been in a trial in months—because he wants me to help him escape."

"That's not true," Artur said. "You're being kept alive because you are participating in a longitudinal study of the drug. You are here because I am monitoring your brain over a long period of time. All of you have to get it through your heads—there is no way out of this facility. There is nowhere for you to run. If the guards don't get you, the drones will. And if by some miracle you escape the drones, you will be out in the wilderness all by yourself. You wouldn't last a week."

"You must know where we are," Brady said.

Artur heaved a sigh. "Yes, I know where we are."

"Where?"

For a long moment, Artur was silent, then he said, "We are on the Kamchatka Peninsula. Hundreds of kilometers away from any sort of civilization."

"Kamchatka Peninsula, where is that?" asked Emily.

"Russia."

"Russia?" said Emily in disbelief.

Artur continued, "This place was designed to keep people inside. You can't *reason* with the people who run sharashkas. Once you've been placed inside, there is no getting out."

"*Reason* . . ." Marko said, then grabbed his cell bars and pressed his face farther into the light. "Of course."

"What?" Brady asked.

"Devil's Breath."

Artur looked up curiously at Marko. "What about it?"

"It made me useless, it made me obey your every command, it made me tell the truth. I had no control of my actions."

"Scopolamine and sodium pentothal," Artur said.

"Yes!" Marko said excitedly. "You can use it on the general and his men! You can use it to get us out of here. They come here by helicopter, right? I can fly us to safety—we could even steal a helicopter from Yermakova's fleet."

Suddenly, the doors to the cellblock opened. Footsteps could be heard coming toward them.

"I only have one dose left of Devil's Breath—there are nearly a hundred personnel in this facility."

"You hate it here!" Marko hissed. "We need your help—"

A voice broke through the darkness, "*Doktor, idi s nami!*"

Artur turned to the voice, then looked at Marko. "The general is summoning me."

"You are a coward," Marko said.

"I am trying to survive—just like you," Artur said, then walked out of the cellblock.

Chapter 58

CAPTAIN YERMAKOVA SAT in the control room and fingered the key hanging from her neck. The drone operators and technicians were at their stations, bent over their work.

It had been nearly ten hours since General Sokolov killed William French in the white-tiled room. The barbarity of Sokolov's actions had driven Yermakova up to her executive living quarters, where she'd calmed her nerves with a glass of vodka. She'd planned on staying in her residence for as long as possible, but Sokolov's men had quickly kicked her out so the general could sleep.

The general had looked terrible as Yermakova grabbed some personal items and left her quarters, heading to the control room, where she sat now—deep in contemplation.

One thing that Yermakova despised was needless torture. Science experiments and sport were one thing; they had a purpose, but what Sokolov was doing downstairs was sickening.

She understood that Cassandra's father supposedly killed Sokolov's son and Sokolov was hell-bent on revenge—but why kill William French?

And more importantly: *Why had Putin authorized all this?*

Her thoughts went back to the FAPSI line when Sokolov had ordered her *intelligentsia* to find the man in the picture—Cassandra's father. KODIAK had located the man and his family, and Sokolov had sent in his Vympels to extract him.

Now, KODIAK had gone dark and Yermakova feared the worst.

Another thing irked her: Sokolov and his men were able to extract Emily Gale, but where was James Gale aka Robert Gaines? Had the Vympels been unable to extract the father?

Did something happen?

In order for Sokolov to execute a mission on foreign soil, he would have to ask Putin for permission. She knew that the general and the president were extremely close, but she couldn't figure out a scenario where the president would authorize such a brazen mission.

Vladimir Vladimirovich Putin was an extremely calculative man. The fact that the president would authorize an SVR-led extraction on the Gale family, after Cassandra was already taken, didn't fit into Putin's modus operandi.

Yermakova flipped through Cassandra Gale's dossier and got to the picture of her family. She stared at the image of her father.

Sokolov wanted you, so why aren't you here?

Yermakova fought the urge to walk over to the FAPSI line and dial the Kremlin directly.

No.

What she needed to do was gather more information first.

In the front of the room, she could see her GRU lieutenant, the point man of the sharashka's *intelligentsia*, huddled over his workspace.

"Lieutenant Klimentiev, a word, please." The lieutenant hurried to Yermakova and stood at attention. She spoke softly, as to not be overheard by any other technician in the room. "Lieutenant, I have an assignment for you. I need you to do this quietly." She handed him the picture of James Gale. "The general and his Vympels ran an operation to capture this man. I want you to figure out why he is *not* here. Scour the news in America, see if anything of note happened in Alaska. Find out why Viktor Sokolov was unable to extract him. Then get back to me."

As Klimentiev saluted and left the room, she looked at the monitors on the wall in front of her. They showed the night-vision drone feed that scanned the top of the facility and the surrounding wilderness. Yermakova noted the harshness of the wild terrain, then her attention went to the concrete bunker at the top of the mountain that served as an elevator entrance into the facility. Next to the bunker was the emergency hatch that had been closed after Subject 8831's escape attempt. *Idiot girl*, Yermakova thought, then gazed at the two helicopters on top of the facility used to bring in Emily Gale and General Sokolov.

She made a mental note that both helicopters needed to be covered in camouflage netting as soon as possible, but telling Sokolov and his men to do anything was proving incredibly difficult. Upon their arrival to the sharashka, Yermakova had forbidden Sokolov and his Vympels from bringing weapons into her facility.

Challenging the general had almost proved disastrous, causing a standoff on top of the mountain between Sokolov's men and her guards. After nearly twenty minutes of debate, it was decided that all firearms would be locked in the facility's armory, but the Vympels would be able to keep their combat blades.

The compromise made Yermakova feel like she was losing control over Post 866.

She turned her attention away from the monitors and the technicians below her, and fingering the key around her neck, looked at the small green door on the west wall of the control room.

Only *she* had access to the room.

Only *she* held the key and knew the codes.

As the director of Post 866, it was *her* responsibility to enact the fail-safe switch if she ever felt the sharashka was compromised.

She hoped it would never come to that.

Until then, she would have to see what information Lieutenant Klimentiev came back with.

Chapter 59

AT TWENTY-FIVE THOUSAND feet, Gale deployed his chute and relaxed, breathing slowly from his oxygen mask. The air was frigid, nearly -60 degrees Fahrenheit. He was glad he was retrofitted with the necessary SEAL-issued thermal-wear to keep him warm. Gale double-checked his GPS bearings with his backup wrist compass and reoriented himself so he was parachuting west along the predesignated route. According to his calculations, and glide ration indicator, It would take him just under twenty-five minutes to reach Site X.

Back at his time in Delta Force, before he'd been scooped up by agency recruiters, Gale had always loved HAHO jumps. Developed and tested in the late sixties, HAHO jumping was created for US Special Forces operators to deploy at high altitudes far away from the reaches of enemy radar and to "glide" into hostile territory undetected.

The minutes ticked by, and Gale kept his flight path on course as he floated into Russian territory. Through his NODs he could see the ground, and he used the larger terrain features he'd memorized earlier from the satellite photos to make sure he was gliding to the correct location. When his altimeter told him he was at two thousand feet and his GPS indicated he was roughly a half mile from Site X, an old sense of excitement coursed through his body.

Then he spotted the mountain.

My target.

Pulling on his left parachute cord, Gale circled in and noticed what looked like a concrete bunker built into the mountaintop just like the OVERDRIVE case file had detailed. As he got lower, he could make out four helicopters, two covered in camouflage netting and two others sitting one hundred yards from the concrete entrance, just as they were shown on the CIA's satellite imagery. Strangely enough, there were no guards or visible detection devices of any kind outside the entrance.

Gale landed softly on the peak, detached himself from his parachute, and oxygen tank, then unclipped the HK 416 from his parachute harness and brought the stock of the weapon into his shoulder. Double-checking the settings of the holograph site on the HK, he moved quietly toward the hatch he planned to breach.

WHITE HOUSE
SITUATION ROOM

"We've got a confirmed landing, sir," Susan Carter said from her seat in the Situation Room. She had been watching Robert's live descent into Site X from her secure computer.

"Good, put it on the big screen," President McClintock said, coming into the Situation Room.

Carter rerouted Robert's live feed from her secure laptop so it displayed on the Situation Room's main screen. The smaller, ancillary screens showed a live feed from the command center at Fort Bragg where JSOC commander Spear kept in constant communication with the SEALs now on the navy carrier southeast of the Kamchatka Peninsula. The rest of the screens showed live infrared and thermal feeds of Site X.

The select members of the National Security Council sitting in the Situation Room included: General Bridgewater, Director of National Intelligence Nagle, SecDef Macy, and National Security Adviser Thomas Bowman. To the president's left was his chief of staff, Morgan Fray, who looked despondently at Prescott McGavran, seated next to Carter.

"Commander Spear, notify both the NSWDG and Blue Squadron commanders to get ready, this could happen fast," President McClintock ordered.

"Yes, sir," Commander Spear said through the screen.

Carter watched as Robert scanned the area, then moved forward. Taking out two brick-shaped plastic explosives from his cammies, he began priming and double-priming them over the hatch.

McGavran had had a great debate with Commander Spear on whether the explosives would be able to breach the steel hatch that supposedly led to the sharashka's emergency stairwell.

McGavran had insisted that it didn't matter whether the explosives worked in opening the hatch. If it did, great, if not, the explosion would be so deafening it would only be a matter of seconds before the alarms would sound and Robert would be apprehended.

Either way, Robert would enter the sharashka. The mission, after all, was to obtain a proof-of-life of Americans inside.

All eyes in the Situation Room were on Robert as he finished setting the explosives and backed up.

Ten seconds later, an explosion blew the hatch off its hinges, the downward force of the blast cratering the ground around it.

They watched as Robert heaved the broken hatch aside and jumped down onto a spiral staircase that seemed to descend forever.

As Robert found purchase on the first landing, the resounding wail of an alarm sounded from the screen in the Situation Room and a bright, strobing light flashed in Robert's feed.

"Okay, gentlemen," Carter said, "let's begin."

Chapter 60

GENERAL SOKOLOV SAT at the end of the bed in Yermakova's suite and breathed in deeply as Yermakova's scientist pressed the cold stethoscope to his chest. Sokolov eyed the scientist curiously—something about him was eerily familiar.

"What is your name?" wheezed Sokolov.

The scientist pulled the stethoscope from the general's chest and frowned. "My name is Artur. Tell me, General, how long have you been sick?"

"That is none of your business," snapped Sokolov, who was still feeling weak even after nearly ten hours of sleep. "Just give me one of your cocktails. I need energy to continue downstairs. How are the prisoners?"

"They are fine," Artur said and went to his little black bag.

Sokolov again tried to figure out why the scientist looked so familiar, then gazed around the room. His four Vympel operators guarded the door and Dmitry clicked away on his tablet from a chair. Artur returned with a milky vial and syringe.

"How long have you worked under Yermakova?" Sokolov asked.

"Eleven years."

"And she gives you the freedom to conduct your own experiments?"

Artur didn't respond, and Sokolov chuckled. "Back when I ran Post 866, I had some of the most brilliant minds in all of the USSR working in this facility.

They did groundbreaking research for the state. We were organized, effective—not like this clown show."

Artur injected the cocktail into Sokolov's shoulder, and the general instantly felt a cold wave rush to his brain. He felt refreshed, alive. Looking at the scientist, he said, "You remind me of someone—"

As he said it, a muffled bang resounded from above. Dust fell from the ceiling. Everyone looked up. Sokolov looked at his Vympels.

"Find out what that was!" he shouted.

|||||||||||||||||||||||||||||||||||||||||||||||||||||||||||||||||||||||

POST 866
CONTROL ROOM

Captain Yermakova had been pacing around the control room and checking her watch constantly during the last twenty minutes, until the door to the room whooshed open.

Lieutenant Klimentiev entered in a hurry. "Captain, I have some news!" He held out a tablet and handed it to Yermakova.

On the screen were multiple American press articles of a plane crash off the coast of Alaska. Yermakova scanned the clippings. Each article reported that a private jet had crash-landed on Middleton Island with one reported survivor and five casualties.

"Who is the survivor?"

"Authorities have not released a name yet."

Yermakova cursed under her breath.

"That's not all, Captain. Keep looking through the tabs."

The next tab showed a news clipping of a shooting in Eagle with two Canadian citizens confirmed dead. The article was sparse in detail but Yermakova could fill in the blanks. This was the work of General Sokolov and his Vympels.

Yermakova handed the tablet back to Klimentiev and pointed to the FAPSI line. "Get me Kryuchkov!"

As Klimentiev rushed over to the FAPSI line, Yermakova began to feel herself shaking.

She'd been tricked, taken advantage of. KODIAK was most certainly exposed and probably dead. The plane crash and the events in Eagle had most definitely cast a spotlight on her operations. *I will be ruined.*

"Captain, I have Captain Kryuchkov for you!"

In a rage, Yermakova grabbed the receiver, not caring that the technicians in the room could hear her. "Kryuchkov! I want to know why General Sokolov is at my post! I want to know why his Vympels have been operating in the United States—get me the Kremlin!"

As Yermakova took a breath to continue her verbal assault on the captain of the FSB's Department Fifteen, she heard a sound that made her blood run cold.

A muffled *boom!*

For a paralyzing moment, Yermakova locked eyes with Klimentiev—then the alarms in the control room began to blare. The screens in front of the room all woke up, flashing red warning displays.

"There's been a breach in the emergency stairwell!" a technician cried from his workstation. He toggled through a series of camera views, before settling on the one showing the stairwell.

An armed figure dressed in black dropped to the first landing and slowly began descending the stairs.

Yermakova dropped the FAPSI line, and the receiver clanged on the floor. "Initiate an emergency lockdown, and gas that stairwell!" Yermakova's hand flew to her earpiece and keyed the mike that connected her to all the guards in the facility. "All guards put on your gas masks and proceed to the emergency stairwell. There's been a breach. I repeat, all guards proceed to emergency stairwell!"

Chapter 61

EVEN THOUGH GALE expected to trigger an alarm, he still jumped at the shrillness of the bleating noise and the loud hiss of gas being deployed in the stairwell.

Thankfully, he'd packed a gas mask in his kit. After securing the mask over his face, he looked under the tubes of his NODs so he could see the stairwell through the blaring red strobes that flashed from the walls. Gale readied his HK 416 and tore down the steps two at a time, grimacing from the pain in his hip.

McGavran's OVERDRIVE schematics of the sharashka revealed that Gale would have to climb down at least forty spiraling flights until he'd reach a door for the main level of the facility. From there, he'd have to improvise.

As he bounded down the steps he tried to keep his head on straight and not wonder what the people watching his feed were thinking as they observed him infiltrate the facility. The thought had crossed his mind that maybe they weren't seeing anything, that the video feed from his lenses had cut as soon as he went below ground. The CIA techs had insisted that wouldn't be the case, and that the frequencies that they transmitted through wouldn't be blocked by any terrain or any electromagnetic fields set up to defer communications. Gale could only hope that the CIA techs knew what the hell they were doing. If the SEALs weren't going to come save his ass, he'd be screwed.

On the nineteenth landing, he heard shouts and heavy footfalls pulsing over the blaring sirens and gazed down through the grated steps. Not ten floors below, he saw dozens of black-clad figures thundering up toward him.

Gale stopped, caught his breath, and wrestled through his options.

Engage or surrender?

He knew the 77 grain Black Hills 5.56 mm rounds in his HK would get the job done, but instead he decided on putting his weapons on the landing in front of him. Getting down on his knees, he extended his hands over his head and spoke loudly enough so the nano-microphone embedded on his throat would hopefully reach those keeping an eye on the mission.

"Bear in den. First phase complete."

|||||||||||||||||||||||||||||||||||||||||||||||||||||||||||||||||||||||||||||||||||

EXECUTIVE SUITE

"What's happening!" Sokolov spat at Dmitry.

Three of his Vympels had left the room minutes before to investigate the loud noise that rocked the facility. Moments later, the blaring alarms had sounded.

"I don't know, General!"

Over the bleating noise, Sokolov pointed his cane at Artur. "I know this alarm! It means the facility has been breached!" Walking over to the door that led to the hallway, Sokolov gripped the handle and tried to pull, but it wouldn't budge.

"We're on lockdown," Artur said.

"Can you override it?" asked Sokolov.

The scientist fingered his keycard hanging from the lapel of his lab coat and walked toward the door. He scanned the card for the general, but the scanner blinked red.

Sokolov turned to the remaining Vympel operator next to Dmitry.

"Open this door, Lieutenant."

The Vympel reached into the pocket of his black cargo pants and produced a small brick of C4, stuck it to the door, and motioned for Sokolov, Dmitry, and Artur to take cover in the next room.

Thirty seconds later, the C4 blew the door off its frame.

Sokolov hobbled through the smoky room and into the hallway.

"Take me to Yermakova!"

|||||||||||||||||||||||||||||||||||||||||||||||||||||||||||||||||||||||||||||||||||

EMERGENCY STAIRWELL

Gale had not attempted to resist; he needed to save his energy for what was to come.

The black-clad figures had swarmed him, dragging him down the rest of the stairs. As soon as they had gotten to him, they'd secured his weapons, ripped the helmet and night-vision goggles from his head, but kept the gas mask on. Then a blackout bag was fitted over his head, and plastic cuffs were fastened to his wrists.

Gale had expected to be searched extensively and relieved of all his weapons. What he hadn't expected was the blackout bag.

It was impossible to note all the direction changes after he had left the staircase.

He remembered what BLUEMAN had detailed for him all those years ago on those snowy park benches in Moscow. How the scientist described the layout of Post 866. All the horrors that took place inside. The rooms with the experiments so heinous and vile, even BLUEMAN had trouble telling the young CIA operative what he'd witnessed.

Suddenly, Gale was forced to stop. He heard an electric bleep and the sound of a heavy door opening.

Boot steps echoed around him and he was forced to sit in a chair.

The blackout bag and gas mask were whisked from his head and the first thing Gale saw was the plump face of a woman with thick eyebrows and bushy brown hair.

"Who are you?!" the woman cried in Russian, as four of the helmeted figures dressed in black military fatigues cut the cammies off Gale with surgical scissors.

The woman rounded on Gale and looked him dead in the eye, then her eyes grew wide in what could only be disbelieving recognition.

Gale kept eye contact with the woman so everyone stateside could see her clearly.

The woman stumbled with her words. "How . . . how did you find this place?"

"Tell Viktor I've come for my daughters," Gale said in perfect Russian. "Tell him if he wants to settle our score, he can settle it here with me."

Chapter 62

THE WIND THAT blew softly through the open French doors smelled of seawater.

President Putin loved that smell. It reminded him of his childhood vacations when his parents would take him to the beaches of the Black Sea.

As he grew older and accrued vast amounts of power and wealth, he realized that it was those fond childhood memories that meant the most to him, and the reason why he dumped so much money into re-creating those happy times.

The Residence at Cape Idokopas, often referred to as Putin's Palace, or *Dacha Putin*, was built during his first presidency. The twenty-six-thousand-square-meter Italianate complex located on the coast of the Black Sea near the village of Praskoveevka was built for one simple reason. *Nostalgia.*

The president of the Russian Federation yearned for his childhood years. And now, as the richest man in the world, he'd gone to great lengths to tap into those happy times.

As it was always done in Russia, the construction of the five-hundred-million-dollar compound did not come directly out of his pocket, but from subsidiaries that he threatened, bribed, and cheated to get the palace built.

Out of the twentysomething such compounds that he owned, Idokopas was his favorite. It was his reprieve from his hectic life in the Kremlin.

As Vladimir Vladimirovich Putin lay in his bed, his body on top of the silk sheets, he breathed in that salty air and felt a sense of calm that could only be achieved postcoitally.

Half under the sheets next to him, a lithe figure stirred, exposing a slender back. Young and fit. Not a day over twenty.

Putin traced her hourglass frame with the back of his hand.

Like all the women he shared his bed with, the president had specifically chosen her to accompany him to his secluded compound.

The fashion model had caught his attention the month before. He'd seen her first in a perfume ad and again walking the runways of Moscow's most famous fashion shows. Her pouty lips and voluptuous figure had awoken something inside the president.

She'd been easy . . . Putin thought as he stroked her luscious black hair. He had lavished the young woman with gifts: flowers, chocolates, shopping sprees, and a new apartment in Zamoskvorechye, the up-and-coming neighborhood south of the Moskva River.

When he was confident the young supermodel was smitten with him, he'd made his move and invited her to Idokopas.

And what a little minx she'd been, Putin thought as he got out of bed, put on a satin robe, and padded out of the French doors to his balcony.

He looked up at the stars and breathed in the cool night air.

"Mr. President," a familiar voice said behind him.

"*Der'mo!*" Putin swore in surprise, turning to face his chief security officer, Sergei Antonov. "What is it?"

Antonov walked onto the balcony, a tablet in his hand. "Mr. President, there is an urgent matter that needs your immediate attention."

Putin sighed, retying his robe, looking through the French doors at the sleeping supermodel. "Can it wait?"

"*Nyet*, Mr. President."

Putin closed the doors. "What is it?"

"I've received an urgent message from Captain Kryuchkov of the FSB's Department Fifteen. It's concerning Post 866. Captain Yermakova has sent word wondering why General Sokolov has been authorized to send his Vympels to the United States. She is wondering why you have authorized him to use the sharashka."

"My *dyadya* is at his *dacha* in the Khimki."

"We thought so, too, Mr. President. I sent a team there as soon as I got the message. The general is not there."

Putin tried to channel the breathing exercises his new judo instructor had been coaching him on.

The bastard had gone after Robert Gaines! The old fool!

Antonov handed him the tablet. Putin gazed down at a series of American press clippings.

"Captain Yermakova is claiming that this was caused by General Sokolov and his SVR Vympels."

Putin read the clipping in translated Russian and looked at the carnage of the private jet.

"We believe that plane is one of ours, from the fleet of the oil minister—"

Putin felt his blood begin to boil.

His *dyadya* had betrayed him.

"What are the Americans saying? Have they identified the dead as SVR operators?"

"*Nyet,* not officially. I've contacted the SVR chiefs and they've combed through our recent foreign intelligence lines. No word yet that the Americans know these were our men."

The Americans aren't dumb. They must know.

"When was this crash?"

"Two days ago, Mr. President."

"Get me a secure line to Captain Yermakova at once. I want two units of the Forty-Fifth Spetsnaz on choppers to Post 866 immediately!"

"*Da,* Mr. President!" Antonov said, and opened the French doors, scurrying away.

Putin gripped the marble balcony ledge and swore loud and long, his voice carrying out across the calm waters of the Black Sea.

His uncle would pay for this treachery.

Chapter 63

CAPTAIN YERMAKOVA STOOD in the middle of the initiation room and glared down at the man in the chair. His face was painted green and black, but Yermakova recognized him almost immediately.

"Did you hear me?" the man asked. "Tell Viktor I'm here!"

The blaring alarm muddled Yermakova's thoughts. How the hell had this man found the facility? How had he gotten past the drones undetected?!

She glanced around at the dozen guards who circled the man, then whipped around to Lieutenant Klimentiev. "Tell the drone operators I want them scanning the sky in a hundred-kilometer radius. Send guards to block every exit. Everyone else is to remain in their residences."

"*Da*, Captain!" Klimentiev said and ran out of the room.

Then she turned to her guards. "Check him for any sort of tracking devices!"

A guard took a wandlike device from his pocket and scanned it over Gale's body, head to toe, "*On chistyy*." He's clean.

"How did you find this place?" Yermakova repeated.

"My fairy godmother led me here. Where the hell are my daughters!"

Yermakova took a step back, her fingers instinctively going to the key hanging around her neck.

"*Uydi s moyego puti!*" a voice called from the door. General Sokolov and four Vympels appeared, followed by Artur. The general pushed the guards aside and stopped dead in his tracks.

"How—" an exasperated Sokolov said, his face breaking into a large smile as he took a step forward. "Do you know how long I've fantasized about this very moment?"

"Where are they!" Gale roared.

"Patience, my old friend. They are waiting for you downstairs. They are a little worse for wear, but they will be excited to see you."

"General!" Yermakova barked. "The facility has been compromised. This man did not come here alone. He had help. We need to evacuate immediately!"

Sokolov didn't seem to hear her.

"General, listen to me!"

Sokolov turned around abruptly and snapped at his Vympels, "Escort Captain Yermakova out of my sight!"

"Guards!" Yermakova yelled.

The dozen guards in the room unlatched their nightsticks and Sokolov laughed. "You think your guards with their little cattle prods will be any match for my men?" Sokolov snapped his fingers. "Kill the imbecilic guards."

Captain Yermakova barely had time to react; the speed at which the four Vympels moved was astounding. Blades flashed, dispatching her guards one by one. Yermakova let out a squeal as one of the Vympel operators grabbed her and pushed her to the floor. As the screams of the dying guards permeated through the room, Yermakova knew if she stayed, there was a good chance Sokolov would order her killed, too.

Crawling, she scrambled to the door, pushed Artur aside, and ran down the hallway. She took the first set of stairs that would take her to the control room. In her head she tried to figure out how many Vympels Sokolov had brought with him to the facility. Eight? Nine? A dozen?

Knowing she now had short of forty guards at her disposal, she wondered if they could stand a chance. She keyed the earpiece that connected her to her guards' helmets and was about to order every one of her men to descend on the room when the door above her blew open and Lieutenant Klimentiev entered the stairwell, looking like he'd seen a ghost.

"Captain, thank God!" Klimentiev huffed. "The president is on the FAPSI line. He's demanding to speak to you!"

Chapter 64

"IS THAT THE general?" White House chief of staff Morgan Fray asked in disbelief, pointing at the large screen in the Situation Room.

Carter watched intently through Robert's POV as an old man in a drab green military uniform hobbled into the crowded room flanked by four soldiers and a man in a white lab coat.

The woman with the bushy hair who had been yelling at Robert turned around abruptly.

Carter began typing a request to her operations center in Langley, asking for a positive facial recognition. "Getting confirmation."

On the main screen, a heated argument broke out between the old man and the bushy-haired woman.

"What are they saying?" asked the president.

Carter closed her eyes and focused on the angry diatribe coming over the feed. "The woman wants to evacuate the facility—" Carter's computer beeped and she looked down. "Operations has confirmed the facial recognition. That is General Sokolov."

"Hold on," Bowman shouted, "something's happening!"

Carter turned back to the feed. Robert's POV became jumpy as chaos erupted in the small room. Four of the soldiers who had entered with the general had unsheathed knives from their belts and were dispatching the guards surrounding Robert as the bushy-haired woman was thrown to the ground.

"Whoa!" cried Nagle.

"What's going on?" asked the president, as the violence waned and a blackout hood was thrown back over Robert's head.

"They're moving him," Prescott McGavran said. "General Sokolov has just ordered him to be taken downstairs to his daughters."

Chapter 65

EIGHT OF SOKOLOV'S Vympels entered Red Block and marched to the cells. Two Vympels to a prisoner, they grabbed Cassie, Emily, Marko, and Brady and stress-walked them out of the cellblock, blackout hoods over their heads.

Cassie could hear Marko and Brady struggling behind her. Ahead, Emily whimpered. They entered an elevator and Cassie felt it rise.

When the elevator opened, they marched for another couple of minutes until another door opened and Cassie felt the familiar coldness and the smell of ammonia hit her nostrils.

The Vympels made her sit down in a chair and secured her wrists to the armrests and legs.

Through the hood, she could hear a blade running over a whetstone.

Sokolov barked an order in Russian.

Cassie gripped the chair as a hand clamped over the blackout bag and tore it from her head.

She opened one eye, and then another—her brain not registering the scene that was playing out—a familiar figure hanging from the ceiling.

"DAD!!!!!"

WHITE HOUSE
SITUATION ROOM

"Enough of this," President McClintock said, pointing to the screen showing Commander Spear. "All operations are approved. Tell the SEALs to do what is necessary."

"Wait!" Director Carter pleaded. In the last five minutes, the team in the Situation Room had watched as Robert was moved into a white-tiled room, his wrists cuffed behind him and a leather gag forced into his mouth. A chain with a hook was placed through his cuffs and a winch cranked him into the air. "We need confirmation on the daughters!"

As if on cue, the door to the room flew open. Four hooded figures were escorted inside by eight soldiers. The soldiers sat the figures down into chairs placed before Robert.

On the left side of the screen, General Sokolov was sharpening a long knife on a whetstone. The man in the white lab coat stood next to him, his hands shaking as he opened a box full of syringes.

Suddenly, the hoods were thrown from the figures and Robert's POV became even more erratic.

Two men and two women sat bolted to the wooden chairs.

"Do we have a positive match?" asked SecDef Macy.

Carter's computer dinged twice and she looked down. "Positive identification on Cassandra and Emily Gale." The computer dinged again. "Another positive match on Paul Brady."

President McClintock stood up from his seat. "Commander Spear, tell the SEALs they are cleared to use all rules of engagement needed to rescue those hostages. They are a go."

"Copy that, Mr. President," Spear said through the screen. "Blue Squadron is a go. I repeat, Operation SLEEPING BEAR is a go, hostage-rescue ROEs are in effect; good luck, gents."

POST 866
TORTURE ROOM

Gale thought his veins were going to pop out of his throat as he screamed through his gag.

Emily's and Cassie's faces had turned from surprise, to shock, to desperation.

Cassie's body was filthy, her face covered in bruises; a white bandage covered her left arm. She looked like she'd lost nearly twenty pounds since the time Gale hugged her good-bye in Montana more than two weeks before.

Tears rolled down Emily's face as she gazed up at her father. Gale was so overcome with emotion that he almost didn't feel the vibration in his stomach—alerting him that the SEALs had just left the navy carrier.

Thirty-eight minutes.

He just hoped he would make it that long.

Sokolov marched in front of him, the newly sharpened knife in his hand.

Chapter 66

CAPTAIN YERMAKOVA HAD only heard stories of Vladimir Putin's temper but now she was witnessing it firsthand as the president berated her over the FAPSI line.

"You will do everything in your power to detain Viktor, do you understand me, Captain?" Putin roared after Yermakova had detailed for him the events since Sokolov arrived at the sharashka.

"*Da*, Mr. President. I will try, but he has his Vympels with him."

"You will do more than try, Captain. I want Viktor stopped and alive, is that clear?" Putin then told her he ordered two squadrons of the Forty-Fifth Spetsnaz Brigade from Vladivostok to the sharashka. They would be at the post in two hours. "I want Viktor secured before they get there!"

Yermakova saw her career flash before her eyes.

"Do I have any reason to doubt you, Captain Yermakova?"

"*Nyet*, Mr. President, you can count on me, but—" Yermakova caught herself, wondering if it was an appropriate time to alert the president of James Gale's arrival at the sharashka. It was only a matter of time before he found out. If she didn't tell Putin now, it would be *her* in the cellars of Butyrka—she just had to frame it correctly.

"But?"

"Something serious has just occurred, Mr. President." She took a deep breath and looked around the control room. Lieutenant Klimentiev and all the technicians hung on her every word. "It has just been brought to my immediate attention that the post has been compromised, sir. An American, led here by General Sokolov and his men. General Sokolov is calling him Robert Gaines. Currently, the general has Gaines and his daughters prisoner in the basement cells. We've been infiltrated, sir."

The silence on the other end of the line lasted nearly ten seconds.

Captain Yermakova could hear the sharp breathing coming over the phone, then, calmly, Putin said, "Captain Yermakova, I hereby order you to detain Viktor and bring him to Vladivostok and initiate EL-5 on Post 866 immediately."

Yermakova grabbed the key around her neck. "Mr. President?"

"Captain Yermakova, if you wish to keep your life, you will do as I say, understand?"

"*Da*, Mr. President. Of course."

"Contact me when you are en route to Vladivostok. I will reroute the Spetsnaz to meet you there. They will take Viktor to Moscow. Now, go."

The line went dead and Yermakova put the receiver on the table.

EL-5 was the old code word used by the KGB to trigger complete termination of a mission, asset, or installation that had been compromised. It was a kill switch, a self-destruct sequence.

Captain Yermakova was the only person in the facility who knew the code and held the key to initiate EL-5.

"Captain?" Klimentiev said.

Yermakova held up a hand to silence the lieutenant. She needed to think. Under the guidelines of EL-5, the whole facility was to be destroyed including all personnel.

It was no secret that Post 866 was an old missile silo that used to house one of the USSR's biggest ICBMs, an R-9 Desna, which had the capability to reach the United States during the Cold War.

After the missile was supposedly moved to another location in the early 1970s, the KGB, at the behest of Viktor Sokolov, turned the facility into a sharashka. Upon taking over Post 866 eleven years before, Captain Yermakova was given instructions on how to initiate EL-5 in case of an emergency, as well as the standard operating procedure for her, the director of Post 866, to escape in a reasonable amount of time. She knew once EL-5 was initiated, she had twenty minutes to get out of the facility and as far away from the blast radius as possible.

"What did the president say, Captain?" Klimentiev asked.

"Nothing—" Yermakova said, aware that everyone in the control room was watching her. She needed to figure out how she was going to initiate EL-5, detain Sokolov, and get him into a helicopter within twenty minutes, all without causing a panic.

It is impossible. There were too many variables and too little time. She would have to get creative.

"Lieutenant Klimentiev, how many men loyal to General Sokolov are currently inside the sharashka?"

"Fourteen men. Twelve of them Vympels, one assistant, and one helicopter pilot."

Yermakova did some quick thinking. She would have her guards rush the white-tiled room to eliminate Sokolov's Vympels and detain the general. Only when Sokolov was captured, and his men dead, would Yermakova initiate EL-5. But that, too, would be delicate. She needed to make sure her GRU subordinates wouldn't panic. "Lieutenant Klimentiev, I have been ordered by the president to detain General Sokolov and take him personally back to Vladivostok."

Klimentiev's face flushed, and she heard mumbles from the technicians.

Yermakova continued, "In order to do that, I will order the guards to the armory. I am going to insist that live rounds be used in this delicate operation. I am also ordering that all GRU personnel be sent to their residences while the operation is in effect. It will be a complete lockdown—the only way I can ensure the safety of GRU personnel."

"Even the technicians?"

"And yourself, Klimentiev." Yermakova put a hand on the lieutenant's shoulder. "I am putting you in charge of the safety of all GRU personnel in this facility. I will have our pilots fly General Sokolov and myself to Vladivostok. Once there, I will coordinate to get all personnel evacuated from the post in a timely fashion." She leaned in and whispered in Klimentiev's ear, trying to sound as earnest as possible. "We need to make sure our people don't panic. They will be safe in their residences."

Klimentiev shot a worried look at the two dozen GRU technicians below them in the control room. "If the technicians are to leave their stations, who will man the drones? Who will surveil the peninsula in case the Americans plan another infiltration?"

"Trust me, Lieutenant. My orders come straight from the president. These are his wishes."

Still uncertain, Klimentiev nodded. "*Da*, Captain. I will get everyone secured in their rooms and send the pilots above ground to ready your helicopter."

"*Spasibo*, Lieutenant. Notify me through my earpiece once everyone is safe. Then I will send in the guards to arrest Sokolov."

As Klimentiev burst into action, rounding up all the technicians in the room, Yermakova watched them go before gazing at the green door on the west wall of the control room that led to the EL-5 kill switch. With the Vympels out of the way and all GRU personnel locked into their quarters, Yermakova could initiate EL-5 and take Sokolov to the helicopter without anyone trying to stop her.

Then her mind went to the knockout gas. The facility was constructed so that every room contained vents that could deploy the gas. The only problem was that each of Sokolov's Vympels carried a gas mask.

No, she would take more drastic measures. She would kill the Vympels.

She keyed her earpiece and alerted all the guards to rendezvous at the armory in five minutes. If everything went accordingly, she would have Sokolov in custody in ten minutes, and EL-5 initiated in twenty.

In a half hour, she would be on a helicopter heading toward Vladivostok and Post 866 would soon be reduced to rubble.

Toggling through the switchboard in front of her, she brought up the live video feed of the white-tiled room. Sokolov and his men had Robert Gaines hanging from the ceiling and the prisoners of Red Block locked to chairs in front of him.

She would have the guards leave the prisoners in the torture room—no need for unnecessary bloodshed. They could die just like the rest of the GRU personnel.

Yermakova walked out of the control room and headed for the armory.

Chapter 67

AS THE COMMANDER of Naval Special Warfare Tactical Development and Evaluation Squadron Two, Commander Seamus Cafferty had reached a rank in the SEAL Teams that didn't necessarily require him to be "boots on the ground."

Usually, when reaching the coveted role of squadron commander, a SEAL officer was "freed up" to position himself anywhere on the battlefield in order to focus on the successful execution of a mission.

More often than not, squadron commanders led their team from a safe distance, instead of breaking down doors and kicking ass.

Cafferty thought that was bullshit.

When he'd been handed the command of SEAL Team Six's Blue Squadron in Virginia Beach three years prior, he'd made it known to both his superiors and his men that he wouldn't be hanging back.

Ever.

The Idaho native believed that in order to lead, you had to be willing to show your men that you were still able to get down and dirty.

Cafferty looked at his watch from within the UH-70 stealth Black Hawk and keyed his throat mike, alerting his SEALs, "T-minus twenty!"

He switched from his line-of-sight frequency to SATCOM. "Commander Cafferty to Commander Spear, do you copy?"

"Good copy, Commander Cafferty."

"Any activity on the thermals?" Cafferty was referring to the US spy satellites using their thermal imagery to gaze down on Site X.

"Affirmative. Thirty seconds ago we picked up two hostiles exiting the main entrance of Site X. They have entered the Kamov Ka-82K stealth helicopter and started its engines."

"Copy that," Cafferty said, then changed back to his line-of-sight frequency to alert his men. This would slightly change things. The SEALs would have to get out of the UH-70s weapons hot. After conferring with Lt. Commander Anderson in the UH-70 next to him, it was confirmed that Anderson and his team would hit the hostiles in the Kamov first, then form a perimeter while Cafferty and his team infiltrated the facility.

Cafferty then gazed around the UH-70 fuselage that housed his men. They were flying low over the ocean and should be reaching the eastern shores of the Kamchatka Peninsula in roughly five minutes. These supersecret, high-speed stealth helicopters could reach speeds of up to 220 miles per hour undetected by even the most sophisticated of radars.

A third and fourth UH-70 would take off from the carrier in minutes just in case the first two teams ran into trouble and needed an extraction.

Cafferty tried shutting his eyes and visualizing the upcoming mission. He'd had the CIA's schematics of the old missile silo already committed to memory—a gift he possessed that had helped him more times than he could count during his time in the SEALs. But one thing nagged at him, one aspect of the mission that he hadn't told anyone about.

During their briefing at JBER, Commander Spear had informed the SEALs that one of their own was possibly in the facility, a former SEAL named Paul Brady. Eighteen minutes ago, right before the president had given the green light, they'd gotten confirmation that Paul Brady had been spotted inside the Russian installation.

Seamus Cafferty knew Paul Brady.

Pretty well, actually. They'd been on the same boat team for most of BUD/S and had even served together for six years in SEAL Team Two. Paul Brady was a stand-up guy, a hell of a friend, and had been a damn good SEAL.

Unfortunately, they'd lost touch over the years when Cafferty entered SEAL Team Six and Brady had stayed with Team Two. Last Cafferty heard, Brady had gotten out of the Teams and lived with his family in San Diego.

He couldn't believe his ears when Spear confirmed that Brady was one of the Americans inside.

Cafferty thought of what Brady would say when his team infiltrated the old Soviet silo.

Knowing Brady, he'd just crack his signature wiseass smile and ask what had taken them so long.

Chapter 68

GALE GAZED DOWN at the knife in Sokolov's hand as the old general waved it in front of him

"I was telling your daughters a story before you arrived. I was telling them who you really are, what you really are, but I feel like it would be better hearing it from you, not me." The general snapped his fingers and a Vympel operator took the leather gag from Gale's mouth.

Gale sputtered and took in his daughters. "Are you two okay?"

Both girls looked to be in shock.

Gale didn't have time to really take in the other two men in the chairs because Emily asked him, "You were in the CIA. You murdered all those people?"

"I was doing my job, Emily. The people I killed were bad men. They had their hands in murdering women and children."

"You lied to us," Cassie said, evenly. "You lied to us about everything. Mom didn't die in a car accident—"

Sokolov let out a loud laugh. "A car accident? That's what you told them?" He walked up to Emily and stooped down so his face was in front of hers. "You don't remember me? You don't remember that night in Paris?"

Emily shook her head.

"I killed your bitch of a mother. I killed her in that fancy apartment. I remember you quite well—"

"Stop it!" Gale demanded.

"Or what?" Sokolov countered.

Gale took in the room. He counted twelve Vympels and another Russian who was preoccupied with a tablet. Standing next to a long metal table filled with torture equipment was a frightened-looking man in a white lab coat. Gale briefly locked eyes with the man and felt a vague sense of familiarity come over him. Before he had any more time to think, the general pointed at his daughters and went on.

"Your father and I have a very complicated history. Tell them, Robert."

Gale tensed his muscles, trying to alleviate the searing agony in his shoulders and then snarled at the general.

"You don't want to talk?" Sokolov taunted him. "Maybe I can inspire you." He brought the curved blade to Emily's little finger and pressed down with all his weight.

Emily screamed as the finger rolled off the chair's armrest and fell to the floor. Gale went berserk—thrashing and kicking.

"Tell them, Robert! Admit what you did!"

Emily's screams caught in her throat and her head lolled, as she almost passed out from the pain.

"ADMIT IT!" the Russian thundered.

"I will, just don't hurt my girls!" Gale said, his eyes plastered on Emily's bloody hand. He knew the SEALs were on their way. He needed to stretch out every moment he could and try to control the situation to keep his girls alive; so he decided to talk. "He's right. I was an assassin. I wasn't born James Gale. I was born Robert Gaines. I was stationed in Moscow in the eighties on an assignment to find the Soviet sharashka known as Post 866. This sharashka."

"Go on."

"It was rumored that this place housed American prisoners. The Soviets were rumored to have performed grotesque medical experiments on Americans for decades under the command of this man, and his son, Evgeny Sokolov. For years I tried to find this place, until one day, I met a man, a scientist—who had worked here. He offered to give me the location of Post 866 in exchange for helping his family defect to the West, but—"

"But?"

Gale explained that the scientist was discovered by the KGB and brutally murdered by Evgeny Sokolov. Gale tried to get the scientist's family out of Moscow, but the KGB had already snatched them up. Gale owed it to the scientist to do everything in his power to save the family—so he went after Evgeny Sokolov. He captured him days later in Finland and made a deal with the KGB. Gale would hand over Evgeny Sokolov in exchange for the scientist's family. The swap was set up and Gale moved his own daughters and wife out of Moscow to Paris, hoping to keep them safe from any reprisals from the KGB. At the swap, the CIA let Evgeny go, only to have the scientist's family executed during the exchange by the KGB. "They killed the young girls first, then the mother. Simultaneously, this man came after you," Gale said, looking at Sokolov. "This man killed your mother—and he almost killed the two of you, but our men were able to scare him off. I told you your mother died in a car crash to protect you."

"Then tell them what you did!" Sokolov roared.

"After your mother died, I went after Evgeny. It was a sanctioned operation. I tracked down every KGB agent associated with the kill order on the scientist's family and your mother. I killed them all, and eventually caught Evgeny." Gale described that he had received intelligence that Viktor was at his *dacha* in the Khimki Forest outside of Moscow. Gale took Evgeny and marched him through the snowy forest for most of the night until they got to the *dacha*. There, Gale killed Viktor's security, tied Viktor up, and brought him outside, binding him to a chair in the freezing cold and made him watch as his son died of hypothermia at his feet.

"You let him die like an animal!"

Gale roared back, "He died from the cold! Your son murdered Dr. Pyotr Yakonov and his family like animals! His daughters were ten and twelve!"

"They were traitors. Vermin!"

"They were innocents!"

Sokolov rushed forward and pressed the curved blade to Gale's throat in fury.

"They had names," Gale sputtered. "Natalia Yakonov, Klara Yakonov, Alvetina—"

A commotion sounded to Gale's right, as the man in the white lab coat suddenly lost his balance and put out a hand to catch himself on the metal table.

"Artur, what the hell is wrong with you?" Sokolov spat.

The man tried to regain his composure, but it looked like he had lost control of his legs. When the man didn't reply, Sokolov pointed at his soldiers. "If he doesn't have the stomach for this, get him out of here."

Two Vympels grabbed Artur by the arms and threw him into the hall, shutting the door behind them.

Sokolov rounded again on Gale. "Tell them what happened next."

Gale recalled that fateful night. "Somehow, the KGB caught wind that I was at the general's *dacha*. They came for me in helicopters. Chased me through the forest with men and dogs. I was able to get to a river. I was shot through the hip and fell into the water. Somehow I survived and was able to make it to the extraction. From there, I made it back to Washington. I had the CIA give us all new identities—new lives in Montana. I never wanted you girls to know what happened . . . what I was."

A long silence followed, then Sokolov spoke, "For three decades I've grieved for my only son. For three decades I've lived with the pain of seeing him die in front of me, bloody and helpless."

"The world is a better place without Evgeny Sokolov in it," Gale said. "I would do it all over again if I had the chance. My only regret is leaving *you* alive."

Sokolov smiled. "And yet, here we are: full circle. A father is about to watch helplessly as his children are murdered in front of him." Sokolov walked over to the metal table and snatched a meat cleaver, walking back over to Cassie. "I'm going to chop them up slowly. Bit by bit. And you are going to watch, Gaines. I am going to cut them up into little pieces—then you will be taken to Moscow to spend the rest of your days dying of old age in a cell too low for you to stand and too small for you to stretch out. You will spend every second of the rest of your life thinking about this night and how you could do nothing to stop it."

Sokolov grabbed Cassie's little finger and raised the meat cleaver in the air.

Gale watched helplessly as the sharp metal flashed through the air and landed on his daughter's finger with a sickening thud.

Chapter 69

ARTUR STUMBLED DOWN the hallway outside the white-tiled room and made it to the stairwell that would take him to the floor that housed his laboratory.

Body trembling, he willed his legs to move up the staircase until he reached the desired landing. Moving down the hallway, he rounded a corner and was met with a circus of black-clad guards, all armed with AK-15s huddled outside the armory surrounding Captain Yermakova, whose deep voice shouted out commands.

If it wasn't for the ringing in Artur's ears, the pounding of his heart, and the all-around despondency of his mind—he would have heard Yermakova order the guards downstairs to the white-tiled room.

As Artur continued forward, the guards broke off from Yermakova and pounded down the hallway toward him. Skirting their advance, Artur dipped into the side hallway that led to his laboratory and scanned himself inside.

When the lab door shut, his knees buckled and he felt his world tip. He met the cold linoleum floor on his hands and knees and crawled his way to his workstation, inching closer and closer to the mound of letters that always occupied the top of his desk.

He grabbed a handful of the letters and brought them down before him. Holding the thick, worn, wrinkled papers, Artur let out a heart-wrenching sob. For a long moment, Artur clutched at the letters and let himself succumb to the wave of earth-shattering emotion. General Sokolov's words held him tight, shaking him, pounding him into oblivion.

He sat like this for half a minute, before his heartbeat slowed and steadied.

For a moment, Artur felt like he'd entered some sort of limbo, an otherworldly space between his conscious and subconscious.

He floated in that ether for a few seconds. Basked in the serenity of it, until the floodgates opened and another, more complex emotion took over.

Rage.

White hot and searing, it bubbled up within him so raw that he was brought back to reality. His attention narrowed and crystallized, a plan forming in his brilliant mind.

Artur opened his eyes and stood. Wiping the tears from his face, he shoved the letters into his pocket and then turned to the computer at his desk that housed all his research. Plugging in an external hard drive, he started backing up the computer, then turned to face the rest of the laboratory.

His eyes flickered to his bunk in the far corner of the room, then to the gurney where Subject 8831 had woken from her surgery. Artur strode to the gurney and stopped before the tray that contained his surgical equipment. Snatching one of the remaining surgical knives, Artur walked over to his bunk, ripped off the sheets, and then plunged the knife into the middle of the mattress and tore sideways.

Pushing his hand inside, he moved his fingers around until they stopped on something cold and metallic.

He pulled out the MP-443 Grach pistol and held it in front of his face, remembering when he had stolen the weapon six years before, right from under Yermakova's nose.

The computer dinged, indicating that all his research was fully loaded onto the external hard drive. Thrusting the hard drive into his pocket, and tucking the pistol into his waistband, Artur walked over and stood on the spot where Subject 8831 had killed the guard.

The plan for what he was about to do next was shaping quite well in his head. He knew the layout of the sharashka probably better than anyone, probably even better than Yermakova herself. As the lead scientist, Artur had access to nearly every room, corridor, and lift—even during a lockdown. It was the reason why Subject 8831 was able to use his keycard to get into the emergency stairwell during her escape attempt in the first place.

But while Subject 8831 might have been brave in her escape attempt, she'd been completely shortsighted.

Artur was anything but.

His eyes flitted to a small black box next to the surgical tray and the words of Marko, the Ukrainian subject in Red Block, came back to him.

I'm a helicopter pilot. You're keeping me alive for a reason!

Marko had been right. Artur was keeping him alive for a reason.

Marching over to the black box, Artur flipped open the lid and grabbed the only remaining vial of clear liquid from within.

He snatched an empty syringe, extracted the liquid from the vial, and put a safety cap over the needle.

The scopolamine and sodium pentothal glistened under the laboratory's halogen lights and Artur visualized the final piece of his plan fitting together perfectly in his mind.

Turning off the lights to his lab for the last time, he stepped into the hallway, looked up and down to make sure the coast was clear, then headed to the armory.

There was something there he needed. A key that dangled around Captain Yermakova's neck and a password embedded in her brain. Artur hit the hallway running, a sense of anger, purpose, and revenge burning through him.

Chapter 70

CAPTAIN YERMAKOVA SHUT and locked the door to the armory and then stepped back into the hallway. She'd just received confirmation from Lieutenant Klimentiev that all the GRU personnel were locked inside their residences.

Tapping through the lockdown procedure on her tablet, she made sure that the fail-safe process could not be overridden once the GRU personnel heard the EL-5 countdown sequence through the facility's intercom. It had been laughable how easy it was to convince Klimentiev that her actions were for the safety of her subordinates.

Fools.

Minutes before, the last group of guards had left the armory, armed with live rounds to eliminate Sokolov's men and capture the general. Yermakova figured it was best to return upstairs and watch the show from the safety of the control room.

As soon as Sokolov is captured, I will initiate EL-5.

The guards will bring Sokolov to me, then I will take him to the surface and fly him to Vladivostok.

Two of her GRU helicopter pilots were already warming up her chopper above ground.

A flutter of excitement bubbled in Yermakova's stomach at the thought of successfully delivering the general to Putin.

It will show that I am faithful.

That I can get things done.

Surely, her success would overshadow the blunders of the last few days. Yes, Post 866 would be destroyed, but she could find another role once she was a member of the *siloviki*.

Still daydreaming about her future, Yermakova looked up from her tablet and jumped in surprise at the person standing in front of her.

"Artur!"

The scientist stood in the middle of the hallway, his posture rigid.

Yermakova cocked her head. "What is it? What's wrong?"

Artur reached into his lab coat, pulled out a clump of letters, and held them out for Yermakova to see.

"Did you know?"

"Did I know what?" Yermakova asked, feeling that early bubbling of excitement suddenly sour in her stomach. She looked down at the letters in his hand. "Artur, I had nothing to do with that. Minister Antonovich was the one forging the letters, not me—"

"But you knew they were fakes!" Artur's free hand flew from his waistband and suddenly there was a pistol pressed to Yermakova's forehead.

Yermakova's hand instinctually went to her earpiece that linked her to the guards. But Artur beat her to the punch and stripped her of the device, before pushing her against the door of the armory.

His pistol still pressed to her forehead, Artur's eyes went to the chain around her neck. "Give it to me."

"Give . . . give you what?"

"The key."

"I . . . I don't know what you're—"

Artur's hand flew to the key dangling around Yermakova's neck and ripped it free of its chain. Yermakova tried to snatch it back but Artur pushed her hard against the door.

"You can't—"

"I can't what?" Artur demanded. "You think I don't know what this key is for? You think I don't know about EL-5 and the green door? The R-9 Desna warhead rigged below the facility?"

Yermakova felt her eyes widen in surprise. "Comrade, wait—"

"I will no longer be your prisoner."

A syringe materialized in Artur's hand. Before Yermakova could object, he bit off the safety cap and stabbed the syringe into her neck.

Chapter 71

CASSIE LOOKED DOWN at the bloody nub where her finger had been and felt like she was going to faint.

Her sister's screams had stopped just seconds before when General Sokolov had substituted the meat cleaver for a rubber truncheon and beat Emily until she had passed out.

Frankly, Cassie didn't know how much longer she herself could stay awake. Her mind felt like it was on the verge of giving out. One of Sokolov's men moved forward with a hot iron and cauterized the wound on her hand, causing Cassie to scream from the agony and the smell of burning flesh.

Sokolov now turned on her father, beating him with the rubber truncheon until one well-placed blow collided with his jaw and he went limp.

Let it end, Cassie thought as she felt herself slipping. *Please just let this end.*

"Cassie," Paul Brady said next to her, "stay with us."

She was so exhausted, it sounded like the former SEAL was a thousand miles away. She lolled her head in the direction of Brady and Marko next to her and caught movement behind them.

Through the bulletproof window embedded in the door of the round white-tiled room, Cassie could faintly make out a series of black helmets and reflective visors peering in from the hallway.

Sokolov's Vympels, who held positions around the entirety of the room, had their eyes on their boss and hadn't seemed to notice.

Cassie squinted at the door, trying to figure out what was going on, when the helmets and visors suddenly disappeared.

"Brady, something is—" But Cassie couldn't get it out, because a resounding *BOOM* cut over her voice, and the door to the room was blown inward.

Sokolov's men instinctually went for their combat knives as something was thrown through the smoke-filled doorway. It clattered under Cassie's chair and stopped before the general's feet.

Cassie recognized the grenadelike object a tenth of a second before it detonated and the room suddenly disappeared in an explosion of deafening sulfuric whiteness.

For a while, there was nothing.

As the seconds ticked by, Cassie struggled to move. Struggled to regain even one of her senses—

Then, something registered—

A faint staccato broke through her delirium. It pulsed, and grew louder, then her vision came back online.

Dozens of Yermakova's black-clad guards swarmed into the room, firing live rounds from assault rifles. Cassie watched in disbelief as Sokolov's dazed soldiers were cut down one by one.

Cassie clamped her eyes shut, waiting for the bullet that would end her life.

But it never came.

When the gunfire stopped ten seconds later, someone was whimpering to her left.

Cassie allowed one of her eyes to open and she saw General Sokolov and his assistant huddled below the metal table containing the torture devices. Having taken the brunt of the stun grenade's blast, the general bled from his nose and looked confused. His assistant, on the other hand, continued his whimpering and in a frightful, high-pitched voice, began pleading with Yermakova's guards in Russian.

The largest of the guards stood before the metal table and pressed a hand to his earpiece under his black helmet.

Cassie took in her father, her sister, then Marko and Brady. Her father and sister were still unconscious and luckily untouched by the bullets. Marko and Brady blinked at her.

"What . . . what's going on?" Brady groaned, as Cassie's attention went back to the large guard standing before the metal desk. The guard had lowered his hand from his earpiece and was barking orders to the other guards.

Immediately, four of the guards pulled General Sokolov and his assistant from below the table and dragged them to the middle of the room. Cassie saw that Sokolov's nose continued to bleed heavily as his eyes focused and settled on her. He muttered something unintelligible under his breath as his hands were wrenched behind his back and zip-tied.

His assistant was forced down on his knees next to the general. His body shook like a leaf.

The large guard stood behind the assistant, raised his pistol, and fired into the back of the assistant's head.

Cassie was too far gone to flinch at the noise. Too overwhelmed and exhausted to notice that her father was being lowered by the guards from his position in the air. And too broken to realize that the cables holding her to her chair had been cut.

"He's doing it!" she heard Marko say. "The crazy scientist is helping us!"

Strong hands helped Cassie to her feet. She looked around the room, her bare feet fighting for purchase on the blood-soaked floor.

General Sokolov, Brady, and Marko were being led out of the room.

Another group of guards carried Emily and her father.

Cassie took a step forward to follow, but lost her balance. She was caught by two guards, who stood her upright.

Fighting to stay on her feet, she staggered out of the room and into the hallway.

She hadn't made it twenty steps when the lights suddenly dimmed, and an unfamiliar alarm shrieked through the facility.

The alarm blared, once, twice.

Then a woman's voice cut over the alarm and in Russian, said:

"EL-5 initsiirovan. Dvadtsat' minut do detonatsii."

WHITE HOUSE
SITUATION ROOM

The large screen in the Situation Room showing Gale's POV suddenly went dark as Gale's eyes closed and he lost consciousness.

Within thirty seconds, two loud explosions consumed the audio then an eruption of gunfire rippled through the feed.

"Can someone explain to me what I'm hearing?" asked President McClintock.

"I don't know, Mr. President," replied Carter.

"Commander Spear," the president asked. "What is the SEALs' ETA?"

"Eight minutes, Mr. President."

The room went quiet as faint voices, some in Russian, some in English, could be heard over the feed. Someone was whimpering, pleading, then a sharp gunshot echoed through the room.

"*He's doing it!*" an accented voice said in English. "*The crazy scientist is helping us!*"

Carter shot a confused look at McGavran, who looked just as puzzled.

There was a scuffle of boots, the moving of chairs over the audio, and then two shrill bleats of an alarm sounded, followed by a woman's voice saying something in Russian.

"What did that say?" asked DNI Nagle.

Carter blinked, not registering the voice.

"It said that EL-5 was initiated," McGavran piped up. "Twenty minutes until detonation."

"They're blowing the place up," Carter said.

Chapter 72

THE INJECTION OF Devil's Breath into Yermakova's bloodstream put her into a near zombielike state. Her face drooped and her shoulders slumped over. The injection was meant to make the GRU captain completely submissive to Artur's orders, but Yermakova was doing her best to fight the drug.

In the minutes since leaving the armory, Artur instructed Yermakova to escort him to the control room. He studied her reaction as her body twitched and jerked in protest of the Devil's Breath, but she had reluctantly succumbed to his orders.

When they had arrived at the control room, Artur was stunned to find the place completely devoid of its GRU technicians. He was even more surprised to learn that Yermakova had previously ordered all GRU personnel to be put into lockdown in their residences.

"The guards leaving the armory, where did you send them?" Artur asked.

Yermakova's mouth twisted, fighting to stay mute, but she spit out, "Down to the white-tiled room to detain General Sokolov and eliminate his men."

"Detain Sokolov? Why?"

"It was my orders."

"Orders from whom?"

"President Putin."

Artur hadn't expected that answer and inspected Yermakova's face for any signs of deception. When he found none, he slid over to one of the workstations and turned on the video feed from the white-tiled room. He watched in real time as the door was blown off its hinges by the black-clad guards. Watched as a flash grenade was thrown inside and detonated. The video feed cut out abruptly, then returned, showing Sokolov's men being gunned down. As the violence abated, Artur noticed Sokolov and his assistant huddling under the metal table.

Artur suddenly had an idea. He took Yermakova's earpiece from his pocket and handed it to her.

"Tell the guards to dispose of the general's assistant. After that, tell them to bring all the prisoners and General Sokolov to the control room, unharmed."

Yermakova's face jolted again in protest. Artur grabbed her by the neck and repeated his order more forcefully.

Relenting, Yermakova inserted the device into her ear and began relaying Artur's orders. The scientist used that time to walk to the west wall of the control room and stopped at the green door. Taking the key that had hung around Yermakova's neck, he unlocked and opened the door to find a cement room the size of a broom closet. On the wall opposite him, a red box was welded into the concrete. The red box housed a keyhole and a simple black keypad.

Artur called for Yermakova to come into the room.

Holding the key, he asked, "Did the president order you to initiate EL-5 and bring Sokolov to Moscow?"

"To Vladivostok," Yermakova said.

That was why all the GRU technicians were locked in their residences. Yermakova needed them out of the way so she could carry out the president's orders.

The president will get his wish. Well, sort of, Artur thought. Inserting the key into the red box, he said, "Enter the code to initiate EL-5."

Yermakova's hands shook as she punched in a series of numbers on the keypad and then turned the key.

At once, the lights in the facility dimmed and a high-pitched alarm blared twice. Then, a woman's voice cut over the facility's intercom:

"*EL-5 initsiirovan. Dvadtsat' minut do detonatsii.*"

Artur couldn't help but smile.

So far, his plan was working much better than expected.

|||||||||||||||||||||||||||||||||||||||||||||||||||||||||||||||||||||||||||||||||

KAMCHATKA PENINSULA
UH-70 HELICOPTER

Commander Cafferty pressed his earpiece deep into his ear and focused on Commander Spear's update coming over the SATCOM frequency.

"Commander Cafferty, this is JSOC, over."

"Copy, Commander Spear, go ahead."

Spear's voice caught static then normalized. "We've got a situation, Commander." Spear updated Cafferty of the twenty-minute detonation sequence at Site X.

Cafferty looked down at his watch; they were now seven minutes from their destination. "We have twenty minutes until detonation, Command. I say we stay on mission, over."

Cafferty could see his men through his NODs looking at him from the dark fuselage of the helicopter. He knew the Night Stalker pilots were also hearing his transmission as well as the pilots and Lt. Commander Anderson in the UH-70 next to him.

These types of thing always happen, he thought to himself. Things change, nothing goes as planned. Luckily for Cafferty and his men, this is what they trained for. With seven minutes more of flying time, they'd have less than thirteen minutes to secure the hostages and get the hell out of Dodge.

"Copy that, Commander," said Spear over the comms. "You are still a go."

Cafferty switched the frequency over to his team and updated his men on the detonation sequence. Cafferty put a twenty-minute countdown on his watch and took a deep breath, doing the math in his head.

Alpha team was composed of eight men including himself. Eight men that would go down the hatch and into the facility.

"Six minutes until landing," the Night Stalker pilot alerted him.

Commander Seamus Cafferty wasn't blind to the fact that this change in circumstances had severely hindered their chances of success. That getting all the hostages into the choppers in time was highly unlikely. There were simply too many intangibles. Too many blind variables.

But dammit, Paul Brady is down there.

Americans are down there.

He looked over his SEALs. The seven men staring back at him were the best in the world. Professionals fully cognizant of the dangers that came with the job.

"Five minutes," the Night Stalker pilot relayed.

It was time to go to work.

Chapter 73

"EL-5 INITSIIROVAN. SHESTNADTSAT' minut do detonatsii."

Sixteen minutes until detonation.

Cassie heard the woman's voice in Russian again as she was led up a set of narrow stairs. Two guards supported her by the elbows as she climbed. She could hear the rest of the guards marching above her and wondered if her father or sister had gained consciousness yet.

Soon, Cassie made it to a landing and a door was held open for her. The guards helped her forward as they stepped into the familiar large, circular room Cassie'd taken Artur through by knifepoint during her escape attempt.

The circular room had been busy the last time Cassie had been in it. Now, it sat deserted. Cassie looked across the room and saw another guard holding a door open for them.

Staggering forward, Cassie relied on the strength of the guards.

Her mind was too depleted to think clearly; she needed all the energy she could muster just to get one foot in front of the other.

After crossing the circular room, she was helped into a hallway and led to another open door.

Stepping inside, Cassie couldn't help but gasp.

The room looked like a NASA mission control center. Different levels of workstations descended down into the room, all facing a massive wall littered with LED screens.

"Here, sit down," a voice said to her right, and Cassie saw Artur put a chair in front of her. "We won't be here long."

Cassie sat. Dozens of the black-clad guards stood at attention along the back wall. At her feet, Emily and her father were unconscious on the floor next to a bound and gagged General Sokolov.

"I knew you would help us!" Cassie heard Marko say. The Ukrainian was standing next to Brady, both of their eyes glued to Artur, who grabbed Captain Yermakova.

Yermakova swayed on her feet and looked like she had contracted a serious bout of food poisoning.

"*EL-5 initsiirovan. Pyatnadtsat' minut do detonatsii.*"

Fifteen minutes until detonation.

Artur said to Yermakova: "Order the guards to leave their weapons here and secure themselves in Red Block."

Yermakova turned, almost trancelike and repeated Artur's words with a slur to her speech.

Cassie watched the imbecilic guards drop their weapons and file out of the room.

"How did you—" Brady started, but Artur cut him off, motioning to Marko.

"Captain Yermakova has two of her helicopter pilots in a Kamov Ka-82K stealth helicopter on top of the facility. If they refuse to fly us, would you be able to fly that chopper?"

"I can fly anything."

"Good."

"She's helping us too?" asked Brady, looking at Yermakova.

"She is under the spell of Devil's Breath."

"You took my advice," marveled Marko.

Artur crouched down to inspect Cassie's unconscious father and sister. "I don't have any more of my drugs. They will have to be carried out before the detonation."

"Detonation?" asked Brady.

"The facility will self-destruct. We have fifteen minutes."

"Where are we going?" Cassie asked, weakly.

Artur didn't reply because a hoarse coughing took over the room.

Cassie saw Artur's face turn sour. The scientist stepped over Cassie's father and sister and stood over Sokolov. For the first time, Cassie noticed Artur was holding a pistol in his hand.

"*EL-5 initsiirovan. Chetyrnadtsat' minut do detonatsii.*"

Fourteen minutes.

Artur stood over the general, and for a long moment, he didn't say anything.

The old general's face was covered in blood. His emaciated features—his sunken cheeks, arthritic gnarled fingers, and liver-spotted nose made him look like a corpse. Artur calmly cut Sokolov's zip ties and turned the old man so he was lying fully on his back.

"Look at me," Artur said, in English.

The general let out a cough that sounded like a bullhorn, but his eyes eventually settled on the scientist.

"You still don't recognize me, do you, General?" Artur asked, his voice calm.

Cassie watched as the general's eyes flickered from Artur's face, to the gun in his hand, then back to his face.

"Nyet."

"Let me jog your memory, no?" Artur pulled out a stack of envelopes from his lab coat and dropped them on the general's chest.

"What are these?" Sokolov wheezed.

"Look at them."

Sokolov's eyes focused on one of the envelopes, then his eyes grew wide. "You're—"

"The son of Pyotr and Natalia Yakonov. Brother to Klara and Alvetina."

Cassie felt like the air had been sucked out of the control room. Even in her state, she remembered the names her father had mentioned in the white-tiled room. His old asset and the family he swore to protect—the family murdered by Sokolov and his son.

Sokolov didn't move.

"For thirty years, I believed my father died in an accident at his lab. For thirty years, I have kept up a fake correspondence with my mother and sisters. For thirty years I have kept the hope alive that I would see them again. That I could be free of the state's sharashkas. But you slaughtered them. You forced me to live in this horrible existence."

Sokolov grunted in disgust. "I didn't force you to live this existence. Your traitorous father did that. He killed your sisters and mother as soon as he opened his mouth to the Americans."

Artur raised the pistol and aimed it at Sokolov's head.

Sokolov smiled. "Do it! Shoot me and get it over with. The sooner I get to see my son—"

The gun shook in Artur's hand, and Cassie could see the white of Artur's finger tightening around the trigger.

"Wait!" Cassie said. "Don't kill him like this."

The whole room turned to her. "He killed my mother, too. Don't let him off this easy."

Sokolov hacked out a cough. "You don't have what it takes to put a bullet in me."

Artur looked to Cassie. "What do you suggest?"

"You asked Marko if he could fly that helicopter"—she pointed to the screen showing the Kamov Ka-82K on top of the mountain—"which means you have a plan to get us out of here?"

"Yes."

"Where?"

"East. There is an American chain of islands nearly five hundred kilometers east of us. We will give ourselves over to the Americans once they spot us on radar."

"*EL-5 initsiirovan. Trinadtsa' minut do detonatsii.*"

Thirteen minutes until detonation.

"Take him with us, then. Let the bastard pay for his crimes. Give him to the American government."

Artur returned his gaze back to the general, who now looked worried at Cassie's proposition, then Artur lowered the pistol.

"*EL-5 initsiirovan. Dvenadtsat' minut do detonatsii.*"

Twelve minutes.

"We need to hurry," Marko said, grabbing an AK-15 left over by the guards. Brady grabbed one, too.

"What are we going to do with her?" Brady asked, looking at Yermakova.

"She dies with this place," Artur said.

"Fine," Brady said. "And what about them?" He pointed to Emily and Cassie's father.

Cassie was getting to her feet, and only half listening to Marko, Brady, and Artur discuss how Emily and her father were going to be carried to the elevator and onto the helicopter when she saw something on the main monitor in the front of the room that made her breath catch. "I think we might have a problem."

The men turned their heads to her and she pointed at the monitor showing the night-vision drone feed depicting the top of the facility.

All eyes turned to the screen, which was now showing two helicopters that had appeared out of nowhere. The choppers circled the top of the facility, then bright tracer rounds shot out from one of the helicopters and peppered the cockpit where Yermakova's pilots warmed up the Kamov Ka-82K.

Within seconds, the Kamov and its pilots were obliterated, and both invading helicopters had landed on top of the mountain. Dozens of armed figures spilled out of the choppers, half of them forming a perimeter on the mountaintop, the other half storming through the emergency hatch and into the facility.

"Russians?" asked Marko in disbelief.

Artur shot a panicked look at Yermakova. "The president sent reinforcements?"

Yermakova shook her head. "No. He recalled them back to Vladivostok."

Artur swung on Sokolov. "Your men?"

Sokolov just laughed.

Artur turned back to the surveillance feed. "I don't understand how they could have gotten by the drones—"

Another monitor next to the main screen flashed awake and showed eight heavily armed men descending the emergency stairwell.

"What are we going to do?" Marko asked.

Artur said, "We don't have a choice. We have to fight back." Turning to Captain Yermakova, he ordered: "Gas that stairwell and have the drones fire down on those men!"

Chapter 74

THOUGH THE PEOPLE in the Situation Room could not see the happenings in Post 866 due to Robert being unconscious, they could sure hear what was going on.

"Did I hear that correctly?" asked President McClintock. "They're going to use a drone to fire down on our men? Commander Spear, did you copy that?"

"Loud and clear, Mr. President. I have already alerted the SEALs of the threat."

"And you aren't pulling them out?" asked Fray.

Spear replied, "That's not how they operate, sir. Those SEALs have a mission to carry out. They have men to support and hostages to save. An impending threat on their lives doesn't change things."

"Well, surely we could do something!" growled DNI Nagle.

"It's in God's hands now," replied Spear.

Carter could hear the strain in Spear's voice and understood that emotionally Spear would have loved to pull his men out of harm's way. But she also understood the mentality that was hammered into each and every SEAL's psyche from the moment they entered BUD/S—*the group before the individual*. Bravo team leaving Alpha team down in the facility would be the biggest sin a SEAL could make. They'd rather die supporting their teammates than leave them high and dry.

Carter had heard stories of individual SEALs jumping on live grenades to save their brothers in combat. She hoped to God she wouldn't have to witness such a sacrifice firsthand.

||||||||||||||||||||||||||||||||||||||||||||||||||||||||||||||||||||||||||||||||||||

POST 866
CONTROL ROOM

The voice over the facility's intercom alerted the group in the control room that EL-5 would be initiated in eleven minutes.

Cassie watched the feed from the control room as it showed the armed men charging down the emergency stairwell.

Artur spoke rapid Russian to Captain Yermakova as she began punching keys at the main control station, readying the drone and gas attack on the incoming assailants when Brady screamed: "STOP!!"

Cassie, Artur, Yermakova, and Marko all looked at the former SEAL.

"Those men aren't Russian!" Brady said.

"What are you saying?" asked Artur.

"Those helicopters—those are UH helicopters—classified stealth choppers used by United States Special Forces. Those men"—Brady said, pointing at the screens, a wicked smile spreading on his face—"are Americans."

"How do you know?" asked Marko.

"Zoom in on the figures coming down the stairwell."

Artur directed Yermakova to zoom in on the men coming down the stairs.

"See, there!" Brady cried. "Eight-man SEAL Team. Their weapons, all variants of the HK 416. Their getups—all SEAL issued. That's an elite team, a DEVGRU assault team."

"What are you saying?" asked a confused Artur.

"They're here to save us," Cassie said. She had been standing over her unconscious father and sister, looking down at them one last time—accepting the fact that she only had minutes left on this earth. "They're here to save us."

"We need to meet them at the bottom of the stairs," said Brady. "We can take the elevator to the surface with them, right?"

Artur blinked twice, then nodded slowly.

"Leave all the weapons here," Brady ordered, "take off whatever clothing you can. Show them that you are unarmed. They will treat us like a threat until they can confirm we are not one." He pointed down to Cassie's unconscious father, sister, and Sokolov. "Help me carry them. We need to hurry."

||||||||||||||||||||||||||||||||||||||||||||||||||||||||||||||||||||||||||||||||||||

POST 866
EMERGENCY STAIRWELL

Cafferty led his men down the winding staircase. He'd counted nearly thirty revolutions and his legs were starting to get heavy.

A woman's voice spoke something in Russian every minute they'd been in the facility.

Probably the countdown sequence, Cafferty thought, looking at his watch, which told him they had eight minutes until detonation.

Through the pulsating alarm, and the red flashing lights, Cafferty gazed down through the grated steps and could finally see an end to the staircase ten twists below.

At the bottom of the staircase was a landing and a red door.

His explosives point man primed and double-primed the door in less than fifteen seconds, and they'd formed a stack behind the breacher and readied themselves for the explosion, which came three seconds later.

The massive red door blew off its hinges. Cafferty and his men burst into a hallway that led to a large circular room where they expected to meet face-to-face with hostiles.

What he hadn't expected was a half-dozen disheveled figures lying on the floor.

Cafferty and his men quickly secured the room before he flipped up his NODs onto his bump helmet.

Two of the figures seemed to be unconscious—one was Robert Gaines, the other was a young woman.

"What the fuck took you so long?" a familiar voice said to Cafferty's right.

Though he looked like he'd gone through a meat grinder, Paul Brady's smile lit up the room.

"You think I'd miss this?" Cafferty said, offering a hand and helping Brady to his feet. "This everyone?"

"Yes, sir," Brady replied. "All hostiles are either dispatched or locked away and this piece of shit is coming with us." Brady motioned down to a cadaverous-looking man at his feet who wore a blood-soaked green military uniform. Cafferty at once recognized General Sokolov from his briefing.

"Copy that, but we got about six minutes to get everyone up those stairs and out of the blast radius—"

"I got a better idea," Brady said, turning to a tall skinny man with glasses. "Artur, have Yermakova get that elevator open."

In accented English, the tall skinny man asked one of Cafferty's SEALs for the tablet he'd taken off a sickly looking woman with bushy hair.

The SEAL handed her the tablet and she clicked away.

Moments later, the massive elevator door to their right opened.

Brady took the tablet from the woman and told the SEALs to zip-tie her and leave her in the facility. Cafferty did the honors, and when everyone was inside the elevator, Cafferty looked around, his eyes landing on Paul Brady and the woman standing next to him. He'd seen her picture in his briefing.

Cassandra Gale.

As the elevator began to rise, he took in the state of the rest of the hostages. In all the years that Seamus Cafferty had been on the SEAL Teams, he'd been personally involved in dozens of hostage rescue missions. From Somalia to Pakistan, he'd seen hostages tortured and starved, beaten and malnourished.

The hostages before him were no different.

He just couldn't believe he was witnessing this in modern-day Russia.

Chapter 75

PRESIDENT PUTIN PACED in a secure bunker fifty feet below his Idokopas compound and felt his blood boil as the thermal imagery satellite feed booted up on the screens in front of the room.

"Mr. President," Sergei Antonov said. "We've got the live feed up now."

Still in his satin robe, Putin stopped pacing and took in the sight on the monitor showing the events taking place on top of Post 866. There were two new helicopters on top of the mountain, and at least eight heat signatures forming a perimeter around them.

"Those are American soldiers and their two American choppers?" Putin roared.

"*Da*, Mr. President. Yermakova's Kamov Ka-82K has been neutralized by the Americans."

Putin stepped forward and yelled at the technicians in the room in charge of manning the satellites looking down on Post 866, "And why don't we have control of the drones over the sharashka?"

"They seem to have been overridden from inside the sharashka just after EL-5 was initiated," a petrified technician replied.

Putin swore loudly as he watched over a dozen heat signatures burst out from the facility's main elevator entrance and run toward the American helicopters. "They're out," Putin said under his breath. "How much longer until the EL-5 detonation?"

"Four minutes, Mr. President."

"They will make it out of the blast radius. Scramble the MiG-35s out of Vladivostok. I want those helicopters blown out of the sky," Putin said, watching the last of the figures load onto the birds and take off east toward the Pacific Ocean.

Sergei Antonov lowered his secure phone. "Mr. President, the MiGs are scrambling now. They will make contact with the American helicopters in ten minutes." Watching the American choppers fly toward the Pacific, Sergei Antonov asked, "The MiG pilots want to know if they have permission to engage over international waters."

Putin turned around so fast his satin robe nearly untied itself. "You tell those pilots to down those choppers by any means necessary. I don't care if they kamikaze into them!"

"*Da*, Mr. President," Sergei Antonov replied, and then relayed the message.

Putin returned his attention to the satellite's thermal imagery. The countdown sequence to the EL-5 detonation had just ticked down to under three minutes.

Vladimir Putin could feel the blood pounding in his ears. Under no circumstances could those helicopters make it back to the United States.

It would be the biggest embarrassment of his career.

He would not let that happen.

Chapter 76

THE SPEED AT which the UH-70s flew east was mind-boggling to Cassie, who sat squished between Paul Brady and another SEAL who looked like a bearded heavyweight cage fighter and smelled of chewing tobacco.

In front of her, in the dim light of the rising sun, Cassie watched as four other SEALs worked on her unconscious father and sister, both lying on their backs in the chopper's fuselage, oxygen and IV lines attached to their faces and arms.

On the other side of Brady, Commander Cafferty leaned forward and pointed at his watch, alerting everyone that the facility, now miles behind them, would detonate in thirty seconds.

Not knowing how big the shock wave would be, the SEALs quickly buckled themselves to the fuselage as well as made sure that both Emily and her father were properly cinched down.

Cassie leaned forward and tried to view the other UH-70 roaring next to them, but was held back by the monstrous SEAL next to her. She was hoping to get a glimpse of Marko or Artur in the neighboring chopper.

"Ten seconds!" yelled Cafferty.

Cassie shut her eyes and counted down in her head.

Seven seconds later, a brilliant white light erupted through her clamped eyelids.

"BRACE!" someone shouted, and nearly five seconds later, the shock wave collided with the UH-70, throwing it violently forward.

Cassie felt the UH-70 pitch left and then right. Gritting her teeth, she heard the rotors above her stall and felt the chopper start to rapidly lose altitude.

|||||||||||||||||||||||||||||||||||||||||||||||||||||||||||||||||||||||||||||

WHITE HOUSE
SITUATION ROOM

"Someone give me a status update," President McClintock said from his chair in the Situation Room. Sweat dotted his forehead as the sound of the explosion roared over the SEALs' audio-capturing devices.

On the center screen in the Situation Room just moments before, Director Carter had watched as the thermal feed from the American KH-11 spy satellite had turned completely white from the explosion at the facility.

She turned her attention to the screen showing Commander Spear at his station in Fort Bragg.

Carter felt like her heart was in her throat as she listened to the chaos on board the UH-70s. She didn't even notice the phone in front of General Bridgewater had started blinking. The general picked up the receiver and put it to his ear.

The audio feed from the UH-70s suddenly muted. The whole room held a collected breath, then Spear's voice came over his feed, "Mr. President, the UH-70s have regained control. They're currently six minutes from international waters."

Cheers erupted in the Situation Room but were cut off by Bridgewater who smashed his phone back on the table. "We're not out of it yet."

"Meaning?" Carter asked.

"Our navy has reported that two MiG-35 fighter jets have just left Vladivostok and are currently over the Sea of Okhotsk. They're on course to intercept the UH-70s."

"How far out are they?" asked the president.

"Sir, we can expect them to intercept the UH-70s in just under five minutes."

The room went quiet, then the president said, "Where are our F-22s?"

"Currently two hundred nautical miles east of the Kamchatka Peninsula awaiting to escort the UH-70s once they hit international waters."

President McClintock squinted at the general. "I'm not seeing the problem, General."

"What the general is saying, Mr. President, is that by the time our F-22s are able to reach the UH-70s and fight off an attack from the MiGs, the UH-70s will still be in Russian airspace," said McGavran.

Carter watched as the young president ran over McGavran's words in his head.

"Sir," said Fray, "downing Russian aircraft in Russian airspace—"

The president cut off his chief of staff. "As far as I'm concerned, nothing has changed. We are still within our inherent right of self-defense." He pointed to Bridgewater. "You give our F-22s the go-ahead to intercept."

Bridgewater spoke into the phone and then put it down. "It's been done, Mr. President."

"Good. How long until they intercept the MiGs?"

Bridgewater looked down at his computer and frowned.

"Talk to me, General."

"It's going to be close, sir."

"How close?"

"Those MiGs might reach the UH-70s before we do."

Chapter 77

THE NORMALIZATION OF rotor wash and the leveling out of the UH-70 allowed Cassie to unclench her eyelids. A feeling of relief crept into her body.

The SEALs were back to working on her father and sister in the fuselage and she heard Commander Cafferty shout over the thrum of the rotors that they were three minutes from international waters.

Cassie felt Brady's fingers wrap around her uninjured hand and she looked over at him.

"We did it, Cass—"

One of the Night Stalker pilots cursed loudly, ripping Cassie's attention from Brady.

Looking out the window, Cassie could see pink morning light warming the mountainous terrain below them. As she looked toward the pilots, she made out the rising sun and the ocean in the distance.

"We've got a big fucking problem!" shouted the same pilot.

Cassie's attention jumped to Cafferty, who was pressing his headset into his ears, a look of pure concentration on his face.

"What's going on?" Cassie asked Brady.

An alarm whooped through the chopper.

"Two bogeys incoming from the southwest, intercept in ninety seconds!" shouted the other Night Stalker.

This got the attention from everyone in the fuselage and Cafferty ripped the headset from his head. "Command has called in two F-22s to come save our asses!"

"That's good, right?" asked Brady, wondering why his old friend looked so concerned.

"It would be if they weren't going to be twenty seconds late," Cafferty said, putting his headset back on. Unclipping himself from the wall of the fuselage, he poked his head into the cockpit.

Cassie couldn't hear what Cafferty was saying to the Night Stalkers over the sound of the alarm, but it looked like a heated argument had broken out. Cafferty was turning red and jabbing his finger vehemently in their faces. One of the Night Stalkers yelled something forcefully back at Cafferty and the argument seemed to have ended.

For a moment, Cafferty looked down, contemplating something, then he looked up and began to yell orders at his men, pointing at Emily and her father's unconscious figures on the deck. "Give them a shot of adrenaline. Wake them up and get them suited and clipped in as fast as possible!"

Cassie couldn't hear the rest of Cafferty's orders as the SEALs suddenly unclipped themselves from the fuselage's walls.

"What's happening?" Cassie asked Brady, noticing that their UH-70 and the one next to them were now over the ocean.

"ONE MINUTE!" screamed the Night Stalker.

Brady's head turned on a swivel.

"MISSILE LOCK!" the other Night Stalker yelled.

Pandemonium erupted in the fuselage as the large SEAL next to Cassie unclipped her from the wall and reached down for the blue bag he'd been sitting on. The SEAL opened the bag and took out four cold-water immersion suits.

The SEAL threw two of the suits to the SEALs crouched over her father and sister who were now gaining consciousness. He handed the other two suits to Cassie and Brady. "Get these on!"

Cassie snatched the suit and unzipped the front. Stepping into it, she said, "We're all bailing into the ocean?"

"Not everyone," replied the SEAL.

"The hell is that supposed to mean!" Cassie said, zipping up the bulky immersion suit, but the bearded SEAL had turned away from her and began helping her father and Emily get into their suits.

Cassie suddenly felt the UH-70 dip toward the water and she turned to Brady, who had also finished putting his suit on and was gripping a handhold on the fuselage wall as they rocketed toward the ocean.

"MISSILES FIRED!" screamed the Night Stalker pilot.

Cafferty stumbled over to them as the UH-70 and the one next to them suddenly leveled out just above the ocean and went into a hover.

"What the fuck is going on, Seamus!" Brady screamed at Cafferty.

"We're going for a swim!" Cafferty said, and threw his body weight into the both of them.

The twenty-foot fall into the freezing ocean knocked the breath from Cassie's lungs. She thrashed and kicked, her weak body struggling for the surface. When she breached, she saw the rest of the SEALs and hostages dive out of the UH-70s. She thought she saw Artur and Marko, both in their immersion suits, hit the water, but her attention was sidetracked by a loud, whistling noise from the west.

Spitting up seawater, Cassie looked over and saw two contrails arching toward the UH-70s, whose pilots had now, devoid of their passengers, hit the throttle and raced away.

The Night Stalkers are sacrificing themselves for us.

"GET UNDER THE WATER!!" Cafferty roared from somewhere behind Cassie as the missiles screamed over them heading toward the fleeing UH-70s.

Cassie took a big breath and pulled herself under.

The explosions were deafening even under the ocean as the shock waves cut through the water above. Cassie surfaced, only to see two fireballs plummet into the sea, just as two black Russian MiGs rocketed over her head and began to bank around.

"GET BACK UNDER THE FUCKING WATER!!" Cafferty yelled again. "THEY'RE GONNA PUT THEIR CANNONS ON US!!"

As Cassie watched the MiGs complete their deadly arc back toward everyone, she couldn't help but think that this was it.

After everything that had happened over the last couple weeks. After all that she had endured, all that she had survived—this moment in the ocean would be the end.

Cassie closed her eyes and thought of Derrick.

The roar of the MiGs was suddenly overshadowed by the thunderous scream of something else.

Something louder. More powerful.

Cassie snapped her eyes open to see two gray specks to the east closing the gap behind the MiGs.

Four small plumes of orange light erupted from the specks and rocketed toward the MiGs.

A strong hand clamped over Cassie's head, Cassie turned to see Brady as he screamed, "TAKE A DEEP BREATH!"

Cassie gulped in the salty air and plunged back under the water one last time.

Epilogue

NED VOIGT RELISHED the fact that it was January and well over seventy degrees. Taking a puff of his Cuban cigar, he leaned back in the most comfortable seat on his yacht and closed his eyes, letting the warm night air and the faint sway of the large boat against the dock rock him gently.

As his eyes shut, he thought of what his life had been like nearly six months before. The massacre he and his wife had survived in Eagle at the hands of the Russians. Their carefully plotted escape route that had taken them nearly a month to follow. Luckily for them, it had all been meticulously planned. From Alaska, they'd snuck back into Canada on foot, picked up a stashed car, and drove to Montreal before flying to Mexico City. From there, they'd gone to Cuba then sailed to Jamaica and finally St. Thomas.

They'd drained all their Russian-linked bank accounts and moved their money to various banks in the Seychelles—before rerouting and depositing it into several accounts in Luxembourg, which Ned was able to access whenever he pleased.

It was the way he had been able to purchase the seventy-eight-foot luxury motor yacht with the sleek flybridge and even sleeker cherrywood interior.

Ned, or Paul Mathers, as he went by now, smiled at his good fortune and took another puff of the cigar. Tomorrow he and Darlene would sail to Secret Harbor Beach, where they would enjoy their time snorkeling the various reefs.

They'd deserved it, after all.

After more than thirty years working for the Russians, they'd earned this lifestyle.

The fallout from the events of last summer in Alaska had been severe. Both Ned and Darlene had paid significant attention to the press reports following their escapes. Their faces had been plastered on every news media site from Anchorage to New York, and every agency from the FBI to Interpol was looking for them.

But they would never find them.

A plastic surgeon in Cuba had seen to that.

As for the international relations that had soured between Russia, Canada, and the United States since the events of last summer: the plane crash, the incident in the Kamchatka Peninsula, as well as the American government's accusations that Russians were kidnapping American citizens on American soil—well, Ned Voigt couldn't really care less.

It wasn't his concern anymore.

He would spend the rest of his days sailing the beautiful and warm places of the world.

As he relaxed and took another puff off his cigar, relishing his triumph, he didn't notice that his yacht pitched ever-so-slightly against the dock. He wouldn't have noticed anything at all if it wasn't for the soft whimper that resonated in front of him.

Ned opened his eyes and saw his wife silhouetted in the doorway to the cabin; she was backlit, so her face was obscured in shadow.

"Darlene, honey. Why aren't you in bed?"

All of a sudden, a woman's voice, cold and emotionless, spoke from behind Darlene, "You two were hard to find."

Darlene took a step forward. A slender figure dressed completely in black stepped out from behind his wife.

Ned instantly went for the pistol on the table.

"Nah, ah!" the figure said, as the muzzle of a suppressed pistol was pressed to Darlene's head.

Ned froze at the sight of the weapon.

"Who are you, what do you want?"

"You don't recognize my voice?" the figure asked. "I bet you don't. I'm sure it is hard for you to remember, considering all the victims you've kidnapped over the years, am I correct, KODIAK?"

Ned felt an icy sensation course through his body as he pinned down the voice.

"Cassandra Gale."

"Very good."

"What do you want?" Ned asked, trying to sound unfazed.

"We want you," another voice said, from the starboard side of the ship. Another figure stepped from the shadows, his face exposed. The face of James Gale. He, too, carried a suppressed pistol. "The United States government wants you. Turns out, you two might have valuable information—over thirty years' worth of information."

Ned's eyes flickered to his own weapon on the table in front of him.

James Gale raised his gun. "Don't even think about it."

"We have money," Darlene said. "Lots of money."

"I'm sure you do," Cassie said. "Actually, according to your bank accounts in Luxembourg, you're sitting on a small fortune. I think you'd be surprised to see that those accounts are currently empty."

Ned felt himself go weak. *Empty?*

"How did you find us?" Darlene asked.

"A captured SVR general and a scientist we took back during our escape from Russia showed us how to follow the money. Once they traced the rerouted accounts in the Seychelles, finding the Luxembourg accounts was pretty easy."

Ned felt a shiver down his spine. "How did you know we'd be in St. Thomas?"

Cassie pushed Darlene forward. "Don't you remember?"

Ned scrunched his brow.

"The first time we met, you said your dream was to retire on a boat in the Caribbean, maybe even in St. Thomas. You said you never wanted to feel the cold again. Turns out, it's not so hard to follow the sales of luxury yachts when you have the resources of the United States government at your disposal."

Ned cursed himself for his carelessness as he remembered that conversation over six months before.

"Tell me," Cassie continued. "Did you know what fate you were sending your victims to? Did you know what the Russians were doing to us?"

"No."

"Liar," Gale said.

"I didn't know. I . . . I still don't know."

"The truth will come out soon enough," Cassie said. "You both will pay for what you did to William French, my dog, and all your other victims."

"Your dog!" Ned half laughed, leaning forward and extinguishing his cigar in the ashtray near his pistol. "Please tell me this whole charade isn't about a dog."

"It's about what you did to your countless victims, the pain you put my daughters and son-in-law through," Gale said.

"Ah, so he survived, that's great to hear. But I have to tell you, that wasn't us who planned on shooting Peter Trask. Those men who shot your son-in-law and your *dog* were *not* my men."

"We know that," Cassie said.

"Then you know we are not at fault! So whatever you are going to do, you might as well get on with it!" Ned said and jumped for his pistol. Grabbing it, he aimed it at Gale and pressed the trigger.

Click! Click! Click!

Ned looked down at the weapon in shock as another figure stepped out from the shadows behind Gale.

Paul Brady wore all black, just like the rest of them. He gazed at Ned, relishing the panicked expression on his face. "We unloaded your gun earlier this evening. Funny you didn't notice."

Brady snapped his fingers and suddenly a half-dozen figures sprang up from the water and jumped on the boat. They wore rebreathers on their faces and black wet suits and sported HK 416s that they aimed at Ned and Darlene.

"You'll never make us talk," Ned said, defiantly.

"You're right. *We* won't make you talk, but I'm sure they will."

The operators descended on Ned and Darlene, zip-tying them as they forced them to the ground. After cuffing them, they stood them upright and walked them off the yacht to the dock.

They watched them go, then Brady said, "Now, what?"

Cassie stepped forward and grabbed Brady's hand, giving it a small squeeze. "Well, you keep telling me how you want to see Montana."

Gale shoved his weapon into his holster, glad to see his daughter so happy, then looked at Brady. "You've never been to Montana?"

"Can't say I have."

"It's a terrible place, not beautiful at all," Cassie said with a smile.

"Funny," Brady replied. "Almost every Montanan gives me that same reply."

"Our way of keeping people out," Gale said. "C'mon, I promised those SEALs a beer if we ever made it out of the sharashka alive."

"Well, then, I guess we should hightail it stateside," Brady said. "Don't want to break that kind of promise."

"No, I guess I don't."

Acknowledgments

I HAD A wonderful writing professor in college who told me that it takes a village to write and publish a novel.

She couldn't have been more correct.

Marianne Wiggins, thank you for not only letting me use your office to write in my free time, but also for your brutally honest teaching manner. Your early support means the world to me.

To Gregg Hurwitz and his better half, Delinah, thank you both so much for your mentorship over the years. Not only did you both practically furnish my apartment after college, you gave me the desk on which I wrote my first novel. But most importantly, thank you both so much for feeding me and giving me odd jobs around the house when I was a starving college student and a struggling writer. Delinah, I'm still keeping that Tupperware!

Andrew Kircher and Connor Lunt, thank you so much for your time helping me on all things aviation. All mistakes are my own.

I would also like to thank some of the early readers of the manuscript, who each gave me insightful notes and comments. Alex Marker, Andrea Sloan, Ben Sembler, Brock Coyle, Francesca Zanatti, Jens Davis, Michael Hewitt, Coley Oliver, Chase Ryan, Krista Zsitvay, Walker Adams, and Steph Irwin. Thank you all so much.

To O and M, my good friends up north. I want to not only thank you both for your decades of service to our country, but also for helping me with all things "Agency" and "Dam Neck" in this book. Again, all mistakes are my own. Excited for the future, and more long hikes up "The Big." *Only Dead Fish Swim with the Current.*

To Robert Crais. You probably don't remember this, but years ago at a book launch I was telling you how I was struggling with the writing process, and you just smiled at me and said, "I know, isn't it great! How lucky are we to be able to write every day? We have the best job in the world." Bob, that really resonated with me and really put things in perspective. We truly are incredibly lucky and fortunate to be able to do what we love. Thank you.

To my superagents Meg Ruley and Rebecca Scherer and everyone at the Jane Rotrosen Agency. Thank you so much for taking a chance on me. Your patience and meticulous help not only through the drafting process, but also guiding me through the world of publishing means more than you both could know.

To Emily Bestler, it has always been a dream of mine to work with you and your team at Emily Bestler Books. Thank you so much for your insight and keen editorial eye.

To Lara Jones, thank you so much for keeping me and everything else on-target.

To everyone at Simon & Schuster and Atria Books, thank you for giving me the green light and being the best in the business at what you do. Specifically, thank you to Libby McGuire, Suzanne Donahue, Kristin Fassler, Dana Trocker, Milena Brown, David Brown, James Iacobelli, Paige Lytle, Jason Chappell, and Laurie McGee. At the time of writing this, we are all still in quarantine. One day soon, I hope to meet and thank you all in person for all your hard work.

Nearly five years ago when I first started writing *Sleeping Bear*, I knew I was taking a pretty big risk. How could I take a "woman goes missing in the woods" plot and turn it into a political/espionage thriller? I had never seen it done before, and quite frankly, it terrified me. I knew that in order to pull it off, I'd have to go back and study the masters. Vince Flynn, Brad Thor, Mark Greaney, Gregg Hurwitz, David Baldacci, and Jack Carr, thank you so much for blazing the way.

To my father, Mark Sullivan. Words can't even describe the gratitude I have for you helping me on this journey. Growing up, you showed me what it took to become a writer. I saw the work ethic it took, the grit to keep going when things weren't going right, the highs and lows. I don't think I could have done this without you. Thank you.

To my mother, Betsy Sullivan. Thank you for being the most supportive, loving mother ever.

To Bridger, Dylan, Henna, Pacho, Mary, Jorge, and Chris. Thank you so much for putting up with me.

To my wonderful wife, Mariafe. You are the most loving, supportive, and incredible person I have ever met. Why you married me, I have no idea, but I feel like the luckiest person in the world that you did. I love you.

To Alan, to whom this book is dedicated. Thank you for all the love and support over the years, not only to me, but to all the others you helped guide into adulthood. We all love and miss you, big guy. Rest easy.

And lastly, to my canine writing partner Arlo. If it wasn't for your incessant whining, crying, and barking in the first two years of your life, this novel would have been completed years ago. But honestly, I wouldn't have it any other way. Now you get to deal with a real sleeping bear, your baby Saint Bernard sister, Matilda. Isn't payback sweet.